The UNFORTUNATE Basil Albright

By
Tony Boucher

Published in Great Britain in 2014
by AGB Publishing

ISBN 978-0-9928737-0-7

I

KURT LEITNER 1
NORMA'S WAKE 2
ST JOSEPHS 4
BAZ'S BENCH (1) 7
THE BIG HOUSE 9
BAZ'S BENCH (2) 9
NEVER A GOOD DAY FOR A HANGING 13
A LONG WALK FROM SOUTH WALES 14
BROTHERS OF THE BOARD 16
TOPPLED PIECES 22
ZED AND BILLY 32
FALLEN RUNNERS 35
GOODBYE OLD MR THOMAS 43
THE HOLE 46

II

A WAR AT HOME 53
MEETING THE ENEMY 68
MRS WATERHOUSE 92
14 MINCHEN STREET 113
MRS BLAKENEY 122
MOST LOSE A COUPLE 128

III

SS CITY OF DERBY 131
RAF SHAIBAH 135
PLAN B 167
P-B4! 222

IV

ROBERT BLAKENEY 225

ONE FAMILY, TWO GRAVES, THREE NAMES 230

IN A DARK CORNER 235

MRS CHATTLE 238

I KILLED A MAN ONCE 243

THE PRIEST'S HOUSE 248

THE TEMPLE 254

EDDIE 273

A DROP OF ACID 279

JOHN WATERHOUSE'S NEIGHBOUR 287

YOU SAID YOU KILLED A MAN ONCE 291

PORK LOIN OR RIB-EYE 299

PASANG 306

THE ATTACK 308

V

HAS THE PAPER BOY BEEN 319

LITTLE DAIBAI, EAMON CARRICK, THE IRISHMAN 321

SUNNYBRIDGE 323

BAZ'S BENCH (3) 328

BAZ'S BENCH (4) 332

BAZ'S BENCH (5) 337

THE SPICE OF INDIA 343

BAZ'S BENCH (6) 350

THE LETTER 355

THE TREES ECHO 361

BAZ'S BENCH (7) 363

WHERE SALMON GO TO DIE 368

THE FAIRY FELLER'S MASTER STROKE 377

A COLD WIND 387

For Dad

With special thanks to Lynda, my rock.

Also by the same author:

driver boy
The Tukul with the Blue Door
The Drowning Mary
(the sequel to The Tukul with the Blue Door)
Anna and the Knight
Alone
Close
(the sequel to Alone)

I

KURT LEITNER

NORMA'S WAKE

BAZ'S BENCH (1)

THE BIG HOUSE

BAZ'S BENCH (2)

NEVER A GOOD DAY FOR A HANGING

A LONG WALK FROM SOUTH WALES

BROTHERS OF THE BOARD

TOPPLED PIECES

ZED AND BILLY

FALLEN RUNNERS

GOODBYE OLD MR THOMAS

THE HOLE

The world was experiencing turbulent times when Basil Albright entered into it. An Austrian, Archduke Franz Ferdinand had just been assassinated, which along with other catastrophic reasons triggered the First World War. Not that this period in history had any direct affect on Baz's early years...

Kurt Leitner knew he was about to die. The green grass was hurtling towards him at great speed as he gripped tightly onto the rim of the gondola. Behind him were the grotesque groans from the collapsing framework as it was being swallowed by a violent fireball. The front of the huge burning structure rearing its head like a drowning animal while the tail section had already succumbed to the clawing flames, crushing the rear compartment and consuming the airmen inside. The remaining crew were stunned into a petrified silence as they clung onto various parts of the front cabin, the angle now so acute some had already sealed their fate by plunging into the rear panel.

Kurt Leitner knew too well he had to get the timing of his jump exact, too early and the fall would break every bone in his body, too late and he would be engulfed by the flames. He waited, his heart pounding through his chest, his eyes bulging from their sockets, sweat streaming from every pore of his body.

He waited.

"Springeeen," shrieked a plummeting voice.

Kurt Leitner leapt outward as far as his quivering legs would catapult him. As he hit the ground his knees buckled under him, causing him to fall heavily onto his side and shattering his wrist. Oblivious to the pain he quickly rose to his feet on his fight for survival.

Kurt Leitner ignored the noise of engines crashing from their mountings and propeller blades snapping on the ground, he ignored the intense heat roaring around the buckling metal, the sparks of flaming fabric swirling in the scorching air, he ignored the hideous screams and cries of his crew mates perishing in the inferno.

Kurt Leitner ignored the lone aircraft landing in the field behind him.

The beginning, according to Basil Albright's memory, was actually not the beginning, it was just his earliest recollection. Not as though anything that happened before was of any great importance. Only what was to follow was going to be so much more.

It was night, well, it was black, and it was quiet, a black so dark and a quiet so silent it felt as though a switch had been pulled on the world. He also knew his time was running out.

NORMA'S WAKE
1918

Baz watched as the Albright family and friends, dressed in their dark attire, began to congregate in the small, dimly lit, front room. Their soulful movements accompanied by a priestly air of calmness and peace.

Looking severe in her dark dress and wearing a small pillbox hat draped with a fancy black cobweb, the prehistoric Mrs Lombardy guided the four year old Baz onto an old wooden chair. The chair creaked so loudly when he sat in it, he wondered if it might be crying in pain. "Chairs don't cry, even if they are sad," she told him, theatrically brushing him under his chin before drifting over to more adult company.

Baz could hear quiet mutterings from mature conversations, words he didn't understand, sympathetic sentences sounding the same and always followed by dignified agreement. He saw sad faces, he heard stories about sons and fathers not coming home, covert glances and whispered words of young men returning with missing limbs or diseases that replaced a bullet wound.

"The world has lost its way."

Why has the world lost its way?

"Oh don't sit there Basil," his mother called out, her words breaking through the air like cracked glass. "Mrs Anderson or Dr Wells might like to sit down. Mrs Anderson would you..."

"No, no, please, let him stay," Mr Anderson answered for his wife.

"All these adults are probably making the poor boy nervous," said Mrs Anderson.

"He's too young to have nerves," announced Baz's mother, sharp words, softly spoken. "Probably best to let him sit anyway, he would only cause some accident somewhere." Not that Baz had caused many, or any at all for that matter, it was just something she liked to say. He wondered why she never said it about Oliver, who created havoc at every opportunity.

In the corner of the room Baz could see the baggy eyed vicar with his white dog collar and effected smug utterances speaking to the Dickensian Dr Wells. Baz watched the doctor's bulbous chin tremble whenever he spoke and the muscles in his temples twitch whenever he listened. Where was your God when Norma needed him? Where were your medicines when my daughter was pleading for her life? Baz's father wanted to say to them: he said neither, clutching his dormant pipe his stance remained upright, the smoldering fireplace dying behind him. Baz knew his father's cries were on the inside that day, his pain hidden from sight.

Standing next to his father was Old Mr Thomas with his bushy moustache and wise old eyes. Baz was glad to see his friend there, he was also glad he was Old Mr Thomas's friend too.

Mrs Lombardy returned to where Baz was sitting.

"Where has she gone? Why did she get all broken?"

"Little boys won't understand."

"Will I die from a cough?"

"Not if you're good Basil."

"Why has she gone to go to a better place? She liked it here with me. Is a better place in a box?"

"So many questions for such a small boy."

"What is soul? Where is heaven?"

Silence.

For Baz it could only have been the cold wind that had taken his sister that day. For him there *was* nothing else, for him there *was* no other answer.

He turned his attention to the tormented expressions of Mr Anderson with his inconsolable wife, her face concealed by her husband's crumpled handkerchief. They were there without their beloved Evie. Baz remembered Norma's distress only last month from losing her best friend to the same cough. That cold wind must have taken their child also.

He looked at Norma's bright face confined to the silver frame on the mantlepiece and whispered goodbye. A goodbye she would never reply to.

Where the twins and his brother vanished to in the daytime was a question soon to be answered for Baz. That word 'school' was about to become a reality.

It happened to be a frosty, late November morning when Baz was first liberated into the wider world. It was ten minutes past eight and the ground floor of 14 Minchen Street had just emptied itself of its occupants.

"Why I have to do this is beyond me, I brought you into this world and that is the most anyone should do for one person," his mother said to him as they stepped out onto the pavement.

Rosemary Albright was a woman finding it hard to come to terms with the fact that giving birth to her last child had done nothing to help her ascend up the social ladder. Not that Baz knew much about how his mother felt about him, he just thought the love she showed the twins and Oliver just happened to be different, although no one ever came close to having the same attention as Norma had.

Baz's mother would never be seen outdoors in anything that might resemble home clothes. She preferred bright summer attire, even during the drab coldness of winter. Her days as a domestic servant had given her sewing skills that would compliment any professional seamstress. After leaving service she had the opportunity to make her own clothes and that she did, lots of them. Although, however much she tried, Rosemary Albright would never be able to reach the heights of sophistication and elegance she so longed for.

The depression that descended on the rest of the country had left a small unaffected area called St Josephs Elementary School. During the eagerly awaited breaks between lessons, the playground was aloud with playful screams of young girls and boys resonating down the street. Pockets of animated children with their marbles and skipping ropes, games of tag, hopscotch and leapfrog, or just random disorderly activity.

Fifteen minutes after their departure, the Albright family arrived at the sober two-storey building. A bleak establishment with grimy, rust coloured brickwork surrounded by a high wrought iron railing.

Breaking through its roof was the towering central clock tower, every morning it would overlook the families arriving, rigorously reminding them of their punctuality. The headmaster was always eager to ensure the clock was regularly maintained to the sacrifice of more important areas in the school. "The day that clock goes out of time will be the day they carry me out of here," he would often declare. Needless to say there was many a pupil that glanced a hopeful eye upward.

Four times a day the clang of the school bell echoed around the school, all play and noise instantly ceased followed by a drum roll of small obedient feet dashing to form their ten lines of twelve children.

Baz stayed close to the twins at the start, an attachment they accepted for the time being.

Ruby and Violet are two years older than Baz. Everyone calls them the twins, not quite identical, very close nevertheless. Although in later years it was Ruby that blossomed first, she had become the pretty one, the one that had all the interest from the boys.

Their temperaments could not be more contrasting. Ruby is prone to outbursts of anger and long bouts of sulking that would befit the most pampered child. She also has a stubbornness so frozen in ice it could test even their father's most placid nature.

It was obvious to all that Violet's level-headed and mild manner was inherited from her father. She was quieter, quick witted, by far the cleverest, the one who had acquired an insight and wisdom well beyond her years.

Together the twins were close, ever watchful of each other. They would gain great amusement when any person, always an adult, mostly teachers, failed to tell them apart. On the downside, it was of considerable annoyance to them when people would call one by the other's name. The law of averages would state that this would only occur half of the time, surprisingly it seemed to happen all the time. Baz thought it was patently obvious which one was which.

His school days were not much different from one day to the next. Break periods spent sitting on his wooden bench, followed by a repetitive reel of morning assembly and lessons that left him none the wiser. To most, it became evident Baz was a boy that appeared to do nothing for fun, even his existence seemed to have stopped registering in the minds of the other children. When I say he became one of the invisible people, believe me, Baz was one of the invisible people.

There was one teacher whose radar Baz was incapable of flying under, especially when she was in need of a target for some ridicule. "Albright is not all bright today," was a favourite of hers and sure to bring on a chorus of smothered sniggers from the other pupils. Her name was Mrs Guest, his form teacher. Baz had never liked Mrs Guest, not many children did. In truth, Mrs Guest was not an easy teacher to like. When she wasn't picking on one particular pupil she would often get the whole class to answer a question together, a kind of group ridicule. Why snare one when you could ambush them all. Anyhow, this usually resulted in a chorus of unharmonious and conflicting, slowly spoken, extended words. Hopefully enough of the pupils would say the correct answer before it reached the end, unfortunately, most of the time, this was not the case.

Mrs Guest had earned the ultimate pupil compliment, a nickname, which took her infamy to a whole new level. Whenever her name was mentioned, the two words 'Mrs Guest...' were always followed by '...who only took prisoners, never guests.' In truth, Mrs Guest had a nickphrase.

What was an anomaly to Mrs Guest, who only took prisoners, never guests, was that nothing seemed to sway Baz. He had this way of gazing impassively past her, as if she didn't exist at all. Seeing a teacher turn their head to see what he was looking at was not an uncommon occurrence in the classroom.

Strangely, on the surface, these episodes were not as they would appear. Yes, Baz did feel unsettled by his teachers taunts, and no, staring nonchalantly past her was not his fault. Baz does look directly at people, this is true, with his right eye. His left eye? That is completely different. Baz has an imperfection that has many names and he has been called all of them at one time or other. 'Cock-eyed monster', 'squinty', 'wonky eyed', just to mention a few. Baz could tell you there are many more and could easily recall every one of them and at any time. The latest 'half moon', he thought was an imaginative inclusion.

And the first person ever to turn their head? Well, that happened to be his mother. It was probably the first thing she had noticed about him. And the second, that was Baz's curved back: the most accurate way to describe it was that his head protruded slightly forward from his shoulders. Not so much a hunchback, just a pronounced curve at the top half of his spine. Turtle like you could say, and many children did. A cock-eyed turtle.

I can tell you this much, many years later, Baz's wonky, half moon, squinty eye, would save his life.

BAZ'S BENCH (1)

There was one thing the other pupils knew about Baz and that was he could keep a secret. They knew this because he never spoke about anybody to anyone. In truth, he never spoke much about anything to anyone. It had never occurred to him when he sat on his bench on that first day his peace would occasionally be shattered by children he hardly knew, telling him things he didn't really want to hear and mostly about children he didn't want to know.

It was after one of these visits Baz was left feeling confused and saddened, although he had no idea why. Maybe it was in the woeful manner that this particular girl had spoken.

She was about the same age as Baz, a delicate, mousy girl with small pale features and a yellow fringe cut in a straight line above her round saucer eyes.

Baz said nothing, he just waited, expecting her to slip back into the sea of children.

"I have lots of dads," she suddenly said.

Baz remained silent, his gaze firmly fixed forward.

"I'm lucky I suppose, having lots of dads."

He angled his head slightly towards her, just managing to catch a glimpse of the fringe and half shuttered round eyes.

"Not at the same time though, you know, the dads," she added.

Baz could feel her looking at him. He felt confused about her having lots of dads. Especially with him having only the one. In fact everyone he knew had only one dad. Maybe she was just lucky.

"Well that's not exactly true. Once I had a dad and an uncle at the same time. Does your mother have lots of dads?" she asked, then paused. "Or uncles?"

Baz continued his silence.

"Thought not, only it's the dad I have now, he keeps touching me and makes me touch him. He makes me do things, I don't like it. I hate it," she said softly. "He tells me not to tell my mum, or anyone." Then she spoke more to herself. "God will punish me if I do." She began to sob.

They both sat on the bench for what seemed ages, Baz trying his hardest to understand the last few minutes.

"Thank you." Were the last words she spoke, wiped her eyes, then ran off.

For a while after, Baz would see a lot of the girl, only in the playground though and some distance away, always appearing to stand out from the crowd. He would see her playing on the hopscotch squares or with a skipping rope, or just standing with a downward gaze, thumb in mouth. Sometimes her large leaden eyes would stare at the other girls, in hope, expectation, maybe envy. All the time, she remained on her own.

As suddenly as the girl had appeared in his life, she vanished. Baz never saw her at school again and never forgot that strange one-sided conversation.

It would not be the last time Baz would hear her voice.

THE BIG HOUSE

The fifteen minute walk to school with the twins gradually became a fifteen minute walk to school without the twins. It began with the twins joining forces with their friends, Baz started to feel increasingly awkward, an outsider, a stranger in strange company.

The twins failed to notice Baz slowly drift behind, ten feet one day, twenty feet the next. Eventually they vanished around the corner of Alders Road, leaving Baz alone in the commotion of the morning melee. For the first time in his life he was alone, a new found freedom, enriched with the pretence of being grown-up. He sometimes altered his route slightly, not too much, not so much as to get lost, just enough to see what else the world had to offer.

It was on one of these diversions he paused on the corner of the considerable Haydons Road, captivated by the sight of the dusty haze rising from this bustling industrial road and the differing shapes and sizes of the large factories bordering the canal side. The heavy work horses kicking up the dry summer dirt as they pulled their carts loaded with the days deliveries. Automobiles and lorries coughing out clouds of thick dark smoke. Herds of labourers disappearing through the towering side gates of the factories.

But it was the building in the far distance that intrigued Baz the most. A huge white stone house facing directly up the road towards him and looking as if it owned all it surveyed. He named it the The Big House. Only in his wildest dreams did Baz think he would be able to live in a place like that.

BAZ'S BENCH (2)
1921

It was another unremarkable day. Baz sat on his bench unaware that one more encounter would have such a profound effect on his life. A boy appeared at his side with an incoming nervous gaze that made Baz feel uncomfortable, an intrusion for a short while that he managed to ignore with his well practiced nonchalance.

"William Waterhouse old boy."

A short, slightly built, well groomed individual with soft delicate features, white wispy hair and pasty transparent skin that appeared to have that just washed look. Apart from his bright blue eyes and a slight pinkness on his cheeks there seemed to be no colour to him whatsoever, as though he had spent most of his life cooped up indoors, hidden away in the shadows. Baz also thought a not too strong wind and that would be the last anyone would see of William Waterhouse.

This time he said it slightly louder. "William Waterhouse." But not too loud, God forbid he would want to bring any unwanted attention to himself.

"No, I'm Basil Albright," replied Baz, feeling slightly glad he wasn't the intended beneficiary.

"You can call me Will old man," making eye contact with Baz for the first time. He then whipped his head around in a state of panic, a leftover from his previous school, turning back with a sense of relief.

"William, that's my name, people call me Will though. Other than my parents, they call me William, sometimes Mummy calls me Will, mostly when father is not around. Then it's William." The boy took a deep breath and held out his hand.

Avoidance was now impossible. Baz reluctantly gripped the outstretched hand belonging to William Waterhouse. You could count the number of people Baz had shaken hands with in single figures, mostly uncles. "You can tell the strength of a man's character by the firmness of his handshake," his father had once told him. He knew from the moment he touched William Waterhouse's emaciated fingers, it was going to be the limp-wristed, coldest and dampest hand he would ever come into contact with, he wasn't wrong either. Not that Baz had ever shaken hands with a dead chicken's foot, but if he had, then that's probably what it would have felt like.

"I was inaugurated in this establishment this morning," said Will.

"Huh?"

"I started this morning old man."

Explaining the reason why Baz has not seen him before. A perfectly positioned tie crushing the collar of his crisp white shirt, new shiny shoes and long trousers, long trousers! William Waterhouse was certainly a vision Baz would have remembered.

"Can I plant one's posterior here old man?"

"Huh."

"Can I sit here?"

"Sure, why not, I don't own the bench," replied Baz, although if anybody did, Baz would probably have first bid on that claim.

And from that day William Waterhouse became Baz's second friend (Old Mr Thomas being the first).

William explained to Baz how the Waterhouse family ended up in the city. "We lived in the country, I went to a private school."

"Private. You mean you didn't want anyone else knowing about it."

"No. It was paid for by my parents. It was called Graves."

"Graves?" Baz laughed.

"Yes I know old boy," Will said, then solemnly added, "They bury your childhood there."

"Graves," Baz repeated, still laughing.

"Actually its full name was Graveley Manor."

"I prefer Graves," Baz's laugh subsided. "I bet you had a lot of cold winds there."

"Sorry old boy?"

"Nothing."

"My father was the bursar. We lived in one of the houses in the school grounds."

"What's a bursar?"

"He looks after the money, only he never talked about it. He was a lay preacher as well, in case the rector lost the ability to preach." William curled up his hand and acted out the drinking from the bottle sign. "You know, glug, glug."

"Sounds grave," said Baz, chuckling.

"You could say my father's style of preaching was, let us just say, singularly unique. Then my grandmother died and we came down here to live in her house, and here I am."

"And here you are."

It wasn't long before Baz realised Will was more like an adult than a child. He even spoke and wore the same clothes as a grown-up. A tie, outside of school! Not only was he the first boy Baz had ever seen with a cravat, it was also the first time he had ever seen anyone wearing a smoking jacket, man or boy. Although Baz did think that smoking jackets were meant to look slightly more sophisticated than the oversized blue one William wore. "Who stole your hands?" Baz asked him on first sighting.

In some ways Baz was in awe of his new found friend, even if he was slightly neurotic and perpetually on edge. Will had that confidence in his own intellect to quickly reflect any unwanted ridicule, telling Baz it was as essential as a school tie if anyone was going to last his time out at Graves.

Unlike Baz, who preferred to be one of life's spectators, any spare time Will had was devoted to grown up activities, reading novels was one. "The classics old boy," he had told Baz. "The classics are the food of a healthy mind and erudite thoughts."

"Huh."

11

Another hobby of Will's was painting, proudly describing one of his own artworks as, "Observing the interrelation between structure and composition."

"It's a boat Will."

"I know Baz."

"And one that would probably sink."

"I know old man."

Will also taught Baz chess. "Remember chess is like life, you have to cover every eventuality," were his first words. "It is also an art my boy, an art of the most sublime ever created." Baz sensed William's satisfaction in having the opportunity to play against someone his own age, he told him his father was the only other person he had ever played against. "And that soon abated after I began winning."

Baz was left breathless the first time he saw Will's chess set. Thirty-two beautifully carved ebony and boxwood pieces of varying heights and thicknesses. Stallion's heads, bishop mitres, coronets and castle battlements and smaller pieces with tiny spheres symbolising heads. "These are the foot soldiers Baz, weak on their own but together they are strong and brave, ready to sacrifice themselves for the greater good."

At the beginning Baz was quite content just to look at them. "Phenomenal," he said. One of Will's words, strangely said in the correct context.

"A Staunton chess set."

"It's got a name!"

"It's made by John Jaques," Will said proudly, as if Baz would know of any other.

"Two names!"

"Designed by Nathaniel Cook."

"Three!"

Unknowingly Baz had returned that fresh wonderment to Will, it was like seeing them for the first time, something he had lost a long time ago.

"Where's the dice?" inquired Baz.

Whereupon Will suddenly rolled over like a swatted fly, laughing loudly. "The dice! My unworldly young fellow, would you like *your* destiny to be gambled on the throw of a number."

"Then how?"

"This game is all down to you old boy. *You* will only have *yourself* to blame."

"And congratulate if you win," Baz added, redeeming himself.

"You are learning already old man."

"Then how?"

"Listen and learn my good fellow, listen and learn..."

William stared hard into Baz's eyes and spoke without barely moving his lips. "This is a game where you never give up. You fight and fight and continue to fight, you fight to the death. Until all hope is lost, until you can see no ending in sight," Will's gaze softened. "Then you resign my boy," he said grinning. Soon adding, "If he doesn't accept a draw first," his grin evolving into a smile.

Will was amazed by the speed Baz caught on to the game. He had learnt and remembered the moves virtually on the first sitting.

A week later a spark suddenly lit in Baz's mind and he became a chess player, even giving Will a run for his money soon after. When Baz played chess no other world existed. He felt a power. With one insignificant move he could change everything.

NEVER A GOOD DAY FOR A HANGING
1923

Mary Chandler stared into the tear-drop space within the rope and for the first time in just over two years she accepted her fate. That time in her miserable life had finally arrived. Any chance of a reprieve was finally behind her, any hope she once had was now gone. Only a cold emptiness remained.

Mary Chandler looked the best she had done for a long time, her auburn hair had been neatly styled and she wore a blue silk dress given to her by her solicitor's wife. In the last minutes of her life Mary Chandler was determined to have her moment. With a compassionate smile she looked directly into her executioner's eyes. "I do not die alone," were her last whispered words to the sombre man in the black suit.

Like a closing shutter her world vanished as the executioner's hood was finally pulled over her head, followed immediately by the tightness of the rope around her neck.

"Forgive me Alice."

Mary Chandler dropped the eight feet to her death.

Baz never read newspapers, after all he was too young, but the picture he saw under the main headline on the front page 'NEVER A GOOD DAY FOR A HANGING' sent his mind spiralling with confusion. With a flick of his wrists, Baz's father folded the paper in half and what Baz had seen vanished under the layers of pages set down on the kitchen table.

A LONG WALK FROM SOUTH WALES
1925

Old Mr Thomas became Baz's friend as soon as Baz realised friends existed. Wearing his flat cap and knee length blue apron under a threadbare jacket, Old Mr Thomas would push his rickety wooden milk cart up Minchen Street twice a day and warmly welcome the folk carrying their jugs to be filled with milk. Hand painted on the side of his cart in very irregular white lettering was written 'THOMAS'S DIARY-THE SAFEST MILK IN TOWN'. Yes, I know, 'DIARY'. No one had the heart to tell the old milkman.

Old Mr Thomas was very fond of telling his milky tales to anyone that would listen. Unfortunately on the warmer days, especially by the time it got to the end of his round, the creamy liquid was in a very dubious condition.

Baz knew when the old milkman was about to begin one of his stories, the ritual had always remained the same. This suited Baz very well. Baz liked same, same always meant, well, the same. Crouching down to Baz's height Old Mr Thomas would gently tap the top of his arm with his sausage like fingers, then whisper under his thick smokey breath, "Now listen to this boyo."

Apart from the cow that lost his black and white tail by swishing it around too much and only because he had heard it many times before, Baz had great difficulty in understanding any of Old Mr Thomas's stories, especially when the old milkman finished every one with "Now there's funny." Baz couldn't see anything funny in a cow losing its tail.

14

Only this morning, Old Mr Thomas told Baz a story that didn't begin with his usual ritual.

"Why are you a milkman?" Baz had simply asked.

 The old milkman's face went a lighter shade of his normal grey and the sparkle from his eyes melted into a watery glaze. Baz knew that this story was going to be different. This story would definitely not be ending with, "Now there's funny."

"I owned a farm in South Wales with my two no-good brothers," the old milkman began. "The lazy layabouts would spend all our money in the local bar drinking whisky and getting drunk. I was finding it difficult to make ends meet you see. My..." he paused for a second and took a deep swallow, "Our farm was falling into ruin, bills were piling up and the farm had to be sold to pay the debts. I saw the writing on the wall boyo." His face came closer to Baz's and his voice quietened. "It was night time you see. I took six of our best dairy cows while my brothers were out cold, drunk they were Boyo. They never questioned why I gave them a bottle of whisky when they came home from the Stag and Hounds that evening, now there's stupid."

On a dreary night in September Old Mr Thomas and his cows began a long and eventful walk (that's another story) that ended in Baz's home town. The first question anyone would ask Old Mr Thomas after listening to his tale. "Why here?" They could think of a lot finer places to go. With a twinkle in his eye and a wry, slow evolving smile that turned up the ends of his bushy moustache, Old Mr Thomas would reply, "I just followed the cows. Now there's funny."

At the end of the story Baz was none the wiser, all he could think to say to the old milkman was "What ends did you want to meet? Why would someone want to write on a wall?" Although he knew what drunk meant, he had heard his mother say it enough times.

Late in the war the German U-boats were sinking more and more of the merchant ships sailing from America and Canada and the inevitable rationing was introduced in this country. The Albright family along with his other customers were never in need of milk, butter or cheese during this restricted period. Thanks to Old Mr Thomas.

Although Baz had started school he still saw Old Mr Thomas on the morning round and in spite of age restraining Baz's greeting, he was still happy to see his friend, and his old friend was happy to see him.

On a Tuesday in the May half term holiday, in Baz's fourth year at school, Old Mr Thomas failed to deliver the morning round and every round after. In fact, Baz never saw Old Mr Thomas again.

BROTHERS OF THE BOARD

The Waterhouse family home is a large three storey dwelling on the affluent side of town. Light beige stone on the outside and richly decorated on the inside. Baz had the notion he could probably fit his entire house into the drawing room alone.

The two boys were sprawled out on the carpet in the second floor bedroom, both concentrating on the tough battle being fought out between them.

Knight to King's Bishop five. A warm feeling was flowing through Baz's body as he could feel the impending defeat of his opponent. Will widened his eyes and gazed despondently at the hard fought battleground, his defeated pieces scattered to one side of the board.

"Stale bread and sour milk for you Master Albright," quipped Will. A joke that would itself turn stale *and* sour within the hour.

"Is that the sound of defeat I hear?" Baz proudly announced, awaiting his victory.

Will tipped his King over "That's the third time in a row, I must be a great teacher old man," he said graciously.

"No *old man*, I must be a great pupil."

"Five minutes boys." A melodic, feminine voice ascended the stairs, followed by the delightful aroma of roast beef.

Will picked up a pawn, one from the light coloured pieces. "Take this Baz, this will make us brothers." He then took one of the darker pawns, held it out for Baz to see then put it in his pocket. "Now we *are* truly brothers Baz. While we have these we *are* brothers, board brothers." His face lit up as he suddenly declared "brothers of the board!"

Will tipped the rest of the chess pieces into a box then slid it onto a shelf in his cupboard.

With the softness of the lush carpet under his shoeless feet, Baz followed his friend into the dining room. A room in complete contrast to the eating arrangements at his house, it felt as though he was entering into another world.

Baz's home is a rented, small Victorian terraced house close to the industrial southeast side of town.

The large kitchen taking up the entire backspace is the hub of the house, mainly because the stove made it the warmest room. Fireplaces in the other rooms were only lit in times of extreme cold and then only for a short period of time. Ice on the inside of the window panes usually influenced the deciding factor of that decision.

If the kitchen was the hub of the house, then it was the scarred and bruised oak dining table in the centre that happened to be the beating heart. Eating, drinking, reading, writing, studying, talking, arguing, tranquility and peace when possible, were all practised on a daily basis around this family altar.

Baz also discovered that hell itself was situated in his house or on the outside would be more to the truth. Turn right under the small lean-to and there it was, behind a door made from planks of rotting wood with more gaps than his granny's teeth. Normal people called it the toilet, Baz called it hell. A place where you could be eaten alive by the largest spiders known to man. That is if you could fight through the thick netting of cobwebs.

Anyway a two bedroom house inhabited by four children and two adults does not equate very well and the drawing room, along with its heavy brown curtains and stone fireplace had been seconded as his parents' bedroom. The day of Norma's funeral was the only time Baz saw the room in its intended state. Even after the Albright children had flown the nest, Rosemary and Giles Albright continued using it as their bedroom. A decision they would later regret.

The Waterhouses' dining room had deep red and gold renaissance flock wallpaper. A large elaborate framed mirror hanging on a wall gave the impression of a much larger space. Alone on another wall was a small dark painting of the crucifixion in a scuffed wooden frame looking like an ancient relic and appearing important in its solitude.

"You can sit here Basil," said Mrs Waterhouse, indicating to a straight backed chair. As she strolled past the table an odour of lavender drifted under Baz's nose, he always thought Mrs Waterhouse smelt so nice, he thought everything about Mrs Waterhouse was so agreeable. He wished Mrs Waterhouse was his mother, after all, he and Will were brothers of the board. Baz dutifully sat down on the chair, a silver candelabra with tall upright translucent cream candles dominated the space in front of him.

"I hope you boys are hungry," Mrs Waterhouse smiled warmly as she entered the room holding a tray of food, a look that told Baz how happy she was knowing William had a good friend.

Mr Waterhouse, tall, thin, wearing a wide lapelled dark grey suit soon followed behind. This was the first time Baz had ever seen him, apart from the back of his head when he would see him reading in the front room. Will had told him it was the bible, always the bible.

Baz gazed longingly at the food. A joint of roast beef sat on a blue patterned china platter alongside a long silver carving knife. Fluffy brown roast potatoes in a matching bowl, sprouts and carrots in another. A gravy boat popping bubbles from the steaming brown liquid.

Mr Waterhouse sat down last and clasped his hands together so tightly Baz could see the white of his knuckles, cracks appearing by his eyes as he squeezed them shut. Baz thought he might have been in some sort of pain until William and his mother followed suit, heads bowed, eyes closed.

For the first time he heard Mr Waterhouse speak.

"Bless O Lord, this food to our use,
And us to thy loving service;
And make us ever mindful of the needs of others,
For Jesus' sake. Amen."

"Amen," echoed Will and Mrs Waterhouse. Baz moved his lips to say the word, nothing came out.

The second time he heard Mr Waterhouse speak he wished he hadn't.

"In which church does your family worship Basil?"

Baz tried to quell the panic. Lie or tell the truth, tell the truth or lie. The truth!

"We don't go to church Mr Waterhouse."

William stared forlornly down at the table.

Will's mother looked towards her husband. "Lets not talk..."

"Your father must take your family to church on a Sunday Basil?"

"No Mr Waterhouse. My father doesn't believe in God."

"Your father does not believe in our Lord, our Saviour!"

"No Mr Waterhouse," Baz said quietly, barely opening his mouth as he spoke. He then looked at the food, hoping this conversation would soon come to a speedy conclusion. Although deep down he somehow knew otherwise.

"And do *you* believe in God, Basil?"

Now that is a question Baz has yet to answer himself.

On one side he had Mr Minns, the school's religious instruction teacher and a bearer of the most dangerous of combinations, a religious fanatic along with being quite seriously deranged.

He was a squat, balding man with round spectacles that matched his round featureless face. His trousers encircling his pot belly ended up virtually under his armpits, giving him the odd appearance of constantly leaning back. Apart from that the most notable part of him was a thick silver chain dangling from a buttonhole in his waistcoat, a watch concealed in a pocket at the other end, that Mr Minns would regularly pull out and give a long scrutinising look in the cup of his hand. Unfortunately the lesson went on for the same tedious hour as it had always done. The only break from the dullness was the silent laughter and facial expressions Mr Minns's penchant for flatulence would generate. This led to his nickname, which in fact wasn't actually a nickname, more a sound. For example. "Are you going to old Mr...lesson?" In between Mr and lesson would come the sound. The sound only the vibrating of ones spluttering tongue poking out between tight lips could produce. Mr Minns had a nicknoise.

Mr Minns preached rather than taught and his lessons were always void of any questions. God was definitely *not* open to debate. He did peculiar things like handing out tiny pieces of bread to each of his pupils while muttering, "In the name of...," or attempting to imitate a story from the bible he would move small badly coloured cardboard cut outs of religious characters around the black board, half of which would fall on to the floor. It was then his flatulence would be at its most dangerous. Although his worst attribute was the white salivary froth that appeared at the corners of his mouth when he spoke

19

for any length of time, putting most children off looking in his direction. Unfortunately being caught not looking in his direction would trigger Mr Minns's fondness for wielding his cane.

Anyhow, Mr Minns was the last person Baz would listen to concerning spiritual matters.

Then on the other side was Baz's father Giles Albright. A tranquil, private man who had never been far away from the harsh side of life, but lived without any bitterness whatsoever. Behind his remote countenance was a person with an insatiable appetite for knowledge, a self-educated and passionate reader of anything that remotely resembled ink on paper. A walking encyclopaedia which he only liberated on rare occasions. When he listened to people, and I mean anyone, young, old, male, female, rich or poor he had a way of making them feel he was attending to their every word. He was also a man whose intellect should have seen him rise well above his own perceived ordinariness, if only he had the inclination. Hard work was not one of Giles Albright's better attributes. He never gave much, then on the other hand he never asked for much either.

So you won't be surprised that Giles Albright was satisfied with the small things in life. A strong passion for a glass of port, two worn out suits, a threadbare dark green cardigan and a pipe which was rarely lit and rarely missing from beneath his dark moustache. So much so that when his father spoke Baz only saw one side of his mouth move, *even* with the pipe absent. And when I say a glass of port, I actually mean that in the plural. He wasn't a drunk, not as such, he just drank too much, or so his wife would say. The port had done nothing to blur the sharpness of his mind either, Oliver once said. "He's the only man who sobers up as he drinks." Probably the wisest words ever to come from his brother's mouth.

Baz was always enthralled by one odd characteristic about his father. His speech was unlike anyone else he had heard, not his accent (which was a kind of gruff city brogue) but the way he used words. To Baz it was like listening to a whole new way of talking, a lyrical language, a kind of poetry that wasn't poetry. "The best way to get something is not to want it," and "You don't know where you are going to unless you know where you have come from," were two recent additions. Mostly they confused the hell out of Baz, although strangely enough he had heard his father repeat so many, at so many times from an early age, he thought quoting these words of wisdom were a normal part of life, even though he hadn't understood most of them, somehow he knew that would come later.

When it came to religion Giles Albright had seen enough suffering in his lifetime to dismiss any existence of a higher being. In truth, he had a very low opinion of religion indeed and had come to the conclusion long ago that it was just another weapon to beat people with. "Most of the stories in the Bible have some kind of moral that ends in a threat anyhow," he told Baz. "As if people didn't have enough to contend with in life without some preacher adding to it. Remember son, you judge yourself not from what you have done, but what you haven't done. Not from some stranger telling you what you should have done. To be honest with you son if you add all the egos of the Christians in this world together, then you'll probably get their God anyway." He sat back in his chair with a look of pride. His father then took a swig of port, a puff of his pipe and disappeared behind a cloud of smoke.

Baz then asked his father the big question, not where do we come from but...

"...So where does God come from then?"

His father leant forward, his face breaking through the white fog.

"To answer that question you will have to believe in God, and to believe in God you have to have faith," he said, taking his pipe out of his mouth and studying Baz's face.

"And the closer to faith you are the further from the truth you will be."

Baz could smell the tobacco on his father's breath. "You always say to tell the truth."

"Then you have answered your own question son."

Both Baz and his father sat in silence, Baz's head in a spin.

"Well! Do you believe in God, Basil?" repeated Mr Waterhouse.

"No I don't think I do." Baz's eyes lit up when he spoke the words, remembering what his father had said about telling the truth. Thinking of his father at that time was not a good idea either. "Belief in God is just a desperate and hopeless pursuit." Whatever that meant.

Mr Waterhouse abruptly shot up from his chair and called Mrs

Waterhouse over to the dining room door.

"Give the boy some of God's food," breathed Mr Waterhouse through gritted teeth.

Both Baz and Will overheard the whispered command.

"He's only a boy, he doesn't..."

"Give the boy some of God's food, I said."

"We have no fish," said Mrs Waterhouse quietly.

Mr Waterhouse mumbled something to his wife that neither Baz or Will heard.

Early that evening the Waterhouse family dined on roast beef and all the trimmings.

Baz tasted God's food, a tin of sour pilchards and a slice of stale bread.

Will reluctantly made a promise to his father that day.

TOPPLED PIECES
1926

The route to Baz's new school happened to be a precise copy of the journey he had taken for the previous six years. Just add a hundred yard footpath along the side of St Josephs and you reach Victoria Manor Secondary school, commonly known as 'Vicky Hall'. It was also commonly known that whoever went to St. Josephs usually ended up at Vicky Hall.

Everywhere Baz turned he would see William, standing in some corridor, seated in a classroom, or leant up against the wall in the playground reading his latest novel, a classic no doubt.

Will had made that promise to his father, a promise he felt he had to keep. Out of all the long and wonderful words he knew, allegiance was now foremost in his mind.

William Waterhouse had made many sacrifices in chess, but they were nothing compared to the sacrifice he made on one particular day. Will had decided to choose needlework and cooking over Baz's and the other boys' choice of woodwork and metalwork. Baz thought he had been very courageous to have made that decision, he knew the taunting from the other boys would be relentless. William was William though and his verbal supremacy managed to get the better over any situation. "It is me who chose the camaraderie of females my dear boys, it is quite evident you have a preference for what is predominantly the same sex as yourselves, although, for some of you I would surmise that is probably debatable." Luckily for William most of the words flew straight over their heads and by the time they had been left tittering over the word sex he had long departed.

Baz and Will's quick glances at each other imparted the same thought, a pawn in each of their pockets. William Waterhouse and Bazil Albright remained and will always be brothers of the board.

1928

Baz joined the Victoria Manor School Chess Club as soon as he saw the handwritten flyer pinned to the school notice board.

Not only had William taught Baz the moves and rules from this most noble of games he had also given him a book on the various openings.

The Ruy Lopez, Sicilian, Kings Gambit, The Modern Benoni, Caro Kann and many more became words well known to Baz. His capacity not only to remember the openings but also the hundreds of variations within them was nothing less than miraculous, you could say he had a facility that surprised most people, including himself. His only explanation; he didn't have much else in that mind of his.

Baz became the second best player in the school Chess Club. That is if you were to discount William Waterhouse who would have happily chopped off his right arm to become a member. Seeking permission from his father was his only mistake. "No doubt a society for heathens," his father told him in no uncertain terms.

Like everything else at Vicky Hall, the school chess team was usually graded by ability. When I say usually, Mr Humphries tactics warranted some, shall we say strategic re-allocations. Mr Humphries, the teacher who ran the Chess Club was not only a master tactician at chess but very adept at tournament strategy also. Moving the better players to the lower boards assured a definite win, as long as the opposition hadn't done the same. Some would say that was how St Joseph's school chess team got as far as it did that year.

Alan Goldsworthy is by far the best chess player in the team, and the whole school for that matter, including William Waterhouse. Now Alan Goldsworthy *does* have natural ability and in abundance. He also has a self-confidence bordering on smug arrogance. Justifiably? Alan Goldsworthy would think so anyway. As for his personality, no one ever got that close to him to discover whether he was likeable or not. He was a boy that always appeared to be on the edge of the frame. "You, my dear fellow, are a person that is living in a parallel universe, a peripheral member of society." William had once told him. He was one of the few boys whose company Alan Goldsworthy would tolerate, mainly because William was the only boy that could hold his own in a chess match against him.

Even Alan Goldsworthy's dexterity when taking one of his opponents pieces was a sight to behold, as though he lassoed it away. Baz was always amazed how with only one hand he could pick up a chess piece, place it dead centre on a square while scooping up the opponents piece at the same time. Then, flicking his hand over to the side of the board, he would discard the captured piece, incredibly always in an upright position. All this in one precise action and within the blink of an eye. Baz had once tried to get close to that deftness of hand but soon gave up after it ended in an embarrassing chaos of fallen pieces.

Out of the many friendly games Baz played against Alan Goldsworthy he had never won, or drawn for that matter. Whenever Baz thought his game was chugging along nicely, several moves later and at the least expected time, Alan Goldsworthy's bishops, knights and rooks would be all over Baz's pieces like a swarm of locusts, leaving him totally dumbfounded at how he had managed it. It always appeared to start with one insignificant move that Baz dismissed as just a pointless positioning manoeuvre. Only Alan Goldsworthy knew better, his assassin had been put into position, then waiting like a praying mantis he would snatch away Baz's first piece, then another and another. Soon after, Baz's position would be hopeless, leaving him confused but full of admiration.

Two other players, Richard Bacon and John Peters understood the tactics and strategy behind chess and played mainly on board three and four.

The remaining two were David Smith and Philip Phillips. They just knew slightly more than how the pieces moved. These less competent players were given boards five and six and were matched against opposition equal to their strength. Both were generally content to split the point with an early draw. As far as their parents were aware they were playing chess, an admiral pastime for their usually wayward offspring. The perfect alibi for an early escape.

The feral looking David Smith was a law unto himself. He acquired an anger which made him lose any concern over what people thought about him. His chess prowess came in the art of cheating. OK the word cheating is a bit strong, more like distraction. Crossing legs and accidentally kicking his opponent's shins, followed by a not too convincing, "Sorry." Tapping his fingers on the table with a bit too much enthusiasm, or just a simple unblinking glare accompanied with a smug 'I have the advantage' grin, usually when he hadn't, was enough to make his adversary's mind lose all concentration.

As for John Peters, it was also well known amongst the other players in the Vicky Hall team that he kept a book tucked in behind one of the toilet cisterns. This might seem unusual to the ordinary Vicky Hall pupil, unless it portrayed the naked delights of women throwing a beach ball on a page from a Health and Efficiency magazine. But when the book is called 'Chess Openings' by Alfred Emery the reason became evident. Even more so when he vanished for a couple of minutes, usually during a rather difficult opening, returning soon after with either a cheery or dour expression.

However, the Victoria Manor School Chess Club was on a roll. To the surprise of everyone it has advanced through to the semi-finals of the Evening Echo School's Chess Championship, an achievement never thought possible, having never progressed past the first round in the club's six year history.

The school day for the Vicky Hall chess team finished two hours early and one of the classrooms had been transformed into a venue for serious chess play. Two long wooden school desks are placed length to length. A very large and soiled white dust sheet is found in the caretaker's shed and used as a tablecloth to cover the ink stains and illegible hieroglyphics debasing the desktops. Six cardboard chess boards are unfolded and positioned equally apart with the box wood pieces allocated to their individual squares. A chess clock supplied by the local chess association is placed next to each of the boards.

The blackboard is the centre of attention with most of the boys studying the two rows of names written in white chalk.

VICTORIA MANOR v EASTCASTLE HIGH
Board 1   Alan Goldsworthy (W) v Roger Hartwell (B)
Board 2   Basil Albright (B) v Raymond Hodges (W)
Board 3   Richard Bacon (W) v Roland Hope (B)
Board 4   John Peters (B) v Charles Spencerley (W)
Board 5   Philip Phillips (W) v Ian Ramsay (B)
Board 6   David Smith (B) v Egor Cornelius (W)

"I bet that clever looking one with the round glasses is Egor Cornelius," David Smith angrily hissed into Baz's ear. He just thought with a name like Egor Cornelius he could be nothing but clever, although board six! A strategic Mr Humphries style reallocation? David Smith looked thoughtful, reflecting on his strategy, which had nothing to do with chess, Egor Cornelius was without doubt a prime target.

Baz, who had scrutinised every Eastcastle High player and turned many a head in the process, could not understand why every opposing team always looked more intelligent and relaxed than his own ragamuffin side. Especially Vicky Hall's Philip Phillips whose permanent pink nose had a continuous flow of descending mucous, then to the annoyance of everyone that witnessed it, a probing tongue would periodically appear, lizard like, sliding along the length of his top lip, followed by an unashamed swallow. A much needed advantage for Philip Phillips.

Sadly Mr Humphries, the ageing Chess Club founder had aged a bit too much one day and dropped dead a month ago. Two weeks after the funeral the headmaster unexpectedly asked in the staff common room, "anyone play chess?"

Mr Clifford, not wanting to miss a chance to boast, "I once played against a grandmast..."

"Well done Clifford, you now run the school Chess Club," instructed the Headmaster, calmly glancing up from reading his newspaper and enjoying the annoyance shown by the deflated Mr Clifford, whose displeasure was compounded by the fact that he couldn't finish the grandmaster story, especially when most of the staff were within listening distance.

Many say Mr Clifford compensates his short height and goat shaped face with a strictness bordering on tyranny and the surprise appointment by the headmaster had done nothing to help his disposition.

Although he did look on one positive side, as far as he was concerned the Victoria Manor Chess Club represented the schools degree of intellect. If the boys win, it will be Mr Clifford's victory. Also, the frustrated history teacher having never made it to the heady heights of headmaster, never lost an opportunity to show his colleagues what the teaching fraternity had missed out on.

Everything associated with todays match had to be just perfect, or to put it another way, up to Mr Clifford's high standards. He would never swap the board numbers around as did his predecessor; Mr Clifford would always play by the rules. Needless to say Baz was now content with his permanent placing at board two.

"If you are going to be a chess player then you will look like a chess player," he told the boys, whatever that meant. However, the team members were given a dress code. Clean white shirts had to be tucked into neatly creased trousers, not that some of the boys had white shirts or trousers that had any chance of having a crease in, including Baz. School ties had to be worn and knotted at the neck. Then the impossible, polished shoes, ones you could see your face in. William would have been perfect thought Baz.

Mr Clifford tapped his knuckles on the wooden table top, "To your boards gentlemen," he declared with his usual smug tone of authority.

Baz sat down in front of the black pieces and glanced at his opponent for the first time, who nonchalantly returned the look, instantly whipping his head round. Baz thought the tall, older looking boy had a street wise demeanour about him, a kind of upmarket Dickensian pick-pocket.

Baz hoped to instigate an open, clutter free match by exchanging as many pieces as possible early on in the game. Baz disliked crowded chess boards, much the same with people. Anyhow, if the middle game gets clogged up and complicated, then it is possible to think too long and use up valuable clock time.

Every boy is designated one hour to make all his moves. If one of the hands from the double faced clock passes that hour and results in that player's flag dropping, then his game would be lost.

"Start your clocks gentlemen," said Mr Clifford in a theatrical tone, informing everyone of a fondness for his own voice.

The players with the black pieces pushed down their button to start the opponent's clock, apart from David Smith who decided to thump the button, causing his opponent to flinch nervously.

Tick tick tick.

Each orderly row of the two facing wooden armies was quickly interrupted by the move of a single white pawn, except for Alan Goldsworthy who played a knight. Battle commenced.

Tick tick tick.

Only a cough or a dejected sigh broke through the silence, apart from Philip Phillips's gurgling as he tried to reverse the everlasting flow.

The only activity was the movement of a player picking up a chess piece and placing it on the chosen square. David Smith plonked his down with a little bit too much enthusiasm and Alan Goldsworthy did it so quickly it left his opposite number wondering which piece had actually been moved, if any.

Tick tick tick.

Time went slowly for the boy waiting for the opposition's move, and far too quickly when the clock was on their own game. The attention span of some boys was being stretched to near breaking point, agitation started to creep in. A few rose from their chairs and strolled around, scrutinising the positions of other games, a corner of their eye always reserved for their own board, waiting for the flick of their opponent's arm.

An argument had taken place when David Smith had accused Egor Cornelius of taking his hand off a bishop without moving it. After a short while David Smith gave his opponent the benefit of the doubt, or more to the truth felt he had done enough to unsettle him. He then decided to crouch on the chair, baboon fashion, a new ploy, never seen before, even by the Vicky Hall team. Desperation must be creeping in thought Baz.

Tick tick tick.

Board five was close to agreeing a draw. Philip Phillips's opponent had clearly had enough of the constant sniffing, licking, sucking, gurgling and gulping. Hands are shook, then wiped. A whole point halved.

Victoria Manor's board four's position seems hopeless. Now that John Peter's book behind the cistern was past any use, his game had gone down hill rather swiftly.

Alan Goldsworthy has an air of victory, each piece placed with the authority and confidence of someone smelling his opponents defeat.

The scantness of board six suggests an endgame had been reached with neither player wanting to concede defeat, or accept a draw for that matter. It is a game that could go in any direction and David Smith's character matching aggressive game has given him the slight advantage. He has a pawn close to reaching the eighth rank, metamorphosing the lowly ranked piece into an all powerful queen and the immediate demise of the opposition.

Tick tick tick.

Baz is coming out of a congested middle game, not the game he had wished for. Pieces lost and gained are identical, the position is equal. He has a secret weapon, his bishop covertly waits one square away from the corner of the board, ready for that diagonal swoop into the enemy's territory, creating havoc and mayhem amongst his opponent's pieces. Baz is confident of victory, an open endgame would suit his style of play. If the match was won by one game it would be his game. Baz could hear the applause, he could see the looks of admiration, he would greet the praises heaped upon him with an air of apathy, Basil Albright would be revered throughout the whole school.

After making a strong move, the Eastcastle High player opposite Richard Bacon on board three has sat back with a look of self-satisfaction. Unfortunately, in his smug contentment he stupidly forgot to push down the button to start the Vicky Hall player's clock. Richard Bacon, who had noticed this lapse in concentration, sat with his arms crossed, a fake attentiveness fooling his opponent. Patiently he waited while his rival's time wasted away. The player for Eastcastle High thought his move so good the Vicky Hall player had no answer to it. In silence they both waited.

Tick tick tick.

Baz had been in deep concentration for the past hour, he could feel his muscles begin to stiffen, his mind wander. He had just deployed his bishop into enemy territory, a move that will hopefully give him the advantage.

While he waited and so as not to displease Mr Clifford, Baz ran his fingers through his hair, tucked his shirt into his trousers, straightened his tie, slid back his chair.

"What the hell!" came a shout.

"No!" from another.

All the players with the exception of one sprang to their feet with either a look of shock or delight.

"I don't believe it, I was winning." David Smith cried out. The first time he had done so in match play.

A howl from Richard Bacon. "My opponent's time was tick...!" Halting mid-speech with a sheepish grin. His opponent looked down at the clock face, surprised to see his own clock hand edging ever closer to the flag. Less than a minute until it dropped.

Alan Goldsworthy had remained seated, emotionless. Not a single flinch. His stare remaining on the scattered pieces. Although his opponent, not surprisingly, had stood up, quietly savouring the moment.

Every single piece from every single game had fallen as if they had been mowed down in a hail of gun fire. It was carnage in wood.

Each player's gaze slowly followed the pleats made from the dust sheet, like the wake left behind a boat in water, gradually narrowing as the sheet finally ended up in a point at Baz's waistline, and there it disappeared, tucked into the top of his trousers as Baz rose to his feet and took a step back.

At that moment in time if a hole had opened up and swallowed him whole Baz would not have been disappointed.

The school hall was crowded that morning as it was for assembly every morning.

In one row at the back of the raised stage sat twelve teachers, their level of importance graded towards the centre. The larger more ornate chair in the middle of the line was empty, as it usually was at this time. Behind the wooden lectern stood the portly figure of the headmaster, his shaggy moustache and bespectacled round face protruded upwards.

With a businesslike air the nine men and five women looked down on the hundreds of attentive school children.

30

The vast majority of the pupils sat cross legged on the wooden parquet floor in order of age. The youngest at the front having to strain their necks at the most acute angle if they were to see anything of the headmaster presenting his instruction for the next hymn. The sixth form pupils, sat on a single line of chairs at the back, their numbers greatly diminished from children dropping out in the previous years. The need for money at home outweighs any requirement for education and only pupils from more affluent families remained.

Behind them, at the back of the hall, equally spaced out stood three other teachers, observing any wrongdoing that may occur in the horde of children before them.

What harmony there was had begun to wander and the headmaster managed to coax the last hymn out of the children.

As he did every morning he remained standing, always having one last fragment of wisdom to share before he dismissed the restless assembly.

"It is with regret that I have to tell you the school chess team under unfortunate circumstances lost their semi-final of the Evening Echo School's Chess Championship."

The murmurs of children buzzed around the hall like a swarm of hungry wasps. Some pupils began pointing, some held hands over their mouths trying hard to muffle the sound of their tittering. All eyes directed towards one forlorn figure.

"Quiet!" the Headmaster shouted. "Eyes forward."

With eyebrows curled downward he stared around the hall.

"Mr Clifford informs me it was a tight match right up to the end."

Suppressing their urge to laugh, some children began to tremble.

"Remember children it is not the cloth that maketh the man but the way he wears it."

An explosion of laughter reverberated around the hall.

Baz shrank to the floor, oblivious to the Headmaster's rage.

Baz did not play for the Victoria Manor School Chess Club again.

As much as he tried, he failed to ignore the weeks of ridicule and taunting that followed.

William Waterhouse took over board two.

Eastcastle High in a hard fought battle won the final of the Evening Echo School's Chess Championship.

ZED AND BILLY

Noah Golby crouched in front of the ramshackle stable and patted Queenie just below the knee, "Com'n me old girl," the rag-and-bone man said and with a helping tug the old mare dutifully bent her leg. She had repeated this same deed a countless number of times and always with the same look of boredom and weariness. If Queenie could talk they would probably be the most forlorn uttering anyone had ever heard. In truth, Queenie is very well cared for, some say better than the rag-and-bone man himself. After all, the family business would be nothing without her.

Leaning on a broom handle in the junk filled yard and watching his father, was the dusky, shadowy figure of Zed, Noah Golby's son and successor. A tall, powerful boy with thick black hair and smokey eyes. His dark gypsy like features gave most people the impression his appearance was just down to being unwashed.

Zed's strength, well beyond his fourteen years of age, came from helping his father on the rag-and-bone collections. The combination of their understanding and teamwork had evolved over the last couple of years. Having to hoist heavy metal objects on and off the cart, sometimes without a word being spoken, had developed as close a relationship as a father and son could ever get.

Zed always kept himself to himself. Even more so after the death of his mother just over a year ago. If anyone thought that Baz didn't talk much, then Zed spoke even less. No one ever knew what Zed was thinking and he much preferred it that way, a conviction he held throughout his entire life. When he did speak though, it was always with the greatest respect and politeness, whatever the person's age or position in life.

The rag-and-bone man's yard is entered via two large wooden gates. Whether they were open or shut was an indication of the Golby's presence. I know, closed gates at a rag-and-bone man's yard, you would be surprised how many people want to steal another's rubbish. Either side of these stood an eight foot high wall, the decaying and crumbling bricks, along with its ramshackle two storey wooden shack of a house set against the furthest wall, gave the appearance of a medieval ruin. A flight of wooden stairs butting up against the outside, led to a front door on the first floor and the Golby's living area. The ground floor was kept as a lock-up for valuable items and keeping saleable clothes away from the elements.

The yard itself was a vision of organised chaos. There was Queenie's stable, the lean-to under which the cart was kept, and several piles of scrap metal heaped up against the wall. Alongside them were more recognisable items, a street gas lamp, a washing-mangle, old vehicle parts, even a badly stuffed mountain wolf baring two huge fangs: Noah Golby was sure that even in this inanimate condition it would frighten away any unwelcome intruder. Tucked into the right hand corner was an abandoned gypsy caravan, now beyond repair and use. Its once ornate paintwork and carvings barely visible, its fractured wheels propping it up at the oddest angle, a long and hard travelled life now a bygone memory.

Few visitors would brave the damp and rotting smell of the yard. Buying and selling was the name of the game, although money usually only travelled in one direction. Noah Golby's bartering skills would impress even the most souk hardened Arab. It wasn't unusual for someone to enter the yard with the sole purpose of acquiring some vehicle part, then leave with a hat stand once belonging to the Duke of Westminster or a rare persian rug with great mystical qualities, without knowing how they actually obtained them in the first place.

Noah Golby gazed down at the underside of Queenie's hoof. "'E'll need a new shoe lad," he said to his son, stroking the fractured metal.

"Go and find some'ing to pay the blacksmith with."

Zed disappeared into the piles of metal, returning a minute later with an old rusty and twisted iron gate.

"This do Dad?"

"Good lad, now off to school with you, I don't want you skulking 'round the yard all day."

"Blacksmiths Dad? With you?"

"Na, me and Blacky got some'ing to discuss."

There were tricks of the trade Noah Golby had yet to enlighten his son about. Usually after he had returned with a cart full of lead and somewhere in the vicinity a roof had begun leaking.

"Anyway, I don't want them suits comin' 'ere asking questions like last time."

Zed reluctantly retreated to school, the first time in a long while.

Stan Keenan took a swing at his son Billy. Although he had missed him by a mile, the momentum spun the inebriated father around full circle, resulting in him being splayed out onto a small table. A bowl of cold porridge, several empty bottles of ale and the contents of an ashtray were launched into the air, finishing up over the bare floorboards. At the same time Stan Keenan was ever mindful not to spill any whisky from the metal mug held in his left hand.

With a resentful hard glare, Billy slowly backed off from his wretched father. "You couldn't knock a fucking rattle out of a baby's hand, you pitiful excuse for a human being," he spat. Then left the squalid basement flat.

Billy was not afraid of anyone, least of all his father. A bulldog of a boy, not very tall but stocky and thick set with a forehead appearing to have been carved from rock. He had large bloated hands with thick fingers and arms that were wider than most boy's legs. His deep set eyes were so thin and sunken below his strong neanderthal brow, you would think he was observing the world through narrow slits.

Billy has had very little in life, materially or emotionally: any hope he did have in this world soon evaporated with the sudden disappearance of his mother six years previous. Since that day his father progressively took solace in the bottle, leaving Billy to provide for himself.

Everything Billy owns, he has acquired himself and not always by the most honest means. His tactics were simple, intimidate! Just by being Billy Keenan. If you have spots, food, fair hair, too much weight, pocket money, too little weight or just plain and simply an existence, then it could be your time to be confronted by Billy Keenan. Fortunately for Vicky Hall he attended school as many times as his father was sober.

Waiting outside at the top of the steps were two of his like minded acquaintances, Frank Harman and Marvin Elwood. When I say acquaintances they were more like his followers, his disciples. They were nothing without him and profited far more with him.

Both boys were taken aback when Billy suddenly announced,

"we're going to school."

"What!?" declared Marvin.

"Why would you want to do that Billy?" inquired Frank, displaying his usual baffled expression.

"Food, you fucking brainless morons."

"Why don't we go behind the Bridge Cafe like last time?"

"Because of a carving knife and a very pissed off chef holding it. That's why fucking not."

FALLEN RUNNERS
1929

It is a miserable rain drenched afternoon and Baz is third in a line of four boys standing one behind each other. Either side of him are countless rows of similar lines.

The scene is reminiscent of a great weaponless army waiting on a field of battle. At the given command it would be ready to charge a nonexistent enemy and to everyone present that day, the feeling of an unexpected outcome was just as intense.

All are wearing an assortment of coloured shirts or vests and shorts, some sporting, some just your ordinary schoolwear that had seen better days, also a variety of footwear from running shoes, plimsoles, football boots and even old worn-out school shoes. Pinned to the front of each shirt is a square of white material with a bold black number painted on it. Baz is number 1157 which baffled the hell out of him as he didn't think there could be more than a few hundred boys there.

At the apex of the wall of runners is a continuous movement of rising and falling heads as the boys spring up and down like disembodied heads bobbing on a wind blown lake. Some loosen their muscles by shaking their legs as though they're trying to remove some unwanted object from their toes, only resulting in flicking wet mud on the boy in front. Many just stand motionless, hands on hips, looking down at the soggy ground, lost in their own trepidatious thoughts.

To the sides of the field are the spectators, some under umbrellas, others clutching a newspaper or some kind of bag held aloft their heads. The majority are school staff with a few selected pupils hoping to enjoy an afternoon off from teaching or being taught. Anything to get that much needed couple of hours away from lessons. All had been deceived by the light cloud cover as they departed their schools a few hours earlier.

A sporadic and spontaneous sound of clapping and shouts of encouragement punctured through the rain.

"Come on Meadowbrooks!"

"You can win this Haversfield!"

"Don't fuck up this time Albright!" yelled David Smith.

Facing this horde of sopping runners is a treacherous hundred yard run across a rain soaked field with uneven clumps of long tufty grass. Followed by a steep, strength sapping narrow hill rising to a tree lined verge where a sharp left turn will take them into dark woodland. Two and a half mud-caked miles later they will exit an opening out of the same woods from the foot of the hill, followed by a deadly hundred yard sprint to the finishing line. Most boys will be so shattered at this point in time, they probably won't even be aware of their own existence.

Lining each stage of the route are the all important markers, pupils and teachers who have volunteered to hold a white piece of card painted with a red arrow indicating the direction to follow.

Out of the four runners representing their school the highest three positions will be added together, discarding the fourth and worst placing. The team with the lowest number will be declared the winner of the City Schools Team Cross Country Race. More important to the Vicky Hall team, a place in the top twelve will ensure they proceed through to the South East Championship. All four runners from this same team will do their utmost to beat each other. Individual pride is also at stake.

The Vicky Hall line up is headed by the self-obsessed sixth form pupil Peter Sandford, a boy that appeared to have arrogance down to the finest of art forms. His first loathing was being beaten at anything, especially in a race by an insignificant fifth former like Basil Albright. On the several occasions this had happened, it had left Peter Sandford with his second most loathing, having to explain his misfortune.

Stood behind Peter Sandford was the gormless and nervous Lester Brown, a very tall and gangly sixth former with a long neck and coat hanger shoulders. An odd shaped individual who appeared to have amassed all his weight around his haunches. His long loping stride was the only attribute that made him the long distance runner he was. Unfortunately for Lester Brown it was also his height and the distance the oxygen had to travel that made him finish any race as though he had shrunk to half his size. Even though Baz had beaten him every time, it was his sixth form status that earned Lester the second place in the line. Baz's only view was of Lester Brown's stinking unwashed vest, black shorts cut down from old school trousers and a pair of hefty rugby boots, it was like standing behind an agitated ostrich with constipation.

Behind Lester Brown was Baz. The solitary life of a long distance runner was something that suited his disposition. This was Baz on his own, no one to interfere, just him and the demons within. Other runners have said that they think so much about other things they actually forget all about the running. For Baz it was the opposite, all his thinking was on the running, entirely and completely, nothing else, just concentrate on the running. And staying power, Baz had staying power in abundance: for him it was simple, start moving, put one foot in front of the other, hopefully quicker than anyone else, repeating this procedure until you are told to stop, hopefully ahead of everyone else, simple. Having a light frame with a large pair of lungs also helped, along with a determination bordering on sheer doggedness, the refusal to accept your body is about to cease up at any moment. What's the worst that could happen? Dropping dead from exhaustion, it had crossed his mind on several occasions.

Last of all and at the rear of the line is Reggie Haller, a fourth year pupil and an exceptional athlete for his age. A boy who excels at all sports and one of those boys you either hate or admire because of it. Baz couldn't think of a sport he wasn't good at. Because of his age he was devoid of the strength to be a threat to any of the other Vicky Hall runners, for this year anyhow. Annoyingly for one individual waiting at the front of the line, Reggie Haller knew which strings to pull.

"Fast start today Sandford?" yelled Reggie Haller.

"Shut up Haller," snapped Peter Sandford.

"Yeah, shut up Haller," echoed Lester Brown. His vomit regurgitating nervousness distracting him from knowing what Reggie

Haller had actually said.

"Don't want Albright to beat you again Sandford?"

"Shut the fuck up Haller."

"Yeah, shut up Haller."

"We've all got the..."

"Shut up Albright."

"Yeah, shut up Albright."

"Shut up Brown."

Waiting just left of the boys was a dark suited, bowler hatted man with a large umbrella standing on a grocer's box, a silver whistle poised in his lips, an outstretched arm aimed a starting pistol upward. The man's cheeks ballooned out and a piercing shrill filled the air. For what seemed an eternity he waited for all movement to cease. "Ready," he hollered with the bellowing voice of a Shakespearian actor.

Bodies hunch over in readiness. Baz had moved slightly to the side of Lester Brown knowing the ostrich's acceleration was not the quickest, especially after his experience in the last race when he ran straight into his back.

Seconds felt like minutes.

"Set"

No time to think.

"Crack!" The sound of the pistol blasted a hole in the sky.

The mass of runners surged forward, an unstoppable tidal wave of bodies. On his first stride Baz was side by side with Lester Brown and ahead of him on his second, tucking in directly behind Peter Sandford, the sixth formers spiked shoes flicking wet mud onto his face.

The stampede to the base of the steep incline stretched out the field. Baz was taken aback by the speed the race had started, a pace so fast it felt more like a sprint, far to quick for him to keep up. Those initial doubts rearing their ugly heads again, Baz always had to conquer them at the beginning of each race.

An arrowhead had been created as the leading runners closed in towards the foot of the rising hill. Baz reached the same spot seconds later and saw about thirty runners climbing above him. He drove on and up, each step sapping another small fragment of strength, still he managed to overtake several more runners. By the time the brow of the hill was reached most had slowed to a near walk, their laboured gasps soon turning into desperate grunts. Baz veered left onto the ridge and spotted the leaders disappearing into the trees, their close proximity inspiring him to make a quick recovery.

The fast start had taken its toll on Peter Sandford and Baz quickly took advantage of his sluggish pace, passing him easily on the narrow path.

He penetrated the woods as the sun began to break through the clouds, from overcast daylight to dappled tree lined shadows. Under his feet was a six foot wide mud sodden track. Ahead, mature birch and oak trees overlooked the pack of leading runners trudging and slipping precariously along the path. Tree roots casually emerged out of the ground, then plunged back down like slippery wooden snakes, ready to trip any unsuspecting athlete. Concentration had to be at its sharpest. Some straddlers unable to compete with the pace began to fall further back; Baz picked them off one by one, he was now in fifteenth place and closing fast.

A marker diverted them to the left.

A picture of a boy's rotting maggot eaten body entered Baz's head.

I know, a strange image to have in the middle of a cross country race. Baz always took very special care to look out for the markers, he also took particular notice in which direction the other boys were running. There was a very good reason for this. It was all because of a story Oliver had once told him. One Baz remembered well, mostly because in those days it was rare for his brother to speak more than two words to him. Oliver said he had been in a race many years ago when a boy got so far in front of the others he found himself running alone. A young marker, thinking the race hadn't reached him yet, had been taking a pee behind a tree. Instead of veering off to the right as the runner should have done, the boy ran on ahead. "How would he know otherwise?" Oliver told Baz with an innocent shrug. "That boy was never seen again. Not until his rotting maggot eaten body was found many months later by a man walking his dog." And it was this image that had always stayed with Baz, especially when confronted with a boy marker.

The spaces separating the front runners were beginning to widen as they were directed from out of the cover of the trees and back into open sky, emerging at a narrow footpath in an opening between two woods, a path just wide enough for two runners abreast. Baz had dropped behind a boy with an odd running gait, about the same height and stature as Baz but only the bottom half of his body moved, as though rigor mortis had set into everything above his waist, his elbows locked tight, his arms held rigidly in front of his chest, his hips and feet just skimmed across the ground. Could be his undoing with those plunging snakes thought Baz.

As they entered the woods again, a marker was looking down at his paint smeared board, the dripping red arrow virtually dissolved by the constant pounding from the rain. The boy with the strange gait ran to the right. "No! No! Not that way!" the marker yelled out, managing to point in the correct direction just as Baz reached him. In the corner of his eye Baz could see the boy vanishing into the distance.

The thin line of runners broadened and the pace quickened, strength of character tested to the limit, lungs starting to ache, muscles being drained, knees beginning to jar as legs ran away with themselves on the steeper descent.

Further down the hill another marker directs them back into the woods. This time the trees were more dense, the shadows darker, the mud wetter and deeper. Baz could see the eight boys in front slogging through the mud, some out of position, some creating a sloppy sucking noise with each trudging stride. Some moved over to the side, avoiding the heavy going at the centre. Behind he could hear the rasping gasps of runners, their presence spurring him onward. Ahead he could see the brightness from the widening space between the trees. The edge of the wood was now in sight, no more than a hundred strides away. Then the final sprint to the finish and glory.

"Baaaaz, proteeeein."

Baz quickly looked up and no more than ten feet in front of him was Donald Brooks, his outstretched hand clutching a half wrapped, half eaten bar of chocolate.

Donald Brooks is not the sharpest tool in the box. His power of thought could only extend to having the afternoon off school by volunteering as a marker in a cross country race. If his thinking goes beyond a certain boundary, well, it gets a bit murkier. Very much like it had this particular afternoon.

Baz had no time to consider the situation. After all, it was only a bar of chocolate, he could just take it and chuck it into the undergrowth further on. Only that combination of a swift glance and a grabbing hand caused a split second loss of concentration and that was all it needed.

The ground suddenly disappeared from under his feet and the unsuspecting Baz dropped like a stone into a foot deep muddy rain filled ditch.

Donald Brooks stared at the fallen runner trying his hardest to extract himself from the gooey mud. Only the blazing white of Baz's sorry panic-stricken eyes identified him as being a member of the human race.

Baz looked up in horror, a continuous flow of mud caked soles was all he could see. A swift rise to his knees was soon accompanied by a loud thud and a shooting pain in the side of his head. Baz did not see the runner tumbling head over heels into the mud, bringing another handful of boys down with him. He did recognise the howling of Peter Sandford though.

Baz quickly rose again, just managing to get into a standing position. This time he was hit smack on by another runner who rebounded into another, then into another, sending the towering Lester Brown toppling into the thick undergrowth like a shot giraffe.

A traffic jam of runners started to collect before the writhing pile of fallen bodies, a heaving bottleneck of cursing mud splattered, steaming schoolboys. The more agile ones like Reggie Haller managed to avoid the confusion by swerving into the trees and leaping over the bracken like fleeing gazelles.

Baz finished the race in sixty-seventh place, dazed and with a golf ball size lump above his left ear. Lester Brown loped over the line in seventy-fifth place and the mud covered Peter Sandford limped in at one hundred and eleventh. Young Reggie Haller came in at a commendable thirty-first. Out of the thirty teams Vicky Hall finished twenty-sixth.

Bazil Albright and Donald Brooks made a pact to never, ever, at any time in the entire future of the universe, reveal what happened.

Apart from one unforgettable morning, assembly was as it had been for most of the term, tedious and dull. Hymns were sung, awards and praise doled out, sermons preached. The teachers sat on their normal chairs in their usual places, occasionally a small change in the order as one had been promoted. The Headmaster, was as expected, stood behind his lectern, gripping the sides with his pudgy fingers. His roaming stare enough to bring order to the rows of school children.

"...Who has made all things well," came the dissonant sound from the hall as the last line of the last hymn was sung, followed by the usual fidgeting, coughing and sniffing.

The Headmaster stood silent for a few seconds. Glaring down at the children, his patience was rewarded after a short moment of shuffling.

"It is with regret that I have to tell you the school cross country team failed to make it through to the South East Championship."

What happened next took the wind right out of Baz's sails.

Some children turned towards him and began giggling, a covert point with a finger, a knowing whisper and Baz immediately knew Donald Brooks had broken their pact.

'I should have known Donald Brooks couldn't keep a secret. What was I thinking of? Jesus Christ not again, Peter Sandford is going to kill me. Always in assembly. I hate fucking God. Just because I don't believe in him does not give him the right to treat me like this. Fuck, fuck, fuck!'

The Headmaster continued, "I would like to finish this assembly with an old Chinese proverb, it may lessen the pain of losing for those who took part." The Headmaster gazed down at a piece of paper and began reading. "Aiming for your goal and missing it is better than aiming for a ditch and hitting it."

And for those in the know, like it had in one other assembly that year, an explosion of laughter reverberated around the hall.

That afternoon Giles and Rosemary Albright were summoned to the Headmaster's office, although it was only Baz's father that made the journey. Another pact is made, this time it is kept.

Mr Clifford gladly volunteered his services, a certain chess match not forgotten.

With the stinging still fresh on his palms Baz found it difficult to write five hundred lines of, 'I will not use abusive language in assembly.' Although in a strange way he did enjoy the repetitiveness.

GOODBYE OLD MR THOMAS

Giles Albright arrived at Old Mr Thomas's home on a grey Saturday afternoon. A dilapidated, tiny, old stone cottage in the most impoverished part of town and only a stones throw away from the railway sidings. The paint that was still remaining had virtually surrendered to the weather, awarding the whole place a look of resignation. The small brick chimney poking through a haphazardly tiled roof would normally never be seen without a steady flow of smoke rising out of it. That was until today.

The end terraced cottage was the last from a row of four. The other three are unoccupied and are now pretty well uninhabitable. All four stood on the side of a dead-end road opposite a small area of grassy wasteland where the old milkman grazed his four cows. A rickety cowshed Old Mr Thomas had built himself stood to the rear of the cottage, a place where, twice a day, every day, he would milk his cows before he released them onto the wasteland to set off on his daily rounds.

Giles Albright stood facing the front door and was feeling none too happy about disturbing the old milkman. Tapping softly on the wood he peered through its grimy, cracked window pane.

The vision awaiting him that Saturday afternoon shocked him to his bones.

On the other side of the tiny front room and through its open door into the kitchen he could see the grimy black boots, dark trousers and waistcoat all belonging to and worn by Old Mr Thomas. He could see the grey of his shirt sleeves hanging by his side and the outline of his broad working man's hands. The milkman's head and shoulders were hidden by the wall above the kitchen door but the overturned chair and the clear empty space under old Mr Thomas's boots were patently evident.

Giles Albright, dreading the sight that was about to confront him, stepped into the death smell of the cottage. Reluctantly he stood in the kitchen doorway and gazed up at the contorted and crusty grey face of Old Mr Thomas. Above him a rope descended from the darkness of an open trap door in the ceiling and like a stubbly snake, wound itself around the neck of the old man.

Giles Albright arrived at Noah Golby's yard less than one minute after his gruesome discovery. Noah and Zed were unloading the cart after the Saturday morning round. Queenie had her huge head lowered and was busily chomping on a pile of hay, aware of but ignoring the advancing Giles Albright. Zed was the first to see him approach and instinctively knew this visit was different. Giles Albright's stare, stained with sadness was steadfastly aimed at Noah Golby. Zed said nothing, only the direction of his gaze made his father aware of the visitors presence.

"A'ernoon Sir."

"Hello Mr Golby, sorry, Giles Albright, Minchen Street." He paused for a moment. "May I have a few words please?"

Both father and son gazed accusingly at each other with the same suspicious concern at each others misdemeanour. The rag-and-bone man listened as the visitor made him aware of the demise of Old Mr Thomas. The conversation concluded with one short nod of agreement.

"Watch the yard son, me and Mr Albright are goin' to the old co'ages."

Zed obeyed without question and watched his father approach the cart with Giles Albright in tow.

"Com'on old girl, we got work to do," he said. A cloud of horse dust wafted into the air as he patted Queenie on the shoulder.

"Put one foot on the wheel sir and pull yourself up, thats it sir, you're a natural."

"Fear is not of death but life itself," Giles Albright said quietly, as he sat on the cart.

"Sorry sir."

"Nothing, Mr Golby."

Noah Golby made a clucking sound, flicked the rein and the cart trundled forward.

To Giles Albright, the scene was no less tragic the second time he saw it. He gazed down at the bread knife in the rag-and-bone man's hand and then into Noah Golby's eyes.

"A terrible sight sir, so it is, a terrible sight." Noah Golby said as he uprighted the toppled chair. "I'll 'old him sir, you cut the rope." He passed the knife over to Giles Albright and wrapped one arm around Old Mr Thomas's legs, with his other hand he gripped tightly onto a fold of cloth from the back of his waistcoat.

44

Giles Albright stood up on the chair, and began sawing through the rope, one by one each strand snapped. He looked at the old milkman and remembered the sympathetic and wise words he had said to him at Norma's funeral. He remembered the times he had listened to his tales, always told with a smile and a glint in those wise old eyes. He remembered the kindness he had shown to his family throughout the rationing at the end of the war.

Giles Albright finally sliced through the rope and Old Mr Thomas dropped by a few inches. They carefully laid him on the stone floor and removed the rope from around his neck, a bed sheet was draped over his body. Noah Golby crossed his chest and the two men looked down in thoughtful silence.

"Thank you Mr Golby, as I promised, I know Mr Thomas would have wanted it. He told me how you had helped him," said Giles Albright through the bounce of his pipe.

"Not a lot 'ere of much good Mr Albright." Something Noah Golby would always say when he was called to a house clearing, even if there was a solid gold statue standing in the corner. "Anything metal, save it going to waste sir," he added.

The concern Giles Albright had over how particular the rag-and-bone man might have been was soon quashed when the cart was loaded with everything from saucepans, an old wood burning stove, milk churns, bottles, the bed frame, even the stained and grubby kitchen sink. Giles Albright was beginning to think that the only thing remaining was going to be Old Mr Thomas himself.

"You had better leave the churns Mr Golby. The cows will need milking."

The two men walked in front of Queenie on the short journey back to the yard.

"Why?" asked the rag-and-bone man.
Giles Albright took the unlit pipe out of his mouth and gazed into the scorched emptiness of its bowl.

"Large dairies and their new vehicles Mr Golby, bottles in crates, pasteurisation."

"Pasteurisation?"

"Safer milk."

"Poor old sod," Noah Golby said quietly and more to himself.

"The milk round was all he had. It's a changing world out there Mr

45

Golby."

"They'll always be junk sir," said Noah Golby, hopefully.

In the months after the funeral, Giles Albright, along with Baz, would occasionally look in on Noah and Zed Golby. The two men would sit on wobbly old chairs by an old beer barrel precariously held together by its remaining rusty ring. They would drink tea, sometimes port and puff at their pipes like two tribal elders.

Baz was in Baz heaven, he couldn't think of anything more rewarding than repairing broken household objects.

As always, Zed never said much, he was glad to provide the brawn or dab some paint when needed, and for the first time was happy to have someone his own age to hang out with, as was Baz. Zed had always been a solitary boy, in a strange way that was what Baz liked about him, he felt they were kindred spirits. Their lack of conversation was probably one of the reasons they got on so well. The boys, although happy in each others company *in* the yard, away from it they kept themselves very much to themselves. As they had always done.

THE HOLE

"I see food!" said Billy Keenan to his two chums just minutes after arriving at Vicky Hall. In fact, what Billy was actually seeing was an old cracked leather satchel with bulging sides and straining straps. And to the hungry penniless Billy that could mean only one thing.

"Lets go hunting," he said, stomping through the crowded playground and parting the children like Moses at the Red Sea. Billy was a boy on a mission and his calling hung off the back of an unsuspecting schoolboy.

"What's in the satchel Albright?" said Marvin Elwood standing behind Baz while fingering the straps.

Baz spun his head around and found Marvin glaring at him with a heinous smirk, not unusually Frank Harman stood to the side of his accomplice, displaying his usual vacant expression. Baz, bemused by the situation knew these two guttersnipes by reputation, he also knew they were all mouth and no action.

Billy, out of sight, had circled around the preoccupied victim and was now standing behind him, carefully squeezing the satchel for any identifiable contours that might resemble food.

Baz spun around again and was shocked to see himself looking straight into Billy's hard cold eyes. Billy Keenan does not turn around for anyone or for any reason, especially not a half moon eye.

"You heard Albright. What's in the fucking satchel?"

"Nothing that would interest you Billy," said Baz, respectfully.

"Give it to me Albr..." said Billy, suddenly stopping mid-sentence.

On this particular morning there was one pupil in the entire school none of the other pupils could see, or teachers for that matter, but he could see them.

Vicky Hall has a bicycle shed, a three sided structure cobbled together with planks of wood that had a convenient gap to observe any approaching enemy, namely teachers.

The telltale sign of rising smoke is the usual indication of pupil presence and for the past few minutes Zed Golby had been standing in that exact same place, puffing on his roll-up and surveying the area for any advancing foe. What had caught his eye was the rare appearance of Billy Keenan and his two stooges standing in a circle, surrounding some unsuspecting victim. Normally at this stage Zed would ignore this occurrence. He and Billy Keenan avoided each other like the plague, it was a kind of mutual understanding, an unwritten agreement. So much so that neither had ever spoken a single word to each other. It wasn't until a gap appeared through the horde of animated school children did this island of menace become clearer and Zed became aware of who the unsuspecting victim was.

Zed Golby took one last puff of his roll-up, dropped it to the ground, pivoted his right boot over it and left it amongst the growing pile of stubs.

"Give it to me Albr..."

"Let go Keenan," Zed said with such force it startled everyone present. Also being the first time Billy and his two accomplices had ever heard him speak.

"Keep out of this Golby," snarled Billy.

"Let go Keen..."

47

"I said let...

'Clang clang clang!' The sound of the morning bell resonated around the playground and the children were sucked into their orderly lines.

"Behind the hole, four o'clock, be there!" Billy dictated to Zed as he swaggered his way out of the school exit with his two lackeys in tow.

Apart from Baz and Zed, the playground quickly cleared, only one other person remained.

"You don't have to go Zed. It's not your fight, it's mine. Besides if I run they'll never catch me," said Baz.

"No place to run behind hole Baz. Four o'clock. You be home." Zed also left the school knowing too well the consequences if this dispute wasn't brought to some kind of conclusion.

It was only when Baz was left standing there that he realised he had no idea where or what the hole might be.

Throughout the day every streetwise pupil was sought out. "Do you know where the hole is?" Baz asked.

"Only the one in your head Albright," the favoured response.

"You're the second person to ask me that," had been the reply on three occasions.

Then it occurred to him. Alan Goldsworthy. Why didn't he think of him at the beginning. Alan Goldsworthy knows everything.

It was ten minutes before four and Baz stood facing the hole. Only at that moment in time, it wasn't a hole. It was a ten foot high wall running alongside the canal footpath, a thick shrub concealing the lower bricks. Baz looked across the oily black water of the canal and saw the imposing furniture depository, exactly as Alan Goldsworthy had described. Baz looked from side to side, it was clear, without another thought he darted behind the shrub, and there it was, the hole! Or to be more exact, a two foot irregular square of missing bricks creating an entrance to a potholed wasteland half the size of a football pitch. For the past ten years the area had been turned into a wilderness of weeds and wild thorny shrubs, interrupted only by the odd patch of barren stony areas. A dumping ground for discarded rubbish from unwanted bottles to rotting mattresses, even an old rusted automobile carcass lay in a deep gully, its rusty underbelly on display to the world.

Baz crouched on all fours and crawled unseemly head first through the opening. On the other side he emerged into a clear area of rubble laden land, at least twenty foot square and surrounded by a jungle of monster weeds, large spiked nettles and thorny shrubs, all growing out of proportion to any other plant he had ever seen before.

He had never felt so alone, or so vulnerable.

In the distance he could see the tops of white chimneys poking above the green wilderness, there were at least half a dozen of them, tall, ornate, frozen in time. But what gave the place the most eerie feeling was a mildewy stone statue of an angel with out-spread wings, surrounded by four open mouthed cherubs, each one damaged, a nose, an arm, a leg, a wing, were all missing in one form or another, a centre piece for what was once a magnificent fountain. The entire object being gruesomely strangled by a tangled, creeping shrub.

Baz ducked behind a dense bush and there he crouched, waiting.

Minutes passed like hours. The eerie silence was only broken by the occasional fluttering of a bird's wing or the rustling of some unseen creature rummaging around in the undergrowth.

He then heard whispered voices coming from the other side of the hole. After a long deep gasp of air, he held his breath. And there he remained as frozen as the angel behind him.

Four small white fingers appeared around the hole, then like a cork from a bottle, Frank Harman unceremoniously popped through the opening, followed by a scurrying Marvin Elwood. Billy was nowhere to be seen.

For a few seconds the two reprobates stood motionless, their senses opening to the creepy stillness. They quickly separated, Baz had lost sight of Marvin but could clearly see Frank searching round the edge of the area.

"Ouch! Fucking thorns," complained Marvin, too close for comfort.

Baz remained as small and silent as humanly possible. Squeezing his eyes shut, a strange hope that if he couldn't see them, then they wouldn't be able to see him, or was it that he just didn't want to see them finding him. Either way he knew it would only be a matter of time.

Suddenly Frank called out. "Look what we got here Marv, we got ourselves a rat."

"Oh yeah, a real living, breathing rat."

Baz hesitantly opened his eyes, expecting to see Marvin or Frank staring down on his sorry, hunched up body.

"Hey Billy, its all clear, only come and see what we got."

Billy struggled to squeeze his burly torso through the hole. At one point nearly wedging himself in, putting him in a even fouler mood than his usual disposition.

Baz could see Frank, then Marvin. Then!

Jesus Christ! What is he doing here?

Frank Harman had grabbed William Waterhouse and yanked him into full view of the helpless Baz. The whole miserable situation felt reminiscent of a prisoner being brought forward for execution. Billy stomped toward Will, stopping only inches from his face. He then asked the exact same question Baz would have liked the answer to. Except not in the intimidating way Billy Keenan asked it.

"What the fuck are you doing here?"

In truth, Baz would probably have not said it much different.

Will remained silent. Baz couldn't work out whether it was out of plain stupidity or fear. Or both.

"I said, what part of the fucking ground did a worm like you crawl out of? *And* who the fuck are you anyway?"

Will, again, remained silent.

In truth, William hadn't the foggiest idea why he was there. He could only put it down to the guilt he had gnawing away inside of him ever since he abandoned Baz all those years ago.

"I said..."

"I am, my acrimonious adversary, a friend of Master Albright," he then stood as straight as a die with his chin held high. "We are brothers of the board," he added proudly "And my name is not your concern old boy."

"Old boy!" Billy laughed. "Then I'll have to beat it out of you, *old boy.*"

"In that case I've come to make up the numbers."

"Yeah, three against one, great fucking arithmetic, *old boy.*"

"Make that two!" shouted Baz springing up from behind the bush like a jack-in-the-box.

"Bloody hell, they come in fucking pairs," announced Marvin.

"This is my fight Billy," said Baz, striding forward, unstrapping his satchel and spilling the contents onto the ground. "Look, this is what you want to see isn't it?" Pointing defiantly to his muddy screwed up running gear, some dog-eared school books and a half eaten rotting apple which Baz had forgotten was there. "Fill your face, fat boy." Thinking if this is the day he was going to die, then he was going down with pride and dignity, if not with a great deal of stupidity. It was also the first time Baz had ever seen someone's face go from a blotchy red to an all over beetroot.

"If Golby sends you two gob-shites to fight his battles," snarled Billy, clenching his fist.

Baz couldn't believe how many thoughts could enter ones mind in a tiny fraction of a second. 'If I run that would mean leaving Will. Maybe Will deserves it. He deserted me. No, I couldn't do that, it wasn't his fault anyway. I wouldn't be able to live with myself. Anyhow, run to where? Zed was right, there is nowhere to run in the hole. If I stay and beg for mercy then I would be forever more at Billy's beck and call. I would have to leave the country. And if I stay and fight, how much damage would Billy have done before I'm scarred for life, before every bone in my body is smashed into a thousand pieces.'

A smirking Marvin and Frank could smell the imminent blood.

"I send no one." A voice punched through the air. "Zed Golby fights his own battle."

Billy spun his head around. The ridge where the voice had come from was deserted, apart from an old bicycle frame and a dead shrub.

"Zed Golby fights his own battle." Zed was now standing as large as life and no more than six feet in front of Billy.

For a few seconds the whole world appeared to have stopped, the birdsong, the rustling from a slight breeze, everything had frozen, as if the reel from a movie had got stuck.

"Aaaargh" Billy screamed as he turned and ran towards Zed, his head down like a charging bull.

Zed's first punch rebounded off the top of the much shorter boy's stooping head. Then a thudding pain as Billy planted a strike into the left side of his rib cage, and another into his right. Zed sprung backward, pushing down on the back of Billy's neck, a strike on the right side of Billy's chin, his face distorting out of all recognition and splattering blood over the leaves of a nearby bush. Like an unstoppable train, Billy advanced, blow after blow flying indiscriminately into his adversary's body. Zed winced again as another hit him hard in the ribs. Then with all of his formidable strength he bent down and wrapped his arms around the tops of Billy's legs. Lifting him up he threw him onto the ground, Zed fell on top, both boys writhing around in the dirt. Zed rose first, thrusting one knee into Billy's cheek and pressing his hands on the side of his face, rubbing it like a cheese grater into the stones. Billy's knee thumped into Zed's kidney sending him flying sideways, hollering in pain, his hands scuffing on the stony ground. Staggering to his feet and panting heavily, Zed saw Billy hauling himself up, holding a large boulder. Without pausing, Zed launched the toe of his boot into Billy's mouth, two small white objects flew through the air, a dark thick string of frothy mucus followed, his whole face turned red. Then dazed and breathless he gazed up at Zed with a desperate look of resignation.

"I think he's got the message," yelled Baz running in front of Zed and holding him back, feeling the fire drain from his body.

Zed dropped to his knees, clutching his side, his head bowed low. An act he would repeat once more in his lifetime.

———————

Dear Margaret Studd, Daily Tribune.

Basil Albright has been a pupil in my school for the past four years. I have found Basil to be an extremely reliable and capable student in both woodwork and metalwork lessons. His enthusiasm in after-class contributions including tool repair and maintenance has been invaluable to his teacher.

Basil has also distinguished himself highly in out-of-school pursuits such as the chess and the cross country teams. I have no hesitation in recommending Basil for the position of apprentice press engineer with immediate commencement.

Yours sincerely

Malcolm Jaimeson

Headmaster

Victoria Manor Secondary School

II

A WAR AT HOME

MEETING THE ENEMY

MRS WATERHOUSE

14 MINCHEN STREET

MRS BLAKENEY

MOST LOSE A COUPLE

A WAR AT HOME

1936

The first time Baz heard the name Adolf Hitler, he thought of it as just the same as any other foreign name, like Mahatma Gandhi or Charles Lindbergh or his neighbour Mr Batushanky.

The first time he knew of the book Mein Kampf he thought it was the same as any other story, like The Adventures of Huckleberry Finn or Gulliver's Travels.

The first time he heard about the Third Reich he thought about the last war.

1940

Baz decided there had been enough killing in the world already for him to add to it. Not realising most people would call him a coward, ignorant, even irresponsible, or worse, a pro-nazi or fascist. I would call Baz a brave man. Not in the same way as a soldier or sailor or airman, but in a way where it is more courageous to stand by your principles and take the abuse and humiliation that would inevitably follow.

Baz had made a decision. The Daily Tribune would have to do without one of its engineers for the time being. Wars are not won by fixing printing presses.

It was a February mid-morning, Baz had begun a walk starting from his home in Minchen Street, a determined pace in his stride.

On the streets he could see faces masked with despair, dark expressions conceding to the horrific realisation of times ahead, harsh reminders of just over twenty years ago now repeating themselves. Some were already kitted out in their uniform of greys, blues, greens and browns. Norma's funeral was the last time Baz could recall such wretched expressions. A vague memory but not forgotten. He also knew many would not see these streets again.

Baz entered the grubby grey stone building of the Employment Exchange.

53

A short queue had already lined up in front of a solid wooden desk, a metal chain hanging from a crossed beam in the ceiling held up a white sign with stencilled black lettering. 'REGISTER HERE'.

Baz looked down the row of people, a varied cross section of the social standings in the area. One man wearing his one and only ill fitting Sunday suit, others wore working jackets, heavy boots and flat caps. In front of them was a young woman with her warm winter coat and perfect make-up. Two upstanding gentlemen, one wearing a long overcoat and bowler hat, the other, a smart expensive suit, an umbrella pressed stiffly against his neatly creased trousers. Their web of contacts not stretching far enough to avoid the experience of having to register.

Sat under the sign and behind the wooden desk was an attractive young woman. He thought her soft fair skin, large eyes and faultless features held a beauty beyond any other he had seen in female form.

Behind her were a number of other desks, all occupied by older men, some in military attire, others official looking in dark suits. Most of these had someone sitting opposite them, questions were being asked, notes were taken and papers exchanged. Then the person was moved on through a door at the side, soon replaced by another.

Baz eventually took the three steps forward.

"Name?" she asked. Not even a glance up.

"Baz."

"Name?" she repeated, louder.

"Basil. Oh! Basil Albright. With one 'l', the Albright that is. Not the 'l' in Basil," he said with a smile, feeling proud his humour appeared to have flowed effortlessly. Until she looked up with the sourest expression. Slowly and quietly he repeated, "Basil Albright."

She froze for a couple of seconds, pen poised mid-air. She was not used to men looking past her.

"Basil Albright. With one bloody 'l' in Albright."

"Correct, one bloody 'l'," said Baz.

"Address?" she said irritably.

"14 Minchen Street."

"Age?" her voice getting less patient.

"Twenty-six."

With a quick glance she looked up again. "Male." Then quietly added. "Possibly."

Leaning to one side she looked down at the queue forming behind. An urgency had now appeared in her voice.

"Are you applying for military service?" she said quickly.

"Yes. No, I mean."

"Are you applying for civilian employment?"

"No."

"Then *what* are you registering for?"

"I just don't want to kill anyone," Baz said, with a shrug of his shoulders, thinking no more of his answer. He even thought she may respect him for it.

"Are you a CO?" she said abruptly.

"A what?"

"Do you object to fighting in the war?"

"If it includes killing anyone, yes."

"So you are a CO, sit over there and wait to be called." Loosely pointing her pen over her shoulder.

Baz sat next to a streetwise looking youth with unruly brown hair. The lad was leaning forward, staring pensively at the floor, his chin cupped in his hands and clutching a piece of paper. He looked at Baz, then with one shake of a wrist he flapped the sheet in the air.

"Conscripted," said the young lad, rolling his eyes.

"Oh."

"They said I have a choice, Army, Navy or Air Force. Everyone wants the RAF or Navy. If I choose the Army I'll probably get the posting I want."

"Do you know the posting you want?"

"Yeah, back home."

"Oh," repeated Baz.

"And you?"

"Sorry? Oh volunteer, well no, that's not quite true. I'm a C.O, that's it, a C.O."

The young lads next action confused the hell out of Baz. Without warning or even a summons by one of the officials, the lad shot to his feet as if he had sat on a hot cinder. With a look of disgust, he cast a glare towards Baz, then quickly moved to a chair further down the row. A whispered comment to an old man prompted a similar unpleasant glare.

Baz remained on his chair. The names of the people that had sat before him had already been summoned. One by one the names of the people seated after him were called. Baz continued to wait.

Two hours had passed and a sign nailed to a wooden plinth is placed in the open front doorway. People came in from the street, looked at the notice and walked away.

The girl rose from behind the desk. Baz could now see the full extent of her elegance. The olive green suit buttoned tight at the waist portrayed a slender and shapely figure with a narrow waist. She lifted her arms and pinned a beret to her neatly styled brown hair. Then with a not so graceful movement, picked up a bag from under the desk and clomped out of the building like an old shire horse. No one's perfect, thought Baz.

"Basil Albright!" A shout tore through the air.

The one remaining official was staring in his direction. Not the most welcoming of looks, thought Baz, considering he was here to volunteer his services for King and country. Baz strolled over, pulled the chair from under the desk and sat down.

The official took a silver watch out of his waistcoat, snapped the lid shut and quickly returned it to its pocket. "What is your religion?" the man said in a condescending manner, followed by a puzzled glare at Baz's eyes.

Baz paused for a moment and wondered what religion had to do with anything. Anyhow, from past experience Baz always thought carefully before answering this question. "I don't have a religion. Write atheist or nonbeliever if you want, I don't care. They're both the same."

"You're not a quaker then?"

"No, I'm an engineer. A print..."

"Or a Jehovah Witness," the man interrupted.

"Witness to what?"

"None," the official mumbled to himself as he wrote.

He then repeated the same watch staring routine as he had done before. "You'll get a summons to a tribunal in the post," he said. Then with a vigorous drop of his hand, he stamped 'CO' in large bold letters on the piece of paper and rose to his feet.

"Summons, tribunal?"

"Goodbye, Albright."

"CO?"

"Goodbye!"

POST OFFICE
9th March 1940
TELEGRAM
PRIORITY CC- MR MRS ALBRIGHT 14 MINCHEN
STREET
=DEEPLY REGRET TO INFORM YOU THAT YOUR SON
LEADING SEAMAN OLIVER WALTER ALBRIGHT
P/JX145642 HAS BEEN MISSING PRESUMED
KILLED ON WAR SERVICE LETTER FOLLOWS
SHORTLY=
COMMODORE DEVONPORT

Baz had told no one about what had happened on that day at the Employment Exchange. Whether it was out of shame or embarrassment, or simply that he wasn't able to explain something he did not understand himself. It was not until he picked up a newspaper a few days later and read an article tucked away on page five that everything came to light.

SQUADRON LEADER RESCUES CO

A highly decorated fighter pilot came to the rescue of a man being beaten by four yobs.

Squadron Leader Paul Batty chased the youths after they had punched and kicked the victim, his body covered with tar and goose feathers, the word 'conchie' (conscientious objector) was painted on his forehead. The perpetrators were later arrested but released on the same day, without charge. The staff at the hospital where Squadron Leader Batty took the victim refused to give treatment, he then went on to take him to The Society of Friends (Quakers) where he was given a bed, cared for and fed.

It was later found that the beaten man is Mr Tom Wright, a teacher from Warwick. A local newspaper had written an article about him headed 'CONCHIE TEACHER REFUSES TO FIGHT FOR HIS

57

COUNTRY' after Mr Wright refused to sign a statement declaring 'I hereby solemnly and sincerely declare that I am not a conscientious objector or a member of the Peace Pledge Union.' Although, he later stated that he was not a member of either, adding "He just didn't think it was right that he should be asked to sign it." He was dismissed from his job at the school and refused to sign up to any of the armed forces, saying "All I wanted was my job back." In the following days after publication Mr Wright was flooded with abusive and threatening mail, some included a cutting of his picture with a Hitler style moustache drawn on it, excrement was wiped over another. To avoid any more antagonism Mr Wright moved to London without telling his family of his destination. This resulted in him not receiving the summons for the tribunal hearing. A week later Mr Wright was arrested and sent to prison.

Although Baz had heard the words conscientious objector in passing, he hadn't really paid much heed to it. He just thought people object to most things most of the time anyhow. After all, it was only human nature and being conscientious about your objections didn't seem such a bad thing.

It was only by luck he had read the article at all. Under normal circumstances he never really took much notice of newspapers, even though he had worked at one for years. Baz thought it best not to know what was happening in the world, he found living his own life hard enough.

After reading the article he realised the seriousness of the situation. Abusive and threatening mail, letters with excrement wiped over them, but what hit him like a bombshell was that word prison. It was then he felt helpless, he thought life was going to deal him his worst blow yet.

Baz had felt guilty that he hadn't yet informed his parents, especially his father, who he knew would be more saddened that Baz hadn't confided in him.

Only this envelope had 'HMSO. If undelivered return to the Harvest Inn Law Courts' stamped on the back.

Now it was out in the open. In some ways he was relieved they had seen it, the problem of telling them, or not telling them, had been decided. In his defence he had known they were both deeply upset after receiving the telegram about Oliver. Not wanting to increase their torment anymore had been done out of kindness, so he had told himself anyhow. He felt it would be much worse to let them worry over something they would need an explanation for.

Baz sat down at the kitchen table and slid the envelope in front of himself. For a short moment he just gazed at it, as though it would divulge its secrets there and then.

It was Baz's mother that spoke first. "I told you he would drag us through the mud. Law courts! What's the foolish boy done now?" She scowled. Then she sat behind her sewing machine and fiddled with some tangled thread. "I can hear the neighbours now," she added under her breath.

Giles Albright was seated beside the kitchen table, his smoking paraphernalia spread out in front of him. A pipe, an old blackened cloth, a scratched and dented silver baccie tin surrounded by hundreds of tiny strands of tobacco. Since the beginning of time Baz could remember these same objects in the same place at the same table and in the same condition. He could only think that his father had acquired them looking that way.

Baz explained the events that unfolded in the Employment Exchange, even adding the infatuation he had with the girl. His mother had to stop him sharply when the account was getting too detailed. "She wouldn't be interested in you," she sneered.

"Love is not love which alters when it alteration finds," his father had said with a glint in his eyes, then added, "William Shakespeare."

Baz would have to think about that one.

He told them about the reaction of the young lad. He told them about the man seated behind the desk and the way he kept looking at his watch. "His lunch was far more important than my future."

Baz's explanations for not wanting to kill anyone were not as convincing as he would have liked, although he talked from the heart and listening to himself, he heard nothing that made him think differently.

"Violence never solved violence," he said, looking solemnly at his father, then added, "Giles Albright."

Baz heard a high pitch whistling noise as his father sucked through the unlit pipe. He had seen it lit so rarely these days.

"Norma, now Oliver, we've lost so much already."

"You'd have him dead already, he's probably playing one of his stupid jokes again," his mother said. "You wait, he'll be home for

Christmas, I'll have my favourite son back, you'll see."

Baz ignored her as he had always done, it had been inbuilt. "It's the people at the top, they started it, let them fight. Do you think I owe them anything? I owe them nothing. It's us, the people at the bottom that get the raw deal. Friends and foe. We're all made from flesh and blood, we all have the same emotions. That man who sank Oliver's ship was under orders, he was just as scared as the next man. Why should I obey an order to kill him when I don't blame him. When I don't even know him. He probably has a mother and father, just like you. Do you want them to get a telegram like that one?" he said, glancing up at the sheet of paper on the mantlepiece.

"What will the neighbours say?" said Rosemary Albright. "They will say 'the mother with the coward son.' That's what!"

Baz glared at her. She looked away.

"Wondering what the neighbours are going to say will be the least of our worries," his father said, disentangling a wad of tobacco from the tin.

A moments silence. "Was I right?" Baz asked.

His father finished pressing his thumb into the bowl, lit a match and for the first time in days the recognisable glow of red lit up the small chamber. "A man should see what he is and not what he thinks he should be," vanishing behind a cloud of smoke as he sat back. "Wars are all the same. The more there are, the more it all seems too normal, only this war will make it far too acceptable to have others. We can rebuild the houses and the factories but it's the memories that will stay with us, it's the memories that will turn to hate." He paused for a second. "You will be fighting more than one war from now on. Don't let it turn to hate son."

Suddenly, the noise from hard soles clopped down the stairs. Ruby halted on the bottom step and caught sight of the sombre faces. "What? Have you heard any more about Oliver?"

"We were just discussing the war darling," Rosemary Albright said.

"Crap isn't it," Ruby replied, as she moved in front of the mirror. "I'm seeing Peter tonight. We'll probably eat at the station." She put a winter coat over her bottle green uniform and carefully positioned her cap.

Ruby had joined the Women's Voluntary Service a year ago. Her tasks were varied, from sorting bundles of clothes shipped over by the

American Red Cross, to more recently, evacuating children from the city. Most leaving their homes and families for the first time. Their world now in a small scuffed suitcase and a cardboard box strung around their necks. Ruby's bubbly and extrovert nature made her very adept at easing the separation from their families. Although she never revealed her distress on the railway station platforms, more than once she had returned home withdrawn, sobbing in the solitude of her bedroom.

"See you later, don't wait up," she shouted back, departing swiftly through the front door.

All three replies were said in unison, all were different.

Baz gazed down to the envelope, sliced it open with a kitchen knife, unfolded the letter and held the sheet of paper in front of his eyes.

"Fourth of June."

———————

The tribunal hearing occupied a twenty foot square, oak panelled room. Glossy varnished floorboards loudly echoed the sound of anyone walking on them. Apart from a few well trodden rugs the whole establishment seemed to have the same wood adorning every wall and floor. Baz thought it would be impossible to be anywhere in this building without someone else knowing about it.

After a short pause to scrutinise Baz, an old clerk with a severe face and a stiff limp came to the door and called out his name; without waiting he returned to the room. A point of his willowy finger indicated to a side row of desks. Other than that, he showed no interest in Baz whatsoever, other than contempt, that was obvious.

Sunk into the far wall of the room was an imposing white marble fireplace with grey veins grazing its surface. A set of brass weighing scales stood at the centre of its deep mantelpiece. Above them hung an elaborate coat of arms mounted on a deeply carved wooden shield.

Running parallel with three walls were a number of desks that had been pushed together to make a 'U' shape. A dark green baize cloth covered the end row of desks running in front of the fireplace wall. Equally spaced along these were three large, blue jotting sheets with their corners tucked into leather mats, three glass ashtrays and half filled tumblers sat beside them.

Baz had never seen so much oak in one room. Apart from the windowpanes and fireplace, the only break from the wood was the ornate cream plaster rose above a small brass knob and chandelier and a plate surrounding the light switch.

He stood with a large window behind him, the warm glow from the sunlight offering a false sense of well-being. Another beam penetrated through a mist of dust, its broad ray hitting part of the wall opposite, highlighting the squares of unfaded wood where paintings had once hung.

Facing him on the row of desks opposite were the old clerk and a middle aged woman with timid mouse like features. She was absorbed in official papers, occasionally looking up with a disconcerting glance. The old clerk still avoided any eye contact, Baz thought he was probably a war veteran, wounded in the leg. Conscientious objectors were not going to be his favourite people.

Two constables had entered the room shortly after Baz, followed by three men in ill fitting suits. One had a light brown raincoat draped over his arm and a floppy trilby which he removed cowboy style. Journalists, Baz thought, then remembered the newspaper article and that word prison again. One of the policemen remained at the door until everyone had settled, he quietly shut it and waited, his legs astride, his large hands clasped in front. The other constable stood menacingly to the side of Baz. The journalists sat scattered on plain wooden chairs situated either side of the entrance door, notepads and pencils at hand, ready to debase Baz's very existence. He could read the headlines now, 'conscientious objector sentenced to life'.

A rectangular door size hole suddenly appeared in the far corner of the room. An overweight, dark suited clerk carrying a thick pile of papers appeared, soon followed by a large formidable looking woman with an enormous frontage, then two other men, one with shadowy afternoon stubble and years of hard labour etched into his face, the other was clean shaven, much older, more distinguished looking with swept back, steel grey hair. The door virtually vanished into the wall as the clerk shut it behind him, only the brass knob gave any indication of its existence. Everyone rose to their feet as they entered the room.

The clerk placed some official looking sheets of paper on each of the jotting pads and pulled out the seat for the woman, the chair almost disappearing beneath her huge frame. It was only after the distinguished looking man sat down, that everyone else followed suit.

The clerk then walked to within a couple of feet from where Baz stood and meticulously divided his stack of papers into four orderly smaller piles.

"Stand up straight!" he said abruptly, as if he was talking to a school child.

Grimaces were etched into every face in the room as a loud grinding sound penetrated the air from the scraping of Baz's chair.

The rotund clerk spoke in a precise voice that dominated the entire room. "Basil Albright. Application for exemption from combative duties on conscientious grounds. This is a pre-court hearing. Judge Barmby presiding."

His statement was immediately replaced by the ruffling of paper and the clearing of throats. The thick serious air gave way to a business like manner, as though it was just another days work for all concerned.

Seated in the centre was Judge Barmby, the chairman of the tribunal and the first to speak.

Prior to this appointment, Judge Barmby had been a high court judge, rising to that position through a lifetime of privileged hard toil. Making friends in high places, calling in and returning favours. He was a master of manipulation. A man who knew when to give and when to take. He had reached the summit of his profession many years ago and enjoyed the authority and power over his court, demanding respect from every individual and never failing to get it. Judge Barmby knew he would always have the last word. Listening to the ranting of hardened criminals and the manoeuvring of a barrister's evidence was an everyday occurrence for this extremely astute man. Judge Barmby was no ones fool and neither did he suffer them. His only regret in life? Not giving longer sentences.

He also knew the people before him at these hearings were not real criminals. Being of a certain religious persuasion, belief or opinion is not a crime. Helping the war effort was his main aim, finding round holes for round pegs was his objective. Although, Judge Barmby disliked cowards intensely.

The room fell into an absolute silence as the judge prioritised his paper pile. Looking at Baz over his half moon spectacles and with a matter-of-fact exactness he finally spoke. "Mr Albright, I see by your submission that you have no character witnesses." His gaze held longer than usual as he studied Baz's eyes.

"No," Baz replied.

"You have no letters of support from a lawyer or union representative or a doctor? Or anyone?"

"No."

This hearing will attach a lot of importance to witness statements Mr Albright."

"I have no need for someone to speak for my conscience."

Judge Barmby took off his spectacles and stared at Baz once again. "So be it," he said. "I see by your notes that you are void of any religion and your objection is purely on conscientious grounds."

"Yes."

"Please tell the tribunal what your conscience is telling you?"

Baz had thought about this answer many times, especially in the last few days, repeating the words over and over again in his mind until they had become well and truly embedded.

"I have a conscience, I can tell you that much. How do I prove that I have a conscience? Maybe that's why I'm here, maybe that's the question. If I were to kill someone, then I might as well not have a conscience," Baz answered, hoping the words had come out right, and also in the correct order.

"Thank you for that well rehearsed statement Mr Albright," said Judge Barmby. "Mrs Mann, Mr Meyer, have you any questions?"

"You know why you are here young man. You are here because you refuse to fight for King and country?" said the large woman.

"I am here because I refuse to kill. Why would I want to kill some-one   I don't know? I don't even want to kill someone I know *and* I don't like!" Although Baz didn't really know enough people not to like any.

Mrs Mann was just expecting a simple yes. "We may have to kill to save our own souls, to save our land," she said. "It is not only us that have made sacrifices. Our Lord *also* gave his body so we could be saved."

"Then who else is idolised by millions? Who else has his own inner circle of disciples? Who else wants to conquer the world just like your religion? Who else has had millions that have read his book?" Baz said.

"Sorry?"

"Adolf Hitler!"

The journalist's pens began burning into their notebooks.

"That is quite enough," interrupted Judge Barmby. "Carry on Mrs Mann."

Mrs Mann was a representative from the Church Parish Authorities and well read on all relevant religions, more so these days on the Jehovah Witnesses and the Quaker movements. Her only role was as an adviser to Judge Barmby, who knew her experience in court protocol was limited. He also knew she liked the sound of her own plum filled voice far too much.

"No! Mr Chairman, I would like to hear more. Carry on young man," she said, hoping Baz was about to dig his own grave.

"You said 'to save our land', our land will always be here. It is us we will destroy, you, me and everyone else. If there is a soul, then they will be with your God. Isn't that what you want anyway? Or are you worried you will be sent to hell, because we have this desire to kill each other?" he paused. "Well don't send me to hell. If everyone thought like me there wouldn't be a war, and yet here I am being condemned for it." Baz held a finger against his chest. "He who has never killed anything." Baz was proud of never having knowingly or consciously killed any living thing, not even the smallest insect, not even the most annoying fly or wasp.

"It is called defence of your country," she said.

"Then blame the people at the top, it is them we should blame, it is them that should be here, not me, I am not responsible for starting the war."

"It's our people at the top that will unite the world and it is our people that will give us victory." She then allowed herself a smug smile. "We must *all* row the boat in the same direction."

"Then this boat is being rowed towards hell," he replied, sounding more like a bad amateur actor.

"No Mr Albright, this boat is going around in circles because people like you are rowing it in the opposite direction."

"Soon there will be no one left to row them."

"It doesn't sound as though you want *us* to win this war?" she said abruptly.

"*Us*...I want peace to win the war, that is what I want to win. If everyone adds to the killing then no one will win, until we are all dead and there are no degrees to death. It is final, it is only in death we will be united."

She cleared her throat with a high pitched cough, "Would you call yourself a rational thinker, young man?" More bait.

"Rational thinking stops in times of war." Baz bit in.

"Then *are* you a fascist?"

"Fascism, socialism. Left, right. Up, down. Black, whi..."

"Are you a..."

"Thank you, Mrs Mann," interrupted the judge. He had heard enough.

Judge Barmby knew from his time as a barrister never to get into squabbles with defendants. He wanted straight answers for straight questions.

"You were not conscripted," the judge said.

"No Sir."

"So you had not received any conscription papers?"

"No Sir."

"You volunteered yourself?"

"Yes Sir."

"Why did you volunteer after everything you have just said?"

"I have, I *had* a brother in the navy. I just thought, if he's going to be on a ship then I want to make sure it's a safe ship. Its probably too late now."

"Too late?"

"Missing, presumed killed."

The judge gave Baz a long glare. Sympathy was a weakness in court, solely for the jurors.

The man sitting to the left of the judge curled his finger in front of his mouth and coughed through the small hole. A seasoned negotiator, Mr Meyer was a low ranking member of the General Council of the Trades Union Congress and had a strong belief most situations could be resolved amicably.

"If I may, Mr Chairman." he said overemphasising the words above his strong East London accent.

"Of course Mr Meyer."

"You have been a member of the PEU for ten years?"

"PEU? Mr Meyer," said the judge.

"Print Engineers Union, Mr Chairman."

"I have," said Baz. Wondering how the man knew.

"It seems to me Mr Albright you wouldn't mind being part of the machine. You just have no wish yourself to run anyone over with it?"

More father-like quotes thought Baz. Then decided Mr Meyer was probably on his side. "Yes."

The trade union man leant across to the judge and spoke in whispers.

"Mr Chairman, we are an island. In my opinion the battle for this land will be fought in the air. We will need all the planes we can get. Aircraft need mending Mr Chairman. This man is an experienced engineer, they will need as many people like him on the airfields as they can get. They are called volunteer aircraftmen. Ground crew Mr Chairman." Mr Meyer paused for a moment. "If we are going to send our men on ships, let's make sure it is a safe ship. The defendant said it himself Mr Chairman."

"Thank you Mr Meyer, I get your drift."

"Drift," Mr Meyer puffed out a laugh. "Very good sir."

The judge threw a stare at Mr Meyer, then turned his attention towards Baz. "Safe ships Mr Albright, safe aircraft."

"Sir?"

"I have taken into consideration that you did volunteer your services in the first place. On the other hand, whether out of ignorance, or as you say, your conscience, you *did* refuse combat duty. In plain words Mr Albright, as Mrs Mann put it, you refused to fight for King and country. Although, it has been drawn to my attention you have certain skills that will be very useful to the war effort and for that reason I will exempt you from combat duties. I strongly advise you to accept my recommendation, failure to do so will result in very serious consequences."

Prison, thought Baz.

The judge studied Baz's face for any reaction then continued.

"Mr Meyer, under my authority as chairman of this hearing, you will make the necessary arrangements for Mr Albright to train as an RAF volunteer aircraftman."

He stared long and hard at Baz, "Good luck Mr Albright."

————————

WAR ORGANISATION
OF THE
BRITISH RED CROSS SOCIETY and ORDER OF ST. JOHN
OF JERUSALEM
WOUNDED, MISSING AND RELATIVES DEPARTMENT

Mr & Mrs G. Albright,   18th July 1940
14 Minchen Street,
London.

Dear Mr & Mrs. Albright,

We deeply regret that the Admiralty have now found it necessary to
presume the death of your son, Leading Seaman Oliver Walter
Albright, following the loss of H.M.S. Arrowhead.
From eyewitness statements and naval notifications it has left the
Admiralty with no choice but to abandon any hope that he could have
been a survivor from this ship.

We sent your son's name to the International Red Cross Committee In
Geneva, asking that enquiries should be made for him in all known
German Prisoner of War camps. Unfortunately the International Red
Cross Committee have not been able to trace your son as a prisoner of
war.

We wish to assure you that your son will not be forgotten by us; his
name will always be kept on our records, and should we have any
further information concerning him we will not fail to write to you at
once, though it would not be kind for us to encourage you to hope that
any more enquiries would obtain further news of him.

May we ask you again to accept our heartfelt sympathy in your great
sorrow at the loss of your son, who has given his life so bravely in the
service of his country.

Yours sincerely,
Elizabeth Humphries
Chairman

68

A train platform with long name boards. Then a cropped woodland, roads and rust coloured houses, more hills, another station, this time stopping for a couple of minutes until the thudding from the doors had ceased and the gradual woofing from the huge steam engine as it pulled away from yet another station.

With the lack of sleep from the previous night and the rhythmic swaying from the train, Baz's eyes had began to feel like lead weights. His thick grey uniform trapping in the June heat did nothing to help matters either, the chafing from its abrasive material at the start of the journey had begun to drift away with his consciousness.

Every now and then a noise in the carriage or the sudden drop of Baz's head would rouse him from his half slumber. At one time and to the amusement of the other passengers he had head-butted the window with a sudden lurch forward, leaving a golf ball size red blotch on his forehead. He had also given up concentrating on his book long ago, after reading the same sentence over and over again and never knowing what was written anyhow. In truth, the only reason he took a book with him was to avoid unnecessary eye contact with strangers.

More annoyingly, after leaving the last station he had dutifully given up his seat to an unappreciative sulky mother with two crabby children. Baz thought the woman didn't seem to be a terribly good mother, tugging and smacking the children for the slightest misdemeanour. The lack of affection from either side made him wonder if she was actually the mother at all. As he stepped into the corridor, knowing he wasn't going to share a compartment with the youngest infant's persistent crying throughout the journey, softened his irritation slightly.

His mind drifted back over the last months from the day he had received his call-up papers. The relief in having not been sent to prison had been replaced by a period of time where his life would be out of his control and his destiny mapped out by others.

He thought about his time at RAF Cosford, the place he had left only two days before, an airfield purposely earmarked for the training of aircraft technicians and pilots. A prime target for German bombers was his first thought.

Baz left the airfield as an aircraftman 2nd class (AC2). The RAF had a nickname for every rank, in fact, as he discovered, they had a nickname for nearly everything and everyone. Baz's rank was the lowest, an AC plonk, he just thought life was continuing as it had always done.

The only person at RAF Cosford who knew about him being a conscientious objector was Warrant Officer Miley. Every airfield has a Warrant Officer Miley, a snake eyed man who was void of any emotion whatsoever. A man with the hardest stare, the straightest back and the coldest disposition Baz had ever seen.

It was on the last day when Baz was summoned to the Warrant Officer's office. The conversation began with, "Sergeant Bonner recommended that you are promoted to a LAC," he paused. "But you're not a Leading Aircraftsman, are you Albright?" Not only had this man never turned around at any time, he also never seemed to blink. "And we do not promote conchies, do we Albright?"

"Yes sir, no sir."

"Do you know a Mr Meyer?"

Baz thought about the tribunal. "No sir, yes sir."

"Well, he seems to know you. He asked that your convictions go no further than this office. I wanted to ignore his request at first but as the course progressed I saw you in a new light Albright. We need good aircraft technicians, that is why it stayed in these four walls. If it slipped out, well," the Warrant Officer paused. "No one likes a conchie Albright," and for the first time he revealed what Baz thought might be the faintest of human qualities. "He told me you had lost a brother not too long ago. A navy lad?"

"Yes sir."

As Baz was leaving the office, Warrant Officer Miley asked, "Why Albright?"

"A pretty girl, a long queue and an old man who was late for his lunch. Sir."

Countryside and houses were replaced by railway buildings as the train drew alongside the platform. The clunking of couplings was soon followed by the hissing of steam as the engine gradually ground to a standstill.

Baz stepped out through the tall doors of the station building and took a long deep breath from the clean village air. The peaceful blue sky and the reds and browns of the late summer leaves turning for autumn gave no indication of the violent times being played out above.

Two frightened and bewildered children were collected by a stout man driving a huge shiny black saloon. An old couple walked away hand in hand with another child. RAF personnel and civilians departed in various modes of transport or ambled away under their own steam. Baz waited by the station entrance.

"Are you off to the airfield old boy?" A voice broke through the air from behind.

Baz turned his head and saw a white cravat bulging out like a frog's throat sac, below that, the gold wings of a pilot's badge.

"Me. Yes Sir. The airfield. RAF Coltishall."

A tall willowy man in his mid forties stood before him. His sunken outdoor face had a friendly charm about it. Deep crows feet broke away from his eyes like a chipped windscreen and awarded him the appearance of wearing a permanent grin. A quiff of dark wavy hair had fallen over his forehead as he took his cap off and tucked it under his arm.

"Wing Commander Batty," extending one arm and pushing back the fallen lick of hair with the other.

Baz shook his hand. "Aircraftman Albright. Sir." Accepting the gesture. Jesus Christ! A Wing Commander, he thought. Then saluted.

The Wing Commander gazed down the short dusty station road. Baz remained where he stood, waiting patiently for his dismissal. No one walks away from a Wing Commander. Even he knew that much.

"Good show staff, couldn't do without you chaps. Salt of the earth." His words spoken as though they were tucked away behind his thoughts. "Ah good, here is the old girl now."

A matt grey saloon car with large identification stickers stuck to the front wheel arches entered the station road at breakneck speed. As it screeched to a halt with the rear passenger door perfectly positioned in front of the Wing Commander, a small gust of dust blew up around the two men.

An attractive lady in a WAAF uniform rose from the driver's seat and rested her arms on the roof of the car, cradling her chin on top of her hands, a playful grin accentuating her high cheek bones, her round soft eyes followed the Wing Commander's every move.

"Sorry Sir, operations, then eggs."

"Eggs. Ha! Hope you didn't break any on my behalf old girl?"

"Don't be silly Sir, eggs come before Wing Commanders. You should know that."

"Quite right too. This is Aircraftman Albright. We'll drop him off at staff digs," said the Wing Commander, taking Baz's kit bag and along with his own leather suitcase stowed them away in the boot.

"Hello staff," she said, carrying a smile that nearly melted Baz's knees. "Both of you get in the back, I don't want you sitting on my eggs."

Baz had no idea how to greet a WAAF officer, especially one like Mary and ended up delivering a tentative raised hand somewhere in between a salute and a wave.

"Hope that isn't a Heil Hitler, staff?" she joked.

"No, no, I didn't..."

"Don't worry about Mary old chap. If she had her way, she'd have all the top brass saluting her."

"Saluting Sir?" Mary flashed a smile at the Wing Commander. "Is that what you call it?"

The car sped off at the same speed it had arrived, not even slowing as it rounded the corner. Listening to the shaking and rattling he thought it would be a miracle if the eggs didn't get back scrambled, then thought it would be a miracle if he didn't either.

The quiet solace of the village was soon replaced with a noisy commotion as the airfield loomed closer. To the side of the road, workmen in muddy overalls were busy digging trenches and laying cables, others erected metal mesh fencing between tall standing concrete posts. Roads had become occupied with trundling grey trucks and fuel browsers, smaller cars and motorcycles were trying to overtake larger vehicles. Everyone of them being left behind in the wake of the Wing Commander's car.

It was to Baz's great concern that Mary talked constantly through the entire journey, mainly small talk, regarding social life at the airfield, appearing to know everyone who is anyone, and although her hands moved the steering wheel around with ease and confidence, it did nothing to ease Baz's anxiety. As far as he was concerned, he was going to die in a road accident with a Wing Commander and a beautiful woman. Could be worse he thought. Sometimes she would look over her shoulder and ask Baz some trivial question, for a few death defying seconds the vehicle would be left to its own devices. Baz replied in quick one word answers, hopefully saving his life and that of the Wing Commander. His only hope was that the Wing Commander recognised this act of foresight.

The vehicle turned a corner into the entrance of the airfield and a vast expanse of grass was stretched out in front of them. Baz could see the sleek contours of twelve Spitfires parked in a row to the left of the control tower. Hurricanes appeared to be waddling over the ground towards the runway. The recognisable shaped nose of a Blenheim bomber poked out from the inside of a hanger.

As their vehicle hurtled into the internal area of the airfield a guard at the entrance stood to attention and delivered a stiff salute, the Wing Commander returned a raised hand in a half gestured acknowledgment. Throughout the whole ordeal, he appeared to be as relaxed as he was before he had entered the vehicle. An elbow propped on the door armrest, his chin cupped in the palm of his hand, a pensive stare through the passenger window. A man in his own private thoughts. It was only when the vehicle stopped alongside a brown brick building that he woke up to the world around him.

"Looks like your stop old boy."

———————

William Waterhouse leant forward as far as his harness straps would allow him and looked up through his canopy to the sky above. He could see them now, a swarm of small crucifix shaped objects silhouetted high overhead. It seemed like there were hundreds of them, some larger than others, all flying in an orderly formation. Occasionally they would vanish in a haze of cloud cover, only to reappear again seconds later.

Will knew that in a couple of minutes time, he would be in the hardest battle of his life. All his senses had to be at the pinnacle of their awareness. The culmination of all the chess games he had played throughout his life would not even get close to the concentration he will need for this combat. The smallest mistake would not mean the loss of a pawn or knight or even the game, but probably his life.

The only battle he had at that moment in time, was with himself. He wondered why he had ever become a fighter pilot in the first place. It was his father who had pushed him into it. "My son the RAF fighter pilot. He will be fine. God is on his side." What else could a son from a good family do in times of war.

Only Will thought a fighter pilot was the last vocation a coward like him would have wished for, and compounded that thought with: it was also a coward like him that couldn't stand up to his father.

Will had the urge to turn his Spitfire around, fly back to the airfield, face the consequences. He would still be alive after all.

He remained in formation.

The last few months had been spent in training. Try to escape was his initial thought, hide away on a remote island somewhere in Scotland. He soon accepted the realisation that there was no choice but to remain, accept his fate. Even during that time he experienced losing two friends in unnecessary flying accidents. Something he had to deal with in his own way, a sadness that gave him an inner determination to continue, if only in their memory. Or maybe he just wanted to prove something to himself. They were better pilots than him and they died through their own mistakes. A thought Will took to bed with him every night.

During one terrifying time he thought his number was up when he managed to get lost high above the English countryside, no identifiable landmark to pinpoint his position and down to his last drop of fuel. He got back to the airfield by the skin of his teeth, only by following a river in the right direction, it was fifty-fifty, he could have chosen either way. Maybe God *was* on his side.

In truth, Will liked the environment of the cockpit, the solitary pilot. Only him in control, no one else to make mistakes, no father to stick his nose in. Everything had to be done just right; under the security blanket of normal life it would have been something he relished. This was why he made it through the training when many failed. 'I *am* a good pilot'. He had to convince himself.

He also knew it was a time of war, it would be over soon. Not really worth worrying about, everyone would have come to their senses by the time his training had been completed.

Will looked over his port wing. The other eleven aircraft were alongside him. A squadron of Spitfires flying in formation, ten thousand feet below their enemy and five thousand feet above the English countryside.

He had only arrived at the airfield that same day, no time to settle in, no time to get to know any of the other airmen, managing only to remember a few of their names, they were now his family, his brothers in the air, each watching the other's back.

Will also knew only too well that he was replacing a pilot killed in the last action.

A muffled voice crackled over the radio transmitter, just about audible through the static.

"Badger from Leader. We'll go from above. Keep close. Over." A pause, the same voice. "Control from Badger Leader, Enemy in sight. Too many to count. Two o'clock Over."

"Understood Badger Leader. Good luck. Over."

"Badger from Leader. Look out for stray bandits. Over."

In several minutes, Will's squadron ascended to twenty-five thousand feet and were above and behind the enemy.

"Control to Badger. Friendlies coming up at seven. Over."

"Badger Leader to control. Understood. Friendlies rising at seven. Over."

"Leader to Badger. Many bandits. Repeat. Many bandits. Stay close. When I say go. Break in sections. Then you are on your own. Good luck chaps. Over."

"Green one to Leader. See you in the pub for noggins. Over."

"Leader to Green one. I'll have a pint waiting for you Pat. Over."

The voice vanished as fast as it had appeared.

The only sound Will could hear was the droning of his Merlin engine. He glanced at the dials in his cockpit. Oil pressure, check. Revs, check. Water temp, check. Gun button, on. All OK. Check, check, check.

Will relaxed and let the aircraft fly itself. In a strange way he felt an inner peace. He began to feel content, a kind of fulfillment. Maybe I have excepted my fate, maybe this is all I have to give to the world he thought.

What will be, will be.

The voice appeared again, a nervous urgency about it. "Green one to leader. Bandits broken! Repeat. Bandits broken! Over."

"Leader to Badger. Hold fast. Over."

Will looked through the clear perspex of his canopy. He saw Hurricanes and Messerschmitts twisting and turning like gnats. It reminded him of all those years ago when strolling with Baz on a hot summer evening along the canal near his home, both swatting at the midges with flying arms, each tiny insect avoiding the boys as though they were playing with them.

Amidst the furore are white streaks of tracer bullets and the bright flares of gunfire lighting up the sky, the occasional smoke trail as some unfortunate descends from the skirmish to an early grave.

"All Badger. Tally Ho!" was the urgent shout through the radio transmitter, followed by a carefully spoken, "Good luck everyone."

Will was acting as wing man to Red section. Blue 1 and Blue 2 were the first to break, their port wings dropped then vanished out of sight. Red 1 and Will immediately followed behind them.

As they got nearer he saw Red 1 break away and head towards a German bomber straying from formation. Its lower gunner firing unceasingly at the approaching Spitfire.

Will shouted into his oxygen mask. "Red 1. Bandit at ten oclock. Break Red 1. Break Red 1!" Will saw him swiftly bank away, his bullet tracers missing the bomber. A German fighter in hot pursuit.

He looked to his starboard and saw a Messerschmitt fighter coming up from below. He rammed his stick hard to the left, full throttle, hard down on the rudder peddle, a steep turn to port. The Spitfire was on a circle so tight the g-load was making his fighter plane shudder like a car on cobble stones. Will saw the oil streak on its underbelly as he watched the German fighter fly overhead. His first encounter with the enemy. "Missed me," he said, spitting vomit into his mask.

Will looked around. No Red 1. He was on his own. The rest of the squadron were mixed up in the mayhem of battle.

A thousand feet below a small number of Heinkel bombers were splitting away from the main group, already being pounded with gunfire from Hurricanes. Some of them had smoke trailing behind their engines. Others banked to one side and dropped from the sky, the occasional white material billowed open as a crew member vacated their stricken aircraft. More Messerschmitts entered into the confusion, a last attempt to protect the few remaining bombers.

Will saw some German aircraft turn around and head back home, low on fuel or maybe they knew they were no match for the British fighters. He yanked his joystick to one side and flew into the fracas. There was no time to think, every movement had to be spontaneous but calculated. Smoke was coming from a Hurricane's engine. Too late, a Messerschmitt had finished it off, firing a burst of bullets into the cockpit. He could see the splatters of red inside the canopy, the head of the pilot slumped to one side. Will flew towards a Heinkel, the upper gunner saw him, bullets shot past, some passing through his starboard wing. Will banked hard to port.

The first William Waterhouse knew of the impending disaster was the fast oncoming roar of another aircraft's engine, followed by the sudden appearance of the British blue, white and red roundel. Then a loud crash as he collided into an aircraft crossing his path. Will's starboard wing sliced through the tail section of a Hurricane, at the same time shattering half of his own wing. A loud thud as a propellor blade struck the metal framework of his canopy and the Hurricane vanished as fast as it had appeared. It was all over in a fraction of a second.

The initial impact threw Will into a sudden lurch forward followed by a slow spiralling spin that quickly caught speed. Any movement on the joystick made no difference whatsoever, there was only one direction this fighter plane was heading and William Waterhouse knew it. At first he felt deep shock, soon replaced by a heart pounding panic.

Forcing each foot hard onto the rudder pedals, first one, then the other, with both hands gripping tightly onto the joystick he pitched it left, then right, hopelessly trying to take some sort of control. Nothing. It was only his harness stopping him from being thrown around the cockpit like a rag doll. His head left free to be brutally tossed from side to side.

Will's aircraft was in free-fall, dropping at hundreds of miles per hour. Rolling and vibrating violently, the inevitable impact imminent. The blood draining from his face, he was slowly losing consciousness. William had only one choice.

It was a fight for survival. Pushing his head back and straining every muscle, he reached out and pulled the engine cutout. The engine stopped, followed by a quiet eerie sound of the wind rushing past.

He yanked out the oxygen hose and threw off his mask and goggles.

The juddering shape of the canopy jettison handle was to the front right of him, a sense of relief as his right hand lunged out and clutched the round red ball. A hard tug. Nothing. The canopy hadn't budged. Another hard tug. Nothing. His heart was about to explode. He tried the canopy winding handle. No movement. He pulled harder. Not the tiniest fraction of an inch.

In desperation he tried breaking the hood with his fist, each strike becoming his only chance of survival. With both hands wrapped around the release handle he tried one last hard tug, still nothing. A hopeless firm backward push with the flat of his hands on the underside of the canopy, a futile last attempt that only managed to exhaust any of the hope he had left. He was falling from the sky, trapped in his coffin.

Will cried out. He cried out for life. He cried out for his mother.

The end, only seconds away.

He closed his eyes. His last image was of Baz waving at him from the outer rim of the airfield, a beaming smile across his friend's face. Brothers of the board.

A cold wind blew through William's cockpit.

"OK Chaps." Wing Commander Batty looked down into the eyes of one runner, then the other. "These are the rules." He stretched out his long arms and placed a hand on each of their shoulders. "You are to complete one full circuit of the airfield, staying within ten feet of the outer perimeter. The first man to pass under the flag is the winner."

The Wing Commander casually walked away from the flagpole and sauntered up to the top step leading to the mess hall door. Above the heads of the two runners was the Union Jack calmly swaying in the early morning breeze. He turned, "On the word go you will start the race."

Flying Officer 'Birdie' Anderson had complained to the Wing Commander that he was above racing against an inferior rank, that the AC2 had been disrespectful. Wing Commander Batty knew exactly what had happened, he also knew this race had to go ahead. Even a pilot under stress cannot think he can strike a subordinate rank and get away scot-free. This was his way of disciplining the man. Saves all that paperwork. Also good entertainment.

The mainly grass airfield of RAF Coltishall is shaped like an elongated diamond, the grass runway extended between the two furthest points. Most of its buildings are built around the near side angle, opposite them are a few dispersal huts. All in all, the perimeter is about three and a half miles long, mostly soft grassy earth.

"Get ready chaps," said the Wing Commander. "Steady old boy," as he spotted 'Birdie' Anderson inching forward. "Go!" he shouted, as he sliced his hand downward.

It was a fast start, too fast thought Baz, but he always thought that. He had remembered being at the start of a race many years before, he knew how that one had panned out. The Great Chocolate Bar Disaster of 1929. Although Baz was the only one that knew it by that name. The other kids had called it something else.

The beginning of the race was run behind a large grey hangar, then between two armoury sheds, reaching the outer limits in only a few minutes. Both runners were evenly matched as they rounded a corner towards the inner fence, soft doughy earth soon replaced the hardness of the concrete.

Baz decided to tuck in behind the airman, weigh up his stamina, note his style. He was fit, there was no doubt about that, but heavy footed, too much exertion and action for a long distance runner, his movements were forced rather than natural. In contrast Baz had a peculiar hunched gait, like a tortoise on two legs, as though his body would get lost if it wasn't following his head.

The airfield was angled with a slight upward slope towards the top point of the diamond, it was there they would pass the end of the airstrip.

In front, Baz could hear the rasping breaths of the airman as he forced deep gulps of air into his lungs, his stride was beginning to look laboured, his arms had dropped.

Baz positioned himself to the outside and just behind, as if to overtake on the longest route. He gradually quickened his pace, the airman sped up to fend off Baz's threat. Baz increased his pace again. Again the airman kept Baz at bay; he felt pleased, the lead had remained his. The increased pace had not let up though and the flying officer was beginning to suffer. Baz managed to quicken his stride, just short of a sprint. The pilot remained on the inside, he had the advantage, no one knew about out running the enemy with tight turns more than 'Birdie' Anderson.

They soon passed round the top of the runway.

Baz quickly darted behind the airman and into the inside. Baz could hear the panting, he could sense the heaviness as the exhausted pilot slowly faded away behind him. They were now on the downward straight on the opposite side of the airstrip. Baz took a quick glance over his shoulder. The airman had slowed, his head angled to one side, his action had become sluggish. This victory is going to taste sweet.

Immersed in their own personal battles, the two runners were oblivious to the hell breaking loose behind them, airmen had begun sprinting to their aircraft, some already seated in their cockpits, thumbs up for the ground crew. The airfield was awakening to the swarming of aircraft. Black smoke blasted from exhausts as engines exploded into life. Aircraft bounced awkwardly along the uneven grass of the airfield. The sound of engines surged as they throttled for take-off, propellors merged into roaring, spinning circles.

When Baz reaches the next bend he will be exactly halfway and very much in the lead. The field on this side was home to a Hurricane Squadron already on the move. Like a stubborn spoilt child one aircraft had remained where it stood, its cowlings removed, the naked guts of its engine in full view, mechanics scurrying around, hurriedly pulling and poking into the mass of metal. Another aircraft squatted patiently on the earth, waiting for its master.

In front was the dispersal hut, Baz then remembered the last time he had approached this same building.

After a good nights rest and an hour until the start of his day, Baz departed his quarters to begin his first ever run around RAF Coltishall. Something he needed to do to shake away the cobwebs from the previous month. To be alone for a short while, a rare luxury in this people cluttered environment. He needed to come to terms or even understand what was happening in the world. The Germans want Britain for themselves and bombing the airfields to eliminate our air power was their first strategy. Baz was well and truly on the front line. Anyone else would take this personally.

Baz paused momentarily and soaked up the tranquility and colour from the low light of the chilly September morning, the sun had only just risen, illuminating a thin mist hovering slightly above the expanse of grass before him. Even in the normal quiet and calm of the early morning, this day felt different, peaceful, serene even.

Baz started off slowly. A leisurely jog alongside the high wire fence, behind it he could see the crop fields of the neighbouring farms and the odd copse lining their borders. He could see down the length of the runway, the grass worn and flattened by the constant take-offs and landings.

Minutes later, Baz headed along the second straight towards the first sign of human life. Mingling in front of a dispersal hut were a handful of pilots, primed for that crucial call to scramble. Eight Hurricanes neatly parked in two rows, a couple of ground crew showing more then a passing interest in one of them.

As Baz got closer to the dispersal hut he was aware off one airman staring in his direction. Although seeing an aircraftman in his PTs, running around an airfield in the middle of a war, especially on a cold September morning, was not an everyday occurrence: it would be unusual for anyone *not* to be slightly curious.

A plum filled public school accent was fired in Baz's direction. "Don't you salute an officer when you see one?" A flying officer stood sanctimoniously with both hands on hips.

Baz saluted the officer while still on the run.

"Stop there!"

Nonchalantly, Baz slowed to a halt and turned around.

"Stand to attention when you salute an Officer."

To tell the truth, pilots are not Baz's cup of tea. Don't get me wrong, he knew they were courageous, flying in the worst extremes of weather, putting their lives on the line every time they were called out on operations, not knowing if they were going to be alive tomorrow. Being airborne in one of these tin cans, tens of thousands of feet in the air, is bad enough, then having someone doing their utmost to blow you out of the sky!

But on the other hand, Baz also thought of them as toffee nosed, stuck-up, self-righteous, smug. Everything he disliked about a person. Baz repaired these tin cans, they just flew them, in his eyes that made him just as equal, if not less heroic.

Baz stood rigidly to attention and gave the stiffest of all salutes.

"He's taking the sodding piss...and look at me when I'm talking to you boy."

It was the word boy that annoyed Baz the most, coming from someone probably younger than himself. He wouldn't have minded old boy, but boy on its own, that was something else. Anyhow, this was Baz, not one of his servants in some colonial outpost.

"I said look at me when I'm talking to you."

"I am...*Sir*."

"No you're not, you little. I've a good mind to..." The Flying Officer began walking towards Baz with his gloved hand raised.

"I have heard you are a good runner Anderson," interrupted a voice from the dispersal hut doorway. A figure standing tall, casually resting his shoulder against the wooden doorframe, a cigarette theatrically poised between two fingers in front of his mouth.

None of the fighter planes in the airfield would be flying without aircraftmen like Basil Albright and Wing Commander Batty knew it. He also did not like officers flaunting their position over lower-ranks, we are at war with Germany, *not* each other. It also didn't help the Flying Officer's cause being an old Eton boy. The Wing Commander was educated at Harrow. If it was good enough for Churchill.

"Yes Sir," replied 'Birdie' Anderson, saluting.

"Relax old boy. Run for your school, Eton, wasn't it?"

"Yes Sir." Wondering how he knew that.

The Wing Commander took pride in knowing the history of all his airmen, he needed to know what they were made of, what to expect from them when confronted with the enemy. He wanted men to shoot down the enemy, *not* be shot down. He also knew that 'Birdie' Anderson was a good pilot, returning from six sorties to date was no mean feat.

"You obviously like running, staff?"

"Sir?" Baz replied with a salute. Hoping very much the Wing Commander wasn't going to shake his hand.

"Good show." Knowing this dispute had to be resolved. Wing Commander Batty disliked loose ends intensely.

Baz took another quick glance over his shoulder. The Flying Officer had dropped even further back. In a strange way Baz felt sorry for him. Convincingly beaten by someone lower-classed, lower-ranked.

Maybe I should have stopped and saluted him. No, he got on his high horse, he deserves to be humiliated, teach him a lesson, he should have given me a closer race. I'm not to blame for being the better runner. Anyway, the Wing Commander thought this one up.

As he approached the other end of the airfield he could see the fighters queuing up, not unusual with aircraft taking off and landing all the time.

The ground had become heavy going, large tufts of grass begun to jar his knees, he wasn't sure whether his foot was going to land high or low, he felt himself losing co-ordination, he started to feel loose-limbed, ungainly.

Another quick glance behind. The airman was just passing the dispersal hut.

Baz arrived at the top of the airstrip. In the corner of his eye he saw two spitfires accelerate down the grass track, a space between wheel and ground, both vanished into the glare of the sky. He felt a relief as the higher ground became firmer. All the muscles in his legs were starting to ache and it felt good to look down at the gradual descent, but more importantly he could see the Union Jack gently fluttering in the distance.

He also saw a Spitfire squadron taxiing up the airfield, waddling like ducks out of water. He thought aircraft always looked so clumsy and obstinate on the ground, however graceful they may look in the air. He could see the pilots constantly glancing left and right, checking their distance.

There was something different about the aircraft bringing up the rear. Baz could see the pilot staring in his direction, an oxygen mask hanging down, flying goggles perched on his leather flying helmet. The airman began to wave frantically.

Baz slowed, he didn't know any pilots, not ones that would wave to him anyhow. His pace decreased to a near halt as he tracked the movement of the aircraft, then stopped altogether. It was those mousy features, that pasty face, the wispy strands of blonde hair poking out from under his helmet.

"William Waterhouse, Jesus Christ, it's Will."

Ignoring his exhaustion he turned and began running alongside the aircraft. "Wiiiiill!" Baz yelled, beaming a wide smile.

As the Spitfire turned onto the top of the airstrip Will raised his hand and slid his canopy shut, something he had done a hundred times before. A proud thumbs up for Baz, the aircraft sped down the airstrip, the tail lifted and the aircraft was slowly sucked into the grey.

Baz looked down to the airfield buildings and more importantly what was to the side of them, the flagpole and the designated finishing line. It was then he saw Flying Officer 'Birdie' Anderson.

It seemed to Baz there was hardly any time between the air raid siren blaring and the first bomb dropping. A loud explosion rocked the front of the control tower, followed by a spray of concrete debris flying indiscriminately through the air, a lucky escape for the men inside.

More bombs began falling, some missing the airfield altogether, one landing in a neighbouring farmer's field. Oblivious to their impending fate, several cattle were dismembered where they stood.

Baz leapt into the safety of a ditch, yelling out as his bare legs shared the waterlogged space with a nettle bush. One explosion, far too close for comfort, pelted him with cascading soil. It was his overwhelming fear that carried his exhausted body the rest of the way to the shelter. In two leaps he bounded down the ten steps, virtually falling head first through the small metal door and there he stood, scratching and panting, his sodden running gear clinging to his body, his legs smothered in deep red blotches.

Inside the shelter a bare flame flickered from a gas lamp on the floor, its light casting sinister dark shadows up the walls and onto the arched concrete ceiling.

"Glad you came dressed for the occasion staff," announced a female voice.

"Yes sorry, long story."

A head leant forward. a yellow light cast over the features of a perfect face. It was Mary. "Yes Staff, I *have* been told it."

Through the dull, smokiness he could make out two long benches, one on each side and running the length of the shelter, both crowded with women wearing blue WAAF uniforms. From under the peaks of their caps, soft pale faces stared towards him.

"I prefer more flesh on my man," said an older woman, a nervous laughter echoed around the shelter.

"And all the same colour," said another.

Muffled booms could be heard behind the chatter. In the past few weeks the sound of the air raid sirens was becoming more frequent. Some were just empty warnings, others were the real thing. As was this days raid. A loud resonating boom. It felt as if a bomb had exploded directly above them.

After a relieved silence, Mary spoke again. "And did the earth move for you Staff?" Another burst of nervous laughter echoed around the shelter.

"I'd better go and see if I can help outside, you never know, an aircraft may need glueing together or something," said Baz, sounding more schoolboy than aircraftman.

"OK staff, you be careful out there. I'll be sure to tell the Wing Commander what a hero you are."

Mary Wallace was one of the first WAAF to be posted to RAF Coltishall and the longest serving out of the eighteen there. A well respected and popular officer amongst the other women, well liked by those lower ranked than her. Superior ranks thought different. They saw her as a loose cannon, a party girl, not appropriate for the rank of an officer, although her special friendship with the airfield's charismatic and highly decorated second-in-command made her virtually untouchable.

Baz could have chosen a better time to leave the shelter, although he did catch sight of the enemy for the very first time. Flying at roof height directly towards him was a German Messerschmitt 109, the rattling sound of its machine guns blasting sporadic flames of bright light from both wings, the face of the pilot clearly visible in the cockpit, his large manic eyes trained on anything that moved. Unfortunately, in this case it happened to be a fleeing aircraftman named Basil Albright.

The first bullet that hit Baz entered through his left side, ricocheting off his bottom rib and out again into his lower left arm, on its travels it shattered every bone it came into contact with. An inch to the right it would have missed him completely, an inch to the left and Baz would be dead. In the minutest fraction of a second later another bullet entered his shoulder and exited out the back. The force spun Baz around and dropped him onto the hard concrete at the top of the steps, and there he lay, staring down at the blurred greyness of the shelter entrance.

At first, he just felt a cold numbness, followed by a severe excruciating pain, as though someone had left hot embers simmering inside his body.

Then nothing.

For the first few days Baz drifted in and out of consciousness. The couple of times he became aware, he experienced an entirely new degree of suffering, one that made him oblivious to his own cries. For those short periods it was just him and the pain, two very reluctant bedfellows.

In the morphine induced spells of time where reality ceased to exist, Baz was unaware of the battle his body was experiencing. A fight that he could win, or he could just as easily lose. If the medical staff couldn't stave off the infection, his life would be in the balance and the odds heavily weighted against him.

On the third day he managed to open his eyes long enough to have some grasp on reality, albeit a very meagre and unusual one. Through his barely conscious haze he could see a glow of light shining from above, followed by the soft silhouette of a beautiful angel looking down on him.

"I'll get the Matron," said the angel.

A minute passed by.

The silhouette of another angel appeared above him, not so beautiful as the first. She looked older, rounder, with large breasts and a voice that was as sharp as a razor blade.

"Good afternoon Basil," she said loudly, then after studying his eyes for a couple of seconds she turned to look above her.

"I don't think he's with us," she said to the other angel.

Baz was in a place with a wonderful translucent white light, a place where angels can talk to you. "You are in hospital Basil. You have had an operation," she said speaking in a precise and distinct manner, mouthing each word as though Baz would be able to see them if he couldn't hear them. He could do neither. "You were shot by an enemy aircraft. The doctor had to remove a bullet. You are going to be fine Basil." She studied Baz one more time. "Do, you, understand, me?"

He didn't, the words arrived but vanished into the ether somewhere. Baz gave her a muffled groan instead. Angels should not be ignored, whatever they might be saying.

For the rest of the day Baz caught sight of several angels of varying shapes and sizes. Angels nevertheless.

Then he met God himself, dressed in a white coat. Hung around his neck was a 'Y' shaped device. An unusual crucifix? What else? A small silver bell hung from the bottom of the cross, God pressed it on Baz's chest. Searching for my soul Baz thought, feeling relieved when God smiled and nodded to one of the angels. Baz was delighted, his soul was still there. On one occasion God spoke to Baz. "I bet you'd sooner be round the fireside Mr Albright." God spoke in a Scottish accent. He preferred talking to his angels though, probably instructing them with some holy order.

Another morphine induced night and Baz had dreamt he was walking up the aisle of the ward, naked as the day he was born. It wasn't a steady sure footed walk, more like a hunched, dragging your feet, on the path to hell walk. Baz wasn't in his body though, he was hovering above, looking down on himself, being pulled along by a silver cord stretched to its limit, looking as if it was about to break and he would just drift away. The angels were floating with him, laughing and pointing at the state of his wretched flesh.

He woke that morning to find another shorter God standing at the side of his bed. 'Two Gods! Jesus!' This one was also dressed in a white coat and had the same soul finding crucifix hanging around his neck. He didn't say anything, just a prolonged stare over his spectacles, then studied a clipboard hanging from the end of the bed. A list of my sins Baz thought.

Baz was also relieved when he didn't take his soul either.

Later on in the fourth day they stopped giving Baz the morphine injections. The hallucinations subsided. Angels became nurses and the Gods had stopped searching for his soul. The white hazy light gradually cleared, which left Baz with the feeling he had a heavy weight pressing down on his body, his mind trying to beat its way through his skull. The pain grew intermittent in its agony, from intolerable to unbearable, the slightest movement bringing it on with a near death vengeance.

The first bullet that had entered Baz rebounded off a rib, breaking it in several places, tiny splinters of bone had to be searched for and removed, the surgeons had a lot of prodding and poking to do. The same bullet exited through Baz's side and lodged itself in his ulna, an inch below the elbow. This two inch piece of German metal also had to be removed. The second bullet passed straight through his body just below the shoulder bone, ripping muscle tissue on its way, awakening every nerve ending in its path.

The visit of Violet on the seventh day had lifted Baz's spirits. She had travelled up by train in the morning and had planned to stay for a few hours over lunch. Returning to London mid-afternoon, arriving back home before dark descended. Baz had scolded her for travelling just to see him on such a miserable day. But especially because of stray enemy fighter bombers flying low to evade our radar, purposely targeting trains, easy to detect with their billowing plumes of smoke.

"Two of us getting shot by the enemy in the same week would not look good," Baz had said to his sister.

"If you remembered to duck, we would not have had anyone getting shot in any week," she replied with a hint of a smile.

Violet had become an English teacher. She even dressed like a teacher, plain looking, always preferring to wear simple earth or grey coloured clothes. Three years ago Violet fell in love with a man as unfussy as herself. A year later Violet Albright became Mrs David Peveler. Violet Peveler, the accountants wife. Then the war came and she left the classroom of a girl's school for a job in Whitehall. The underground war offices. No one knew that though, not even Baz. Her husband David was somewhere in France. No one knew that either.

Violet peered over to the bed next to Baz. The dark green screen surrounding it had been permanently pulled around ever since Baz became aware there was even a bed there.

"Who is your neighbour?" she asked with a raise of her eyebrows.

Baz shrugged his shoulders, not the ideal movement when a bullet had only passed through one a week before. "The nurse told me he's an airman," he said, grimacing. "His aircraft got hit while taking off, burst into flames, apparently his aircraft was one of the last to leave the airfield. Or not to leave. All he does is moan. I heard him tell the nurse that he wanted to die."

"Poor man."

"They sometimes wheel him away, some kind of bath. You can hear the screams a mile away."

"My god, how awful."

"You can't see him though. He's completely wrapped in gauze and bandage, even his eyes. Jesus, I would hate to be like that."

"Poor, poor man."

Baz insisted they only talk about nice things for the rest of the visit.

Before the sun had risen on the ninth day there was quite a commotion surrounding the bed next to Baz's. A nurse had carried two lamps behind the green cloth screens, Baz could see the faint silhouettes of medical staff scurrying around.

Baz stared up to the ceiling, thought about home and drifted off into a deep, dream free sleep.

It was only when a nurse pulled back the black out curtains and allowed the morning light to infiltrate the ward that Baz awoke to see the screen gone and the bed empty. The prolonged eye contact told Baz everything.

On the eleventh day Baz managed to get out of bed. At first the nurses had helped him by taking his weight and sliding him hunched up onto the heavily cushioned chair. He would sit there unable to move, his arm protecting his heavily bandaged torso. The twelfth day Baz managed it on his own, half killing himself in the process.

Only Baz remembers that day for another reason, a day he had two other visitors. The first he knew of their arrival was when he saw a couple of men standing to attention with a sharp salute. Seconds later he saw Mary and Wing Commander Batty at the end of his bed.

Mary was the first to speak, "Hello staff."

"Hello." Baz replied in surprise, then looked towards the Wing Commander.

The Wing Commander neither answered or saluted.

"Hello Sir. Sorry Sir. Consider yourself saluted Sir."

Mary sat down, crossed her legs, and slid her hand along the underside of her legs. Baz thought everything Mary did was so graceful, so feminine. He also thought he detected a glint of delight in her eyes when she caught him staring at her knees. Only her demeanour had changed from the fun loving WAAF Officer Baz knew. She ran her fingers nervously up one arm. "Sorry we haven't come earlier Staff."

"I hadn't expected to see you at all. No, sorry. I mean, its great..."

"I know what you mean Staff. It's me who should apologise. I should never have allowed you to leave the shelter that day."

"Shelter?"

A moments silence.

"You don't remember?"

"What shelter!?"

Mary leant forward, filling the space in front of him with the smell of fresh flowers. His eyes followed her every movement, examining her slightest gesture. Morphine didn't have a patch on Mary.

"What's the last thing you remember Staff?"

Baz paused in thought. "The race. I remember the race. Who won? I must have won, I remember being in the lead. Then I stopped. I remember William, my friend William Waterhouse. He was in a Spit', he was waving at me from his cockpit." Baz paused for a while. Mary waited. "After that...nothing," he said quietly. "Can you let William know where I am? It'll be good to see him." Baz glanced towards the Wing Commander, he looked so remote, so distant. "Do you know what happened after that?"

Mary explained everything from the reason for the race to Baz leaving the air raid shelter. "We heard the machine guns, the sound was terrifying. Then the sound of your scream." Her eyes narrowed. "It was awful Staff. We thought..." she paused, as though to compose herself. "We thought you had been killed. A couple of girls volunteered to help me leave the shelter and get you. The only thing I remember was the amount of blood on the steps, there was so much of it. Let me tell you staff, we didn't wait around. You were back in that shelter as quick as a wink. A couple of my girls are trained in first aid, they were gems. We needed cloth, lots of cloth. The only thing we had for bandages were our shirts. As soon as one got soaked in blood we needed another. Nearly every girl in that shelter had removed their shirt by the time we had finished. It must have been quite a sight."

Baz nodded in agreement. A pain shot through his shoulder. "Shame I wasn't conscious at the time," he said, with a grimace.

"When the bombing stopped young Lizzie ran to get a truck, and you think I drive fast Staff." She checked to see if Baz had accepted her smile. Then waited while Baz took it all in.

"And here I am?" he finally said.

"And here you are Staff."

"Thanks Mary." Baz perked up. "Who won the race by the way?" Baz sensed an awkward silence.

"No one knows old boy," the Wing Commander finally spoke, his words sounding heavy.

"What did the Flying Officer say, Sir?"

Mary gazed up with a sadness in her eyes.

"The Wing Commander blames himself."

"Sorry? Blames himself for what?"

"Robin Anderson died yesterday morning..."

Wing Commander Batty interrupted. "Flying Officer Robin Anderson ran to the other side of the airfield to collect his Hurricane, his fitter said he was panting like a rabid dog. He didn't even bother to change out of his PT kit when he got in his aircraft. He probably would have frozen to death if he..." The Wing Commander suddenly stopped. His mouth turned down. A deep breath. "There was a Messerschmitt 109 taking pot shots at anything that moved."

"Yes sir, I know, I've met him."

"Birdie got onto the airstrip and was throttling up for take off when the 109 fired at him. The hurricane's fuel tanks were full." Wing Commander Batty looked down to the floor. "It burst into flames. It must have been terrible. The fitter said his clothes were alight when he jumped from the wing. How he survived those burns. God only knows."

Baz felt a coldness as he suddenly realised who had been in the bed next to him.

"Nine days of living hell and you old chap, I'm so sorry, it is all my fault, if the Germans aren't trying their damn hardest to kill you then I come along and..."

"It was a German fighter that shot me Sir, not you. I don't blame you, I am sure the Flying Officer doesn't, wouldn't have either." Baz shrugged his shoulders and winced in pain again, he wished he could remember to stop doing that.

Baz had heard the stories about the Wing Commander. How he was once a fresh faced pilot in the first world war. A young fearless airman flying a fragile biplane, who famously shot down a Zeppelin bomber over the skies of Kent, landing his plane to protect the lone German survivor from being beaten by four thugs baying for blood, who had stayed with him until he found people that were prepared to help.

It was the Wing Commander who gave the order for the aircraft to take to the skies that day. Seven never returned, seven pilots lost. One of them a much greater loss to Baz than he knew at that time. Nine days later it had become eight.

It was the Wing Commander who had to write to the families. Every letter handwritten, every word heartfelt. How do you justify the loss of a son, a husband, a loved one?

Only two days before, it was the Wing Commander who decided a couple of fighters should take to the air on a stormy day. Their mission to hunt out enemy aircraft entering our skies. Neither returned.

It was the Wing Commander who knew these decisions were unavoidable.

"There is something else Staff," said Mary. "Or should I call you Leading aircraftman Albright.

"Lead..."

The Wing Commander interrupted, "My God Staff you left that shelter to see if you could help, you were nearly killed. You deserve a medal old man. Anyway, your registration papers have been lost. I must be getting absentminded in my old age." Baz then saw a glimpse of the old Wing Commander return. "I've drawn up new ones. Life should be a bit easier from now on. You won't have to fight, your wounds have put paid to that." Then he quickly added, "You are now an LAC, you deserve it. It is the least I could do."

For a short moment the three remained silent.

"William Waterhouse? Sir"

MRS WATERHOUSE

Baz halted on the pavement and faced the six concrete steps leading up to the Georgian terrace house. A sight he had seen many times before.

He knew too well the heaviness of the task that lay ahead and paused to reflect on the reason why he was there. A chapter had to be closed and this was the only way he knew how. There were belongings that needed returning to their rightful home, objects that tied memories to the real world. A conscience needed healing.

Baz stared along the row of three storey houses and the length of black iron railings fronting them, reminding him of times long past. Memories of two boys racing against each other, running with wooden sticks, tapping them along the spearheaded rails. Two excited children climbing the long branchless trunks of the trees lining the avenue, only able to get a little way up at the time, how high and wide they seemed then. It felt like time had passed too quickly, so much had happened. All the fun and laughter had gone. The war had seen to that.

A heavy heart had weighed him down, even more so when he made the decision to embark on this quest six weeks before. The time was getting closer, his nervousness had deepened over the last hour, nausea began to emerge from his anxiety. The reason why he was there was slung over his shoulder, a grey kit bag not belonging to him.

A glance up, a deep breath and Baz took the tentative steps up to the top. Ignoring the lion headed door knocker he rapped softly on one of the dark glossy door panels.

He waited. No answer. He wondered how Will's father would accept this heathen after all that had happened?"

A louder rap. This was a mission that Baz knew he had to complete. He waited again. Still no answer. He knocked again. Nothing.

Nothing but regret.

Baz rolled the tie rope of the kit bag over his shoulder and dropped it onto the cold grey stone.

"Hello," said a small inquiring voice. An eye became visible in the dark narrow gap of the doorway. A woman's eye. A woman's voice.

"Mrs Waterhouse?"

A moments pause. "Basil? Is that you? Basil? My God Basil, it is you," she sounded pleased to see him.

"Hello Mrs Waterhouse."

Her face shone like ivory as the gap widened. Baz could see she was not wearing one of her suits or bright dresses. She had always looked so expensively dressed, always so immaculate. Covering her delicate figure was a brown woollen dressing gown pulled tight around a slender waist. Her dark auburn hair had not been styled in the perfect weave he remembered, never a strand out of place. Instead it had been left to drop freely over her shoulders and cascade in waves over the front of her body, stopping just above the tie of the gown. Baz could never have imagined it would be so long.

"Basil. You are so much older. I hardly recognised you."

"Twenty-six, Mrs Waterhouse." Forgetting her only son would have been the same age. How could she ever forget that?

She remained in the doorway, her eyes fixed on his.

Baz flicked awkward glances over her. She seemed different, cleansed, pure, no mask of perfectly applied make-up to hide her vulnerability, no odour of perfume. A look of a women whose beauty had begun to ebb away into middle age. He noticed small changes, the slight loosening of the skin, two thin creases circling her neck.

"I've brought Will's things," he said. "I thought you would like them back."

"Oh." She stared down at the kit bag. "Thank you Basil. You are a dear. You always were a good boy," she said quietly. "How rude of me leaving you standing there. You must be cold."

"No I'm fine Mrs Water...."

"I insist Basil, I'll heat up some of my soup for you. You've always liked my soup. I remember when you and William..." she halted mid speech. "Oh, never mind that." She threw out her arm and with a gentle grip pulled him into the entrance hall. "Leave the bag in the corner Basil. It is very kind of you to bring it all this way and I expect with your own one as well."

Baz recalled the sympathetic looks from the train passengers on the return journey home.

The hallway hadn't changed at all, it was still as immense and sumptuous as he remembered. It must have seemed like a grand gaping cavern when he was a small boy, an entrance to a fine palace. Only now with all the curtains closed it had acquired a cold and gloomy atmosphere. Baz could see four magnificent paintings remained hanging in their same place, a distinct memory from his childhood. A set of oils depicting wild cats and mounted in ornately carved gold frames. Closest to the front door was a tiger staring fearsomely at its audience, the likeness so perfect it had always sent a cold shiver down Baz's spine, as if he himself was the prey, that same feeling remained. Then another picture of a lion with its flowing mane, standing proudly on a rock, surveying his territory. Further on, a family of cheetahs, the mother looking on at her three cubs playing in the long grass and finally, half way down the hallway was Baz's favourite, a leopard relaxing in a tree, thoughtful looking, its huge soft front paws dangling over a thick branch, how content with life it seemed. These were images that had been embedded in his memory, but not until now had the richness and finery become all too clear to him.

Baz watched Mrs Waterhouse walk along the hall, the lower half of her dressing gown billowing behind her like a ship's sail. She stopped at an open doorway, her hand resting on an inlaid table tucked against the wall. A black and gold vase sat on top, half a dozen drought stricken flowers had slumped onto the wooden surface, around them a scattering of wilted petals.

"Wait in there Basil. I won't be long."

It was the dining room. How could he forget!? There was an odour of stale tobacco hanging in the air, nothing like the sweet smell from his father's pipe. The flock wallpaper was still there, just slightly more faded, also the large mirror hanging on the same wall, appearing to lead you through to another room. The small picture of the crucifixion was missing, the strength of the original dark red patterns on the wallpaper the only indication of its existence.

The dining table stood in the middle of the room as it had before. The candelabra remained, only this time two of the creamy white candles were left at jaunty angles, two were missing altogether. The starched white cloth had gone, leaving the once glossy wood exposed and dull. Only a single dinner mat remained at the end of the table and a plate with the remnants of yesterday's supper. Next to that was a small crystal tumbler holding a tiny amount of clear liquid. A single cigarette poked out from a crumpled packet.

Baz remained at the open doorway. Across the hall was a pair of open double doors leading into the drawing room. Baz recalled that neither he or Will were ever permitted to enter the room. The only time he remembered seeing it was when peeking through the open doors at Mr Waterhouse sitting on a snug chair with his back to them, reading a black bound book. He recalled Will's words. "The Bible, always the Bible."

Only there was no Mr Waterhouse, nor that smell of polish and fresh fruit. The furniture was still placed in perfect uniformity as he remembered, no clutter lying on the table tops as it was in the dining room. Unknown to Baz it had always looked like this, Mr

Waterhouse had insisted on it, a clean house evokes a pure God-fearing mind he used to remind his family on a regular basis.

"He's gone Basil," she said, standing in the kitchen doorway, steam rising from a bowl. "John...Mr Waterhouse, he's gone. Gone to his sisters."

"Oh, is she ill or something?"

"No Basil, he's gone," she said, walking past. "He has left me Basil." She stopped, "In truth I told him to go. I couldn't stand to look at him any longer, he killed my William."

"I don't..."

"No! You don't know the truth Basil. William didn't want to become a pilot. *He* forced him into it. John as good as shot down the plane himself." The hate in her voice was plain to hear.

Together, they walked to the table, Baz slowly lowered himself onto the seat and began spooning up the soup, failing to sip the liquid without slurping. Even then, he still felt like a boy in her presence.

Her eyes followed the rise and fall of the spoon. "You don't know how I have suffered. My marriage was forced upon me Basil. My parents wanted me to become a classical pianist." She puffed out a cynical laugh. "Fat chance. Marriage was all that was left. There was no other alternative for a failure like me."

"You're not a..."

"My parents worst nightmare would have been their daughter marrying below her station. John was found you might say, two families wanting to keep their class pure."

For the next half an hour she freely bared her deepest hidden feelings, as though her words were being liberated for the first time. She described how their relationship had became a loveless union, void of any warmth or physical passion. His spoon poised in mid-air, he could feel himself blush. She told him all their conversations were polite, if not limited, always one-sided. "He didn't beat me Basil, if that is what you are thinking."

"No I never thought he..."

"Not with his fists anyway." Speaking as if it would have been better if he had done. She said she had been oppressed by a man that placed God before her. "Any opinion I had would be subjected to the writings of the Bible before they were allowed into any discussion. John wasn't close to God, Basil. I mean wouldn't *you* want to love

God? Not just believe in him."

"You're asking the wrong person."

She grinned, "Yes I remember."

"Why didn't you leave...?" He felt glad when she interrupted him.

"Leave him! I had nowhere to go Basil. My parents would have disowned me. All the friends I had before the marriage stopped visiting us. Being on my own is something I am used to, even when I was with John."

She said that it was only when William was born her life became fulfilled, the reason behind her loveless union. "William had become my life." She felt she could talk to Baz about William, something she could never have done with her husband. "John didn't like children Basil. I know that sounds strange but it is true. All he wanted was an heir, someone to carry on the Waterhouse name. He loved him alright, from a distance I mean. It was me that gave William the hugs and kisses. It was me that gave him the love."

"I would have felt very lucky if you were my mother Mrs Waterhouse."

"You are very sweet Basil," she said, placing her hand on his arm. "As William became older things changed, that is when John wanted to take over his life. He wanted William to become a man when he was still only a child." Baz remembered the cravat and the smoking jacket. "All William wanted was to make his father proud of him. Everything William did was to earn his approval. That is why he became a pilot, just so his father could say his son was a hero. Who in their right mind would allow their son to fly in times like these? Who Basil? Who?..William didn't, I knew he didn't. The only reason he is dead now was just to please his father, he died *just* to please his father." She stared down at the table, her eyes like fading jewels. "All I wanted was William to be William and not stop being William. When you two became friends I couldn't have been any happier. I saw my son find his childhood again, it was wonderful. John hated it. That is why that day, you know, that dinner, the pilchards, it wasn't just about God. It was about you giving William his childhood back." Baz could see her eyes well up. "William missed you terribly after his father stopped your friendship. He went into his shell. It was horrible Basil, I felt so helpless."

Her fingers trembled as she slid a cigarette from the packet and struggled to strike a match, a flame eventually danced into life, highlighting her skin in a yellowy orange glow. "All I wanted from life was a child and a loving husband Basil. I miss William terribly. I don't know if I can live without him Basil." She leaned over and held the match against a candle wick. "For my son, for your friend," she said.

Baz watched as the flame came to a standstill. He told Mrs Waterhouse about the time behind the hole. "He was like a prisoner," he could picture it as if it was yesterday. "He was very brave Mrs Waterhouse. Somehow he knew I would be there, I think he wanted to protect me. It takes a very brave man to stand up to Billy Keenan." He then told her how he and Zed became good friends. Baz grinned. "If there were two people that were poles apart, then Zed and Will were it." Baz paused for a moment. "I hate pilchards Mrs Waterhouse."

She finally lit the cigarette, leaving the smell of sulphur hanging in the air.

"A Wing Commander Batty sent me a letter Basil." The smoke escaping her mouth with the words.

Baz was drawn to her lips as she talked, since she had mentioned the letter they appeared to have swollen, like two glistening fleshy pads. A strand of moisture stretched away as she took the cigarette from her mouth, only breaking off as she blew the smoke towards the ceiling. "He mentioned you in the letter Basil. How you were the last person to see William alive. You don't know how happy that makes me. To know he was with someone he knew. A good friend I mean. The Wing Commander said it would have been instant. William didn't suffer." Baz could see wetness lining her eyes as she spoke. "The letter was the first I heard, you know, about William. Reading it was the worst moment of my life Basil. It was a very kind letter though. The Wing Commander sounds like a good man."

"One of the best Mrs Waterhouse," Baz felt proud to say. "It was the Wing Commander who also told me about William." Baz paused. "I'm very sorry about William, Mrs Waterhouse, Will was my best friend. He will always be my best friend. We were very much alike. He was one of the best too, Mrs Waterhouse." Then realised how self-righteous that sounded.

"Thank you Basil, that's very kind of you to say so. It is just that I can't believe I won't see him again. The mornings are the worst, when I wake up. It's like not realising he has gone, then being told about it all over again. Sometimes I don't want to go to sleep, and if I do, I don't want to wake up." She briefly placed her hand on top of Baz's fingers and gave them a gentle squeeze.

The touch made him feel uncomfortable. "I always have the pawn to remind me of William." His face opened with a quiet proudness. "We were brothers of the board, Mrs Waterhouse."

"Brothers of the board?"

"It was a kid's thing." He told her about how they had each taken a pawn from the chess set and swore an oath that they would always be brothers of the board. "We were too much like wimps to draw blood, you know, like blood brothers." He slid his hand from under hers and pulled out the small wooden piece from his pocket. "William had the black one."

"He probably had it with him." She said quietly.

"Probably," he added, even quieter.

She took a small sip from her glass and held the liquid in her mouth, appearing to pluck up courage before swallowing. Another longer sip, no waiting this time. Her tongue wiped along her top lip.

"I'm so sorry Basil, how rude of me. Would you like a drink? There isn't any ale I'm afraid. Gin or whisky is all I have. I prefer gin myself. Mothers ruin and all that. I think it is going to help me to forget." She playfully shrugged her shoulders "It doesn't work though."

"No thanks, I'm not much of a drink...."

"I won't hear of it." She rose from her chair and disappeared into the drawing room. Baz could hear the distant opening and closing of cabinet doors. She returned and deposited a nearly full bottle of whisky, a much emptier one of gin and another crystal tumbler on the table.

Baz raised the glass to his mouth and allowed the tiniest drop of liquid to enter between his lips, swallowing more saliva than whisky. He tried it again, it tasted good, the whisky warmed him up inside. He took a longer swig, then another.

"And what about you Basil? What are you doing now?"

"Drinking your whisky."

She laughed out loud, it sounded false. "No, sorry. I mean in the RAF?"

"Oh, I'm an Aircraftman, a Leading Aircraftman."

"A Leading Aircraftman, that sounds important."

"Not really Mrs Waterhouse."

"Please, call me Margaret, it sounds so formal saying Mrs Waterhouse all the time. I want us to be good friends Basil." She hesitated before releasing the next words. "William told me about the tribunal?"

"Oh that."

"Not John, he didn't tell John, just me. John would not have approved." Puckering her lips and shaking her head. "Although the Bible does say thou shall not kill and love your enemies. He would only quote the commandments when it suited him. Fucking hypocrite."

Baz was astounded she knew such words and even more amazed to hear her use one. The gin, he thought.

"William said you were very brave to stand up for your principals."

"Well, it wasn't quite like that, Mrs Waterhou..."

"Margaret."

"Margaret."

"You have a nice nose Basil, like a girls." She looked at him with a doughy gaze. "How are your family?"

The proceedings were published in the local newspaper, appearing two days after Baz had departed for his training detail. He knew nothing about the trouble that followed.

The word 'conchie' had been hurriedly splashed over their front door in white paint, unfortunately it had dripped over the normally pristine step, upsetting his mother even more. Human excrement and white feathers were sent to them in the post. Over time the abuse quietly died down, stopping altogether when Zed Golby put the word around that they should be left alone. The rag-and-bone man's son had become a force to be reckoned with in the area. His father hadn't been seen for a long while, some credulous people even thought he had gone to fight. Zed had managed to avoid conscription, after all, there was nothing to say he actually existed at all. Anyway, he had taken advantage of the war and expanded into the black market. A natural progression for his line of business, he had thought.

"They're fine thank you. Well, Ollie, he..."

"Ollie."

"Oliver. My brother."

"Oh yes. I heard. William had told me that too. I am very sorry. I know exactly how your Mum and Dad must feel."

"Violet's doing something in London, office work I think, and Ruby's in the WVS. The war hasn't changed my mother and father's life much," Baz perked up slightly. "Dad has even had time to paint the front door."

"Oh, that's good," she said, stubbing out her cigarette.

"Mrs Water..."

"Margaret."

"Margaret, I should be getting back home."

Baz rose from his chair and lifted his jacket from the backrest. Mrs Waterhouse swigged down the last of her drink and followed him out into the hallway.

Baz felt a sadness that they were parting company, he had felt comfortable in her presence, something very few people could do.

For Mrs Waterhouse, that brief moment with Baz had pushed the darkness to one side. That knot in her stomach, that heaviness in her heart had remained but Baz had given her a momentary release from the anguish.

"Basil. Would you mind taking William's kit bag upstairs for me. It looks very heavy for a feeble woman like me."

"No Mrs Water...Margaret. I mean yes, of course. Where would you like me to put it?"

"William's bedroom please Basil, if you don't mind. It is very kind of you."

Baz began the short walk he had trodden so many times, savouring every step, somehow he knew he would never take the same journey again. It wasn't until he entered the bedroom a wall of sadness hit him. He stopped as so many memories began flooding back. This was the place where he had discovered fun and laughter, but most of all, friendship. Everything that was lacking outside of these four walls. It was the place where he and Will had become brothers of the board, something Baz felt was closer than just normal companionship. As though he was his real brother. Now the room was like a pining pet that had been abandoned by its master.

As a child Baz always thought Will's bedroom should have belonged to a much older boy, maybe a man. Now as he stood in the doorway, it appeared to belong to someone much younger. How much I must have grown up he thought to himself.

The sturdy wooden desk with its powerful turned legs stood in the same place. The shelves sat precariously above the bed head, crammed with what looked like the same leather bound books as before. "The classics old boy." Set out on the centre of the desk was something he recognised immediately. The Staunton chess set. Made by John Jacques. Designed by Nathanial Cook. "The King of chess sets," he whispered to himself. Only this one had a gap in each of the front rows, as if two teeth had been pulled out.

Baz picked up the four inch high black King and rubbed his thumb over the wooden figure, stroking the contours on its smooth surface.

"Old memories Basil?"

Baz turned with a startle. "Sorry Mrs Waterhouse, I was..."

"Margaret."

"Margaret."

Smoke drifted up from a recently lit cigarette. "You have a sensitive touch Basil." Her voice sounding like pure silk. "Keep it Basil."

"I couldn't. Not the King on its..."

"Please. I would like you to have it, take the whole set, I don't play. What use would it have for me?"

"I couldn't Mrs...Margaret."

"William would have wanted you to have it," she pleaded. "You must have it. Please, I insist, after all, you have one piece already."

Baz paused for a second. "Thank you, I promise I will look after it. If there is anything I can do for you."

Her eyes were drawing him in, searching his body.

"I must be making my way..."

"There is one thing Basil." She paused for a moment, her stare now anchored on his, she then walked away. The lower part of her gown billowing behind her, just as before. Only this time the entire gown from the shoulder down was free to flutter behind her, as if the entire sail had become untethered. She stopped in front of a closed door and stared back. A turn of the brass knob, a stretch of her arm, and the door slid into the room. For a few seconds her gaze hung on him, then she stepped in.

Baz tried to make some kind of sense of what had just happened, he stared at the abandoned entrance, waiting for her to reappear, it remained vacant.

Gingerly he made his way along the landing, the floorboards creaking noisily underfoot informed her of his approach, he stopped at the entrance and held onto the door frame, feeling as though it was about to suck him in. It was then he saw Mrs Waterhouse standing in the centre of the bedroom, an image of such beauty it nearly brought him to his knees. Her dressing gown had fallen to the floor, laying in a careless crumpled pile behind her bare feet. Her long unbridled hair rippled over a wafer thin, shimmering silk nightdress, outlining every contour of her body, a trace of smoke drifted upward from a half stubbed out cigarette.

From the age of seventeen Margaret Waterhouse had been married to a mechanical man, a puritan, a husband that considered sex was for procreation only. When the day of judgement comes, God will view this mere mortal as only serving him. William had been born over three years later, copulation after that had become nonexistent. Now the experiences she had missed out on had left her with a deep yearning. A long, suppressed desire, one she thought she never had.

Mrs Waterhouse took a deep breath and released the thin straps from her bare shoulders, a helping tug at her breasts and the nightdress fell to the ground. Her modesty now abandoned, her radiance exposed in its full magnificence, Baz felt he was looking at a beautiful marble statue. A glance at the dressing table mirror, a back view, a narrow slice of curved spine, a top of the plunging cleft.

"Take your shoes off Basil," her voice was assertive, confident. Not to comply was inconceivable.

He crouched down and ineptly slid his footwear off.

"Socks."

He obeyed.

Mrs Waterhouse moved forward with short measured steps until he felt her breath on his mouth. He stared down at her open lips, at the shameless white flesh only inches from him, the two pink jewels, the prominent triangular fleece. He could feel the warmth, he could smell her fragrance, as if she had been sprinkled with nature itself.

A sensation was beginning to move parts within him, feelings he only recognised from waking some mornings, and that one time at the employment exchange.

She placed a hand on each of his shoulders, her thumbs tucked under his collar, a slow gentle push and the jacket fell from his back. The shirt buttons followed, two she fumbled with, Baz helped. It was only when the faded blue shirt was pulled down over his arms did she see a dark brown embossed mark of tight skin inches below his shoulder.

"You poor boy. What have they done to you?" she said in a soft whisper, gently touching the cherry round scar with her fingertips. "Those nasty Germans, you poor, poor, boy."

Baz remained silent. Words did not seem appropriate.

She gently kissed the impaired flesh, once, twice, three, more, every one followed the outline of the scar. Then like a mother undressing her child she pulled the vest over his head, her eyes slid down his boyish bare chest until she saw the other bullet forged scar. This one was more pronounced, purple in colour, resembling a fossilised line of stitches imprinted just below his rib cage.

"Another one. My poor love." Softly spoken, a blend of surprise and relish. She dropped to her knees, planting more kisses around the scar. Her fingers tugged the belt out from under the brass buckle, at the same time unbuttoning his trousers. She tucked her fingers into the top of the material and yanked his remaining clothes down to his ankles.

Baz sprung free, exposed, erect, vulnerable, available, awkward.

She nestled her cheek on his stomach and stared down, her soft hair stroking his skin as she discarded the last remnants of any clothing from under his feet.

A flinch as her hand delicately clasped around him. Her wanton brazenness was even surprising her, she felt shameless, fearless.

Baz felt a moist softness close over him, caressing him, feelings he thought could never exist. He ran his fingers through her hair, stroking her cheek, it felt instinctive, involuntary, natural.

She released him from her mouth and rose to her feet.

Eye to eye, their lips touched, a soft delicate union, a gentle pressure, the moment prolonged. He tasted gin and tobacco, she whisky. His eyes open, hers closed.

She took one step back, then another. The light slipped over her curves like sunlight advancing over hills as she lay down, her long dark hair unfurled indiscriminately over the pillow, cushioning her head onto the soft material. Baz flicked a furtive glimpse as she opened her legs and pulled him on top of her.

"Push Bazil. For Gods sake push."

He penetrated her space. Her back arched, her hips rose up as her shoulders dug into the pillow. She felt like a willing captive, invaded, filled, excited. He moved inside of her, slow at first, then faster and deeper.

Beads of sweat began to glisten on her skin, her hair lay darkened, plastered to her forehead. Her eyes narrowed, her lips widened.

"Thank you Basil." She forced out in one breath.

"No...thank...you...Mis...sus...Wat...er...house."

"Margaret."

"Marg...a...ret."

Baz gripped the pillow as if he wanted to squeeze all life out of it, then one last thrust that released an ecstasy like nothing he had felt before.

Mrs Waterhouse felt warm waves rolling over her body, the last one breaking over her like falling feathers.

She breathed again.

Baz returned home in the evening, still not believing what had just happened, trying to convince himself that it hadn't been a dream. It was only in that last hour he felt the boy had finally been cleansed from his body.

He had left Mrs Waterhouse standing in the front doorway. The look of vulnerability and affection she had willingly given him before was gone.

As soon as Baz pulled out from inside her, she immediately knew what had just happened was wrong. Those waves of ecstasy were replaced with regret and guilt. She, a married woman, had just fucked her dead son's friend. It made William's death seem even worse.

Baz immediately saw her attitude towards him change, she had become subdued, pensive, as though her actions were shameful. Even hiding behind an elaborate Chinese screen to get dressed. Emerging minutes later in a long pleated skirt and a thick woollen cardigan pulled over a high necked blouse, The dressing gown and purple silk nightdress confined to the darkness of her wardrobe. Also gone were the accommodating looks and those soft words, replaced with fleeting glances that established his stage of readiness. Apologising for her transgression as though she had just committed a crime.

"You are a very gentle man Basil, you have a very kind heart. One day you will meet the right girl."

Baz didn't think she had meant it at first. He sensed, maybe hoped she wanted to tell him something else, but didn't, maybe she was too afraid to do so.

His persistent appeals to stay and look after her, that they had forged something special, that they should go somewhere where they couldn't be found. Baz could see he was only pushing her even further away, making her even more committed for him to leave.

Struggling to find any more words he reluctantly submitted to her carefully chosen requests for him to go.

"It is not your fault Basil. It was me, I mean, that was not me, I need to find myself, I need to find the person I lost all those years ago."

"I'll leave the RA..."

"Alone! Please Basil," she implored.

"But you..."

"No Basil. What you are searching for is not here. Not with me. Please *just* go."

He emerged through the front door and descended the six steps into the wretched world he had left a few hours before. Baz somehow knew he would never see her again.

"Basil," she said softly as he stepped onto the pavement. He turned and looked up at her.

"Thank you," was all she said, spoken with a polite smile, the same smile he had remembered as a child.

"Goodbye Mrs Waterhouse."

"Margaret," she whispered to herself as she shut the front door and the outside world behind her.

Baz's experiences in the last hour had made him numb to the drizzling rain and the chill brought on from the fading October light. He had also forgotten the bombing raids on the city had become heavier and more frequent in recent days. Soon the city would be hidden away in its own darkness, then the fear would creep in while the people waited for the sporadic flashes from the bombing and the red glow that never failed to follow. Everyone but Baz.

He pulled his collar up and plunged his hands deep into his pockets. With his head dropped low he pounded the watery reflections. The wooden box with William's chess pieces squeezed tightly between arm and body. Memories and inanimate wooden figures are all that remained of his friend and his friend's mother. Baz smiled to himself, his friend's mother.

Three men passed him wearing tin hats and dark uniforms, their loud chattering and the glint from metal buttons on their tunics were the only indication of their existence. "You'd better get home quick lad. If it's anything like last night you won't want to be out here," one of the men said in a gutteral East London accent. His words encroached into Baz's mind, opening memories of the previous night's bombing. It was twenty-four hours ago when it felt as though the devil himself had woken up.

All Baz wanted to do was walk, in some strange way he thought if he kept moving it would help somehow. "If you think you have entered hell, then just keep walking." Another glorious quote from his father.

He had preferred it when Mrs Waterhouse was just William's mother, everything then was black and white. New emotions had surfaced, ones he couldn't understand or want to understand.

Anything that resembled light was soon engulfed by the darkness. What were buildings, trees and lamp posts had become black featureless shapes. To his right he heard the sound of a vehicle slowly trundling by with its headlamps off, the driver straining to see the white edging on the pavement. A splash of water as Baz's foot landed in a deep puddle, water overlapping his shoe. Minutes later the sky had finally vanished into a vast expanse of blackness, barely leaving a faint glow of moonlight as it struggled to penetrate through the overcast blanket.

A large man in an army uniform collided into him, a polite apology from Baz and some choice words from the stranger as they stepped aside from each other. Not a good time to be in a hurry Baz thought. Stories of folk walking into canals or stepping in front of moving vehicles were common gossip in the shelters. Baz gave himself an inward smile. If the Germans don't get me, then my stupidity probably will.

Baz rounded the corner at the top of Haydons Road. As a schoolboy he had stood in this same spot many times, gazing down this busy road, captivated by its commotion. The same factories remained, a panorama of silhouettes, like cut-outs from a black card. Only, in this time of conflict, the hustle and bustle had faded. In the cold light of day Baz knew it would never be the same again. Most workers have already been conscripted or volunteered, many will never return, he wondered how many had become conscientious objectors. Some factories had been assigned to the war effort, a wood mill used for making furniture was now manufacturing fuselage frames, army uniforms were made in what was once a thriving clothing company, others lay dormant. Baz also knew that their exposed vulnerability would one day succumb to enemy bombs.

Then he saw the distinct profile of the big house and its tall chimneys, even in the dark it remained an imposing sight. He wondered what fate awaited it.

A hard stern voice punctured the darkness. "What's in the box sonny!?"

Baz nearly choked in surprise. Just above his eyeline he could see a thin black strap resting on a chiselled chin. Under the pointed peak of a tall dark helmet were the whites of two glaring eyes.

"Jesus Christ! You nearly gave me a heart attack," Baz blurted out.

"No sonny. If I was Jesus Christ you would probably be dead and I would know what's in the box."

"They're chess pieces." Baz opened the lid and held it out in front of him. "Look."

The pieces appeared to be encrusted with jewels as the torch light caught the raindrops. The policeman aimed the beam into Baz's face, flicking from his right eye then to his left, he quickly turned, the torch light followed.

"Who's shining that bloody light this way? Why don't you just give the bloody hun my name," someone yelled through the inky black.

The policeman flicked the switch off and faced Baz again.

"Are you going to win the war with chess pieces sonny?" he snapped.

"It *would* save a lot of lives."

"Where did you get them from?"

"A friend."

"Where does your friend live?"

"He doesn't, unless you believe in God, then he probably lives in heaven." Baz stared up at the policeman. "He's dead," he added quietly.

The torch was turned back on. "How did he give them to you then?" The look was smug, as though he had just solved a great crime.

"He didn't, his mother did and do you have to shine that torch in my eyes?"

"There are two kinds of people out on a night like this sonny, one are people that wear uniforms and the other wants to rob. And you aint wearing a uniform are you?" the policeman said, as he slid the torchlight up and down Baz's clothes.

"I went round to my friend's house to return his kit bag and his mother gave me his chess..."

Just at that moment the air pulsated with the howl of an air raid siren. Funnels of searchlights began to slice through the night sky, followed by muffled booms rumbling in the distance. The policeman turned off his torch and looked towards the burst of flares lighting up the night sky.

Baz took one step back and disappeared into the dark.

He arrived at his home a couple of minutes later, expecting to find the house empty. Instead, over the distant noise of the siren he heard another sound, a stranger sound, one that was rarely heard in the household, or more to the truth, one that had been kept from him. Through the closed kitchen door came the muffled sound of his parents in heated disagreement. Holding his breath and staring down at the floor he rested his fingers on the inside latch, quietly nudging the door against its frame.

"And he snores," he heard his mother say.

"Well it's better listening to him snoring than a house collapsing over our heads."

"Is it? Is it really! Not if you're stuck in a tin can with that man, and why do we have to do what they say because it's in their garden? And he cheats at cards."

"Well, the shelter is on their land and they are good enough..."

"I haven't had a wink of sleep in days. I want my own bed, just for one night."

"No Rosemary! I forbid it!" A first for Giles Albright.

"You forbid..."

With the flat of a strong hand Baz slammed the door shut.

The Albrights spent that night in the Anderson shelter at the back of their neighbour's garden, with them were Mr and Mrs Downley.

Baz agreed with his mother about the snoring, and the cheating.

On a bitterly cold afternoon, the day before he departed for his new posting, Baz strolled into the yard belonging to Zed Golby. When I say belonging to Zed Golby and not Noah Golby, this is in fact correct. Zed's father had died nearly a year earlier from a long mysterious illness. Handling too much lead, if the truth be known.

Zed's mother had passed away long before that, when he was in his early teens. A vague image of her face was about all he could remember.

The death of his father had a profound effect on Zed, his slow decline had ground the young Golby down until he was on the verge of exhaustion. It was Zed who had to wash his father after the terrible bouts of diarrhoea and tackle the gruelling task of trying to feed a man with no appetite. There were times when his father had forgotten who his son was, staring through him as if he wasn't there. But the worst moment for Zed was the helplessness he felt in not being able to ease the terrible suffering; when he had to listen to his father's groaning and watch his body distort from the severe pain. It was at these times Zed would plead for his father to depart this world. "Die dad die," he would say over and over again, although the rag-and-bone man never heard his son, not until eleven months had passed, Noah Golby finally closed his eyes for the last time.

From that day it would be society that owed Zed Golby.

Baz was taken aback on his first sighting of the yard. If there was ever a contrast with the vision of how it used to look, then this surely was it. Although surprised, Baz had also been impressed, the whole area now looked as though it was owned by someone that had an obsession with cleanliness.

There was one addition to the yard that Baz couldn't help but notice, or more to the truth, hear. As he entered the gates his skin was nearly blown off by the boom of loud barking, a noise that parted the air for miles. It was only the chain, a dubious length of rusted metal straining at every link and appearing to strangle the huge black dog in mid-air that kept Baz from being torn limb from limb.

Neatly written in yellow paint on a plank of wood nailed above a door, was the word OFFICE. Baz remembered it as the stable and without any shadow of a doubt it was no longer a stable. Inside it had taken on a more palatial existence. A solid oak desk stood in the far corner, not dissimilar to how Baz remembered the one in Will's bedroom. A fine leather chair was tucked away behind it, also not a hundred miles away from the one belonging to Will. In front of the desk was another, plain looking chair. From the other corner a warmth exuded from a small grey wood stove, its tottering flue pipe vanishing through the roof.

Baz nervously remained at the open entrance as Zed shook the hand of a short stout man with wide shoulders and a cheap, worn suit. He waddled past Baz, avoiding any eye contact.

Even Zed had taken on a whole new demeanour. His grubby overalls had been replaced with an expensive dark blue suit covering a white silk shirt unbuttoned at the neck, although Zed would never be able to lose those dark gypsy-like features. He also hadn't managed to liberate any more of the English language, nor did he have to, his powerful frame and hard unwavering stare was enough to deter anyone from wanting him to say too much anyhow.

Zed looked him up and down. "Baz," stretching the word in delight and extending his hand.

"Nice dog you got out there Zed." Feeling his fingers being crushed inside a vice like grip.

"Duke, Yeah. Night time Baz, don't come, unless you want to be on menu."

"What about the horse?" asked Baz.

"Steaks, lots of money." Zed froze with a straight face, followed suddenly by a manic laugh, sounding as though it would give Duke's bark a run for its money. "Horse don't protect what you own Baz." He then gazed at Baz's uniform. "Aircraftman." Zed made it his business to know everything about the war, including RAF uniforms, they were popular on the black market and Zed had sold a lot more stranger items.

"Uniform Baz, I buy, good money."

"Not on your life Zed, I'll be shot at dawn."

"Keep bullets Baz, good money."

Baz grinned nervously. "I don't normally wear it away from the airfield but you get the strangest looks if you're not in uniform." It was his turn to look Zed up and down. "Or an expensive suit."

Baz waited for a response, nothing. "Sorry to hear about your father."

Zed stared coldly at Baz.

"Dad said it was a tough time for you?" Baz added, watching Zed roll up a cigarette. "You seem to be doing alright on your own though?"

"I don't need no one Baz."

"Oh yeah. My dad told me to thank you. He said something about not having to paint his front door again. Mind you Zed, I'm sure half the things he comes out with he doesn't understand himself. He also said to tell you to be careful, he said that only fools rush in where angels fear to tread."

Zed tightened his mouth and nodded in agreement.

For the next hour they reminisced over old times, although when their present situation was discussed, Zed kept his words to a more than usual minimum, resulting in them sitting in pockets of silence for some of the time, reminding Baz of old times. A steely glare in Baz's direction would always follow a question that got slightly intrusive. Baz instinctively knew when to stop, even now, as a close friend, Zed could turn him to stone with just one look.

Occasionally the thunder of Duke's barking would indicate the presence of a visitor, appearing at the office door moments later with a ruffled but relieved appearance. It was during these times Zed would vanish, reappearing minutes later as though nothing had happened.

Baz was about to rise from his chair when a very tall visitor with a rod like back, weather beaten face, and a long dark overcoat marched into the office. It was at this stage the barking would normally stop. Only this time it continued, if not louder. In some ways Baz felt thankful he wouldn't be first on the menu.

Zed rose from his chair and strolled to the entrance. "Quiet!" he yelled at the top of his voice, completely drowning out the dog's roar.

Duke lay down on his stomach, sphynx like, both front legs stretched out in front, his head held low, even his whimpering could be clearly heard in the office.

Baz gave a quick glance down at the stranger's black glossy boots. Army he thought, although the dark blue trousers didn't fit in with this assumption. Navy then, Baz felt content. It was only when he heard him speak that the question was answered, with the addition of making the hairs on his arm stand up.

"I've come for my rags Mr Golby."

"Wait here," said Zed and left the office.

Baz stared down at the floor, hoping his face was hidden from the stranger.

"On leave sonny?" The man said to Baz.

"I got shot." That's it! Baz thought. I got shot. I've paid my dues, so leave me alone.

"That was careless?"

"I know."

"A dead man can't play chess sonny."

Baz looked up. "Yes I know." He could see the man studying his eyes.

"You never said goodbye the other night?"

Baz remained silent.

Zed returned with a folded brown envelope. The man took it from Zed and disappeared out of the door.

Baz finally rose to his feet.

"Do you know who that is Zed?"

"Yeah," said Zed.

"No Zed," Baz spoke slowly, "Do you know *what* he does?

"Yeah."

Baz's voice quietened to a near whisper. "No Zed, he's a police...?"

Zed looked at Baz with the coldest stare so far, another man might not have been so lucky.

Baz didn't pursue it anymore. "Don't forget about those angels and where you're treading, whatever Dad meant by that."

"I will Baz. Don't get shot again," said Zed extending his hand. "If do, keep bullets."

Thinking it was probably the equivalent of placing his hand in Duke's mouth, Baz shook hands with Zed, it would have been an insult not to. No one insults Zed Golby.

14 MINCHEN STREET
1941

Giles Albright knew he only had a few more breaths left in his body. He could not see the broken and distorted body of his wife lying only a few inches away from him but he knew she was there. He also knew he would never see her again, or she him.

When the howling of sirens began, so did Giles Albright's power of persuasion to coax his wife into the air raid shelter, a place she had grown to despise, a chore that was also starting to wear him down. So it was no surprise that both had a sense of relief when the shelter had flooded one stormy evening. An uneventful and bomb free night followed, but for Rosemary Albright, a precedent had been set.

Giles Albright also knew in the back of his mind that this moment in time would eventually come, as he knew death would eventually come to everyone. It was only then he had the answer to the question that everyone asks themselves at one time in their life. How?

For the past few months Baz's father had watched the city glow in a burning haze of red, orange and yellow. He had heard the wailing of the air raid sirens followed by the droning of enemy aircraft dropping their death all around him. But not in Minchen Street. Not until this night.

Rosemary Albright and her husband had tempted fate one too many times.

At twenty-past midnight a bomb landed two doors away. A direct hit on the Gibson's house, presumably with them in it, as nothing was ever seen of them again. As the blast blew into the Albright's home, it was their bedroom wall that was to crumble first, quickly followed by the crashing of the wooden floor beams, taking all the contents from the two first floor bedrooms with them.

It was not only his parents that Baz was to lose that night. His prized charcoal grey, drop handled, three gear racing bike had been buckled and twisted beyond recognition, the only part visible and poking out above the rubble like a drowning animal was its contorted

114

front wheel. His lovingly restored record player, another acquisition from the Golby yard, had been completely obliterated by the falling bricks. The extensive collection of gramophone records Baz had collected over the years were fragmented into small black shards. But saddest of all, thirty wooden figures lay scattered amongst the pile of debris, two armies defeated for the last time. The only survivor, a lone pawn safely kept in a leading aircraftsman's pocket.

The top half of the back wall and the whole of the front wall, along with the roof were the last to topple; and that completed the devastation of the Albright's home.

For a split second the massive blast had woken Rosemary Albright from her sleep, all she saw was a blue flash, all she felt was extreme pain as the jagged end of a rafter crashed into her fragile body. Then for her, there was nothing.

All Giles Albright wished for as he lay in the pitch black was that he hadn't survived the immediate impact at all.

After the panic and the confusion came the shivering. All he could feel was the weight of 14 Minchen Street on his chest. All he could taste was a mouthful of dust and burning ash when he tried to breathe. All he could smell was the scorched rotting air. All he could hear was the whispering of a cold wind snaking its way towards him.

Giles Albright knew when the pain passed, so would he.

———————

LAC Basil Albright
RAF Manston
Ramsgate
Kent

To my dearest brother Basil.

As you read this letter your heart will be heavy and your sorrow will be great.

There is no way I can disguise the true heartache it will bring, so I believe as my beloved younger brother you deserve to be told this news from your devoted and loving sister.

It is with greatest sadness I have to inform you that Mam and

Dad were killed two days ago just after midnight. A bomb exploded at number eighteen on Wednesday night destroying half the street, including our home. Mam and Dad were in bed at the time and died instantly, without suffering. Their bodies were removed next morning, I have been told they were both at peace.

First Oliver, now this. The war is truly the worst and I hate it for what it is doing to the world.

This is one of the most difficult letters I have had to write Basil and I hope I will not have to write another one like it.

Your most loving and heartbroken sister.

Ruby

————————

Ruby rested her head on Baz's shoulder and wept.

"Well, that's our home," she sobbed.

No one responded.

Violet, standing on the other side of Baz, affectionately slid her hand around his waist and pulled him closer.

"Mam and Dad never harmed anyone. I hate the war, I hate God, I hate everything. I wish all Germans were dead," exclaimed Ruby, her weeping turning into full blown tears, as it had done for most of the day.

No one responded again.

Her crying had become so frequent that most people had stopped comforting her after the funeral, which, with her attention seeking trait probably made her even more melodramatic.

The three stood facing the pile of bricks and scattered timber that was once their home. The layers of collapsed floor were the only indication of the tragedy that befell their parents. The only disturbance was the rubble that had been removed to retrieve the bodies.

"It's like a bomb hit it," said Baz through his tears.

Violet squeezed him tighter.

Ruby shrieked a sound which neither brother or sister could tell was a burst of laughter or just another fit of crying.

A loving hand was placed on Ruby's shoulder. Standing behind her was Peter, her husband of only one month.

Ruby and Peter had found each other six months before. Or more to the truth, Peter Toulsen found Ruby.

He was a railway worker at Paddington Station, a platform hand, noticeable by his dark blue oversize overalls stained darker by the sooty smoke matching his slick, greased black hair. Peter Toulsen spent most of his day pushing heavily laden trolleys along the many platforms, most of them weighed down with piles of baggage and mail bags. The rest of the time he would be hidden away, smoke rising from his relit roll-up: in a railway station brimming with steam trains, Peter Toulsen knew he was virtually undetectable. It was during one of these breathers that Peter Toulsen had a life changing experience. Through the smoky atmosphere and from across the tracks he watched in fascination at the commotion taking place on the number five platform. What materialised out of the drifting steam had Peter gawking with admiration. He thought he had seen an angel, all be it one in a bottle green uniform, but an angel nevertheless. In fact, what he did see was an attractive young woman helping a crowd of bewildered and frightened child evacuees board a train. Peter was besotted before the flame had reached the end of the cigarette.

"Toulsen! Slacking again. Get them trolleys moved lad," barked the Assistant Station Master.

Twenty minutes later, Peter returned to find platform number five had emptied itself of all but the station staff, it was at that moment he accepted his angel and future happiness had probably drifted up with the steam into the station's vast canopy.

Three days later, fortune had struck Peter Toulsen again *and* on his thirtieth birthday. This time his angel was standing at the station kiosk.

"Hello," he said with a nervous grin.

Ruby looked Peter up and down. "I don't know you," she said.

"You don't need to know someone to say hello," Peter replied with a schoolboy charm.

"Yes, *And?*" she said, forcefully.

"I just wanted to say hello."

"Yes, *And?*" this time rather less forcefully.

"I saw you the other day helping children onto the carriages."

"So you have the ability of sight. Good for you."

If he had thought about his next words Peter would probably not have said them. "I thought you were an angel sent from heaven."

She had never heard words spoken like that before and more importantly, never to her.

Ruby had misplaced dreams of grandeur, and at that time a railway worker did not fit into her plans of ascending into the higher echelons of society life. She hadn't realised it yet but her prospects at best were to marry someone that she would be happy with, someone that just loved her, someone that would accept her impulsive characteristics and fiery tantrums.

"And it's my birthday, one drink with an angel is all I ask," Peter pleaded.

Ruby paused. "OK. One drink, only because it's your birthday."

They sat at a small table in a dark corner of the noisy and smoky station bar. At first Ruby seemed preoccupied, causing Peter's usual confident street-wise words to trip over themselves. Although, it appeared he had an answer for almost everything.

"Why aren't you out there shooting Germans?"

"A gun in my hand would be a danger to anyone within two feet." Anyway, Winston decided that if us railway workers keep the trains running then we'll win the war for him."

"Is it really your birthday?"

"It is, God sent me an angel, isn't that proof enough."

They talked for ages that afternoon, and that evening, and the next day, and the day after that. Ruby married Peter five months later in a wedding dress her mother made out of old net curtains.

For Peter Toulsen, Angel was the only name he called his wife.

As Baz looked down the road he couldn't believe how much devastation could be caused by one bomb. The shockwave had left a ripple of destruction from complete annihilation at the impact site to his own home, only its furthermost wall was left standing, the chimney breast managing to halt its demise. The neighbouring house on the other side of that wall was badly damaged but mainly intact, although uninhabitable. The adjacent house to Baz's home and closest to the explosion was completely destroyed beyond recognition, flattened would be the closest description. This was the home that belonged to Mr and Mrs Downley. Both were bruised and in shock but holed up alone in their Anderson shelter they had survived.

It was at this point Violet had decided to drop the second bombshell on Minchen Street. "There is something I should tell you," she paused. "I know Dad wanted to tell you at some point soon, but, well the war got in the way." She had wondered if she should have said anything at all. Anyhow, since she had started, there was no turning back.

Ruby's sobbing had died down to a red eyed snivel as she gazed over her handkerchief at Violet. "What? What is it Violet? If you know something you must tell us," she said, the thin material billowing with her words.

"Mam and Dad," Violet paused once more.

"Oh for God's sake Violet! It can't be any worse than being told..." Ruby stopped mid-sentence, "well you know...this!"

Violet took a deep breath. "They were never married. There you go, I've said it. Mam and Dad were never married."

"What do you mean they were never married?" said Ruby.

"I'm sorry Ruby. I don't know how to say it any different. Mam and Dad never got married. Mam took on Dad's name but really she was still Rosemary Taylor. I'm sorry I had to tell you."

"How come Dad told you and not me and Baz. I don't believe it!"

"Because I am the oldest in the family." Only by nine minutes if the truth be known. "Why would I lie to you? Dad said that it was something he didn't want to take to the grave with him, you know, after Mam was refusing to stay in the shelter," her words became restrained. "Dad seemed to know their fate, he didn't say it but I could tell."

"He wasn't wrong," said Peter.

"You mean we are bast..." Ruby began.

Without any warning Baz released himself from his two sisters and stepped onto the rubble, stumbling several times as he ascended the mound of debris. At one time his foot slid back, dislodging a few bricks and roof tiles, sending them avalanching a short way down, one brick clopped all the way to the bottom causing Peter to quickly sidestep away, pulling Ruby with him.

"Sorry," Baz called out.

"Who needs Germans," Peter shouted.

Baz reached the summit, standing like a mountain climber proud of reaching his objective. "Not married," he yelled, facing upward. "Not married," he shouted again, followed by loud laughter. Peter's face opened up with his characteristic cackling. The whole bizarre situation finally hit Violet and Ruby, together they began to giggle, soon erupting into uncontrollable laughter. "Not married," Ruby called out in her loudest voice. Tears streamed down her cheeks. Baz sat down on the debris and slowly shook his head. As the laughter receded he released a long heavy sigh. "Not married," he said quietly.

Baz looked over at his buckled bicycle wheel poking out from the rubble. Wrapping his fingers around the rim he felt the airless tyre collapse in his grasp. An image of what the bike used to look like entered his mind, the shiny metal and perfect charcoal grey paintwork, its dropped handlebars, the studded leather saddle. He released his hold, half hoping it would drown under the rubble.

Through a gap in the bricks, Baz recognised the corner of a chequered board poking out from under a piece of wood. Torn and battered, the black and white squares were barely discernible through the grime. Baz removed a brick, then another, and another, until most of the board was visible. He gripped the corner with both hands and gave a quick hard tug. "Damn," he yelled as he sprung backward, a small piece of grubby card his only reward. He plunged his arm back into the mound of rubble, his eyes stared upwards in concentration, a grin appearing on an expression of elation. His arm emerged, immediately he put something in his pocket, then repeated the same manoeuvre again. The third time Baz lay on his front, his arm vanishing up to his shoulder, appearing several times to discard pieces of debris, then delved back down for another rummage. "That's it," he said rising up and brushing himself off. "No more."

After stumbling down the wreckage he hovered his clenched hand in front of Violet. "Take this Vi."

"What is it?"

"Trust me."

They all huddled together in a circle, staring down. Baz held the underside of Violet's fingers and slowly opened his hand over her palm. Violet felt as if something of great importance had touched her, then opening her hand for all to see, she displayed a four inch dark wooden chess piece, the King.

"It's beautiful."

"It's Dad," Baz told her.

Violet's eyes welled up.

He slid his hand into his pocket again and pulled out another piece, one from the lighter coloured wood, the Queen.

"For you," he said to Ruby.

Her face lit up. "Mam," is all she said, then burst into tears.

Baz plunged his hand into his pocket again and pulled out the remaining chess piece. The brothers of the board pawn.

"Who is that?" Peter asked.

"Norma and Ollie," he lied.

Baz had a long hard think before he was about to do what he knew he shouldn't be doing. He had this same feeling the last time he had made this journey. Only then there was a genuine reason.

Maybe he hoped the outcome would be the same as before. Maybe that is all it was, a selfish act. A self-serving egotistic selfish act. Maybe the flow of blood to his penis had taken priority over the flow of blood to his brain. Maybe he would be more confident this time, he knew he couldn't be any less. Maybe he would be able to satisfy her even more. Maybe...

Baz knew it couldn't just be that, it was a lot more than physical pleasure. He had experienced so much then, he had discovered emotions he never knew existed, feelings he has never got close to since. He felt he had touched genuine love. He thought she had felt the same. He thought this time she may welcome him into her life. He...

It was her that was at fault, she seduced him, it was Baz that could live without her. All she had to do was give him some kind of sign that she was happy, a few spoken words explaining everything was good with her life. Or just a simple smile would do. She just had to let him see her again, that was all, nothing need be said. She...

He thought his head was about to explode. Why can't life be simple? Why can't life just be black and white? Why...?

Baz instantly knew as he turned into the wide tree lined avenue and stood in front of the house. He knew when he saw the lowered blackout blinds and the dirty window panes. He knew as soon as he

121

saw the weeds growing from the cracks in the concrete steps. He knew when he sensed the coldness within its four walls.

Baz's knuckles rapped the same wood panel he had touched a few months before. And just as before there was no answer. He knocked again, this time with a force that could be heard halfway down the street. He waited, desperately hoping to see that gap appear in the door again, to hear the welcome of her warm voice once more.

"She's gone." A foreign accent shot out of the blue.

A middle aged face poked from behind a white column framing the neighbour's door.

"A couple of weeks ago," the man said. "Never been back as far as I know."

"Oh. Do you know where she went?"

"Somewhere down south I think, that's all I know, sorry."

"Was she on her own?"

"That's all I know, sorry." The man swiftly concluded the conversation, nearly forgetting his instructions.

MRS BLAKENEY
1942

The doctor and the midwife stared at each other with a look of exhaustion.

"There was nothing we could have done," Maureen Downes said, holding seven pounds and seven ounces of a twenty-two minute old boy. She was a veteran when it came to delivering babies and had experienced everything there was to experience. Sometimes beautiful, sometimes prolonged and exhausting, sometimes quick and uncomplicated, sometimes tragic. There was nothing Nurse Downes had not seen, only for this particular midwife, this day had been the worst.

Mrs Blakeney felt a tightening dull pain just below the bump encasing her baby, then the start of an ache descending from her lower back. It was just after half past three and after wiping away the water running down her thighs she went next door to find Eddie, a fourteen year old evacuee from Dulwich. "Be a darling Eddie and run down to the post office for me. Ask Mrs Ilbrey to telephone the midwife, she'll know why. I'll have a scone and jam for you when you get back." Eddie Wallace looked at Mrs Blakeney's hand resting on her bump, he knew precisely why Mrs Ilbrey had to telephone the midwife.

On a muggy, late Tuesday afternoon in mid-July, Maureen Downes arrived at the sleepy picturesque village of Spade Elm, turning sharply into the narrow country lane where Yew Tree cottage stood. She had managed to get to her destination as fast as she could. Even for a dumpy fifty-seven year old, Nurse Downes could ride her cycle as fast as someone half her age.

"You're right, there was nothing we could have done. Her age, well it wasn't on her side," said the mop haired doctor searching the floor for a clean towel, of which there were none, there were towels alright but none that weren't soaked red. He wiped the blood from his hands on a corner of the bed sheet. Then with a gentle stroke of his fingers the doctor closed the eyelids over the mother's lifeless eyes. After reflecting for a short moment on the grey death mask of her distorted face, he pulled the sheet over her body. "Did you know her?"

"No," said Nurse Downes, slowly shaking her head. "She was one of Emily's. I mean Nurse Dosanjh. And you Doctor?"

"No. Doctor Demant's," he said looking at the thin sheet melting over the woman's body. "And the father?"

"I asked, but she just shook her head. War casualty I assumed. She didn't seem to want to talk about him. She looked upset after I had, I didn't pursue it anymore." Maureen Downes looked down at the baby's face. "Poor mite will be alone in the world."

Doctor Roberts sat down at the dressing table and saw a small envelope with stylish scripted writing. 'To my darling unborn child. Only open when you have realised the truth'. The doctor slid it back into a cubby hole and lit a cigarette.

Pulling out a crisp blank death certificate from his bag and a silver fountain pen from an inside pocket, he meticulously wrote in each column. Under name and surname he wrote 'Margaret Blakeney,' for occupation he wrote 'housewife.' When he came to cause of death he stared at the whitewashed wall and thought for a moment.

Two hours after she arrived at the cottage, Mrs Downes went next door and found Eddie helping his foster mother with the household chores. It was Eddie's lucky day.

"You ever ridden a bicycle young man?"

"You bet lady, my brother had one twice the height as me and I rode that like a good'n," Eddie said with an American twang to his East London accent. He had somehow acquired it ever since his foster mother had taken him to see a film, Sheriff of Tombstone, starring Roy Rogers. Eddie's life changed the day he discovered Roy Rogers.

"Do you know Rambling Down young man?"

"Sure do, deputy New...I mean Farmer Newman takes..."

"Good boy, I think it's the fifth house along the High Street on the left. Hanging on the front gate will be a sign with the words 'Doctor's House' on it. Ask for Doctor Demant. Tell him to come as quick as possible."

Eddie rode the nurse's bicycle the two and a half miles to Rambling Down, only the bike had now acquired a name, Trigger. He had also left a copious amount of bullet ridden red Indians scattered around as he rode over the barren wasteland, at one time nearly toppling over as he flung his loose wristed hand over the handle bars. He reached the doctor's house, dismounting on the run. After some minutes of persistent knocking he sat on the front step, chewed on a blade of grass and waited.

At half-past six Mrs Blakeney was starting to show signs of distress. Nurse Downes had a suspicion the difficulty could be caused by a malposition. Not uncommon, but given the mother's age it was serious enough to call for the doctor. Maureen Downes never took risks.

"I think the little mite has got an arm above its head. Probably wants to try and pull itself out." She patted the sweat from the woman's forehead. "Take a rest dear. I'll just go and give the doctor a call. I'll be back in two shakes of a cat's tail."

The nurse quickly returned and informed Mrs Blakeney about dispatching the excited Eddie. "Doctor Demant is a fine doctor my dear. He'll have the little mite out as quick as you can say Winston Churchill."

Over an hour had passed with Mrs Blakeney asking the same question and the nurse replying with the same answer. "Soon my dear." Small talk and re-examining filled the gaps in between.

It was a relief for both women when they heard a car spluttering to a halt outside. Moments later came the noise of footsteps ascending the narrow wooden stairs. Stooping low, a young lanky physician with unruly hair entered the bedroom.

Mrs Blakeney's bedroom was a ten foot, square room with a low ceiling, just high enough for the doctor to get around without having to bend, although the two wooden beams were always going to be a danger to any part of him above his eyebrows. The woman's bed was nudged up against the wall opposite the door. A wardrobe, a small ornate dressing table which would not look out of place in some grand mansion and two plain chairs took up any remaining space. The only source of light came from a small crooked window made up of lead lined diamond shaped panes. By the number of crucifixes hanging from the walls, both Nurse Downes and the doctor thought Mrs Blakeney must have been very religious. One picture of Christ on the cross looked like a relic from the depths of history.

"Oh, I was expecting Doctor Demant."

"He's been waylaid at St Johns. I came as fast as I could. Nurse?"

"Nurse Downes."

"Hello Nurse Downes, I'm Doctor Roberts." He looked at Mrs Blakeney sitting up in the bed, her knees bent up under a sheet. "Hello young lady."

"Not looking my finest today I'm afraid Doctor," said the woman through gritted teeth and a clammy fringe.

"This is Mrs Margaret Blakeney," the nurse said moving closer to the doctor. "I believe we may have a malposition," she said quietly. "Forty-eight," she added with a lingering stare.

"And the contractions Nurse."

"One minute Doctor."

"Good, looks like you're ready Mrs Blakeney," he said in a loud precise manner.

"Thank you doctor but I'm just pregnant, *not* deaf," announced in harmony with her panting.

"Everything is prepared for you Doctor."

"Thank you nurse."

Mrs Blakeney spoke again. "This is truly a momentous day doctor. Both of you will go down in history. We should all pray." Then began reciting the Lord's prayer. The doctor and midwife ignored her, both had known stranger behaviour in childbirth.

Doctor Roberts took off his jacket and rolled up his shirtsleeves. After vanishing for a minute he returned wiping his hands on a towel.

The young doctor was from the new school of thought when it came to delivering babies, taking a very dim view of the old way, whenever the expectant mother had experienced a complication, however minor, then it would become routine for the poor woman to be sedated and the baby to be extracted from their unconscious body, mostly with the help of forceps. Drug 'em and drag 'em, Doctor Roberts had called it.

He lifted up the sheet and carefully positioned it on her knees, rescuing as much of her dignity as possible. Not that Mrs Blakeney cared a single jot about any self-respect at that moment in time.

The doctor felt inside her cervix. "Four inches, good."

With the tips of his fingers he felt a tiny hand reaching out to him.

"OK Mrs Blakeney, when your body tells you to push, you push."

Doctor Roberts waited. Nurse Downes waited.

Mrs Blakeley could feel a dull ache increase in pain.

"Now relax," the doctor said when he sensed the contraction starting to fade. As soon as the word left his mouth another one had started, this time with a vengeance. "It wasn't like...aarh." The woman screamed. Then she pushed. Then she squeezed Nurse Downes's hand. Then she screamed again. Then she pushed again. Then she screamed louder. Then the nurse freed her fingers from the vice like grip. "There, there my dear."

"Mmm." The doctor hummed, feeling inside the woman. He muttered something that sounded like it had ended in ...itism, then took a metal object resembling a ducks bill from his bag, the other hand grasped a pair of large forceps.

Immediately after the last contraction faded the doctor began to work fast, first the forceps, followed very quickly with "good," which wasn't the exact word Mrs Blakeney would have used as she released such an ear piercing screech it sent the birds fluttering from the trees.

"Sorry, but necessary." The last two words were whispered, more to himself. He opened up the speculum.

With her eyes tightly clamped shut, Mrs Blakeney opened her mouth in a silent scream, a desperate call for help.

After a long breath she started panting again, and with the panting, came the crying.

"Shh, shh dear, it will soon be over," said Nurse Downes.

"I'm dying."

"No my dear, you're just having a baby."

"We're ready now. One last push," said the Doctor.

Mrs Blakeney clasped a hand around nurse Downe's wrist and with the other she held tightly onto a fold in the bed sheet, then inhaled one long, deep breath.

"Push Mrs Blakeney, push, I can feel it coming."

The baby presented an arm to the world, soon followed by a tangle of dark, slimy hair.

Doctor Roberts pulled and Mrs Blakeney screamed.

Then a wet slippery head forced its way through the fleshy exit.

Doctor Roberts pulled and Mrs Blakeney screamed.

A tiny wrinkled baby emerged into the world and plopped itself into the doctor's hands.

Mrs Blakeney screamed yet again.

The placenta followed.

Mrs Blakeney screamed one more time.

The doctor handed the newborn to Nurse Downes. The umbilical cord was clamped and the last physical connection to its mother was severed.

"Help me," Mrs Blakeney cried.

"Now, now dear, you have a lovely boy," said Nurse Downes bending down to make the baby visible to its mother.

"Help me please. The pain, it's the pain," she cried, curling up into a ball so tight it seemed she had shrunk to half her size, her hands sliding down her front as though she was trying to push the pain out.

Nurse Downes froze in shock. "Doctor!"

The entire back of the mother's nightdress was stained with blood, the creased up sheet, the mattress, everything within close proximity had turned bright red. And Mrs Blakeney? She just wanted the torture to end, how it would end was of no importance to her. Her crying had stopped.

"For God's sake nurse, put the baby down and get some towels."

Mrs Blakeney remained silent.

The nurse returned.

"Hold them against the bleeding."

Mrs Blakeney felt a chill slip through her body.

"I'll get a sedative." Doctor Roberts rummaged around in his bag. Pulling out a syringe he plunged it into a small bottle and sucked up the clear liquid, with his hand shaking he united it with a needle and turned to see the mother's face. It was then he knew, it had become ghostly, still, vacant, as if something had been stolen from her. He held two fingers against the mother's sweat soaked neck. "She's gone," he said softly.

Nurse Downes picked up the baby and cradled it in her arms. A tear drop fell onto its forehead. "The poor woman never even saw him."

All the newborn had known of his mother were her screams, a noise that would haunt him for the rest of his life.

"What about the child?" the doctor asked.

"Poor mite will probably go to the orphanage, then the big wide world. If there is anything left of it."

Without any warning, Mrs Chattle, the woman's neighbour appeared in the doorway holding a tray weighed down with a teapot, jug and an assortment of china cups. Eddie close behind her.

"I thought you...Oh!..Oh my God!..Oh my God no!"

"What is it, canna see the baby?" Eddie asked.

The first Mrs Chattle saw were the red stained sheets, then the grey face and rigid body of her neighbour. She stared at the nurse, then the tiny white bundle held in her arms.

"Canna see the baby?" pleaded the muffled voice behind her. "I wanna hold the baby?"

Mrs Chattle felt weak, slowly lowering the tray until all its contents fell onto the wooden floorboards.

"What's happening? What is it? Eddie's frightened words called out as he tried to see through the gaps on either side.

The neighbour turned and held the empty tray in front of the boy. "Come on Eddie, the doctor and nurse are busy. They'll let you see the baby later."

"Are you all right Doctor?" the nurse asked waiting anxiously for his reply.

The doctor turned his gaze away from the whitewashed wall. "Yes

I'm fine. Thank you nurse." Then wrote 'Puerperium Obstetrical Haemorrhage' in the column headed, cause of death. "You're right, there was nothing we could have done."

MOST LOSE A COUPLE
1943

"Most lose a couple." How could Baz forget the Flight Sergeant's words.

It was one week ago when virtually in the same sentence Baz was given two pieces of news, neither did anything to enhance his well being. "From immediate effect you will be Corporal Albright," said the Flight Sergeant, the bags under his eyes appearing to carry the weight of the world.

After hearing of his promotion, Baz's immediate reaction was that he would have preferred to have remained a simple LAC, he was never one for responsibility, or dishing out orders, or any change at all for that matter.

Secondly, and the worst of the news, was his next posting. "We're sending you to Persia, Corporal Albright, Iraq to be more precise, RAF Shaibah, near the port city of Al Basrah. We're sending a load of Spits for the Russians to play with."

Corporal! Persia! Iraq! Al Basrah! Shaibah! Russians! Spits! Play! Baz felt giddy.

The Flight Sergeant continued, "Airfields seem to be very possessive when it comes to letting us have one or two of their aircraft, especially Spits. Anyway, Winston told Stalin he could have some, so we've managed to muster up thirty-five of the blighters from all over the realm. Each one will be broken up into five sections. You know the drill Corp. You'll be travelling with about twenty other men. You will be called the 133 Maintenance Unit. Anyway, the aircraft will be loaded in crates onto some cargo ship, that is when we find one that floats."

Floats! Aren't all ships meant to float, thought Baz.

"You will depart from Liverpool Docks as soon as. Probably going in convoy, with an escort. Safer that way Corp."

"Safer?!" Not realising the word had shot out into the air.

"Most lose a couple somewhere along the way Corporal, law of averages. We'll keep you in the centre, don't want to upset the Russians and lose their precious cargo, do we?"

"No Flight," feeling rather insignificant.

"Oh by the way, I've heard the natives at Al Basrah are a slippery lot. Steal the shirt off your back and without you knowing about it. Handy with the odd dagger as well I'm told."

Baz said nothing. If the ship doesn't get torpedoed, or even sink of its own accord then he'll probably be stabbed by some thieving Arab, and wearing *his* shirt into the bargain.

"Good luck Corporal."

"Flight." Baz saluted and left the room thinking the clock had started ticking on the remainder of his life.

III

SS City of Derby

RAF Shaibah

Plan B

P-B4!

The first time Baz saw the seven thousand ton steam ship City of Derby he thought there was probably more rust than metal. It was floating though, always a good sign.

Baz knew the next few weeks were going to be the longest of his life and had long since convinced himself he would probably die in that time, especially knowing how Oliver had met his fate. Drowning or being burnt to death, even eaten by sharks, Baz had played the different scenarios over and over again until he had exhausted the whole idea of death altogether.

Corporal Basil Albright and another twenty aircraftmen had just followed their kit bags from the back of an RAF transport truck. Baz decided he had never seen a place as hectic as Liverpool docks, or felt anywhere as cold for that matter, a bitterness that only a wind whipping off a winter sea could produce, one that turned his bones to ice.

The port was a panorama of masts, rigging and funnels, all engulfed in the stench of oil, smoke and sweat, but most of all war, it reeked of war. Extending into the damp smoggy horizon was an endless line of ships, at its centre a huge, grey ocean liner devouring never-ending lines of uniformed soldiers trudging up its steep walkways. Above their heads, vast cranes were swinging cargo nets bulging with supplies, dropping onto the decks or vanishing down dark cavernous holds with the sound of echoing booms.

"We'll be bloody safe in that old tub. A German torpedo would probably go straight through it and come out the other fucking side," remarked Paul Morgan in his usual interminable way. Morgan was a rough Mancunian with a music-hall comedian's face and as tactless and uninhibited as any person Baz had ever met, with language to match. Someone who had no respect for authority, probably the reason he had been dispatched to Shaibah in the first place. In truth, Baz thought most of his unit looked as though some hidden transgression had warranted their posting. He wondered what his might have been, maybe there was some other documentation about him being a conscientious objector tucked away in a filing cabinet somewhere in the Air Ministry, only sought out in times like these. Baz was convinced that Morgan wasn't even aware of his language most of the time. He fitted his fucks in like the corn in the inexhaustible tins of corned beef they devoured, you'd never know it was there in the first place.

It was having to listen to Morgan's mind numbing persuasion to swap his dog eared, reclining, naked, parasol holding, stained picture of Madam Roxanne with young Ken Harker's photograph of his fresh faced, swimsuit wearing fiancée Emma that wore everyone down in the back of the truck. Needless to say Morgan won in the end, only under the condition Emma would be returned by the end of the month.

"What about the damn holes it leaves behind Morgan. Haven't you heard holes and boats are not the best of pals," replied Gareth 'Garage' Bryce in a Welsh tenor accent sounding as though he sang every word. Garage had lost his sense of humour somewhere between his home town of Swansea and the many airfields he had been stationed at. Baz learnt that he had four loves in life, rugby, Wales, automobiles, and consuming vast quantities of beer. His one true love, which the war had probably put paid to, was his unwavering devotion to rugby. Gareth Bryce was becoming a name bandied about the streets of Swansea. Above everything else, this was something Garage would never be able to forgive Adolf Hitler for.

On board the ship they were led through the maze of narrow passageways by a boy, or was it a man, or was it a girl dressed as a man. Anyway, he was of Far Eastern appearance with flawless olive skin and wore an oversized dark blue boiler suit. He introduced himself as third mate James Cheng, who they thought spoke with an American accent, whom they later found out was a Canadian of Burmese descent. Baz and his colleagues were finding it difficult to keep up with the agile third mate as he sped through the never-ending aisles like a stoat scampering through its burrows. It was at this time Baz had the strangest feeling the ship was larger on the inside than it was on the outside. Finally James Cheng came to a halt and pointed out four small white doors ringed with large rivets. These led into their quarters, four dark cramped cabins with only enough space for three sets of narrow bunk beds and nothing else. And that's what my coffin looks like, thought Baz.

It was early next morning when the SS City of Derby and seven other ships including the huge troop carrying liner and two Royal

Navy destroyers slipped quietly out of Liverpool Docks into a freezing Irish sea mist.

The ship's crew became increasingly anxious as the convoy made its way to the open sea. Nothing needs to be said for the reason why. U-Boats! Just saying the words put a cold shudder through the men.

A few days passed before they rounded the Portuguese western point of St Vincent. Soon after and through the distant heat haze the Moroccan city of Tangiers came into view. Baz thought the place had a sleepy air about it, especially with the early dusk casting a balmy yellow light and long shadows over the compact sand coloured buildings, giving Baz the impression it had risen straight out of the ground.

Baz woke one morning with the usual rhythmical noise of the engines droning in his ears. Only this morning he heard another sound, muffled voices. The first voice spoke nervously, with Baz just managing to catch the tail end of a sentence. "...mean they've gone?" It was Sergeant Nash.

It was only when the second person spoke that Baz recognised it as belonging to the ship's captain. "I don't know why Sergeant. They can't say anything over the radio. It's too risky, I'm afraid there's nothing I can do about it. My First will work out watch details for your men." The next comment sent a shiver through Baz's bones. "U-boats don't usually come this far Sergeant."

"And what if we see one of these U-boats?" said Sergeant Nash.

"Pray Sergeant...Pray."

It was later, when Baz looked over the starboard railing, the whole horrific reality came to light. More to the truth it wasn't what was there, but what wasn't there that horrified him. Their escort and protectors, the two destroyers, their only means of defence, had vanished with the night. Baz ran to the other side and looked over the port side, it was then he realised the SS City of Derby and the giant troop carrier were the only ships remaining, alone at the mercy of any passing German submarine or aircraft, he could only imagine what the atmosphere must have been like on the liner. It was only a matter of time, he thought.

Baz discovered the destroyers had escorted the other cargo ships into Malta. "People were starving to death. Aircraft needed fuel." He was told.

The two ships spent the rest of the journey with the shoreline out of sight. "If we can't see them, then hopefully they can't see us." James Cheng told them.

Against all odds both ships arrived at the Egyptian port city of Alexandria. Baz learnt from the third mate that their convoy was the first to make it through without being attacked, Baz was only glad he hadn't mentioned it earlier.

Sergeant Nash had given strict orders that no man should venture onto shore after dark, then informed Baz, "Now is a good time for some shut-eye." Baz gladly agreed. "You'd better take this Corp."

"What! I thought."

"It's loaded, any sign of trouble, shoot it up into the sky, they'll run a mile if they know you mean business. Whatever you do, don't let them on the ship."

"Who?"

"The natives, Corporal."

"But I've never..."

"And try not to blow your own brains out...or your balls."

Baz nervously prowled the deck, the gun tucked into his belt, the cold metal against his bare flesh forever reminding him of its presence.

It wasn't too long before the only means of light was a sparse glimmer the half-moon thought necessary to provide. He heard the clunk of a door as the dark profile of a crew member disappeared into a hold and the sound of other others gambling away their meagre earnings. Baz looked down at the shadows mingling on the quay. He checked the top of the walkway, it was clear. Then, as he was about to return to the railings he noticed it nudge down slightly, weight had been put on it, human weight, what else?

"Who goes there?" No answer. "I said who goes there?" A panic had encroached into his words. Still no answer. His fingers curled around the butt of the pistol. A bead of sweat trickled down his cheek.

"Stop or I'll shoot." Baz saw a person rising up the walkway, a scarf wrapped around his head and wearing an RAF shirt. He remembered the flight's words, "steal the shirt off your back," then imagined an aircraftman lying dead in some narrow lane with a dagger stuck in him.

"Stop or I'll shoot!" he shouted holding the pistol aloft. "Stop I say."

"Fucking hell Corp, who do you think you are, some fucking highwayman?" shouted Morgan, appearing out of the shadows at the top of the walkway.

"You Morgan, I could have..."

"Two fucking cigs, that's all, one head scarf, two cigs, fucking bargain Corp."

"Didn't you hear what the Sergeant said Morgan?"

"It *was* bloody light when I stepped ashore Corp." Patting his pocket for the cigarette packet, which had gone! Also the comb, his lighter, young Harker's picture of Emma and the child he had just bartered the headscarf from.

SS City of Derby departed Alexandria Port at first light. It seemed as though no time at all had passed until they slipped past Port Said and into the Suez Canal.

Sergeant Nash introduced a daily program of rigorous exercise, the men's appetites and sleep patterns improved. Unusual ways of passing the time had been thought up, including a joke contest, which Morgan won with the one about the thousand ducks and the twelve inch pianist. Everyone had heard it before but decided it was the best joke anyway and brilliantly told.

Eight uneventful days later and over a month after leaving Liverpool Docks the SS City of Derby anchored in the Shatt al-Arab Waterway, only a short distance away from the port of Al Basrah and fifteen miles from RAF Shaibah.

RAF SHAIBAH

The Shaibah Blues

'Oh a little bit of Heaven fell from the sky one day,
and it settled by the ocean in a spot not far away
And when the Air Force saw it sure it looked so bleak and bare,
they said "That's what we're looking for, we'll put a Squadron there".

So they sent out river gunboats, armoured cars and S.H.Q
and they sent the famous RAF in to the fucking' blue.
But peechi I'll be going to a land that's far remote,

and till that day you'll hear me say "Roll on that fucking' boat!"

> I've got those Shai-bah Blues, Shai-bah Blues
> I'm fed-up, and I'm cheesed off, and I'm blue,
> I tried to learn the lingo but it fairly got my goat.
> The only words that I know are "Roll on that fucking' boat!"
> I've got those Shai-bah Blues, Shai-bah Blues.
> I'm fed up, and I'm cheesed off, and I'm blue.

> So we sent out Vickers Vincents, Blenheim Fives, and Spitfires too,
> and we called up all the Oxfords, Harts and old Valentias too.
> But though we flew to oceans and the desert so remote,
> the only thing it taught us was "Roll on that fucking' boat!"

> I've got those Shai-bah Blues, Shai-bah Blues.
> I'm fed up, and I'm cheesed off, and I'm blue.'

As Baz soon found out, having a song written about his new posting was not done out of endearment. There wasn't one person in Shaibah, who hadn't at one time and seriously meant saying, "Roll on that fucking boat." Only that fucking boat never came, not for Baz anyhow, not for a very long time.

It was an airfield so desolate in its position and so extreme in its environment, Baz was finding it hard to see how any of them were going to survive. As he found out later, some only just managed it and some, well, they never made it at all.

Curiously, RAF Shaibah, despite being solitary was a busy airfield. The higher echelon at the Mediterranean Air Command made the decision to make it the main airbase in all of Southern Iraq, they also made the decision to keep well away from it themselves. Given the choice, anyone in their right mind would. Most were probably unaware of its harshness, the ones that knew, well, they ignored it. After all, there is a war going on.

The commanding officer was Group Captain Rupert Melling, a retired bomber pilot who was never seen without his full uniform, including full length trousers, (everyone else wore shorts) a cap, walking stick and black leather gloves. A sole survivor from a Wellington bomber that had an unfortunate crash landing. "The Bods back home decided that if I could survive those burns then the heat out here would be a doddle," he would say to anyone of rank that lingered too long on the tight discoloured skin marbling the left side of his face. Anyone below the rank of sergeant would be told under no uncertain terms. "The right eye and the right ear work just fine. Never forget that!"

The CO had rules, lots of rules. Abide by the rules, then you would be left much to your own devices. Ignore the rules, then the CO was a master in frightening the crap out of people by showing them the consequences if anyone were to disregard them. Group Captain Rupert Melling had photographs, that is all that need be said.

RAF Shaibah was an island, or it might as well have been. An old 1930's airdrome surrounded by a mud brick, six foot high wall, with squat like turrets every hundred feet or so.

In all directions, as far as the eye could see was an endless and impassable ocean of flat scorched sand, except for the one road that led from Al Basrah. When I say road, it was more like a tyre flattened track with more humps than the camel trains that frequented Shaibah. It was well known that once on the road, either on foot or in a vehicle, distinguishing the difference between the actual track and the desert was nigh on impossible. An abandoned truck, half buried and some distance from the road was not an uncommon sight.

Under large handwritten titles on sheets of paper nailed to the orderly's wall were the CO's rules. On first reading, these rules appeared to have been written for the humour. As the men learnt, they were no joke.

RULES OF THE ROAD

1. Do not walk along the road. If you want to escape from the airfield, it would be quicker to shoot yourself.
2. If you wake up and find yourself alone on the road, pray that it is still a dream.
3. Do not leave your tent if your sole purpose is to pass through the gates alone. Your tent will have one less man, permanently
4. If you pass through the gates alone, pray you have reached total madness. That way you will be unaware of the horrific death you will be subjected to.

5. You may only use the road with the permission of the CO. Pray to God the CO happens to like you that day.
6. You must follow these rules to the letter. If not, please leave anything of use for the next person.

Under each list of rules were the words. 'Roll on that fucking boat.' For the year prior to Baz's arrival, the airfield was primarily used to reassemble bombers for the Russian airforce. Baz's consignment of Spitfires were the first fighter planes to follow that same destiny.

By the end of February, thirty-five Spitfires were assembled and handed over to Russian pilots. These were then flown on to Abadan in Iran, the place where the British blue, white and red roundal was replaced with the red star of the Russian airforce.

As summer approached, June had given Baz an indication of what was in store. A blazing sun pummelled down on any living creature by day, and at night, a thick sweltering air made sleep virtually impossible, the only relief a warm breeze drifting under the tent's rolled up canvas sides. It wasn't uncommon for the men to rise with a dusting of sand covering everything and everyone, usually discovered on their wakening breath.

More rules from the CO.

SALT TABLETS

1. Salt tablets WILL be taken by every man, THREE times a day. The taking of these tablets must be witnessed by your Corporal or Sergeant. These tablets will SAVE YOUR LIFE. 'Roll on that fucking boat.'

The extreme heat was not the only addition in the oncoming months. Another forty-six Spitfires had arrived.

A week later, twelve Russian mechanics had presented themselves to Sergeant Nash. "Show them every nut and bolt, every cable," he told his men. "If the Russians can assemble their own aircraft, then guess who won't be?" adding with a chirp and a clap of his hands, "roll on that fucking boat boys."

On first impression, Baz thought the Russians were much like his own 133 Maintenance Unit. They had a Sergeant and a Corporal and a bunch of aircraftmen. Though the Sergeant was nothing like

Sergeant Nash and the Russian Corporal was nothing like Baz. In stature, the Russian Corporal was a broad shouldered, large framed, hard looking individual with a strong jaw and a quick temper. He had been introduced as Corporal Zamolodchikov. As time passed, Baz never seemed to get any better at pronouncing his name without it sounding like some kind of throat disease. Until one day the Russian Corporal was seen losing it with one of his mechanics and his name was secretly shortened to Corporal Kick-off, although Morgan's translation was slightly more colourful.

Baz felt relieved he was nothing like the Russian Corporal.

Sergeant Tretyakov was in his mid thirties, short, around five foot six, an inch or so shorter than Baz, but much stockier. Baz had the notion that when apes evolved into man, Sergeant Tretyakov had remained somewhere in-between, apart from his face and the palms of his hands, all other flesh had been virtually obliterated by soft, downy, jet black hair. Baz also noticed his jowls had dropped well before their time. Sergeant Tretyakov told him it was a Russian trait. "Lots Vodka we drink. Camels keep water in humps. Russians keep Vodka in cheeks. English keep beer in bellies. Is that how say it Corporal Albright? Bellies," he said, with a hearty, jowl wobbling laugh.

Baz liked Sergeant Tretyakov.

And the rest of the Russian unit? Well, most could muster up some words in broken English, after all, that was one of the reasons they were chosen.

Baz could recognise each of his men in everyone of the Russians. The young Mechanic Rostov was like the lovestruck Harker, both had faces yet untouched by the harshness surrounding them. Baz now believed his young mechanic had changed his devotion from his fresh faced Emma to the sultry Madam Roxanne. Morgan had so far managed to avoid telling young Harker that his Emma was being passed around the male inhabitants of Alexandria.

There was Paul 'Aerial' Morrow, most noticeable by his thick horn-rimmed glasses and mischievous face. Extremely tall and well educated, he was a radio expert who spent most of the time fiddling with some kind of non-descript electrical apparatus. Baz never knew whether he got his nickname from trying to get a radio to transmit through some distant antenna or because of his great height: he settled for a bit of both. Baz also felt he had a flamboyant confidence about him, as if everything had to be overstated. His Russian equivalent was Viktor Gorlovich, who early in their association discovered Aerial's secret. The secret? Unfortunately for an electrics man Aerial was colourblind and could only distinguish the green and red wires by seeing them as differing shades of grey. Not good for someone who spent most of the time poking his nose into a tangled mass of coloured wires. Whenever the English radio man found it nigh on impossible to tell the difference, he had two choices, ask someone, which always happened to be Baz, or risk a silent radio transmitter, not ideal at twenty thousand feet. Aerial made an unfortunate mistake when he actually *did* have a grey wire in his hand. "Now listen carefully Viktor, as this is unique to the Spitfire. This red wire..."

"Grey wire," Viktor said, slightly confused.

"Oh, OK, this red wire then," Aerial said, picking up another.

"Green," Viktor said. "This is green wire."

"This red wire?" Aerial said, sheepishly looking at Viktor for confirmation. After a lengthy stare, Viktor grinned and nodded. The Russian never mentioned it to anyone, although from that day whenever Aerial picked up a wire with Viktor close by, he would always look at the Russian for that verifying nod.

There was another reason Viktor Gorlovich never spoke about Aerial's affliction. Aerial knew something about Viktor Gorlovich.

ALCOHOL

1. Spirits are NOT allowed on the base and the CO does not mean the ones that go bump in the night. Nothing will dehydrate a body quicker than alcohol and when your body dehydrates in Shaibah, YOU WILL DIE! You will stop sweating, this means your body has no natural cooling system. Look at it like an automobile with no water in its radiator, steam will come out of every orifice. You will feel nauseous and start vomiting, this will remove even more liquid. You will then begin to get agitated and confused, you will start to lose control of your thoughts. This will put you in the same mindless state when you had started drinking alcohol in the first place. You may now have reached the point of no return.

At this stage your body will be too weak to take on any liquid. Your kidneys will start to fail and your heartbeat will increase until your heart gets so knackered it will finally give up altogether. THEN YOU WILL BE DEAD!

If you feel the need to smuggle any spirits into the base the CO will be happy to show you the graves of every airman that managed it.

2. Every man will be rationed to ONE bottle of beer a day.

'Roll on that fucking boat.'

In many ways the RAF aircraftmen learnt as much from the Russians as the Russians did from them. Although their enthusiasm for cleanliness seemed to outweigh the importance of the engineering work itself. Order and precision was not so much a necessity for the Russians, it appeared to be an obsession. The reason for this became all too clear to Baz one day.

Twelve Russian pilots had arrived at the airfield from Abadan, nothing unusual about that, someone had to fly the Spitfires out of Shaibah. Only they had brought with them two important looking, big shot officers in long black leather coats and caps the size of dinner plates.

The Russian mechanics had lined up in two perfect rows of six, the tallest at the back and towards the centre with the exact same distance between them. It reminded Baz of chessmen waiting for battle. Corporal Kick-off and Sergeant Tretyakov stood in front, rodlike, as though rigor mortis had set in. Both retaining steadfast stares and a permanent salute glued to their foreheads. With a wobble of his jowls, one officer shouted. Sergeant Tretyakov broke from his stance and led the officers to the nearest spitfire, followed by a low gesture of his hand as if he was introducing it to the two men. The Russian Sergeant then took one step back and waited with the posture of a man who was about to be sent to the gallows. What the Russian officer did next astounded every RAF man that witnessed it. In one slow stroke he rubbed the tip of his forefinger along the leading edge of the Spitfire's wing, ending with it pointing skyward in front of his face. He then turned towards the other officer, who stared wide-eyed at the sandy digit and imitated the same expression of disgust.

The RAF men gazed in wonderment.

"Who was meant to do the dusting this morning?" said Aerial.

"I was on washing up detail," answered Garage.

"I must have missed the aircraft when I swept up the entire fucking desert," added Morgan.

The men stared on in silence.

"Where there's muck there's brass." Harker promptly threw in, immediately followed by a chorus of laughter.

One Russian officer shouted some words towards Sergeant Tretyakov, who marched on to the next Spitfire. The same finger wiping action followed, then a few more barked words to Sergeant Tretyakov who then shouted to Corporal Kick-off, who in turn, shouted at the two lines of Russian aircraftmen.

Three men split away from the front row and ran to where the officers were standing. Corporal Kick-off shouted and the Russian aircraftmen released the engine cowling. The officer looked into the engine. "Niet," was the only word Baz recognised in the verbal flurry that followed.

This went on for all the eighteen fighter planes sitting in their three rows at the front of the hangar.

The two officers, Sergeant Tretyakov, Corporal Kick-off and the three ruffled looking aircraftmen strolled to the entrance of the hangar, the afternoon heat starting to sap the spring from the Russian's steps.

Like a gash appearing across his face the Russian officer smiled at Sergeant Tretyakov, who then turned his attention towards Baz.

"They want this one Bazil," the Sergeant said with a nod towards the Spitfire.

Baz was surprised to hear Sergeant Tretyakov use his Christian name for the first time, more surprising was the way he said it, as if he was pronouncing the country Brazil.

"It's not ready," Baz paused, then added. "Mick...hail?"

Sergeant Tretyakov said something in Russian to the officer and got a reply before he had finished. "They want ready, Bazil."

"Why? there are eighteen perfectly good ones behind you," Baz paused again. "Mikhail."

"They do not like, Bazil."

"Why they do not like? Mikhail."

"They want ready, Bazil," Sergeant Tretyakov said through gritted teeth. You not know bad things for me if not ready."

"Why?"

"Because they can. Because Spitfire belong to them."

"Not over my dead body, Mick...hail."

"No, my dead body, Baz...il."

Baz raised his eyebrows and faked a grin.

"Sergeant Nash," Sergeant Tretyakov said.

"Sergeant Tretyakov," Sergeant Nash said, louder than Sergeant Tretyakov had said 'Sergeant Nash.'

The Russian officer shouted something back at Sergeant Tretyakov, who replied with the word 'Nash' somewhere in the verbal affray. The Russian shouted at Sergeant Nash with the word 'Nash' ending his furious tirade. Sergeant Nash, not understanding a word, apart from 'Nash,' stepped forward. Corporal Kick-off stepped forward, Garage stepped forward, the second officer stepped forward, Morgan stepped forward.

Baz in a flash of light stood bolt upright and saluted. After a few seconds every man present did exactly the same, except the two Russian officers.

Group Captain Rupert Melling, along with his long trousers, cap, leather gloves and walking stick ambled into the midst of the fracas.

"Who is that man Sergeant?" the CO said.

"Sorry Sir," said Sergeant Nash.

"Who is that man there Sergeant?" Group Captain Rupert Melling repeated, pointing his stick.

Sergeant Nash looked around. "Oh that man. Leading aircraftman Morgan Sir."

"Is he one of ours Sergeant?"

"Yes sir."

"Why is he wearing a towel around his head Sergeant?"

Sergeant Nash looked at Morgan and raised his eyebrows. Both stood silent, both at a loss for words and a loss of words is not a situation Morgan was used to.

An uncomfortable silence hung in the air.

The CO continued, "Well?"

"Its my lucky fucking Arab hat Sir," were the only words Morgan could think to say.

"Your lucky fucking Arab hat," said the Group Captain.

"Yes sir, on the assumption I hadn't got shot boarding a fucking ship in Alexandria sir."

"Someone did not shoot you boarding a fucking ship in Alexandria. *Who* did not shoot you boarding a fucking ship in Alexandria?"

Morgan thought for a moment. "Corporal Albright sir."

"Thanks Morgan."

Corporal Albright didn't shoot you. Did you want to shoot this man, Corporal?"

"No Sir."

"I can see the temptation though Corporal."

"Yes sir, me too, but I didn't want to shoot anyone."

"But you have a gun Corporal?"

"No sir."

"Then whose gun was it Corporal?"

Baz stood silent.

"It was my gun sir," Sergeant Nash said.

"Your gun Sergeant?"

"Yes Sir."

"You gave your gun to Corporal Albright to shoot this man?"

"Fucking Aircraftman Morgan Sir," Morgan said.

"You gave your gun to Corporal Albright to shoot *fucking* Aircraftman Morgan."

"No Sir, to shoot an Arab."

"And did you shoot this Arab, Corporal."

"No Sir it was Morgan in his towel...hat...scarf!"

Group Captain Rupert Melling lowered his head and looked to the ground.

"Can someone tell me what is going on here?" turning his attention to the two Russian officers.

"They want this aircraft Sir," Sergeant Nash said.

"Then *why* can't they have it Sergeant?"

"It's not ready Sir."

"How long before we can get it airborne Sergeant?"

Sergeant Nash raised his eyebrows and looked at Baz.

"About two hours Sir," Baz said.

"And another two to polish it," Garage threw in.

"Polish it! It's a bloody aircraft, not Winston Churchill's cabinet table. Two hours, good. Someone translate that for these gentlemen."

Sergeant Tretyakov told the Russian officers exactly what the CO had said, every single word, maybe a bit more, probably the bit about the polishing as well, who knows. All Group Captain Melling required was the few words about the two hours. The red faced Russian officer shot such a lengthy, spit firing, arm waving, temple pulsing, jowl trembling torrent of words at Sergeant Tretyakov that he only managed to stop when the heat had finally exhausted him.

"They will have twelve from behind," Sergeant Tretyakov said.

The two Russian officers turned and marched away, just in time to see a man collapse from the back row of the Russian aircraftmen.

The CO muttered something about not being a grocery shop and left the scene.

"I thought that went bloody well," Morgan announced.

"Take that thing off your head Morgan," Sergeant Nash snapped.

Corporal Kick-off and five other aircraftmen, including Viktor Gorlovich, departed Shaibah two weeks after.

Sergeant Tretyakov had been handed his punishment, which basically meant staying at Shaibah. "Better than the Gulags," he told Baz.

As summer passed, the extreme heat had been replaced by a more temperate climate and that is how it remained through the winter months, until the start of the following year's summer. Baz had lost count of how many fighter aircraft had been assembled and dispatched. He realised the Russians must be losing them at quite a rate.

Back home was becoming a faint and distant memory, he had stopped thinking about the life left behind. Neither Ruby or Violet had written for months, or if they had, their letters hadn't arrived, probably lying somewhere at the bottom of the Mediterranean. Anyway, Ruby only wrote when there was some kind of disaster to report. You'd think in time of war that would be often enough, but Ruby's disasters were different, they had to be a Ruby disaster, so in some ways, Baz thought, it was a good thing.

Not a day went by without Baz thinking of Mrs Waterhouse.

Half of Baz's 133 Maintenance Unit had been replaced in dribs and drabs with new recruits. Aerial, Morgan, Harker and Garage all remained. Sergeant Nash had been sent to Habbaniya, a large airfield near Baghdad.

The most important change in Baz's life happened immediately after Sergeant Nash departed. He became Sergeant Albright. The CO called him into his office. "Seeing as you run 133 Maintenance Unit then you might as well *run* 133 Maintenance Unit," he had said in a matter-of-fact manner.

Corporal Lynch arrived on the same boat as a batch of Hurricanes. A pockmarked overweight man with a bulbous red nose and cheeks covered in tiny broken blood vessels, a sure sign of a man partial to a drink. Baz wondered what past transgression he must have been involved in, maybe he was a drunk, Shaibah was sure to dry anyone out. Baz decided to delegate the paperwork and shift detail arrangements over to the new Corporal, keeping him at a makeshift desk in the shade of the hangar worked out well for both men. That way he might survive Shaibah. Baz was a good Sergeant after all, or maybe he was just a good person.

The natives had been up to their usual mischief, to them it was justified, the servicemen in Shaibah were uninvited strangers. Anything that could be stolen, was stolen, which at one time included a large RAF truck. Blatantly driving it within sight of the airfield the very next day, its open back packed full of ugly black bearded men wearing baggy trousers and long shirts flapping wildly in the wind. They punched their rifles in the air and shouted abuse at the airmen with the few words of English they knew. Mostly taunts about their sisters or mothers and a certain camel's organ.

More rules from the CO.

NATIVES

1. If an Arab is found in the confinements of the airfield without an Air Force uniform, inform an Officer.

2. If an Arab is found in the confinements of the airfield wearing an Air Force uniform, inform an Officer.

3. Do not speak to a native, he will talk the shirt off your back and steal the sugar from your tea: then sell them both back to you.

4. Do not buy liquor from a native, unless you want to use it as aircraft fuel. (Read the rules about alcohol)

5. Do not under any circumstances shoot a native, no matter how tempting it may be. Unless you want another war on

your hands.
'Roll on that fucking boat.'

In the few years Baz had been an aircraftman, he thought he had seen nearly every shape, size and condition of aircraft. Only the state of the Russian Lisonuv that had just arrived, managed to eclipse all of them. The entire bodywork resembled a patchwork quilt of varying shades of browns and greens, with large red crosses painted on white squares each side of the fuselage and tail. The plane banked at such a steep angle as the men watched it approach, everyone thought it was going to nosedive right into the ground, only the aircraft straightened out at the last moment, landing dead centre of the airstrip, managing to create its own sandstorm as it taxied towards the Russian area. The Lisonuv finally hobbled to an ungainly standstill. One of the engines shot out a bright red flame which disappeared in a cloud of dark grey smoke, its propellor spluttering and coughing to a halt. The other engine hissed with a loud sigh as though it was glad its ordeal was finally over, then died.

It was late April and the replacement for Corporal Kick-off jumped from the Lisonuvs rear door. Following close behind him were two dubious looking young Russian mechanics. Much smiling, cheek kissing, back slapping and jowl wobbling were traded between the new corporal and Sergeant Tretyakov. Watching from a distance and seeing the warmth shown in their exchange of affection, Baz decided this was obviously not their first encounter. Sergeant Tretyakov then gave the two mechanics a strong hug, ending with a prolonged grip of the shoulders. The two young mechanics were dressed in ill-fitting and dishevelled uniforms, both unshaven with dark sunken eyes and hollow cheeks. Baz felt the tall one had an air of confidence about him. The shorter, younger, fair haired one had lily-white skin and looked far too frail for Shaibah.

The four Russians departed for the tents with a lot more jowl wobbling, shoulder hugging and back slapping.

"Did you notice something about that aircraft Sarge?" Aerial said as the Russians disappeared out of view.

"Yeah, how the hell did it get more than two fucking feet off the ground?" Morgan replied.

"The red crosses?" Baz said.

147

"No, something else."

A moments thought. "I give in."

"We have been standing here all this time *and* with the aircraft in sight. Right?"

"And?" Baz said, stretching the word.

"Have you seen anyone else jump out of it?"

Baz looked at Aerial, then the aircraft, then Aerial again. Aerial lifted his eyebrows in anticipation.

"No pilots! Shit! No pilots. Who flew it then?" Baz spurted out.

"Well it didn't fly itself," Aerial added.

"Then the Corporal, is that what you're saying? The Corporal brought it in."

"Corporals do not fly aircraft. If corporals flew aircraft then they would be flying officers. That's why corporals are corporals and flying officers are pilots," Aerial said with an annoying air of superiority.

Two weeks had passed and Baz only saw the three Russians leave their tent to visit the latrine or stretch their legs. They always kept well within their own sector, trying to remain as inconspicuous as possible, Baz knew all about inconspicuous, he was a past master at it.

"We need an excuse for you to go over there Sarge," Aerial suggested.

"Why me? Anyway, what *they* do has got nothing to do with us."

"Because you're the bloody Sarge, Sarge." Morgan said.

"Go and ask them for a cup of sugar, that's what my mother used to do when there was any gossip in our street," Harker added.

"We're in Iraq, not some fucking back street in Bradford."

"Sheffield, actually."

"Garage!" Aerial exclaimed, as though a light bulb had just lit above his head.

"We can't send Garage, not the way he is at the moment."

Garage had started to lose weight, everyone in the airfield lost weight, it was inevitable with the rationing they had to endure, especially if a supply ship was late or worse, sunk. Fruit was easy to come by, the many camel trains that passed by always had an abundance of fresh dates and watermelons. Most were willing to part with them at a certain price and arriving at that price could test the fettle of any man. The CO had decided long ago that all the bartering should be done by the few trusted locals working in the airfield.

Anyway, Garage's weight had plummeted at a worrying rate. He had been diagnosed with dysentery, which left him seriously dehydrated and bed bound with severe stomach pains.

"No Sarge, you go over and ask if they have any medicine."

"Medicine or sugar," said Baz, thinking out loud. "They know we have doctors, they even use our doctors! We probably have more medicine than they do."

"Sugar it is then," said Aerial.

It is rare for a person from one country to encroach into another's domain, it was kind of an unwritten rule. Baz believed it was borders like these that started the war in the first place.

The American contingent was very inviting with their large air conditioned huts, beer seemingly on tap and endless movies at the weekends, rumour had it they even had their own ice-cream making machine! Baz concluded the Americans had no reason to leave their territory or encourage others to enter.

Sergeant Tretyakov suddenly appeared as Baz approached and threw out his normal warm welcome. "Bazil, old friend. You now Soviet citizen?"

"No Mikhail, as tempting as that may seem, I'm actually on an errand for some of the lads."

"You here something else?"

"Yes, sugar?"

"Sugar? Bazil," Sergeant Tretyakov said with a smirk.

"Yes, sugar. Mikhail," holding out his metal mug like Oliver Twist.

"Sugar for tea? No tea, English die, yes?"

"Yes, Mikhail."

"No sugar Bazil, sugar not for Vodka."

Baz coughed up a pretend laugh. "Medicine then?"

"Medicine for tea?" said Sergeant Tretyakov, frowning.

"No," said Baz. "Garage has bad belly."

"No medicine Bazil. English have doctor, yes?"

"Yes, thank you." Baz paused for a moment. "How is Corporal Mihailov?" A poor attempt, he thought.

"Good, Bazil."

"And the two mechanics. What were their names?"

"Daniil, Igor."

Yes, they are well. I trust?" Baz said, adding more fake words to his already fake grin.

Sergeant Tretyakov lit a cigarette. "Let us walk my friend."

After twenty or so strides Mikhail stopped and glared at Baz. "The war Bazil, *me*." He gestured with his hand. "*You*, not good." Then he sat down with his back against the wall. Beads of sweat glistened on the soft black hairs. A dark fleecy tuft poked out from the folds of his bulbous double chin, as if he was just coming to the end of devouring a small furry animal.

"You ask me Bazil? Igor? Daniil?"

"Just wondering if they are settling in Mikhail. You know, not getting bored waiting for the next delivery of aircraft."

"You same as English poet Bazil?"

"A poet." Baz frowned." No, why?"

"One line in poem Bazil. Many more words not see, yes?"

Baz thought for a moment. "That's the English Mikhail, never saying what we actually mean."

"I like English Bazil. A cousin told much England. I read English. Dickens I like. I not understand William Shakespeare. He not good English Bazil. Lewis Carroll, I think he like too much vodka. My cousin told, how you say, English humour." The Russian's shoulders shook as he chuckled "If English humour not funny, people still laugh." The Russian slowly shook his head, "I not understand." For a short moment Mikhail stared at Baz, "You ask about Stepan Bazil?"

"Corporal Mihailov flew that Lisunov into Shaibah himself, didn't he Mikhail?" Baz could sense the Russian Sergeant's eyes boring into him.

"Yes Bazil." Without hesitation.

"Quite a feat, seeing he is only a corporal, I suspect there aren't many corporals or even pilots that could get that rust-bucket to fly."

"Rust-bucket?" Sergeant Tretyakov spat out a laugh. "Corporal Mihailov best pilot. He fly anything with wings, bucket no wings Bazil. Corporal Mihailov not corporal, Bazil. Corporal Mihailov is Flying Officer Mihailov," Sergeant Tretyakov said with a proud look of defiance. "Rust-bucket," he laughed again. "English humour, I not understand."

Baz turned to face the Russian Sergeant.

"And the two mechanics?"

"I trust you Bazil, you nice man, you understand life. I tell truth. You know already. I tell you all. Maybe I ask from you Bazil. Stepan and Igor, Daniil. Shaibah not good Bazil, we need get out of Shaibah, out of country. They not stay Bazil."

"We! No one likes it here Mikhail. Can't they go back to Russia?"

The expression on Sergeant Tretyakov's face dropped. "No Bazil!" he said, stubbing a cigarette into the ground. "They die in Russia. That why they here, dangerous here, many officers, many questions. You see officers once, yes!"

"A person can be brave when faced with death but can be just as courageous facing life," Baz muttered, remembering one of his fathers glorious quotes.

"What you say?"

"Nothing Mikhail, I don't think I can help Mikhail, I'm sorry."

Sergeant Tretyakov lit another cigarette.

"You have wife Bazil?"

"No. What has that got...?"

"You have woman Bazil?"

"No."

"You like men?"

"No!"

Sergeant Tretyakov paused for a moment. "I have wife, five children." A sly grin appeared, "how you say? Mistress." His chin held high.

It was a mystery to Baz how he even had a wife, but also a mistress. Women in Russia must be desperate, or short hairy ape-like men with a bad odour are well sought after. Baz remembered when his brother Oliver used to come home on leave from the Navy and boast about his many feminine conquests. Too many to be believed if the truth be known. Baz had never mentioned to a single soul about his one time with Mrs Waterhouse. He doubted if she had either. No one ever spoke about sex in Shaibah, for obvious reasons. A visit to the seedy area of Al Basrah would be the closest any of the men would get, an area both notorious and legendary in its reputation. Baz had never met anyone that had actually been there, rumours and tales were rife though, all eagerly told and all just as eagerly listened to.

"You like women Bazil?"

"Yes, if they are nice."

Sergeant Tretyakov laughed out loud. "Nice! If nice to you, Bazil. If nice to you," he said with wide eyes and just as wide a grin. "Here Bazil," Sergeant Tretyakov said, holding a small battered flask under Baz's nose.

"What is that?"

"Vodka, good vodka. Here Bazil, you like."

"Vodka" Baz whispered. He thought just the mention of the word would get him into trouble "The CO has a rule..." He stopped mid sentence. "Never mind." Baz took a quick swig, surprising himself by actually liking it. Maybe Shaibah does that to you, accepting most things when you least expect to.

"You have woman Bazil?"

Baz rested his arms on his knees. "There was one Mikhail. I thought it was love." He told Sergeant Tretyakov the entire story of Mrs Waterhouse and William, especially the day he returned Will's kit bag. Omitting most of the intimate details, he could feel the vodka liberating his words more than he liked. "I don't think I have ever been the same after that day."

"Then you, how you say? Understand my friend."

"Understand what? What has this got to do with Corporal, Flying Officer Mihailov?"

"Stepan has wife, love much, has son, young girl, Valentina. Very pretty Bazil. How do you say? All boys want her."

"That's how we say it Mikhail."

"Igor is a doctor."

"A doctor!"

"Igor go to front with Daniil. If go, death for both. They live in same village. They friends from child. Igor has wife and baby. Daniil, Igor escape together. They get caught, if lucky, get executed. If not, Siberia, long slow death." Sergeant Tretyakov paused for a moment. "Danill, Stepan's son Bazil." The Russian sergeant waited for a response. None came. "Stepan heard Daniil, Igor talk about escape. Stepan argue long time with them, long time Bazil. He lost argue." Sergeant Tretyakov sighed one exhausted sounding word. "So." He paused again and lit another cigarette, inhaling long and deep on the first drag. "Stepan pilot. Lisunov was at airfield. Airfield, how do you say des...des..."

"Desert airfield. Like Shaibah." Both paused for a moment. "Oh deserted airfield, not in use."

"Yes, deserted. Stepan clever man. Great, how you say, thinker, he master at chess."

"Really!"

"He fix aircraft. Many risks. Many, many risks," Mikhail paused. "You know chess Bazil?"

"Yes Mikhail. I know chess."

"You great chess player Bazil?"

Baz recalled how Will told him never admit to being a great or even a good chess player. He thought he was neither anyway. "I play chess Mikhail."

"Then they move families. Stepan family, also relatives, long way away. Igor wife and baby same. We get Stepan and boys safe place, safe country. Families meet them. After war Bazil, then all alive, all together." Sergeant Tretyakov looked at Baz. "After war Bazil, when that be?"

"Soon Mikhail. What I'm hearing it will be soon."

"Good. Stepan paint red cross on side of fuselage. Stepan and boys took off in Lisunov, great risk when aircraft in air. Look like, how you say? Hospital. Daniil told me German fighter fly close, they see pilot's face. Stepan smile and wave at pilot. German pilot salute, then fly away."

"They refuel in Mahhad. Most risk when in Mahhad. Many Soviet officers. Stepan wore Flying Officer uniform." Sergeant Tretyakov's eyes lit up and raised his hands, "*His* uniform, he *is* flying officer! He said men salute him, he thought funny, if they know truth. Was scared might know officer in Mahhad. Igor in doctor's clothes, doctor's tools and spoke doctor language." Sergeant Tretyakov shrugged, "He is doctor! Daniil was hurt man, how you say...Paish...?"

"Patient."

"Yes Bazil, patient. Daniil not patient. He act like Charlie Chaplin, only he just lay under sheets, lots of bullet holes." Sergeant Tretyakov grinned, "They better now."

"You don't say."

"I use English sarcasm Bazil."

"You did Mikhail. We'll make an Englishman of you yet."

"They had papers, real papers, not real name, that change. Have papers, Russian officer believe everything. Stepan treat Lisunov like woman. Lisunov take off again, now Shaibah."

"Now you know all Bazil. You not agree what they done, how you say?"

"Deserters," Baz paused in thought.

"Desert? Deserted? Deserters? I will never know your language Bazil."

"In my country there are people known as conscientious objectors. They tell the government they have no wish to kill anyone." He turned to look at Mikhail. "Or in my case a young girl more worried about the length of a queue and an old man with an empty belly.'

"Sorry Baz, I not know what you say. Old empty man, young girl."

Baz grinned. "It's not important Mikhail."

"These con...consh. Do leaders execute them?"

"No, some go to prison, some get given jobs where they won't be sent into combat, like aircraftmen."

"Maybe you work with consh..?"

"Maybe."

"Your country, good country Bazil. Maybe I put my friends there?"

"Maybe. Your friends Mikhail, their secret, it is safe with me but I don't know how I can help?"

"Plan not finish Bazil. We have friend. He has boat."

"Has he painted a red cross on that as well?"

Sergeant Tretyakov laughed. "English sarcasm?"

"English sarcasm Mikhail."

"You say one thing but mean something else and then understand what person has said. What is black, is white! What is up, is down! English strange. In Russia, no sarcasm. You teach me Bazil?"

Baz chuckled, "You cannot be taught sarcasm Mikhail. To master it properly you have to be brought up with it. It has to be spontaneous." Baz shrugged, "Otherwise it just doesn't work."

"Spont...an...ous. I learn English first my friend."

Baz grinned. "The Lisunov, why not fly the Lisonuv out of Shaibah. That would be the quickest way out."

"That plan, how you say? Plan A. Lisunov no good, dead. Now Plan B, friend's boat."

"We could fix the aircraft."

"No airfield where they go."

"What about a field? They could land on a field."

"Yes, many field Bazil."

"That's it then, they can land on a field."

"Fields on mountains."

"Oh," Baz said awkwardly. "Boat it is then. Where are they going to Mikhail?"

"Maybe tell you soon Bazil. Not now my friend." His words slowly falling away.

Without any warning, Sergeant Tretyakov quickly rose to a stooping position, his eyes targeting a small boulder ten feet away. He crept forward like a cat on the prowl, pausing once to pull out a short bladed knife, his eyes remaining steadfast on the solid quarry. With the knife gripped tightly in his hand he hovered menacingly over the dusty grey stone.

Baz thought the heat had finally got to the Russian sergeant, or the vodka.

In one swift action the Russian sergeant kicked the rock over, then with great speed and accuracy he lunged the knife downward, his whole body falling, rising immediately with a self-satisfied grin, but more importantly, a writhing and squirming scorpion impaled on the point of the knife. Mikhail slid the scorpion from the blade with the sole of his boot, then swivelled his whole weight on top of it, squashing and twisting the creature under foot with a death crunching noise. "This what Stalin do to Russian people Bazil."

Baz stared at the grimy twisted body of the creature. "Do you believe animals have souls Mikhail?"

"Soul? No soul Bazil, much pois, how do you say? Pois..."

"Poison Mikhail."

"Yes poison, like Stalin, it has poison Bazil. No soul." He paused for a moment. "God make poison, not soul."

Both men sat in silence.

"I will help you and your friends but can I ask a small favour in return?"

"Ask anything Bazil."

"Not you Mikhail. Igor whats-his-name, the doctor."

"Doctor Serebryannikov?"

"You know Garage? One of our men." Baz lifted his arms and puffed himself up. "Garage is ill and he's not getting any better. The British doctor gave him some pills, told him to take two a day and stay in bed. He might as well take two pear drops for all the good they're doing."

"Pear drops?"

"Sweets."

"Ah sweets, sweets I like. Igor look at your friend, Bazil." Mikhail looked long and hard at Baz. "Plan B," the last words he spoke to him that day.

As the sinking sun bathed the airfield in a liquid gold light the two men rose and went their separate ways.

Despite their pleading, Baz said nothing to the men about the mysterious Russians.

Next morning, Mikhail and Igor turned up at the RAF tents. Baz was given a slight nod and a longer than normal glance by the Russian sergeant. The decision to tell the men why the two Russians were there, or not to say anything at all, had weighed on Baz's mind most of the night. He chose the latter. Why an ordinary Russian mechanic happened to be examining one of their friends? Well, that would simply be explained away by saying he was a medical student before the war. Not yet being qualified would counteract any claims of why the Russian services had not commissioned him as a field doctor.

Baz entered the tent with the two Russians. Aerial, Ken Harker and Morgan soon followed.

"What the fucking hell is..."

"Shut up Morgan!" snapped Baz.

Baz looked to the far corner of the tent towards a camp bed. Garage was just visible through the mosquito net, a ghostly figure laying motionless under a white sheet. Baz turned his gaze towards the Russian doctor, no words needed to be said.

Igor carried an air of intelligence as he strode towards the bed, even if it was blended with a smug arrogance, then flung the mosquito netting over its tie rope like a fisherman casting a net.

The Russian doctor knelt down and pulled back the sheet.

"What the fu..."

"I said shut up Morgan! That's an order," Baz snapped again.

Igor held Garage's eyelids open and studied the bloodshot eyes. His words became hurried and anxious as he looked up and spoke to Sergeant Tretyakov. His expression sent an uneasy wave throughout the tent.

"Has he..." the Sergeant said as if he was pulling the words out of his mouth.

"Yes. We told the English doc..."

"Da."

Igor said more words in Russian.

"Has he, how do you say?" Sergeant Tretyakov said spluttering his tongue.

"Yes. Tell the doctor lots!"

"He's a fucking doctor?!" exclaimed Morgan.

"No Morgan, he's a fucking train driver."

"Train driver," the Russian sergeant aimed a glance at Morgan. "Sarcasm."

Igor placed two fingers on Garage's stomach, pressing softly in several places until Garage let out a muddy groan. He pushed down again, held it for a moment, then released it. Garage cried out.

Igor spoke in Russian again.

Sergeant Tretyakov translated, "How long pain Bazil?"

"Three or four days."

More words in Russian.

Sergeant Tretyakov translated, "Ask man cough."

Baz bent down with his mouth close to Garage's ear. "Cough Garage, cough for the doctor," he whispered, as though a mother was instructing her child.

Garage coughed, screwed up his face in pain and rattled out another hideous groan.

Igor spoke in Russian again.

Sergeant Tretyakov translated, "Move legs? Ask man? Straight legs?"

"Can you straighten your legs Garage?" Baz waited. There was no movement "Try and straighten your legs." A slight shuffle under the sheet was followed by another deathly groan.

Garage murmured, "Let me die Sarge."

Sergeant Tretyakov translated.

Igor spoke in Russian again.

"Has man food or water?"

"Da," Baz replied, then quickly added with the only other word he knew in Russian. "Nyeht." He opened his mouth, stuck out his tongue and dropped his head in a vomiting gesture.

Igor spoke in Russian again.

Sergeant Tretyakov translated. "Not give man food. Not good for man. Get, how do you say, trap..."

"Trapped."

Igor gave Garage several reassuring pats on the shoulder then looked up at Baz, he spoke slower but the words were released with the same stoney determination.

Sergeant Tretyakov translated.

"Man go hospital. Man needs..."

"What is it? What's wrong with Garage?"

Igor needed no translation, around his lower stomach he made a circular motion with his fingers, then with a slight curve of his little finger he held it against the same area.

There was a moments silence.

"Appendicitis," Ken Harker blurted out, "I had it a few years ago, not nice."

Igor held out his clenched fist then quickly opened it, repeating it once more. Ken Harker looked at Baz with a dour expression. "It's burst Sarge. Mine was close to bursting, the doctor said another fifteen minutes then I would have been in deep trouble. He said something like perit...perititis, or something like that"

Before Harker could finish the sentence, Baz had disappeared out of the tent, returning ten minutes later with the CO and the airfield doctor.

Sergeant Tretyakov and Igor stepped back into the shadows.

"Appendicitis you say?" the airfield doctor said looking at the Russians. "One of you has medical training I'm told."

Sergeant Tretyakov spoke quietly to Igor.

"He doesn't speak English," Baz said. "He said it may have burst."

"Perititis," Harker said.

The doctor glanced at Harker. "Peritonitis, then how? Never mind. You say peritonitis," he added, turning his attention towards the two Russians again.

"Well its not fucking dysentery, *is* it?" Morgan snapped.

The doctor began to examine Garage.

"It looks serious, whatever it is," the CO said. "Five minutes Sergeant Albright, have him ready for transport." Without waiting for the doctor's diagnosis, the CO left the tent.

The next day Baz had a request from Sergeant Tretyakov. "Stepan play chess Bazil, Russian against English, vodka against tea, Dostoyevsky against Dickens," he said with a smile. "After dinner Bazil, when heat gone."

Plan B, Baz thought. Whatever plan B was.

With the taste of corned beef and dates still in his mouth, Baz headed towards the Russian sector.

Through the open flap of the smoke filled tent he could make out the outline of the four Russians waiting inside. Sergeant Tretyakov was sitting, as was Stepan, stood at the back were Igor and Daniil, Igor's head hidden in the heights of the tent's interior.

Baz tapped the pole dissecting the entrance to the tent and waited. "Come Bazil," the Russian Sergeant called without getting up. Baz tentatively stepped in as if he was walking onto Russian soil.

Harbouring the same smoky atmosphere and dry musty smell it felt very much like his own tent. He saw a small wooden table with a chess set on top, an upside down box lid with an inch high lip bordering its four sides, its faded checkered squares virtually merged into one dirty brown colour. The condition of the chess pieces was no better, at first glance Baz found it difficult to distinguish between the lighter and darker ones, obviously a chess set that had seen many a battle throughout its checkered history.

Sergeant Tretyakov placed a metal mug in front of the chessboard. "Russian tea," he said. "Sarcasm Bazil, yes?"

Igor spoke first.

"How is big man?" Sergeant Tretyakov translated.

"I haven't heard anything since he was taken into hospital. I'll go and visit him soon." No translation was returned, just a nod.

"Sit, Bazil," Sergeant Tretyakov said, indicating towards an empty canvas chair beside the chessboard. Stepan sat opposite, his arms folded in front, staring down at the four rows of chessmen. Baz sensed that Stepan was a person who calculated everything, not only in chess but life as well.

Baz noticed the lighter pieces weren't entirely complete, there were eight pawns, that can't be denied, but only seven of them were of the same design. The one piece that wasn't? That happened to be a rifle bullet, roughly the same height as the other pawns, a lot thinner though and a dull copper colour. Baz raised his eyebrows and pointed to the bullet, "Is this for the loser?"

Sergeant Tretyakov hacked out a laugh and spoke in Russian but not to anyone in particular. Daniil quickly answered. The Russian Sergeant translated in the best way he could. "Daniil say only taking bad at losing Bazil."

"Then tell Stepan that," Baz said picking up the bullet. The Russians watched with astonishment as he threw it high into the air towards Daniil, landing softly in his hands.

Baz sat back, slid his hand into his shorts pocket and rummaged around. The Russians exchanged baffled expressions, Igor said something in his native tongue, causing the other three to chuckle. Baz pulled out the brothers of the board pawn and placed it on the vacant square. It was slightly taller than the other pawns, just as grubby, but more stable and a lot less intimidating than the bullet. Baz thought it looked proud to be back in its rightful place. No one had ever stopped laughing as fast as the four Russians. Igor spoke first.

"Igor ask, how do you say? Magic?" Sergeant Tretyakov said.

Baz smiled. "No Mikhail, it once belonged to a friend." Baz glared at Stepan. "He was a pilot, he was killed flying a spitfire." Then added after a moments pause, "he was shot down," knowing the Russian didn't understand a word, but said it anyway.

Stepan's expression changed as he picked up the pawn, studied it with a look of contempt, and placed it back on the square.

"William! The pawn has a name, the pawn is called Will. Tell that to Stepan, Mikhail," Baz said forcefully.

Sergeant Tretyakov recalled their conversation from the day before. "William, Mrs Water...William? " he said.

"Yes! Mrs Waterhouse's son, my friend William."

"William is pawn?"

"No! William is, was a real person. The pawn is called Will, after my friend William."

"Mrs Waterhouse Bazil, she like queen?" said Sergeant Tretyakov with a smile.

Baz glared at the Russian Sergeant. "Yes Mikhail, she like queen."

"Your sarcasm Bazil. I will never know it."

"That was *not* sarcasm Mikhail."

Stepan snatched one dark and one light pawn and hid each piece away in the clutches of a fist. He then stretched his arms out in front of him. Baz nodded at the one on his left, Stepan opened up his hand

and displayed the slightly lighter of the two chess pieces. "The pawns are the souls of chess," he said to Sergeant Tretyakov, thinking back to what Will had once said. Baz realised he only said things like that when he felt nervous, and he always felt nervous before a chess game.

Stepan spun the board around, the pieces wobbled and slipped. Baz now had the lighter pieces in front of him. He touched, straightened and adjusted every single one until they were central on their own square and facing their enemy. It was a ritual he had done before the start of every chess game, probably a symptom of his nervousness again, until he was satisfied perfection had been achieved, and Baz's perfection had to be nothing short of perfect.

He clutched his hands and tapped them on his lips, then rested his nose on his fingers. Never rush the first move. "Regretting the first move is like regretting you were born," a William quote.

Baz thought on. Stepan sighed, more than once.

Baz slid his king's pawn two squares forward. Without any moment of hesitation Stepan followed with the same move. The Russian's confident and assertive slight of hand reminded him of Alan Goldsworthy. Baz's king's knight. Stepan's queen's knight. Both lifted high over their respective pawns and into action. Baz glided his bishop along the long diagonal until it faced the Russian's knight. Again, without any thought, Stepan moved his outer pawn one square forward where it threatened the wooden clergyman.

Baz was pleased, a classic Ruy Lopez. He had two choices, take the knight or withdraw. Baz as always, much preferred an open uncluttered game, an exchange of pieces would certainly help, but his knowledge of the opening, if he didn't, was far greater. He retreated his bishop onto the edge of the battleground. Stepan brought his second knight into play, protecting the central squares. Baz knew this strategy well. William had told him many years ago 'Hold the centre old boy and the game will be yours for the taking.' He also said to tuck the king away at the earliest opportunity. Baz crossed his hands with a king and a rook held in each, his sovereign now safely out of harm's way, he could concentrate on attacking his opponent's army. Stepan pushed his bishop in front of his king, holding the two long diagonals. With a nudge of his finger Baz slid his newly placed rook to where his king once stood, that all important central flank now stretched out in front of it. "Hold the centre my boy," Will's voice echoed again. Another of Stepan's pawns stepped forward two squares, threatening Baz's wayward bishop. Baz retreated it once again. Stepan crossed his king and rook, his king was now safe. Game equal. Baz's bishop was under threat of being trapped, he pushed a pawn forward, an open door, a safe haven for it to step back into. Then came Stepan's next move. Baz stared down in astonishment, a pawn sacrifice! This is not what he expected. Stepan was giving away his queen's pawn. For what reason? He wants to gain a move, he wants to put Baz on the defence, he wants to be the aggressor, he thinks he is going to get the advantage.

Baz thought long and hard, he had seen this position in only a couple of books. Marshall's attack, that was it, Marshall's attack. The American grandmaster Marshall had played it against Lasker in a 1924 tournament. He remembered another game against Capablanca a few years earlier. What happened next? Baz had vague images of the games. The pawn was taken by the white pawn, he remembered that much. Black knight takes, white knight takes his other pawn and opens the flank for his rook, also opening up the whole game. Who will have the advantage? Baz's rook will be left stranded and isolated in the centre, he could always retreat it, a move wasted. What the hell he thought, after the damage is over he'll be a pawn up and have the uncluttered game he wanted. Baz and the Russian quickly played their next five moves, both players had calculated most of them beforehand. Baz retreated his rook on the last move, just as he intended, he sat back and considered the position. Still equal, he thought.

Then he saw Stepan's next move.

The Russian had brought out his queen and placed it threateningly close to Baz's king. The row of three pawns protecting his monarch looked more than vulnerable, cowering at the mercy of a much more powerful foe. Damn! Baz thought after spending some time evaluating the position. He looked at Stepan. The Russian sensed the intrusion but continued to gaze down. Another eight moves. Stepan attacking. Baz defending, his pieces slowly being hemmed in by the black enemy. It was then, twenty-four moves later, Baz felt as though a pack of wolves were manoeuvering into position for the final kill, surrounding their victim, his opponent's wooden assassins could smell blood.

It was then his position felt completely hopeless. Will's words continued to ring around his brain. 'Let your opponent have his checkmate old man. It is good for the soul.' What soul!?

Baz moved a pawn one square forward, unprotected and alone it was ready for the taking, a move that would signal the end of the game, a speedier death. It was the pawn from William's chess set, a noble sacrifice he thought. Stepan ignored it and played an insignificant pawn move instead. Baz stared down in amazement, the Russian had made his first mistake, he pushed Will's pawn forward again. Again, Stepan ignored it. Again, another square forward. Again, another snub from the Russian. Baz was now two squares away from metamorphosing his pawn into the all powerful queen, he pushed the pawn forward. With a slow, exaggerated arc of his arm, Stepan plonked a bishop directly in front of the pawn, its path now blocked by the cleric.

Baz looked up at the Russian, Stepan returned the gaze. For a moment they just stared at each other. It was then Baz knew Stepan had complete control of the game, he had always had complete control of the game, Baz looked over at Sergeant Tretyakov.

The Russian Sergeant remained silent.

"The pawn is Stepan and Igor and Daniil, isn't it Mikhail? The bishop is me. I'm right aren't I? If I don't help them, they will remain here, eventually they will get caught."

Sergeant Tretyakov said nothing.

Baz stared down at his fallen pieces, "So what is plan B Mikhail?"

"One of your men is in hospital?" Stepan said, through a strong Russian accent but in near perfect English.

"What?!" Baz looked around, thinking someone else had spoken.

"His name is Garage, strange name for an Englishman Sergeant Albright."

"What?! Yes, you speak English and he's Welsh."

"He is in the isolation hospital in Al Basrah. Igor saved his life?"

"Where did you learn English like that?"

Stepan turned to look at Igor. "They took him to hospital with a burst appendix?"

"Yes they did and you didn't answer my question."

"You made a deal with Mikhail?"

"I did. Where did you learn English like that?"

"London."

"London?"

"University."

"Oh, when?" The questions arrived in Baz's mind as fast as they were departing his lips.

"Is Garage a Welsh name?"

"No, and when were you in London?"

"Before the war. How is this man Garage? Sergeant Albright."

"I don't know. How come you went to London University?"

"It was Birkbeck College actually and it is a long story. You would like to know how this man is?"

"Yes I would and how come you went to Birkbeck College?"

"My parents lived in England for a long while."

"Where?"

"Chesham House."

"Where's that?"

"London, Belgravia, it was the Russian Embassy."

"The Russian Embassy!" Baz quietened down, "The Russian Embassy?"

Stepan gave a deep sigh. "My father was an attache at the Embassy for many years. He was very important, only a few of the staff were allowed to bring their families. We lived in an apartment close to the embassy. It was a large house with beautiful furniture, we lived in luxury while the rest of the Soviet Republic were starving. I remember the ambassador's apartment was on the top three floors, I will never forget his name." Stepan paused, he lowered his head as he spoke. "Rabokov, Konstantin Rabokov. He died in 1927, the same year my..." Stepan swallowed before he finished the sentence. "There was also another family in the same house, with younger children, they lived on the ground floor. They used to pay me to look after their children, a boy and a girl. Nice children. We used to make model aircraft and take them out in the garden, some even flew," Stepan said with an inward grin. "It was many years we were in your country, I do not remember exactly how long. My father also spoke your language, he taught me English in the evenings, he taught me chess also. I think I was a good pupil."

"You *were* a good pupil and he *must* have been a good teacher," Baz said.

"My father was involved with the trade agreement between Soviet

Russia and England in the early twenties, we saw many important people. A man called Krasin instructed my father on what to do. Leonid Krasin was a very important man. My father did a lot of the translation for him and they spent many hours in the drawing room alone. He never spoke about his work to me though, or my mother. When my English became good enough I got a scholarship to Birkbeck College. I learnt mechanics, flight mechanics, for me they were good times, happy times. I grew to love your country Sergeant Albright," Stepan stopped.

A moments silence.

"Thank you for answering my questions Stepan."

More silence.

"That is not the end Sergeant Albright." Stepan examined Baz's expression for a sign to continue. "In 1924 Lenin died, Vladimir Lenin, our great socialist leader, Vladimir Ilyich Lenin," Stepan said, slowly shaking his head. "In 1924 we were all called back to Moscow, all the embassy staff, everyone of us. Alexei Rykov took over as leader after Lenin's death but it was General Secretary Stalin who controlled the politicians, pulled the strings as you English say."

Both Igor and Daniil twitched nervously after hearing Stalin's name.

"Yes Sergeant Albright, the same Joseph Stalin who is now working with your leaders, the same Joseph Stalin who tortured and murdered thousands of his own people including..." Stepan paused for a moment. "My father sent me away in 1927 to an uncle. At that time I didn't know why but he said there was some confusion with his time spent in London, it would be better if I wasn't involved. I never saw my father or my mother again. I tried to find out what happened to them. It was very difficult without the police finding out who I was, they had ears and eyes everywhere."

"But you were only a student in London." Baz said.

"And my father was just a diplomat and my mother was just a mother. What you were made no difference to Stalin. They were accused of spying for the English. It was Nabakov who told the police that, Nabakov was tortured until he told them what they wanted to hear. Also the family on the ground floor, all dead. Nabakov died while under arrest. My parents were executed or sent to a gulag. Either way, they are dead." Stepan looked long and hard at Baz. "And that is how

I speak your language Sergeant Albright."

Baz paused, "I'm sorry Stepan. Why didn't you leave Russia earlier?"

"My parents were watched everywhere they went. My father had suspicion that something was wrong. If he hadn't sent me away to stay with Mikhail's family then I would have met the same fate."

"The uncle?" said Baz.

"Yes Bazil, my father," Sergeant Tretyakov said.

"It was Stepan who taught you English Mikhail?"

"Yes. Me not good, how do you say? Stu..."

"Student Mikhail."

Baz noticed the Russian flying officer had never smiled once. "Yes, I would like to know how Garage is," he said.

"Plan B," said Sergeant Tretyakov.

"Who is in command of the airfield Sergeant Albright?" said Stepan.

"Group Captain Melling is the Commanding Officer."

"He good man," Sergeant Tretyakov said.

"Ask him if you can visit your friend in hospital, ask him for a truck, bring along as many of your men as you can. Maybe some will want to visit," he paused, "some nice Arab ladies.

Five more rules direct from the CO.

LADIES OF THE NIGHT

1. See the doctor before visiting any brothels in Al Basrah.
2. Catching a disease that will make your penis fall off will not get you out of Shaibah. Unless you are in a wooden box.
3. Avoid full physical contact if possible. Have some 'lip action' or a 'handshake.' Both will get the same result. It would be cheaper and you will have a lot less worry.
4. If you must have full physical contact then little Johnny must wear an overcoat. Unless you would like the doctor to squirt some poisonous liquid into your penis.
5. See the doctor a week after visiting any brothels.
6. Remember a bob for a blob could mean no knob.
'Roll on that fucking boat.'

"We must have truck the day after tomorrow, Friday morning."

"Two days!"

"You must persuade the Commanding Officer Sergeant Albright. *You* will see your friend."

"I can only ask."

"You made a deal, remember, Igor saved your friend's life."

"It easy for you Bazil, I go, I come back with you. One truck, drive to Al Basrah, see friend, drive back to Shaibah. It easy Bazil," Sergeant Tretyakov said. "You will see friend."

"What about my men? They will ask why four Russians came with us and only one has come back."

"You will think of something Sergeant Albright, you are the Sergeant."

"What about you and Daniil and Igor? Where are you going after you have left us?"

"It is better you do not know. If people ask questions then it will be easier for you."

Baz looked down at the position on the chessboard. "You could have easily taken my pawn and won the game Stepan. I would still have helped you."

"How could I take the pawn Sergeant Albright? It is your friend, it has a name. William, yes?"

"It's only a pawn, just made of wood, not flesh and blood. Keep it with the chess set, that is where it belongs, that is where William belongs."

PLAN B

The morning of Plan B felt a lot longer than usual. The sunlight had just begun to invade Baz's tent and his normal early rise had been even earlier. He always thought of the beginning of the day as his favourite time, the cooler air, the peace and stillness of the airfield, a sense of detachment from the war.

Only today was going to be different. All night Plan B had never been far from his thoughts. He was only going to Al Basrah to see one of his men in hospital, any good Sergeant would do the same. Thankfully it was enough to convince the CO. The Russians just wanted a ride in, that's all there was to it. After that, if they wanted to rendezvous with a boat, then that was their problem. As Sergeant Tretyakov had said, "It easy for you Bazil."

Baz had begun to boil the water for his tea when Morgan stirred, only to quickly doze off again. Morgan would never wake completely, not until he had gone through the ritual of smoking his first cigarette. Aerial and young Harker were wherever their dreams had taken them and Corporal Lynch looked as he always did, a white faced corpse lying face up with his mouth wide open for any intruding insect seeking a dark moist haven, only his drowning pig of a snore suggesting he had not yet arrived back with the living. There was a ghostly atmosphere as the translucent fine netting shrouded the occupants in the mellow light of dawn.

Baz kept the excursion to Al Basrah solely confined to the men in his tent: as far as the CO knew, it was *their* friend from *their* tent they were visiting. The story why the four Russians were accompanying them, well, at that moment in time Baz didn't have one. He could say they were departing the airfield, travelling by boat from the port and leave it at that, after all, it *was* the truth.

The start of plan B would begin with Sergeant Tretyakov asking for a lift into Al Basrah for the four Russians, that would make it seem that Baz had no prior knowledge of the plan. If there was room in the truck, which of course there was, then how could he refuse.

Two hours later Morgan had cooked breakfast as he did every morning: eggs and stale pitta bread were served up, along with an untold amount of tea and the usual inexhaustible quantity of figs, dates and watermelon. On the odd morning they would also have a rasher of bacon, but not today.

Hearing the crunching of gear changes, Baz looked up and saw a veil of brown mist approaching in the distance. A large wheeled, high chassis truck trundled and bounced its way towards Baz's tent, its canvas tarpaulin shuddered and swayed as it negotiated the bumps and holes in the dry earth. Through dirt smeared arches on the windscreen Baz could just make out the face of Corporal Lynch, it had to be the corporal, who else? After all, it was in Plan B.

At the exact same time, Sergeant Tretyakov approached. Baz rose from his chair and met him where their conversation would be out of earshot. They stood face to face.

"Tell men ask go Al Basrah with you, you nod." Sergeant Tretyakov waited. "Now!" Baz returned a sharp, overemphasised drop of his head. "Good. Stepan, Daniil, Igor, me come," Sergeant Tretyakov said, then returned to the Russian camp.

Corporal Lynch dropped the great height from the truck's cabin and strolled over to where the other aircraftmen were. At the same time, Robert Lamb, a welder with a raffish character, one of the later arrivals, had begun interrogating Morgan about the truck.

"We are going to have company," Baz said quickly, after returning to the RAF men.

"Yeah, fucking Shanks is coming with us," Morgan said, with the ability to derail any preconceived conversation.

"That's not quite what I mean."

"Then Shanks is *not* coming with us Sarge?"

"No." Baz thought quickly. "Fine, let the orderly know you'll be leaving the airfield Lamb."

"Thanks Sarge." Shanks slapped his hands together and strode away muttering something about lucky ladies.

"What company Sarge?" said Aerial.

"Safety in numbers."

"What fucking company Sarge?"

Baz shrugged his shoulders as if what he was about to say was an everyday occurrence. "Sergeant Tretyakov has asked if they could come with us, also Corporal Mihailov and..."

"The doctor and his bloody sidekick. Why? You expecting someone to get fucking ill?" Morgan interrupted.

"*Why Sergeant!* Morgan." Baz hated pulling rank. "We're only giving them a lift in, that's all. We have room and because I'm the Sergeant Morgan that's why. I make the decisions, if you don't like..."

"That's all Sarge?" said Aerial.

"Sorry."

"That's all. You said that's all. Was there more Sarge?"

"No, I mean once we're there, they're not our responsibility. That's all, *that's all!*"

"OK Sarge."

"Russians and Morgan, there's going to be some scintillating conversation in that truck," Aerial said.

"And what happens when we get there Sarge?" asked Corporal Lynch.

"This is meant to be a day out for some of you, a break from Shaibah. I'm spending a couple of hours with Garage. You lot can do what you want."

"Al Basrah, great," young Harker said, rolling his eyes.

"No one wanders off on their own, do you understand? You all stay together, the corp will go with you, to make sure you stay out of trouble. Right Corp?"

"Right Sarge."

"Like being back at bloody school."

Baz gave Morgan a long, hard look. "Like not getting robbed Morgan, like staying alive, like keeping your shirt on your back, like not getting a dose of the clap," Baz exhaled a long nasal sigh and pulled out a small cardboard box from his pocket. "The doctor gave me these. You've seen the rules. If you have to, you know, use them! That's an order. If I was you, I would stay well clear of them, you know, those ladies."

"Ladies of the fucking night Sarge."

Baz looked towards the Russian encampment and nodded.

The truck lurched and bobbed out of Shaibah with the ten men inside. Baz had insisted that Morgan sit in the front cabin with Corporal Lynch. Not the normal arrangement as Sergeants usually had that privilege, nevertheless, Morgan seemed happy with the situation, the Corporal a lot less so. Baz chose to sit on the wooden bench in the back alongside the other three RAF men, facing the four Russians, their kit bags held tightly between their legs, conversation was sparse.

Twenty minutes of a bone shaking ride later, Corporal Lynch stopped the truck outside the hospital entrance.

The firmness of Baz's grip as he shook hands with Daniil and Igor said everything that needed to be said. When he took Stepan's hand he mouthed the words, "Good luck. Look after William."

Baz dropped out of the back and thumped the side of the truck.

He entered the hospital alone.

Sergeant Tretyakov and the three Russians decamped from the truck just before it entered the heavily guarded Royal Navy compound at the port, just as Baz had instructed.

Plan B was for the Russian Sergeant to escort his fellow countrymen to the boat and find his way back to the hospital where he and Baz would be picked up. Before they left, Baz voiced his concern about the Russian Sergeant making it through Al Basrah alone. "I have nothing, if want nothing, I give nothing," he said. "Maybe I give wife for camel." Then tutted and shook his head. "Not mistress though." He perked up, "Two camels and a goat for mistress."

Corporal Lynch parked the truck in the security of the compound and the five RAF men made their way to the entrance.

———————

Stretched out in front of Baz was a long corridor with stained, cracked white tiles adorning its walls from floor to ceiling. A central ornate frieze of embossed green tiles extended the entire length of the aisle and dissected the walls into equal halves. The only interruption to this mass of clinical ceramics were paint peeled cobalt blue doors and randomly situated wooden benches. On the right, a row of windows, most with broken panes or no glass at all. Large, brightly coloured pots lined the wall opposite, spouting thick green leaves that fanned halfway across the corridor.

Crowds of natives in long robes thronged around the rows of wooden benches. Baz thought the patient's entire family were there, even distant relatives, all talking at the same time, he was grateful he couldn't understand anything that was said, then wondered how anyone else could either.

Several hospital beds covered with varying coloured cloth in degrees of dishevelment were shoved up against the opposite wall. Some were empty, others occupied with desperate faces staring out through frightened eyes. As Baz passed one bed, a young Arab boy reached out his arm and opened his hand. "Sorry," was all Baz could think to say as he sidestepped the outstretched limb.

Baz slowly navigated his way through the congested aisle, trying his hardest not to make contact. As he got further along the stench became almost unbearable, not one smell but a blend of many, disinfectant, ether, vomit and faeces. But the worst was death, he could smell death, or what he thought was death.

He passed an old man sitting alone, appreciating the slight breeze wafting through a broken window. The long hard years had etched a map of deep wrinkles into his sun dried, sucked-in face. Under a black and white headscarf his black, sunken eyes stared up at Baz, displaying a kindly expression, he smiled, exposing his one yellow tooth jutting down from a dark gum. Then, through a shaking hand, he lifted his stick and pointed it towards an open door at the end of the corridor.

―――――――――

The four Russians made their way along the quay at a steady pace, their confidence marred only by a slight nervousness. The only people that could give them trouble at this stage were the few military police patrolling the docks, most of these were Indian Sikhs left over from the 1941 campaign, and thankfully for the four Russians, mostly interested in what the locals were scheming.

Two large cargo ships were moored up against the port dock, the larger some way in the distance. The first one they passed was sitting high in the water after just unloading its freight. An old work horse of a steam ship that had somehow managed to survive the submarine infested waters. As they approached, Stepan looked up and saw a cloud of cigarette smoke engulfing three crewmen as they leant on the ships railings. Stepan heard their banter, "*English*," he whispered without turning his head. A couple more crew appeared in front of them, one looked like a girl, and with a fleeting glance at the four Russians they hauled themselves up the steep walkway, finally vanishing into the hull.

Stepan looked at his son and smiled.

―――――――――

"Where do we go for a *fucking* good time in this God forsaken place?" Morgan asked the Royal Navy guard standing at the entrance to the compound.

"I think what this ignorant aircraftman is asking Lieutenant, is where a man can get some light refreshment in town, maybe a beer or two?" Aerial said, adopting his usual superior prose.

The guard remained silent with his rifle held close to his chest, its barrel pointing toward the baking sky. Under the peak of his cap his slit like eyes scrutinised the five RAF men one by one, returning to the two chevrons.

Corporal Lynch was an innocuous man, someone with the gift to escape most people's attention. A man who throughout his sixty-three years of poor lonely existence had neither wife or children, or wanted either for that matter. He was a man who slept alone, ate alone and for most of the time drank alone, preferring to shape his own destiny, mainly in the public bar at Flannigans. Corporal Lynch continued walking past the guard with the men in tow.

"You want women?" the guard called out.

Aerial stopped and turned his head "We may want to consider some female company."

"You all look like you fucking need it," said the guard.

"We all look like we need fucking," replied Morgan.

With a couple of firsts, many seconds, a lot of thirds, one fourth, and copious amount of lefts and rights, the guard gave them directions.

"Did you get all that?" asked young Harker, still wondering why he was there in the first place. Since leaving Shaibah he had never thought of his Emma so much and couldn't understand why Morgan still hadn't returned the photograph of his beloved fiancée.

"If you get lost, head for the minaret. That's the tall building over there." The guard pointed at a pencil like object in the distance. "Then go northeast, that'll bring you back here."

The port road into town was a wide, palm tree lined avenue with the tall minaret projecting up at the furthermost point.

"Down this road, second right, third left then when the road splits take the left fork," said Shanks.

"Second right then *fourth* left and I don't remember anything about a bloody fork in the road," argued Morgan.

"We are all agreed on second right," said Aerial.

"Right," said Shanks.

"*Second* right then," Morgan added forcefully.

They turned into a narrow lane with single storey mud walled houses bordering a rutted street. Large opened double doors left dark hollow spaces, entrances where old men sat on makeshift seats, behind them white sacks with rolled tops displaying red, orange and green spices.

A donkey with long lopsided ears and a nodding head pulled a flat wooden cart along the lane towards the aircraftmen. An old woman sat on the front corner of the cart with a leg dangling precariously close to a wheel. With only the faintest of movements she would flick a long thin leafy branch on top of the donkey's head, each time his ears would twitch and his miserable expression would become even more forlorn. A stray cat, of which you could count the number of ribs through its matted fur, sprung onto the back of the cart, sniffed around and leapt off again, finally curling up in a ball in the shadows.

As Baz arrived at the open door he turned to show his gratitude towards the old man, to give him a wave of thanks. Only there was an empty space in front of the window, he had vanished into thin air, along with his chair. If only the smell and noise could leave as easily, Baz thought.

"Mishter Bwyce?" a sharp voice grated from the door entrance.

Baz turned to see a short middle-aged woman with a doughy face encircled by a beautiful blue headscarf. "Mishter Bwyce?" she repeated, her eyes lingering on his. "Misshter Bwyce?" she said for the third time.

"Mister Bryce. Oh, yes. Mister Bryce, thank you," Baz replied.

She led him through a large white room with two small windows at the far end. It felt much hotter after leaving the coolness of the corridor but a lot less noisy, unfortunately the stench had remained, if anything, the heat made it worse.

There were a dozen or so beds, all with a minimal amount of space separating them, just enough for a doctor or nurse to stand. Four doors were evenly spaced in one of the plaster chipped walls, more beds were tightly packed in between them.

The patients that Baz could see were locals, all lay on top of the bedding with most wearing their own clothes, their legion of relatives stifling the air around them. The few that were conscious appeared to stare into some kind of void, one was busy bent over the side of the bed, noisily throwing up into a bowl. The others, well, they were wherever their dreams had taken them behind shut eyes.

Baz had known many of the diseases first hand from the men back at Shaibah. Mostly diarrhoea related, also dysentery, waterborne viruses and a few cases of malaria. Sandfly fever was common and difficult to prevent, tiny insects small enough to find their way through a mosquito net, ready to suck the blood and deposit their deadly virus in any unsuspecting victim. The men who had become ill were given a few tablets and told to rest; if their symptoms worsened they were taken to the Service's Hospital. A few suffered bad bouts of depression after the fever had subsided, as if Shaibah wasn't enough to make any man reach the ends of despair. Mental illness was not recognised, suicide was.

Garage was a special case. After Igor had diagnosed him with a ruptured appendix, he was quickly taken to the service's hospital situated at the large army camp west of Al Basrah. An army doctor's expertise was in the treatment of burns, bullet and shrapnel wounds, some became knowledgeable in more common diseases but peritonitis, that was a whole new ball game.

Garage's appendix was removed immediately on arrival but the paralysis was worse than the doctors feared. He was quickly transferred to Basrah Isolation hospital where Dr Mahendra Chopra, an eminent doctor specialising in the effects of snakebite poison and insect transferred diseases appeared to be Garage's best hope of survival.

The nurse stopped at a closed door.

Baz pushed the door open and peered into the small room.

One by one their steps faltered as they got closer and one by one they hesitated to a near stop. The second, larger cargo ship was gradually looming as the three Russians made their way along the quay. The name on the ship engulfed them with a sickening dread. One was more fearful than the others, he had good reason to be.

"Soviet! Shit! What do we do now?" said Daniil in Russian.

"That's the least of our problems," Sergeant Tretyakov said, his lips hardly moving. *"See that officer in the leather coat? Remember the story I told you, when those two Russian officers came to the airfield?"*

The three remained silent, not wanting to hear what he was about to be say.

"He is one of them!"

"Shit!" Daniil said. *"What if he asks questions? We are not meant to be here remember. He is Soviet, he is bound to ask lots of questions. Shit!"*

"We are just four aircraftmen checking on our next delivery," added Igor.

"We are just four Russian aircraftmen. We are not English. Soviet aircraftmen do not wander around ports checking on deliveries with three kit bags thrown over their shoulders," Daniil said behind tight lips. *"You're a doctor, what do you know about fucking aircraft deliveries."*

"And you're a fucking expert are you? Why don't we just cut behind the buildings? Come out past the ship."

"Too late. Just keep walking. I'll do the talking and for fucks sake look normal," said Sergeant Tretyakov.

Stepan spoke in a whisper, *"This is my fault, I should have allowed for this in the plan."*

'TRANSBALT'. The huge, rust ridden lettering on the side of the ship was directly above them as they stepped into the shadow of a crane.

"Third left, fourth left, that guard was taking the bloody piss out of us," expressed an irritable Morgan as the aircraftmen arrived at a T-junction.

"We could always go back," said young Harker nervously glancing behind him. "To be honest I don't have much experience with women. None, if you really want to know the truth," his words softening.

"Don't you worry young Kenneth, we'll make sure you get a fine lady renowned for her delicate touch and sensitivity," Aerial said.

"He needs a fucking shag! Not mothering."

"Actually Morgan, I wouldn't mind having my photograph of Emma..."

"You stick with me Harker, experience is everything," said Shanks.

"Third left, fourth left, at least let's go left," Aerial decided, leading them into another lane, this one a lot narrower with twenty foot high tan coloured walls either side. In the distance it curved so acutely they could only see a couple of feet in front of them.

"Lets hope bloody cyclops isn't around the corner."

"This is Iraq, Morgan, not Greece," Aerial said anxiously as he took slow tentative steps into the unknown.

With a lot of trepidation each man entered the bend. Corporal Lynch brought up the rear, at one stage losing sight of young Harker in front of him. Much to the relief of the five men the tight curve finally straightened out and they found themselves standing under a high stone arch, a small empty square in front of them, each contemplating the multitude of lanes exiting from every side.

"Bloody hell! Which way now?"

Harker wanted to repeat his plea about backtracking but considering how badly things were going, he hoped someone might suggest it for him.

"We are not alone gentlemen," said Aerial, looking at a wisp of dark, dusty hair above a pair of small eyes peering round one of the corners. Two small hands came into view, another two eyes appeared lower down than the first. Suddenly, three boys popped out from the lane, all around ten to twelve years old . The initial two pairs of peering eyes finally stood upright and revealed themselves in their entirety. The shorter one appeared much younger, he had red hair, a lighter skin tone and wore an oversized dishevelled shirt. The others had black unruly hair and dusky skin, all wore long tunics with little colour, apart from the dried on grime.

"I'll fight the little one," said Shanks.

"Maybe they can tell us the way," said Harker.

"What are you going to ask them? Where's the best place to get a shag around here?"

The five aircraftmen carried on walking, passing innocuously through the centre of the square. "Hello," Ken Harker said with a friendly smile as he looked down at the young redheaded boy.

Two boys defiantly stepped out in front of the men.

"Fucking purse snatchers," commented Morgan.

"American?" said the oldest boy.

"No, British."

"Yes, you American."

"No! British. I know what fucking country I come from."

"You like nice pots? Very nice," said another boy, as though he had already said it a thousand times that day.

"No thank you young man," said Harker.

"You like nice Arab scarf?"

"Been there," declared Morgan.

"No thank you," repeated Harker.

"You like nice rugs? American wife like very much."

"We are not fucking Amer..."

"Its very kind of you to ask but no thank you."

"Buy two, I give one free."

"I don't want any."

"Nice Arab jambiya?"

"A jam what?"

"Jambiya. Very sharp," the boy said thrusting his fist down in a stabbing action, causing young Harker to spring back.

"No thank you."

"Spices? Tarragon? Paprika? Turmeric?"

"No."

"You want automobile? My uncle has many."

"What!"

"In these bloody lanes."

"You want opium? Nice opium."

"Now that might be worth..."

"No we don't," interrupted Corporal Lynch.

"You want nice lady?"

Ken Harker and Corporal Lynch remained silent.

A thin piece of frayed, khaki material covered the narrow window, giving the room a dismal atmosphere and allowing only the slightest hint of light to pass through. Under a blue sheet on a bed in the centre lay the contours of a body, the back of a head sunk deep into a pillow. It was Garage's rugby flattened nose that Baz recognised first.

"Garage?" The word hidden under his breath. He waited. Nothing. "Garage?" This time a whisper, thrown towards the bed. Baz waited again. Still nothing.

He took the few steps over to the bed. Garage's eyes were shut, he looked asleep, a calm serenity about him.

It was when Baz's eyes acclimatised to the dark that the shock hit him. He fought to recognise his friend. Even in the poor light he could see his skin had turned a pasty grey, he looked drawn and gaunt, he was half the man and twice the age. Baz lay his hand on Garage's forehead, it felt warm, a sense of relief, he wrapped his fingers around the toes of one of Garage's feet, also warm, not appreciably warm but not cold. He felt the rise and fall of his chest, a shallow movement.

Baz walked over to the window and unhooked a corner from the material, it fell loose, allowing the outside world to illuminate the room. From a dull grey, the walls transformed into a bright green. On a table the other side of Garage's bed, sat a mug and a jug of water, a mass of tiny winged flies floated on top. A wooden chair pushed into the far corner, both the table and seat covered in flecks from the same green paint.

Baz took the chair and sat beside the bed, there he waited. Every now and then he would lower his face and say Garage's name, each time the word would get slightly louder and each time he hoped it would return some glimmer of life into the Welshman. He needed to hear him say something, anything, even a murmur would suffice. Baz knew he wouldn't be able to leave the hospital without Garage knowing he had been there.

He wondered how the others were, if Plan B was going to, well, plan. If the British aircraftmen had got any closer to achieving their goal, whatever that might be.

After a while, and without any sign of Garage waking, Baz gripped the Welshman's massive hand and gave a good firm squeeze.

Garage's eyelids flickered open into two yellow bloodshot slits.

With the massive cargo ship towering behind him, the Soviet officer's glare followed the four Russians as they stepped from under the crane and back into the sweltering sun. If there was a glimmer of consolation, then it was Sergeant Tretyakov noticing the leather coated officer was the lower ranked of the two that had inspected the aircraft. In fact, he couldn't remember him saying much at all.

"Don't forget to salute comrades," the Russian Sergeant murmured through closed lips in his native tongue.

After a barked command from the officer, one of the sailors dutifully hurried over and handed him a few sheets of paper. For the next few seconds he scanned the top sheet, his eyes roaming downward, returning to the top and down again. He then did the same to the sheet underneath, then the next one. He looked up at the four Russians.

Sergeant Tretyakov stood to attention and saluted, holding his hand stiffly against his right eyebrow, the other three followed suit, standing a good ten feet away, a slow tentative salute was returned. Sergeant Tretyakov then slammed his hand against the side of his leg, the other three did the same. The officer let his hand drop, kicking the flaps of his long leather coat as he marched towards the Russian sergeant.

"There are no aircraft mechanics on my list Sergeant."

"My comrades have just arrived Sir."

"You are going to Shaibah?"

"Yes Sir."

"How are you getting to Shaibah Sergeant?"

"British truck Sir. We are to be collected at the Royal Navy compound."

The officer turned his gaze towards Stepan, he felt the officer could see beyond the simple corporal, maybe a pilot can sense another pilot just by looking at him.

"You have just arrived Corporal?"

"Yes Sir."

"How did you arrive?"

"They came on the..."

"Let the Corporal speak Sergeant."

Stepan's mind raced, he remembered Baz's story about his journey to Shaibah, then thought about the ship they had passed earlier. He hoped this would also explain his already dry, tanned skin.

"We came on the British ship from Alexandria," Stepan finally said.

"Alexandria," the officer replied.

Stepan had no idea if there were Russians in Alexandria.

"Then we are thankful to the British." Evidently the officer hadn't either.

"Yes sir."

"What unit are you with?"

The answer to this question had thankfully been conceived a long

180

time ago, it had been in the original plan. *"17th Aviation Mechanics Division, Sir."*

The stare continued. *"I recognise you from somewhere?"*

A dry swallow got caught in Daniil's throat, only just managing to clear it with a disguised cough. Igor looked towards Stepan, his heart pounding through his chest. They knew the next words were about to shape their future.

The Soviet officer turned. *"Sergeant."*

All four sighs were hidden.

"Yes Sir. We once met at Shaibah. You came with another officer to inspect some British spitfires. I must say I was impressed with the thorough way you examined the aircraft. Our comrades must only fly the best...Sir."

"Of course Sergeant, they must. I do not wish to know your opinion on the way I inspect aircraft. Now I have work to do."

The four Russians felt a heavy weight had been lifted as they continued their walk.

"Sergeant!" Came a loud shout from behind them.

Sergeant Tretyakov turned, *"Yes sir."*

"The Royal Navy compound is in that direction."

Nothing was said as the aircraftmen followed the boys through the labyrinth of hot dusty lanes. The only thought going through Ken Harker's mind at the time was that there wasn't a hope in hell they would find their way back out again. He had lost count of the number of lefts and rights they had taken, each lane looked the same to him anyhow.

The leading boy's arms were swinging like pendulums as he lengthened his strides as wide as his spindly legs could muster. All five men were having trouble keeping up with his pace, the dark patches of sweat on their shirts merging into one.

Out of sight, the young red headed lad was grabbed by his shoulder and spoken to by one of the older boys, with an obedient nod he quickly vanished down some narrow steps. It was only then that the pace slowed considerably, none was more relieved than the exhausted Corporal Lynch.

They emerged into what looked like a main thoroughfare, just as dry and dusty as the lanes but much wider with more people and carts indiscriminately passing one another in all directions. There were even a few servicemen, always a good sign thought young Harker, or did they arrive by the same means?

The lead boy abruptly stopped in his tracks and turned to face Morgan.

Holding out his hand he rubbed the small tips of his thumb and fingers together.

"I think the young guttersnipe needs remunerating," said Aerial.

"Nice ladies?" Shanks said. "Nice la...a...dies?"

The boy rubbed his fingers again.

"A bloody farthing each," Morgan said.

"Not on your life," Ken Harker said, "I didn't want to be here in the first place." He looked around, thinking they were probably entertaining the entire street with their shenanigans, nobody was taking any notice, probably an everyday occurrence.

Morgan, Aerial and Shanks rummaged around in their pockets, Morgan finding a tiny dirty brown coin.

"Dollar," the boy commanded, shaking his head furiously and looking annoyed.

"B..rit..ish, no dollar," Morgan said slowly and precisely.

The boys expression changed to one of irritation. "Dollar," he repeated.

Morgan jabbed his own chest. "Bloody British, we are English, no dollar, only King's money." He held the coin in front of the boy.

"Dollar," the boy spat out, looking as though he was about to kill someone.

"Look, bloody King George."

The boy calmed down "You like nice ladies?" he said with a smirk.

"You like a nice smack in the fu...?"

"Yes! We like but no dollars," interrupted Shanks.

"Here look, big coin, buy many things," Shanks said, taking out a whole penny. "This would buy you a portion of chips back home in Blighty."

Aerial closed his eyes and sniffed the air. "Mmm, fish and chips. I've forgotten what they smell like." Receiving a lungful of spices and donkey crap instead.

The boy held up two fingers.

Shanks shook his head and held up one finger.

The boy folded one finger down and pointed first at the penny, then the farthings.

"Where are nice ladies?" Shanks inquired, shrugging his shoulders.

The boy pulled him into the middle of the road and pointed to an ornate stone archway with a white sign hanging under an arch.

"Nice ladies?" Shanks repeated, pointing to the boy and walking his fingers in midair. Then rubbed the tips of his thumb and forefinger together, feeling proud he was giving the lad a bit of his own medicine. "Nice ladies, nice money."

The boy shook his head, "Papa," brushing a slap past his cheek.

"I think he's saying if his Papa finds him down there he'll get a good beating," said Ken Harker.

"More like his Papa doesn't want the boy to find *him* down there," added Aerial.

The pack of boys vanished into the lanes as soon as the coins dropped into their palms.

The five men strolled wearily along the bustling road, the heat, along with everything else was starting to take its toll.

Another spice shop, more rugs draped over open doors, chickens and small animals crammed into small cages like criminals. Their sounds of distress prompting Harker to glare at the proprietor with a look of disdain, quickly turning when an intimidating look was returned. The shopkeepers would rise and call out to the men, "Americans, nice rug." Others picked up a handful of spice and let it fall between their fingers, "For nice American wife."

They finally reached the arch and gazed forward. A short pathway lined with pot plants and an airy ceiling of tangled vine led up to a virtually square wooden door with large iron rivets uniformly embellishing it.

Five pairs of eyes looked up to the sign. 'HOUSE OF CHARMS.'

Whether Garage knew Baz was present in the room, Baz will never know. What he did know was as soon as Garage opened his eyes he inhaled a deep sharp breath, followed by a slow rattling sound, and that was the last breath the Welshman ever took.

All Baz could do was just stare at Garage's body, not believing what had just happened, waiting for some sign of life to return. Only none came. The more he looked the more he realised no one was there, only an absence, as if Garage had just shutdown.

A feeling of sadness began to overwhelm Baz, one he had never experienced before, as though the darkness and misery had stolen something from him. His muscles begun to jerk in tiny uncontrollable spasms, he began to tremble, he felt a hard chill pass through him.

Then the feeling went as fast as it had appeared, as though sucked out in one breath, replaced by a calming warmth, immediately followed by an intense feeling of euphoria.

What Baz did next, or why he did it, he would never be able to explain, although afterwards he thought about it many times. He gazed up to the ceiling, searching for that floating cloud of mist, that ray of light, that indication of the afterlife. Nothing. Baz returned his gaze towards Garage, he would stay an atheist after all.

"Goodbye Garage," he whispered.

Light suddenly flooded the small room, Baz swung round and saw a short man standing in the doorway, his prominent middle straining the buttons of his white coat, his dark chubby cheeks, darker than the rest of his skin, neatly combed, thick, jet black hair, not a strand out of place.

"Dr Mahendra Chopra," he said in an accent that Baz thought sounded different to Arabic. "The nurse said you were here." He held out his hand and studied Baz's eyes. "I am from India," he said with a sideways wobble of his head.

"Basil, Sergeant Albright." Gripping the doctors hand. "I believe my friend has died Doctor." Just like that, as though it was an everyday occurrence.

For a moment the doctor held his gaze on Baz, one eye, then the other, quickly followed by a glance towards Garage. He stepped over to where the body lay, feeling for a pulse he leant over and flicked the eyelashes. Then to Baz's surprise he took a teaspoon from his coat and ran it up the sole of Garage's foot, his expression remaining deadpan throughout. The doctor waited.

"Your apotheosis seems correct Sergeant. It appears your friend has indeed departed this world. I am very sorry." Studying Baz for a reaction, he continued. "To be honest with you Sergeant we have been expecting it for a while. We knew the poison had started to attack some of his organs. The last few days he became disorientated. I am afraid the young man's dreams had become his reality." The doctor waited again. "Your friend was very strong though, he fought very hard, to be honest I am surprised he survived this long."

"I saw him die."

After a short pause. "Then it is good you were with him. I believe he was waiting for you Sergeant. He needed to say goodbye, it is not the first time I have seen this happen, it will not be the last either. He will be with *your* God now."

Baz's reply was immediate, "I have no God Doctor."

"You are not a Christian Sergeant? You do not believe your friend's soul is with his God?"

"No Doctor. If anything I believe the church robs people of their souls." Baz waited for a response. Nothing. "Whatever a soul is?" As if to ask, do you know?

"You were brought up a Christian, Sergeant?"

"I wasn't brought up as anything."

"But you were brought up in a Christian society?"

"That doesn't make me a Christian."

"In a Hindu society we are all Hindus."

"But would you still be a Hindu in a Christian society?"

"You do not have a God Sergeant?" the doctor's large lips stretching into a grin. "There are many to choose from."

"Too many Doctor, ask anyone who God is and you'll get a different answer every time."

"We are lucky, us Hindus have several Gods Sergeant. In a way it makes it easy for us, every answer will be correct." Another head wobble. "Mr Bryce, was he a good man?"

"Yes doctor, he was."

"In my religion we say he had good karma."

"He was a good rugby player."

The doctor smiled, "In my religion..."

"Your religion?"

"I am a Hindu. In my religion we believe what you do in this life will be carried with you into the next, we call it karma. We believe when you die you discard your body like old clothes, then you are reincarnated into a new body as if you are wearing new ones. We call it Samsara." The doctor looked Baz up and down. "Sometimes it is worth changing your clothes, even in *this* lifetime Sergeant."

"Then what happens when you have enough Karma?"

"Then you become one with God, Sergeant." The doctor paused in thought. "We are all born so not to be born."

"Then working here in this hospital, is that part of your karma?"

"Of course, in Hinduism, as in *all* religions, you have to work hard to go to heaven Sergeant." Baz reflected on his own life and wondered if he had done enough good. He hadn't done much bad, he thought. The doctor continued, "If you are good in this life then you will be rewarded in the next."

"But you are keeping people in this world Doctor, stopping them from, as *you* say, being rewarded in the next, becoming one with *your* God."

Doctor Chopra's face lit up as he grinned, the same way his father used to smile at him. "No Sergeant, it is their choice which path they take, I am just giving them a longer opportunity to choose the correct one."

"Then *you* must be getting very close to your God, Doctor."

"I have a very long way to go Sergeant." The doctor stared down at Garage. "I believe your friend waited for you, he knew he would return. For a Hindu, death is not a great calamity, it is but only a natural progression."

"What will return Doctor? Is it...?"

"The soul, Sergeant?"

Baz lifted his eyebrows and nodded in anticipation.

"I do not know."

"Oh, then how do you know there is a soul Doctor?"

"If I am wrong Sergeant, then so are millions of others."

"But if you are right, if you say there is one, why can't you just tell me what it is?"

"All I can say is that it is the *you*, it is the *self* Sergeant. It exists beyond our senses, far from our conscious mind. How could I describe what it is with my meagre thoughts, my humble words." His sentence tailed away as he turned to look behind him, "Please wait Sergeant," he said as he vanished out of the room.

After a minute the doctor returned with two nurses wearing blue headscarfs and full length white smocks.

"Let us step outside, the nurses will prepare your friend."

"Prepare?" Baz asked.

"You will want to take Mr Bryce with you Sergeant?"

Sergeant Tretyakov had no answer to, *"The RAF compound is in that direction."* As much as he tried, in the fraction of a second he had to think of one, none would come.

Stepan, Igor and Daniil, although stopped, remained looking in the direction they were walking. In the distance was a tight curve in the river where they could see the tips of fishing boat masts bobbing and swaying above the rooftops. How close they seemed.

Sergeant Tretyakov marched towards the Soviet officer and saluted once again. He could feel the sweat trickling down his cheeks and into the hair under his shirt, he just hoped the officer put it wholly down to the heat. The Russian Sergeant took out a neatly folded handkerchief and nervously wiped under his chin, leaving small specks of white fabric caught in his stubble.

Sergeant Tretyakov thought fast. *"The RAF truck won't be leaving for two hours Sir, we were going to walk back through town, keep in the shade Sir, this heat is stifling."*

"Very wise Sergeant."

"Thank you Sir," Sergeant Tretyakov said, turning and feeling pleased with himself, if not relieved.

"There is one thing bothering me Sergeant."

Sergeant Tretyakov stopped on the turn, his fingers gripping tightly onto a lit match hovering in front of a cigarette. The words felt as though they had stabbed him in the back.

"Corporal." He said abruptly. Turning his attention towards Stepan. *"17th Aviation Mechanics Division, Corporal?"*

Sergeant Tretyakov, stared at his cousin's face, willing him to say something, anything, as long as it made sense and ended with Sir. He yelped as the flame reached his fingertips.

"And you say you arrived on the British ship from Alexandria?"

Again, Stepan's lips remained sealed.

A crate clattered at the bottom of the ship's hold, followed by an echoing boom.

"There are no Soviet Aviation Divisions in Alexandria Corporal."

Sergeant Tretyakov always took pride in his composure when faced with an awkward situation, only this was unknown territory. His shirt had become completely soaked from the constant sweat, his heart sped up until he could feel it pounding in his chest, he swallowed, tasting vomit. This was it, he thought, this was the end of the road for them.

Stepan's poise slackened. *"You are very astute. We were never in Alexandria and we did not arrive on the British ship,"* he said in such a confident manner it had Sergeant Tretyakov thinking he might even know what he was doing. *"I am in fact a pilot and my colleague over there, the tall one, he is a doctor."*

Stepan studied the officer's reaction. *"And the short one, well, he happens to be Alexander Novikov's son."*

Novikov! The Chief Air Marshal's son, thought Daniil. Has he even got a son?!

Have you gone mad?! thought Sergeant Tretyakov.

I'm impressed, thought Igor.

Stepan continued. *"We flew in from Mahhad in a Lisonuv, our cargo was secret, the only people who know of this, including the four of us, is now yourself."*

"Your cargo, Corporal?"

"The Air Marshal's son," Stepan said in a haughty manner.

Just shoot us now, thought Sergeant Tretyakov.

The Soviet officer took a long glare at Stepan, soon turning his attention towards Daniil.

"We are under strict orders not to tell anyone. In truth, you should not know either but you put me in a position with no way out. You must never repeat what I have just said." Stepan said deflecting the officer's examination away from Daniil.

"You do not give me orders! Corp..."

"Major, Lieutenant."

The Soviet officer's obvious displeasure increased.

"And the doct...?"

"Lieutenant, Lieutenant."

"And the Chief Air Marshal's son?"

"He is the Chief Air Marshal's son."

The Soviet officer stood rigid.

Stepan continued, *"The boy needs medical care, let us say he has not got a strong constitution. Look at him! He would not last long in combat Lieutenant. Our great Chief Air Marshal arranged for him to be posted to Shaibah, out of the way, where no one would know where he was, Lieutenant."* Stepan glared at the officer, *"No one!"*

The Soviet Officer looked at Stepan then Daniil, then Igor, then Sergeant Tretyakov, then back to Stepan again.

A loud snap followed by an even louder crash resounded from the ship's front hold.

"You can ask me about flying an aircraft, you can ask the doctor about medicine, you can ask the boy about being the Chief Air Marshall's son. That is the only proof I have, Lieutenant," said Stepan.

Ask me about flying, thought Stepan.

Ask me about medicine, thought Igor.

What the fuck do I know about Alexander Novikov, thought Daniil?

The seconds ticked by.

Angry shouts came from the ship's deck.

Stepan continued. *"If the boy's father were to find out someone else knew about his whereabouts, well, that someone could get a posting to the..."*

"Sir," shouted a sailor leaning over the ships railing, waving his cap. *"It's a wing Sir."*

The Soviet officer threw a stony glare towards Stepan, turned, strode up the walkway and disappeared into the ship's hull.

Sergeant Tretyakov and Stepan looked long and hard at each other.

A strong, square, wooden door with regimented rows of large metal studs stood at the end of the shadow dappled pathway. Morgan was the first under the arch, followed by Shanks and Aerial. Young Harker and Corporal Lynch waited under the curved stone structure.

Morgan faced the door, clenched his hands but kept them firmly by his side.

"Go on then," Shanks said excitedly.

"Are we sure about..."

Before he could finish, Shanks's arm had cast itself around Morgan and rapped his knuckles on the door. A short tentative wait was quickly followed by a scraping noise and a loud thud. The door swung open, a black skinned Arab with two bloodshot eyes beamed a well practised gummy smile of dark gaps and brown protruding teeth. The man who had the appearance of being a hundred years old, although it was difficult to tell the age of any local over the age of fifty, was wearing an ankle length dark woollen smock and an old frayed suit jacket several sizes too small, only the tightness of its sleeves stopped them from sliding above his elbows. A thick black band circled a red and white headscarf. The Arab stepped back, bowed slightly and indicated with a low wave of his flat leathery hand to enter into the space behind him.

The men were immediately captivated by their surroundings as they stepped in, each looking around in awe, it was a sight that was in complete contrast to anything they had seen before, or thought could ever exist in this town. They had entered a magnificent courtyard with a floor covered in glossy grey speckled tiles and beautiful rugs of vibrant colours. In its centre was an ornate fountain, the soothing sound of water trickled into a small, round pool surrounded by a low wall decorated with symmetric mosaic patterns, a scattering of rose petals floated on top of the water. Nine archways identical to the entrance led to narrow walkways running parallel along the walls. In front of their pillars were large, green leafed plants nestled inside huge colourful pots.

"It's a bloody palace," said Morgan.

"It's wonderful," agreed Aerial. Then with a whisper, "Listen." They stood in silence.

"I can't hear a bloody thing," said Morgan.

"Exactly."

"The war has gone," said Harker, dreamily.

"Everything has gone," said Aerial.

"They must be up there," said Shanks breaking through the tranquility.

"What?"

"The women, they must be up there," nodding towards a rising stairway behind one of the arches.

"You'll soon find out," said Corporal Lynch spotting a small man dressed in a full length pristine white tunic with a neatly trimmed black goatee and a crisp white head scarf wrapped round his head. His hands, heavy with large gold rings, were held out in front, clutching a round silver tray, on top were six small glasses and a tall ornate teapot with a pointed lid and a long spout like a striking cobra.

"Americans?" the man said through his black goatee.

"Why does every fucker?..."

"We are British," interrupted Aerial.

"Ah, *Great* British Empire," the man rolled the words and spoke in such a strong accent they only just managed to understand him, although they were made to feel at ease by his soft tone. "Tea?" he said, indicating for the men to sit at a circular mosaic table. They watched in admiration as he raised the teapot high above each glass and lowered it again, the shaft of liquid stretching and shortening like an elastic band. By the time he had finished, not one drop was spilt and every glass had the exact same amount of green mint tea. They all took a much needed refreshing sip. When I say all, exclude Corporal Lynch, he just held the glass against his lips, when the Arab's eyes turned on him, he took a pretend swallow. Corporal Lynch was a coffee man anyhow, when he wasn't a beer man, but that wasn't the only reason for him not drinking.

"Where are the women?" mumbled Shanks through a closed mouth.

Aerial shrugged and Morgan took another glug of tea.

The man held up his hand and clicked his fingers.

"At bloody last," said Morgan, feeling surprisingly carefree.

"Come to Papa," said Shanks, melodically.

Anticipating a line of attractive women parading themselves in front of them, all five men scanned the courtyard. The only movement was the old Arab scurrying over with another silver tray, with the same bow and smirk as before he carefully placed it in the middle of the table. The Arab removed a blue cloth, displaying a mountain of gold bangles and chains, all with intricate carvings, many with deep red or turquoise coloured stones. He looked at the RAF men as though they were privileged to be feasting their eyes on such beauty.

"I expect he wants us to buy one of these first," said Aerial.

"He's having a bloody laugh," said Morgan.

"These are going to cost more than a penny," said Shanks.

Aerial pointed at a bracelet. "I bet that large green stone..."

"Red," interrupted Shanks.

"Red," Aerial said softly, sitting back in his chair.

Ken Harker's attention was drawn to two small, dark eyes peering round one of the pillars, the same image he remembered from back in the square. As the old Arab passed he gestured with a swift upward swish of his hand. The young red-headed boy sprung out into the open and for a few seconds faced young Harker with a sheepish grin, then soon scampered through a door at the back of the courtyard.

Morgan looked into the man's eyes. "Where are the women?" he said slowly.

"Yes! Woman, wives, nice gold," the man said widening his eyes and nodding vigorously.

"No! Women, where are the women?"

"Yes woman," the Arab repeated, filling up their glasses with more tea.

"Bloody women," said Morgan, standing up and thrusting his groin forward.

"Yes, for wife, very nice."

At the same time Morgan was indulging in this deep meaningful conversation, young Harker had leant over and whispered in Aerial's ear.

"No! We *want* very nice women, you have very nice women here?" said Shanks with a friendly smile, hoping a change of tack might help.

"Yes! Very nice for wife," the man said picking up a bangle.

"Wom..."

"I think we have been led on a wild goose chase gentlemen. Young Ken here has smelt a rat. That small red-headed boy we followed earlier, well, he saw the little scoundrel over there," Aerial said, nodding towards the pillar. "They're all in cahoots, if there are any women in this place, then I'm an Arab's camel."

"Why the little fucking..."

"We'll just take our leave now," Aerial interrupted, rising from his chair, feeling slightly giddy. "Thank you kindly for the tea."

The other men also rose from their chairs.

"Very nice gold, you buy, very nice, you wait," the man said snatching another bangle, his voice mutating into a sinister growl.

It was only when Corporal Lynch leant over the table and stared long and hard into the man's eyes did the Arab calm down slightly.

"Nice rugs, American wife like."

"We are fucking Brit..."

"We are going now," was all the Corporal said, then with a look that could cut through rock he glared at the Arab for a good ten seconds, then began walking towards the door.

"No! Not out." The man animated wildly, then ushered the men towards the back door. "Out," he said thrusting his finger forward.

Dr Chopra had explained to Baz that if Garage's body were to remain in the hospital he would have to be buried quickly and without a religious or military ceremony. Although he did add that a burial in the Islamic tradition could be arranged, but thought it not appropriate.

"Your friend is probably from one of your western faiths Sergeant. Christian? Anglican? A Jew maybe?"

"Maybe he didn't have a faith Doctor."

"Or of the Catholic persuasion?"

"Maybe he was an atheist?"

"He was certainly not a Hindu Sergeant."

"I think rugby was more his religion Doctor."

"Or Muslim, definitely not Muslim."

"Maybe he never went to church. Some people have no need for religion, they are just good anyway. In fact, I think it's religion that turns people bad. No disrespect Doctor."

"None taken Sergeant, but all religions have their merit."

"Mostly holidays Doctor."

"Ah yes," Dr Chopra returned the smile. "What is this religion called rugby Sergeant?"

"It's a sport."

"A sport is a religion?"

"Only in Wales Doctor."

"Ah."

Baz didn't have to think about what to do next, the answer was black and white, religion or no religion, Garage's body would have to be taken back to Shaibah.

"I'll take him with me Doctor."

"Good, now I have to see to the living. I'll send some orderlies. Goodbye Sergeant and may your God go with you," the doctor said, his grin accompanying a longer than normal stare.

"I have no...never mind. Thank you Doctor."

Two nurses entered the room soon after the doctor had departed. Baz wondered if it was fitting that they should be laughing. It was probably all in a day's work to them. You would certainly need a sense of humour working here, he thought.

For the second time that day, Baz stepped back into the dimly lit room. The blue sheet had been removed and Garage was laying on top of the bed wearing his RAF desert shirt and shorts. They had even put his socks and boots on him, which Baz thought appropriate because of the abuse he got whenever he removed them. He also looked more at peace in death than at any time when he was alive.

Baz sat back in the chair, stared at Garage and wondered what it was that gave a person life, what was taken away at death.

The four Russians made a token diversion amongst the corrugated rooftop buildings. After heading inland for a short while, they diverted back to the river, in the direction where the port had ceased to be a port. A place where the date palms had become more numerous, appearing like a firework display of exploding leaves. They passed the occasional reed built house belonging to a marsh Arab family, their dark inquiring eyes following their every move. Even the dry tan colour they had become so accustomed to had transformed into a lush green, for the first time in a long while the Russians could feel soft grass under foot.

It wasn't until they stepped out from under the shade and stood facing the river leisurely drifting past, Igor said what he had been thinking ever since leaving the port. *"There is no turning back now. What if Novikov hasn't got a son? The first thing the Soviet Officer will do is come to Shaibah looking for us and they will only find you Mikhail."*

Sergeant Tretyakov looked pensive, the same thought had also crossed his mind, only he never mentioned it.

"He has got a son," Stepan said, looking towards the water.

Only ten feet away, a small narrow boat with two marsh Arabs drifted quietly by. The two occupants giving the Russians such a long stare it left them feeling nervous and exposed.

"Believe me, I know all about Alexandria Novikov," Stepan said, pointing to a white stone building with an onion shaped dome half a mile down river. *"There it is. That is where they'll meet us. We had better get back under the trees."*

Plan B was back on track.

They returned to the shelter of the palms and advanced a couple more steps when Stepan stopped, turned and looked at his cousin. By his sombre expression Sergeant Tretyakov knew what he was about to say.

"We owe you our lives Mikhail."

"You owe me nothing Stepan."

Stepan gripped his cousin's shoulders and stared into his eyes. *"We owe you our lives Mikhail. You have done more than we could ever ask for, we cannot ask you to do any more."*

"I will go to the boat..."

"No, this as far as you go Mikhail. You must return to Sergeant Albright, go back to Shaibah. There is nothing more you can do for us. Plan B remember." He squeezed his cousin's shoulders, *"We will be fine. You will be fine."*

Sergeant Tretyakov looked at Igor and Daniil.

"We have my Papa, Uncle, he will get us there."

Igor nodded with a reassuring smile.

"Mikhail, listen to me, Novikov, he has a son around Daniil's age, he is missing. I saw that look on your face when Igor mentioned the Soviet Officer," Stepan said.

"Pawn to king five?"

Stepan smiled, *"Pawn to king five."*

"There are many more moves to make Stepan."

"I know, and we have yet to reach the middle game," Stepan's smile widened. *"The war will be over soon, then we will all see each other again."*

Stepan finally wrapped his arms around his cousin.

"Soon, our family will be complete again?" Sergeant Tretyakov said quietly into Stepan's ear. They released their grip and the Russian

Sergeant held on to Stepans's face. *"Good luck cousin,"* then kissed both his cheeks.

Sergeant Tretyakov walked over to Daniil and gave him a firm embrace. *"You watch your father's back."*

"I will," Daniil said, his eyes glassing over. *"Thank you Uncle, for everything."*

Sergeant Tretyakov held out his hand in front of Igor. *"Doctor,"* is all he said, tightening his hold.

"Sergeant," Igor replied.

————————

Morgan had had a few heated words with the Arab about having to leave through the back door, but soon relinquished when he could see the demonstration of hatred towards him had passed all reasoning. The others just wanted to get out, whatever door they were shown.

"Fucking slimeball," were Morgan's departing words.

As they stepped out from the coolness of the courtyard, their senses were woken once again by the smells and noises of yet another narrow dusty lane.

"Left or right?" said Shanks.

Aerial studied the sky, or what he could see of it through the narrow gap the high mud walls allowed. "Left," shrugging his shoulders.

"That Arab could kill, did you see that face, he's going to bloody kill someone one day," Morgan complained. "Sending us through the fucking back door. We are members of the Royal Air Force, not bloody tradesmen."

A small handcart trundled down the lane towards them, piled high with bulging sacks, it only missed the aircraftmen by inches, the boy pushing it rendered completely blind by a sack just inches from his face.

Raised voices of men in dispute could be heard coming from a small opening behind them. In truth, all conversations in Arabic sound like they are in some kind of heated argument. A fragrant, musky smell wafted past their heads as a group of six locals, all men, four sitting, two standing, were engulfed in a cloud of smoke. Their babbling swiftly faded as they spotted the aircraftmen's faces staring down at them. One big, stony faced man with an intense, no-nonsense manner took a step forward and slammed the shutter, nearly flattening Morgan's nose. "Are all fucking Arabs trying to kill me?" he said, irritably.

The aircraftmen continued along the lane.

More Arabs with dry, weather beaten faces, stared unnervingly at the men. Some had their heads enclosed in headscarfs, dark menacing eyes peering at them through the narrowest of slits. Stuffed into their waistbands were long curved daggers.

"Keep your eyes forward, do not make eye contact," Corporal Lynch said.

A high pitched voice sounding more like a plate cracking, sliced through the air. "Americans," a woman of indeterminable age stood in front of an open door as wide as she was tall. Under a long dark tunic her sagging breasts dropped so low they virtually overhung her prominent belly. A shout from above, never to see fifty again, a dark sunken skull with a toothless grin and long boney fingers had leant out of a first floor window. "Hey Americans, you like nice girl?"

A stunned silence was followed by a slow chuckle that soon erupted into laughter.

Wearing a long grey cloak with his face hidden inside a pointed hood, a young Arab passed silently behind them, both hands clenched behind his back, a determined purpose in his step. He turned and vanished through a doorway.

The laughter died down to chuckles and smiles. "We'll go that way," Corporal Lynch said, taking the lead for the first time. Young Harker brought up the rear.

Corporal Lynch had a gut feeling that all was not how it seemed, it had become far too quiet, there were less people around. The corporal's gut was rarely wrong, it had had a lifetime of being rarely wrong, especially in a town where he had yet to see anything that appeared to be as it should.

"Where the bloody hell has everyone gone?" inquired Morgan.

"Prayer," Corporal Lynch said, then muttered, "I hope."

All of a sudden someone let out an air piercing cry followed by a stifled "Help me."

The men spun round and were amazed to see young Harker leaning back. Only this time there was something different about him, apart from the petrified expression adorning his face, he had two heads, one

197

was his, that was true, the other belonged to the grey hooded Arab, his face implanted on the aircraftman's left shoulder. But out of the two, it was only Harker who had a dagger held against his throat.

Another Arab appeared behind them, his head completely concealed with a black scarf, his eyes barely visible. Then another, a black man with a round face, African looking, no headscarf, just a layer of tight black matted hair discoloured by a dusting of sand, his fingers wrapped around the handle of his dagger still tucked into a scabbard. Out of sight from the men, an older Arab, smarter and cleaner looking with dark eyes hidden under arches of thick eyebrows stepped out of a doorway.

The bulging eyes of Young Harker had crossed inward, staring down his nose, trying to catch sight of the cold hard object held against his throat.

"Dollars," the young Arab hissed.

A stunned silence. "We are British, no dollars," Aerial finally said through a faltering voice.

"Look, British," said Shanks, stretching out his arm and shaking a note.

The black Arab reached out and snatched Shank's ten shilling note, snarled some words in Arabic, screwed it up and stuffed it into his tunic. More angry words were exchanged in Arabic. Ken Harker could feel the grip tighten round a tuft of his hair, his head was yanked further back, exposing more of his throat to the sharp edge. He shut his eyes and waited for the sharp stroke of the cold blade to slice into his neck. Ken Harker thought of his Emma, he thought about the life he would have had, then began blubbering like a small child.

"Weapons, dollars, give."

Harker knew the men had no weapons, he also knew they didn't have any dollars, what he didn't know though, was what it was like to have all the blood drain from his body.

Suddenly, all feeling from the blade had gone, in one hazy moment he decided death was not as painful as expected, in truth, it was surprisingly painless. It was death though, he knew this because all feeling went, even the agony from having his hair nearly yanked out.

He opened his eyes and realised the world he lived in before was the same as the one after death, not only the same but he found he had a whole new euphoric outlook on it. Even his colleagues, who had annoyed him so much over the afternoon, seemed slightly more affable.

But it was what Ken Harker saw next.

The first Aerial, Shanks and Morgan knew of something being different was when the Arab's expressions changed from anger to apprehension, all three began to look agitated. The African took a tentative step back, released the hold on his scabbard and let his hands fall to his sides.

The RAF men could clearly see the pupils of the Arab's eyes fixed towards one point behind them. It was only when they looked over their shoulders they saw the white knuckles of Corporal Lynch stretched out in front of him, then the grey metal barrel poking out from his hand.

Everyone present heard the faint click of the hammer being pulled back.

The hooded Arab attached to young Harker spat out a string of angry words, his whole body became tense, the grip on the knife tightened.

"Let the boy go," Corporal Lynch said, slowly and precisely.

The headscarf, staring down the barrel of the pistol, shouted something, turned his head, shouted the same words, turned his head back, waited, shouted again, then quickly ran off. Corporal Lynch aimed the pistol towards the African.

"Let the boy go," Corporal Lynch repeated. Nothing. "Let the boy go!" he shouted, stretching his arm out further, his eyes had become round, large and fierce. Corporal Lynch had the look of someone that was about to fire a gun.

"I'll say it one more time. Let the...."

A voice drifted from the other side of the road, calculated words, calmly spoken. The older Arab slowly turned with a look of distaste and disappeared into a doorway.

Harker was released and the dagger removed from his throat. The hood spat out some words and took two steps back, then walked away with the same purposeful stride he arrived with. The black African followed.

Corporal Lynch lowered the gun. "Let's get out of here."

"Which way Corp?" Aerial's gaze following the pistol being stuffed into the corporal's shorts.

Ken Harker was sobbing uncontrollably "I'm alive," he mumbled to himself.

"Come on young Kenneth, we've got to go," said Aerial.

Ken Harker's knees buckled under him. "I can't walk." Morgan grabbed hold of him and slung a lifeless arm around his shoulder. "Shanks! Grab the other arm. Quick."

"ALLAHU AKBAR." The sound of a man's voice echoed over the rooftops.

"What the bloody hell was that?" Morgan said, studying the sky.

"ALLAHU AKBAR ALLAHU AKBAR."

"God," said Ken Harker.

"ALLAHU AKBAR ASHHADU AN LA ILAHA ILLA ALLAH...ASHHADU AN LA ILAHA ILLA ALLAH."

"Close enough young Kenneth. That is our way out of here."

"ASHADU ANNA MUHAMMADAN RASOOL ALLAH ASHADU ANNA MUHAMMADAN RASOOL ALLAH."

"It's the call to prayer."

"HAYYA 'ALA-S-SALAH."

"It's from the minaret."

"HAYYA 'ALA-S-SALAH."

"The one the fucking guard told us about."

"HAYYA 'ALA-L-FALAH...HAYYA 'ALA-L-FALAH."

"It's coming from that way."

"ALLAHU AKBAR ALLAHU AKBAR."

————————

Baz's head jolted up as he was woken by an orderly walking backwards into the room, he was carrying one end of a long wooden box still smelling of freshly cut wood. Another orderly soon appeared holding the opposite end.

"I had it made especially Sergeant," Dr Chopra said as he followed them in. "He was a big man Sergeant."

"You shouldn't have gone to all that trouble Doctor," Baz said, through bleary eyes.

"What else would you suggest Sergeant? Bind your friend in bandages like an Egyptian mummy."

"Sorry Doctor, thank you, I wasn't thinking. How long have I been asleep?"

The doctor held his gaze. "We are all asleep Sergeant."

"Well at least I can wake up Doctor," Baz said, looking down at Garage's icy grey face.

Holding the four corners of the sheet the two orderlies lifted Garage into the box. As in Islamic tradition, the sheet was wrapped around his body leaving his face clear of any material, the lid was placed back on top of the box and nailed into place. Baz was impressed by the care and reverence given at every stage.

"You may meet him again Sergeant."

"How will I know Doctor?"

"You won't Sergeant and he might be a she."

"If no one has ever known meeting someone from, well, a past life, then how do you know I might meet him *or her*?"

"It is my faith Sergeant."

"It is that word faith again Doctor. Maybe it is more hope than faith, don't you ever question your faith?"

"How can I question something, that has only one answer. Does it matter that he, or she, does not recognise you, or you recognise them? Is that not just to satisfy a desire within you."

Baz smiled. "My father used to say the best way to get something is not to want it." Lowering his eyebrows he quickly added. "Or was it the best way not to get something is to want it."

The doctor smiled with Baz. "Then your father is a wise man Sergeant." The head wobble becoming even more pronounced.

"*Was* Doctor?"

"Then he will have taken his wisdom with him." He waited a second before continuing. "To want to meet your friend again has no importance whatsoever. To know in another life, maybe thousands of lives, or even thousands upon thousands of lives, your friend will become one with God as sure as a raindrop becomes one with the sea, *that* is all we need to know Sergeant."

"My father also said, the closer to faith you are, the further from the truth you will be."

"If you have faith then anything is possible?"

"Even that your religion may be a lie Doctor?

"If you only *think*, then the world will remain just the world. If you have faith then you will see beyond the world Sergeant. I can see you

201

need proof for faith to become the truth Sergeant. As a Hindu I have faith for *it* to become the truth. It is believing your faith to be the truth, that is the real faith."

"You remind me of my father," Baz said. "I didn't understand him either."

"Maybe I am closer to God than I thought Sergeant. Maybe your father is closer to God than *you* thought."

Baz paused for a moment, "Have you ever felt a cold wind when someone has died Doctor?"

"Maybe Sergeant, why?"

Baz shook his head, "No reason Doctor."

The busy main street running parallel with the port was named Dinar Street. Sergeant Tretyakov knew there would be more servicemen in the area, he also knew Dinar Street would return him safely back to the RAF compound. Stepan had put it as route B, in plan B. The first and quicker choice would have been to return by the port, but after their encounter with the Soviet officer that had become too risky. Another alternative was the warren of narrow lanes south of Dinar Street but these were notorious for robbers and skirmishes with feuding tribes. Wandering into unknown territory in Al Basrah was always best avoided.

Halfway along Dinar Street, Sergeant Tretyakov stopped at the corner of a busy junction, a place thronged with market stalls and traders selling their wares from the tops of carts or rugs laid out on the dusty ground.

The Russian sergeant waited for a cart laden with large crates to trundle by. Then as he glanced up the lane he caught sight of the RAF aircraftmen.

The corporal was leading the way and pointing upwards in mid-stride, the others following him were also looking up. Between the two other men was the young aircraftman with his arms draped over their shoulders, his legs tottering as if they had a life of their own. The fifth, taller man, brought up the rear, appearing nervous, turning his head on several occasions to glance behind him.

The top of the minaret came into view just as the RAF group reached the centre of a small square. Corporal Lynch had pointed upward and shouted back to the men. The call to prayer ended some time ago and it was a relief to see the minaret looming ahead of them.

The corporal stopped and turned to young Harker. "Come on lad, you can walk by yourself now." He then started undoing the lower buttons on his shirt. "Look lad." Between his fingertips was a long undefined shaped scar. "The shrapnel is still in there," he said, prodding the tight patch of skin. "Go on feel it."

Young Harker poked his finger into the corporal's flaccid gut, his intrusion halted by a hard object.

"First world war it was, a bomb exploded too close for comfort and blew me into a crater. Two nights I spent in the cold and wet, one more night and I would be dead. Listen lad, I had to walk with half my guts hanging out, over two hundred yards back to the trenches, *and* in the middle of no man's land." The Corporal's expression softened, "If I can do that..."

"Yes Sir," Harker said, finding just enough strength to lift his hand up to his forehead.

"Don't salute me and don't call me sir. I'm a corporal, not one of them officers. Have some water lad and let's get the fuck out of here. I've had enough of this God forsaken place."

———————

Baz sat back down on the chair and leant forward with his elbows resting on his knees. "Maybe I'm missing something Garage," he said. "The doctor is an intelligent man." He gazed down at the coffin and paused in thought. "We've made this a bad world Garage, you're probably better off out of it anyway." He then fell silent.

Twenty minutes had passed when the door slid open and a shadow crept over the makeshift coffin.

A gentle hand was placed on his shoulder. "Your friend Bazil. He dead?"

For several seconds Baz did not reply. "How did Plan B go Mikhail?" he said quietly, not taking his gaze off the coffin.

"Good, no good, good, no good, good," he paused and stared at the box, "No good."

"Good, that's good Mikhail." Baz finally turned to look up at the Russian sergeant. "He died earlier today Mikhail. Where are the others?"

"They truck."

"All in one piece?"

"Sorry Bazil I do not under?..."

"No one hurt Mikhail, they have all their arms and legs?"

"Ah. One piece, I understand. They are one piece."

"Good." Baz quickly rose to his feet. "Let's go and see them."

The two men began the trek down the corridor. For Baz, the walk felt longer than before, his footsteps sounded louder, probably because the constant buzz of talking had diminished.

For the first time in what seemed ages, Baz stepped outside into the bright light of day and was glad to see the five RAF aircraftmen skulking around the truck, even if they did look drained. Baz put that down to the heat.

"How is Garage Sarge?" said Aerial.

"He's dead." Baz replied coldly then turned his attention towards the young aircraftman. "Are you alright Harker? Has someone stolen your blood?"

"It's the bloody heat Sarge. Fucking youngsters," said Morgan rolling his eyes.

"Garage is dead?"

"Give Harker some water Corp."

"You said Garage is..."

"You heard the Sarge! Drink Harker." The corporal shoved a water bottle under the young aircraftman's nose.

"Stay with the truck Corp, you'd better stay as well Harker. Let's go and get Garage."

They returned along the corridor, finally stopping outside the room. He pushed open the door and there on the floor lay the wooden box, incandescent from a shaft of light coming through the window. Sergeant Tretyakov and Baz stood back, allowing the three men to peer into the room.

"Garage is in there?" Shanks said.

"No he's having a fucking cup of..." Morgan began.

"Well his body is Shanks. According to Dr Chopra, Garage is somewhere else," Baz said flippantly.

"Doctor who?"

"It's not important."

"He's probably up there scrambling around on some waterlogged pitch, bashing the hell out of some opponent." In a strange way Baz liked Morgan's remark, especially as he refrained from his usual colourful terminology. He hoped it was intentional anyhow. "Let's hope he's gone to rugby heaven then, right Sarge?"

"Right Morgan."

Aerial and Shanks lifted the rear of the makeshift coffin, Morgan and Sergeant Tretyakov took the front, Baz walked ahead.

As they passed through the ward and into the corridor, Baz was hoping to see Dr Chopra one more time, he felt their conversation hadn't yet been concluded, he would have liked the doctor to say one more sentence, one that would answer everything.

The old man had returned to his same spot by the window. Stopping the procession he lifted his stick in front of Baz's chest and beckoned for him to come closer, Baz bent down until he could feel the stale breath on his face.

"American?" the old man said.

Baz grinned, "No, British."

"Dollar?" the old man said, rubbing his thumb against the leathery tips of his fingers.

"No, British. Pounds and shillings."

"You give?"

"What! I have none."

"You like nice rugs?"

"What?"

"Pots"

"No."

"Nice ladies?"

"No!" Baz said, reeling back and frowning. The old man sat back, rested both hands on top of the stick and exposed his gummy smile.

The funeral procession arrived back at the truck. Corporal Lynch had suggested that if Baz wasn't going to sit in the front cabin, then it would be only fair to have one of the others. "Not Morgan," he added strongly. Harker was the obvious choice, given his condition.

The truck departed the hospital and made a sharp left turn on to the south west desert road. The wind began to stir as it always did at that time of day, Baz said he could set his watch by it, he was told it had something to do with the build up of ground heat and being so close to the sea. Sheets of sand skimmed across the ground, appearing as though the actual land was moving. Revolving spirals of dirt would quickly rise up out of nowhere, glide aimlessly around for a couple of yards then disappear as fast as they had surfaced, 'dust devils' the men called them.

Morgan lit a cigarette, sat back on the bench and put his feet on the coffin.

"You're a cold bastard Morgan," Shanks said. "At least show some respect, the poor lad isn't even cold yet."

"I've had to put up with his bloody feet for God knows how long, about time I got my own back," Morgan replied.

Like a drunken jaywalker, a dust devil had crossed in front of the truck, causing the Corporal to veer violently and flinging the men to one side, everyone held on tightly.

Baz sat on the same bench as Sergeant Tretyakov; Shanks, Morgan and Aerial were opposite, their glare firmly fixed on a gap in the rear tarpaulin, occasionally catching sight of a swirl of sand passing by like a flying bed sheet.

With the road slowly disappearing under a layer of sand the only way Corporal Lynch knew which direction he was heading was by the faint outline stretching away in the distance. His concentration had to be at its highest, one blink could result in the road being lost forever.

Ken Harker's death by dagger was put to one side by the immediate problem of the vanishing track. Bent forward with his nose inches from the windscreen he started yelling instructions. "Too close on my side! Move right, more right, no left, more left!"

The corporal took notice of the young aircraftman on only two occasions. The first was when the road disappeared altogether and he had little choice, the second, not long after the first, was when young Harker yelled, "HORRRRSE!" at the top of his voice.

It was instant, there was not even time to realise what was happening. Aerial, Shanks and Morgan were thrown head first over the coffin. Shanks landed in a corner at the back of the truck, managing to grab onto the metal framework, saving himself from being flung out altogether.

Morgan had a softer landing, thanks to Sergeant Tretyakov. Unfortunately the Russian sergeant could do nothing about the flying aircraftman head-butting him in a place where, given the choice, he would have preferred not to have been head butted.

Aerial had tripped over the makeshift coffin and fell like a plank of wood, smashing his face on the opposite bench and biting deep into his tongue. As he was lying on the floor he felt as though someone had stabbed him through his wrist, then the realisation that he couldn't move his hand.

Baz came off the lightest. The violent sideways swerve of the truck had slung him onto his side, sending him sliding along the smooth wooden bench towards the back of the truck, managing to avoid the flying Shanks, more by luck than judgement.

"Jesus fucking Christ," Morgan yelled, as he leapt to his feet and noticed Sergeant Tretyakov cupping his hands over his groin. "Sorry, thanks."

Aerial remained curled up on the floor. "I think my writh ith broken," he said, spluttering blood.

"Anyone else hurt?" Baz shouted.

"I'm OK Sarge," replied Shanks.

Sergeant Tretyakov sat up, stared long and hard at Morgan, then mumbled something in Russian.

"Let's get Aerial seated..." Baz froze mid-sentence. "Jesus!" His stare fixed firmly on the floor in front of him.

Aerial sprang to his knees, realising what was only inches from his face, then wished he hadn't after a bolt of pain shot up his arm.

With the momentum from the swerve and a lot of help from Aerial's boots, the makeshift coffin had been thrown onto its side, tipping Garage's rigid grey corpse onto the floor.

"Mikhail, Shanks, look after Aerial. Morgan, help me with Gar..."

"Americans?" spat a heavy accent from the back of the truck.

"What?! Who said that?"

Between the canvas flaps a rifle barrel slid into view, a dark finger curled around the trigger, two manic black eyes peering up at them through a narrow slit from a sand covered headscarf.

"Fe el kharg!" the headscarf shouted, pointing his rifle at every man in turn, including Garage's corpse. Even hidden behind the cloth the rage was obvious to everyone, this Arab wanted to shoot someone, that was also obvious.

"What? No! English! English!" Baz shouted.

"He want us out truck Bazil," grimaced Sergeant Tretyakov.

Baz held up his palms. "OK, OK."

"Fe el kharg! Fe el kharg!" the headscarf screamed, again, jerking his rifle to one side.

"Help Aerial to his feet Shanks. I'll drop the tailgate."

"I've broken my arm, no my hodding leg," scowled Aerial.

Baz slid the two bolts at both ends of the tailgate, it was then he realised his predicament. With his attention on the men inside the truck, the headscarf failed to notice that for Baz to drop the tailgate he would have to take a step back. The headscarf remained where he stood, his rifle resting over the tailgate.

"Fe el kharg! Fe el kharg!" he screamed again.

"Excuse me." Baz said nervously, jiggling the tailgate.

The headscarf jumped back, shrieking in Arabic, which Baz could only translate as, "Now you are going to die."

Baz's arm stretched out as he eased the tailgate away, until it got to a place of no return, where the weight of the metal and the angle of his arm were at odds with each other. Three choices remained, let the tailgate go, only Baz knew a loud bang would probably not sit well with a psychopathic paranoid Arab and his twitchy trigger finger. He also knew if he allowed the tailgate to lower any further, the weight would eventually yank him head first out of the truck, appearing like an escape attempt and for one RAF sergeant, certain death. Third choice, pull it back up, at the angle it was at, even the strongest of men, which Baz was not, would find that impossible.

BOOM! The tailgate crashed down, smacking the back of the truck with the sound of an exploding grenade.

Baz waited for the imminent bullet. Nothing. Only the sound of frantic shouting, Corporal Lynch and young Harker came flying into view. Both shoved to their knees by another two irate Arabs, a rifle at each of the aircraftmen's heads.

Baz could see an Arab with a long grey cloak, his face hidden deep inside a hood, a cloth covering his nose and mouth. He was shouting, not shouts of anger, but of elation and excitement as he danced on the spot with Corporal Lynch's pistol waving above his head. The other was a shorter stockier Arab with a black face and thick hands, more agitated than the other two, shuffling his feet and continually looking towards the hood.

Baz had jumped from the back of the truck. Aerial followed, shrugging away any help from Shanks, sliding from a sitting position and crying out as the heavy landing jolted his wrist. Then Sergeant Tretyakov jumped with his legs held tightly together, creasing up in pain as he landed. Morgan and Shanks were last out, soon recognising the unmistakeable grey hood and the African, then the headscarf, who made up the third Arab they had encountered in the lanes. Both aircraftmen could see revenge on their faces.

The outline of another, shorter Arab could be seen through the gusts, he was struggling to hold on to five horses, a rifle hung from his shoulder.

The contours of Corporal Lynch and Ken Harker kneeling with their heads bowed were becoming faint shadows as the sandstorm picked up in its ferocity. Only the black Arab could now be seen behind them, his loose clothing flapping wildly, the dark profile of the rifle pointing at their heads.

Then a stifled attempt to fire up the engine, spluttering and coughing several times as if it was trying to clear sand from its throat. Suddenly it roared into life, quickly turning to a scream as the truck rocked backwards and forwards, its wheels spinning at great speed, digging itself deeper into the sand.

The black Arab hit the top of Ken Harker's arm so hard with the butt of his rifle it sent the young aircraftman sprawling onto the sand, then pointing his rifle he screamed at the young aircraftman to join the other men.

The headscarf shoved them round to the side of the truck, herding them like cattle, bit by bit he pushed them forward with his rifle. With chins buried into their chests and protecting their eyes they slowly made their way round to the front.

"They're going to take everything we got, then fucking kill us," Morgan said as loud as his closed lips would allow.

"Stay together," Baz shouted.

"They're not going to dump me in some fucking desert."

With the rifle in one hand and the corporal's pistol in the other, the hood thrust his hands forward.

209

The gear crunched into reverse and the engine roared, with their hands flat on the bonnet the truck moved back a couple of inches, only for it to roll forward soon after, pushing the men back on their heels.

The hood smacked the butt of his rifle in between an RAF man's shoulder and Shanks fell to the ground in a cry of pain.

"Ed fa'a! Ed fa'a!" the hood screamed.

"Ed fa'a! Ed fa'a!" the headscarf shouted.

The engine roared louder and again the truck rocked back and forth, straining every nut and bolt as it forced itself against the unmovable wall of sand.

"Ed fa'a! Ed fa'a!" the hood screamed again, shoving Aerial hard onto the headlight.

With one last effort the truck finally released a high pitched howl as clouds of smoke billowed from under the bonnet, a couple of splutters later and the truck finally died.

The cabin door flew open and a tall, older Arab leapt out, the lower part of his headscarf fell below his chin displaying a long face with leathery skin. Neither noticing or caring about the angry gusts of sand swirling round him he wrapped the scarf round his face with an overhead spin of his arm, as if he had done it a thousand times before. What he did next sent fear through the men, the horrific realisation at what was about to happen to them. He took the pistol from the hood.

Baz was the first to move, thinking about it afterwards, he thought it was probably the three chevrons on his sleeve that made him do it, someone had to take responsibility after all. Baz stepped forward and faced the old Arab. Even though he could feel the sand blasting his skin, he remained steadfast, upright with unblinking staring eyes. Old leather face pulled his scarf up over his nose, his dark eyes peered through the narrow gap at his victim. In a strange way Baz had accepted his fate, his calmness even surprised himself, he just hoped it was going to be quick and painless. Now I will find out about death, he thought to himself. The old Arab started to frown, appearing to be confused. He lurched his head closer to Baz's face and glared at his eyes, then quickly spun his head around.

It all happened very quickly, nobody had time to think. In one swift movement, Sergeant Tretyakov picked up a handful of sand and threw it point blank into the dark cavity of the hood's hood, who never saw it coming, thanks to his hood. At that same moment, the Russian sergeant managed to grab the headscarf's rifle, quickly whipping it from his clutches.

Baz was a fraction of a second too slow, old leather face instantly turned back and fired the pistol, hitting Sergeant Tretyakov in the heart. Before he was able to release another shot, Baz had thrust the old Arab's pistol arm into the air and twisted him around, both fell to the ground, writhing about in the sand like two scrapping schoolboys. Baz knew if he let go, then that would be it, his life would be snubbed out with one bullet.

In his blindness, the hood was rubbing sand from his eyes with one hand and indiscriminately swinging the rifle violently around with the other. Morgan quickly grabbed the rifle from the Russian's lifeless hand, then with surprising coolness, shot the hood in the back of the head.

Shanks had scampered round the side of the truck and crouched behind the cabin door; through the flurries he could see the figure of the Arab holding on to reins of the horses. He was smaller, much more slightly built than the others, his arm yanked this way and that as the animals were becoming agitated. Shanks made a desperate lunge towards him and grabbed the rifle strap, raising his fist ready to plant the hardest punch his weary body could muster, only his clenched hand remained suspended in mid-air. The Arab was no more than a boy, not even in his teens. His two frightened eyes told Shanks everything, he was not a warrior, he was not a fighter, he was just a boy, there to stop the horses from bolting. After Shanks slid the rifle strap over his head, the boy did not hesitate a second more, releasing the horses he fled into the beige mist.

Stretched on the ground above Baz's head were two arms, one belonging to old leather face, the other was his, gripping tightly around the old Arab's wrist, pushing it hard in to the sand, the old Arab attempting to force his hand round to face the barrel in Baz's direction, each other's strength was being tested to the limit. Baz knew the old Arab was much stronger and it would be a matter of seconds until the gun would be pointing his way. Baz shoved his other elbow hard on the side of the old man's head, forcing his face into the sand, a last act of desperation.

It was then Baz saw it, only briefly, but he saw it nevertheless. Sergeant Tretyakov lay only a foot away, his back towards Baz. There it was, poking out from the Russian's belt. He knew he would only have the one chance, he also knew he would have to be as accurate and skillful as Sergeant Tretyakov had been on that day by the wall.

There was no time to think, releasing his elbow from the old Arab's face, Baz slapped his arm down on the Russian's back and wrapped his fingers round the bone handle. He knew what he was about to do had to be done, there was no choice. In one quick action he pulled the knife from its sheath and plunged it hard into the old Arab's back, again, and again, and again. The first strike scraped a bone, another went into the flesh as if it had entered a slab of butter. It was indiscriminate, it was survival, it was final. The old Arab let out a cry, followed by another, then another, each one diminishing in volume. Baz went on and on, staring into the old man's eyes as he lunged and stabbed, until he was too exhausted to strike again. On the last thrust Baz felt every sinew and muscle in the Arab's arm tighten, then a loud crack as the gun fired into the cloud of dust. Old leather face's arm dropped and the pistol was abandoned to the sand, at the same time expelling a breath so pungent Baz felt sure it was the smell of death. The old Arab stared at Baz, not moving, not blinking, just two frozen eyes glaring in his direction. Drained of all strength Baz dragged himself to his feet and looked down at the blood darkened material flapping wildly in the wind. For a split second he felt an indescribable power surge through his body, as if he had stolen something powerful from the old Arab.

Baz looked around for the rest of his men, first he saw Morgan aiming the rifle through the flurries of sand. After losing his weapon and watching the demise of his two comrades the headscarf had swiftly scampered away towards the horses, only to discover the young boy had gone, along with his only means of escape. Looking down the length of the barrel, Morgan followed the outline of his body as it faded into the distance.

Hardly recognisable through the dusting of sand coating his body, Ken Harker had fallen to his knees with a whimper. Having a knife at your throat and a gun to your head all in the same day had become too much for the young aircraftman. Baz looked at him kneeling in front of the truck's grill, his head dropped low, his hands together in prayer.

Throughout the entire ordeal, Aerial had remained silent, cradling his broken wrist. Like watching shadows behind a beige sheet he had witnessed everything.

Muffled by the wailing wind, Baz and Morgan heard the crack of a distant gun shot. "Shanks?" yelled Morgan.

"Look after Harker," Baz shouted towards Aerial. "Don't move Harker, stay exactly where you are." Then patted him on the back. "I'll come back and get you." Baz paused for a second as he stepped over the mound of sand that was Sergeant Tretyakov, wondering how many more friends did he have to lose that day.

Baz and Morgan edged gingerly along the side of the truck. Morgan stopped as he reached the back wheel, beside his feet was a body lying face up, with relief he saw the loose clothing of the black skinned Arab but more importantly, a small, dark hole of matted blood and sand embedded in the forehead.

As they arrived at the tailgate they could see a familiar shaped profile through the seething beige, he was standing beside a mound of sand. "Shanks," Baz called out. "It's the Sarge Shanks, Morgan's with me."

"The corp," Shanks yelled back, his words nearly carried away with the wind. "He's dead."

Baz and Morgan hurried over. "Are you sure. Where's the bullet wound?"

"He's dead alright Sarge, far as I can see there isn't one."

"Jesus, not another one. Let's get him over by the truck."

Dragging the heavy body over was not an easy feat for the exhausted men. "We'll sort him out later," Baz shouted, as the corporal was propped up against the rear bumper.

They quickly returned to Aerial and Ken Harker, in front of them were the three corpses of Sergeant Tretyakov, the old Arab and the hood, all virtually swallowed by the drifting sand, as though their graves were being made for them.

"We're going to get back into the truck Harker." The young aircraftman remained motionless. "Get up, that's an order." yelled Baz, Harker rose to his feet and waited for the next command. "Follow me Har..." Baz suddenly froze. "What was that?!"

"What was what?" yelled Shanks, lifting the barrel of his gun, pointing it aimlessly into the flurries.

Morgan looked around. "I heard it, a bloody cough, someone in that direction."

"I heard it that time," the butt of Shank's rifle now pressed into his shoulder, his finger poised on the trigger.

"There it is again," shouted Baz.

One of the mounds moved slightly, not the way the wind had been whipping it around, this was different, the actual ground moved, as if the sand was breaking open. Another cough, a splutter, then the sound of spitting.

What happened next was no less than a miracle, Sergeant Tretyakov rose to his feet, sand showering from his body. There he stood, as large as life, tottering on the spot, coughing, spluttering and spitting. A hole in his left shirt pocket, a circle of sand adhered to a wet dark patch around it.

Baz gulped, not noticing the mouthful of sand he had just swallowed.

"Jesus fucking Christ!" Morgan shouted.

Shanks crossed his chest.

Young Harker began praying, again!

With his body swaying back and forth Sergeant Tretyakov remained rooted to the spot. Grinning like a drunk he slowly poked a finger into the bullet hole, watching in disbelief they saw the tip of it disappear into his body. He pulled out a silver flask, and there it was, a small hole, its metal jagged edges pushed inwards. He turned the flask over, instead of the expected hole on the other side, there was a dent, a deep depression had been poked out from the inside, like a large silver blister. He gave it a shake, as if he was jiggling a hand bell. A noise rattled from inside, metal against metal, bullet against flask, life against death. "Vodka gone," he slurred, holding the flask upside down, crunching sand as he spoke.

"Lucky bastard!" Morgan exclaimed.

As they returned to the rear of the truck, Aerial and young Harker looked down at the slumped body of Corporal Lynch.

"Did they thoot him?" Aerial grimaced.

"We don't know," replied Baz.

"The Corporal saved my life," said Harker.

"And the Arab?"

"Right between the eyes," Shanks announced as though he was

proud of the fact, then pulled out a screwed up ten shilling note from his pocket. In truth, he didn't feel proud at all.

"Actually it was a bit to the right," Morgan said.

Exhausted, drained, coated in sand and virtually indistinguishable from each other, the six men sat in the truck, all exhausted to the point of collapse.

For ages, no one moved, no one spoke. No one needed to. Lives had been taken, actions had to be justified, personalities had to be questioned, characters needed to be examined, every man had to come to terms with their own actions. Each in his own way.

Maybe the old Arab wasn't going to shoot me, maybe he was going to let me go, I am no more than a murderer, thought Baz. He strained his eyes sideways to look at Sergeant Tretyakov. It was Mikhail, I just stood there, he was the first to throw sand at that Arab. If Mikhail hadn't. No! The old Arab was definitely going to shoot me. Mikhail saved my life. I should thank Mikhail. It was me or the old Arab. Maybe I should have let him kill me. What have I got? He probably has children, grandchildren, lots of them. But I didn't want to kill him. He wanted to kill me. He was in the wrong. He deserved to die. No! No one deserves to die. He's not dead anyway, not according to Dr Chopra. Jesus, that old Arab has a lot of good karma to collect. So have I!

Baz looked up. "Morgan, Shanks. You've got the guns. Stay awake or give them to someone else," forcing his words out.

"I'm fine Sarge."

"Me too, we should put him back in the box?" said Morgan, looking down at Garage's corpse.

Garage had ceased being Garage a long time ago, even recognising him as the corpse of Garage was difficult. The exposed skin had acquired large blotches of a blue leaden colour and the limbs stretched out with a rigidity that made them look as if they were defying gravity.

"Yeah you're right Morgan."

"What about the corporal Sarge?" Morgan said, placing one end of the lid back on the makeshift coffin while Shanks took the other end. A hammer had been found in the tool box and the nails were driven back in. And that was the last time Baz ever saw Garage.

"The corporal Sarge?" Morgan repeated.

"Leave him. One dead body in here is enough."

The men settled down again, like watching dancing ghosts their eyes fixed on the sand swirling around outside. Baz had thought it best to leave the back flap open, he didn't want a repeat of the first time they were taken by surprise. Having some of the sand join them felt like a small sacrifice to make.

Sergeant Tretyakov found an oily cloth in a tool box and improvised a sling for Aerial. "We are meanth to kill Germanth, not Arabth." Aerial said quietly to the Russian sergeant as he carefully bedded his wrist into the material.

The Russian hunched down at the end of the bench and thought about Stepan, he hoped the three were fairing better than him. He was glad no one had asked about his absent friends, questions would only lead to other questions, he was too exhausted. Anyhow, after what had just happened, absent Russians were probably the last thing on their minds.

Young Harker sat on the floor with his back against the front cabin. After the day's events the young aircraftman had decided God must be testing him, feeling he had failed, left him doubting his own faith. A true Christian would not be afraid to die. Then decided it was only one of his many weaknesses, most of which he had discovered that afternoon.

Morgan and Shanks sat near the back of the truck, a virtual mirror image of each other. Rifles rested on their laps, a finger poised on the trigger. Maybe the guilt would creep in later, maybe not. For the time being, both were just glad to act as the sentries on guard.

"I won't be needing this anymore Mikhail." Baz said as he remembered what was tucked into his belt.

The Russian Sergeant focused his eyes on the blood encrusted blade. "You kill scorpion Bazil?"

Baz remained silent. He then remembered something Harker had said.

"Harker."

"Sarge?"

"What did you mean earlier?"

"Sarge?"

"When you said Corporal Lynch had saved your life?"

"Sarge?"

"You said the corporal saved your life Harker, *how* did the corporal save your life?"

Morgan and Shanks turned wearily towards the young aircraftman. "For fucks sake Harker, we've done nothing wrong." Morgan informed Baz how they had met the Arabs in Al Basrah, telling the entire story in every detail. Shanks and Aerial constantly interrupted, their words tripping over themselves as they attempted to voice their version of events, it felt like a confessional, with Baz as the priest. They told him how they were conned by the gang of boys, how they were led to the building with the courtyard, of the slimeball Arab with the tray of jewels; and of how he had sent the men through the back door and into the lanes, even the two ladies of the night. "If ladies is what you would call them," added Aerial. Nothing was missed out. Harker interrupted Shanks when it got to the part about encountering the four Arabs for the first time. If only for his own sake he felt he had to justify not seeing the hood grab him from behind. It needed more than just a couple of words spoken by another, someone who had no idea how he felt, after all it was him that had a knife at his throat. When he got to the part about Corporal Lynch and the pistol, he let Shanks and Morgan return to the fold; it was then the story finally exhausted itself. They waited for a response. None came.

"And that is how the corporal saved my life," Harker finally said.

It was quite a while before anyone spoke again.

In a dazed stupor they watched as darkness gradually devoured the remaining light, the flying sheets of sand began to merge into the gloom. Soon it will just be the noise and them, soon they will be entombed in black.

Baz's worry was the headscarf, or maybe the young boy. What would happen when they found their tribe? All the men knew that one grenade thrown into the truck would be enough. Or a fire, the fuel tank was probably still half full. Or a hail of bullets fired through the tarpaulin.

The darkness had arrived.

"Tie the flaps Morgan. We'll wait it out," Baz said. He knew this was going to be the longest night of their lives.

Short conversations came and went. Even one about Corporal Lynch, everyone agreed that none of them knew him that well.

Aerial finally asked Sergeant Tretyakov that question. "What happened to your friends?"

217

The answer was quick. "They on boat." His snapped response had the desired effect of finishing that conversation there and then.

It was young Harker who spoke next. "If the Arabs come back and take us, you know, leave us in the desert, in the middle of nowhere... Anyway, if I was to die first." He stopped talking.

"And?" said Shanks.

"I give you permission to eat me."

For a few seconds the occupants of the truck fell into silence. A chuckle broke the air first, it was Shanks, soon followed by Morgan, then Aerial, grimacing at the same time, then Baz. The chuckle turned into laughter, Morgan's characteristic cackling became louder. Sergeant Tretyakov was soon drawn in. "Sarcasm?" he said, which had the desired effect of increasing the volume. "Shhhh," Baz hushed, slowly the laughter died down and everyone returned to their own solitude.

Baz felt an overwhelming tiredness beginning to swallow him. A deep sleep followed.

"Americans!"

His eyes quickly sprung open, and that was the only movement he made. His first thoughts were he hadn't been blown up, or burnt to death. It wasn't a dream, he was sure of that. He also knew by the amount of light streaming into the truck that it was daytime. Someone had opened the back flap. Baz waited for the bullets.

Sergeant Tretyakov sat bolt upright and pulled out his knife, holding tightly onto the tip of the blade in readiness. He crouched down, there was no hiding place in the back of this truck.

The pain in Aerial's arm and mouth had made it near impossible for him to get any sleep, most of the night he had lain in an agonising trance, waiting for daylight, or death, whichever came first. In his entire life he never thought he would want to see a place as much as he needed to see Shaibah. When he heard the word, he sat up quickly, crying out when the sudden lurch shot a pain up his arm.

Ken Harker opened his eyes then closed them again, hoping what he heard was only a continuation of a bad dream.

Morgan had woken suddenly. In a spontaneous reflex action he had sprung up and fallen backwards on to the makeshift coffin, never letting go of his grip on the rifle or losing his aim towards the back of the truck. It was only by luck the gun never fired.

Shanks had spent all night drifting in and out of a half slumber, losing any sense of reality, the word had yet to register.

"American! I'm American! Jesus Mac, stop pointing that gun at me," the voice said in a bronzed Boston accent.

Once he was satisfied a bullet or knife wouldn't be heading in his direction, the American studied the aircraftmen one by one. "J...e...sus! What the...has happened here?" Finding it hard to believe the sight before him.

It looked as though a sand bomb had exploded inside the truck, a thick dusting of sand and dried blood coated everything and everyone. Sergeant Tretyakov's ape like appearance had become more, well, orangutan. The American's gaze lingered on the bullet hole in the Russian's pocket and the dark stain surrounding it, surprised to see the wearer was still alive.

Aerial had faired the worst, his lower face covered in patches of dark brown clotted gunge from the dried blood and still cradling the oil soaked cloth tied over his shoulder.

But it was their eyes that struck the American most. Scared, vacant, resigned, the white's peering coldly though the dark grime surrounding them.

"J...e...sus," the American repeated. "Major John Maschino, 57th Fighter Group." If you could ever have an appearance that was in complete contrast to the aircraftmen, then the Major had it. A fresh eyed, clean shaven, chiselled faced man in his late thirties with an athletic chest, he had a dark brown cap tucked under the armpit of his neatly creased brown shirt. "You guys look like you've had one hell of a party."

Silence was the only reply.

A hidden person spoke from behind the American officer. Major John Maschino took a step back allowing the flaps to swing shut, returning the men into darkness.

It was only half a minute till a ray of sunlight along with the Major's face appeared again. "Who is in charge here?"

A moments silence. "Me, I am," said Baz, without moving a single muscle. "Sergeant Albright."

"There is a man covered in sand down here Sergeant."

What! Baz had to think for a moment. "Oh yeah. That is...that *was* Corporal Lynch."

219

"How did he...how did Corporal Lynch end up like this Sergeant?"

In truth Baz didn't know how the corporal had died. He couldn't say he was shot by the Arab, because as far as he was concerned he hadn't seen a bullet wound, or any blood at all for that matter. The corporal's death was a mystery.

Baz didn't answer. He still hadn't moved.

The hidden voice spoke again.

"Are any of you hurt?" asked Major Maschino.

Baz looked at Aerial. "A broken wrist." Then looked at Harker. "And a broken spirit." He paused and looked around. "Six broken spirits."

The major turned to speak to the hidden voice.

"Tansey! Harrison!" The hidden voice yelled out. Seconds later two men leapt into the truck.

Aerial was helped out first, followed by Harker, the rest declined any offers of help. As their feet touched terra firma, each man in turn gazed down at the corporal's body.

"We were attacked," Baz said as he faced the American officer.

"There are no Germ..."

"Arabs."

"Oh." Staring at Baz's eyes. "Are *you* alright Sergeant?"

"Fine." The easy answer.

A line of three large wheeled USAF trucks sat on the road. More Americans had already decamped and were sauntering towards the half buried truck, all intrigued by the dishevelled condition of the aircraftmen.

"This is the man that has the bro..." Baz began to say.

"Lieutenant Reeves!" The Major yelled before Baz could finish. A shorter, slight man with thin round glasses and soft pink skin came scampering over, then carefully led Aerial away.

The Major looked down at Sergeant Tretyakov's punctured pocket. "Are *you* hurt?"

Sergeant Tretyakov slid out his flask and shook it in front of the Major, the noise of the bullet rattled inside. "I must get myself one of those," the American officer said with an approving nod.

"Not hole," the Russian said. "Not good for vodka."

Scottish, the American officer thought then returned his attention to Baz. "You were attacked by Arabs?"

220

"Three dead, Major, Arabs, three dead Arabs." Baz walked round to the side of the truck, stopping abruptly beside the half buried wheel, his face masked in horror as he glared down at the sand, in fact, all the RAF men froze with the same startled expression.

Shanks began kicking the sand away. "He's gone, how? I shot him right in-between the eyes."

"A bit to the right, actually," said Morgan.

Baz dashed round to the front, the others followed. Again he looked down in disbelief. "The bodies have gone Major. There were two here, I know," he paused. "I killed one."

"And I killed the other," announced Morgan, not wanting to be left out from this clique of assassins.

Baz dropped to his knees and began brushing the sand around. "There it is." Picking up the pistol.

"You killed an Arab with this firearm."

"No, with Mikhail's knife."

Sergeant Tretyakov pulled out the knife, held it up and grinned.

"Then who does this gun belong to?"

"That's another story," replied Baz.

"The Major's attention was drawn towards Harker. "Are you OK son?"

"No Sir I'm not, I nearly..."

"Lieutenant Reeves!" the Major yelled again. "Another one Lieutenant."

"They must have taken the bodies away," Baz said softly.

"And when we were in the truck! Jesus fucking Christ!"

"Something tells me you guys have one hell of a story to tell."

"How long you got?" said Shanks.

"Where are you guys based?"

"Shaibah," Baz told him. "This road only leads to Shaibah."

They tried starting the RAF truck, not surprisingly it failed with a series of loud clunks. After a considerable amount of digging and heaving it was eventually hauled onto the road and coupled behind one of the huge American transporters.

Corporal Lynch was laid beside the coffin.

"Is that what I think it is?" the Major asked.

"If you're thinking it's a coffin, then yes," Baz replied.

"Oh," a moments thought. "Is there a body?..."

"Garage."

"Garage? Garage is a person?"

"He's Welsh, was Welsh."

"Welsh? Is Garage a Welsh name?"

"He played rugby."

"Rugby? Are all rugby players called Garage?"

"No."

"What happened to...to Garage?"

"That's another story."

"Another, that's three so far Sergeant?"

"Believe me Major, that's just the start"

The aircraftmen rode in the back of the USAF tow truck with the Major and three other Americans, including Lieutenant Reeves. It was then Baz realised he may actually like Americans after all.

Fifteen minutes later the convoy of three USAF transporters and one RAF truck entered through the gates of Shaibah.

"Roll on that fucking boat."

P-B4!
1946

Unfortunately while it was in the Mediterranean, the vessel carrying Garage's and Corporal Lynch's bodies back home was holed by a German torpedo, it sunk in a matter of minutes, along with all hands on board. Neither of their bodies were seen again.

In Wing Commander Batty fashion, Baz had personally written to Garage's family. In the letter he mentioned how happy he was to know their son's final resting place would be in his beloved Wales. How was Baz to know the letter would be received after his parents were told of the sinking. Throughout the remainder of Baz's life he never learnt of the two men's watery grave.

There was no next of kin recorded in Corporal Lynch's paperwork. Thinking back, Baz couldn't remember the Corporal mentioning any family, nor could anyone else. In the back of his mind, something told Baz he might have been Irish, or was that just because of the name. Anyhow, in everyone's opinion the Corporal's accent seemed to be absent of any dialect. The CO told him that Corporal Lynch would be buried in an RAF cemetery somewhere in England and Baz left it at that. How Corporal Lynch met his death on that day remained a mystery.

It seemed the little that young Harker had, was stolen from him in that Al Basrah lane, or the desert, or both. Although Baz thought it wasn't so much the two threats to his life that changed young Harker, but the mind sapping gratitude towards his God that made him lose all reasoning. Young Harker became someone else. "Maybe luck or plain old good fortune are not easily defined Harker but they should never be lost to religion." Baz tried to tell him once, his words lost on deaf ears. The young aircraftman remained convinced some indeterminable force had protected him. Twice!

Not on the third time though. Young Ken Harker had been sent home on the same boat as Garage and Corporal Lynch. Still not knowing why Morgan wouldn't return his picture of Emma.

Aerial had had his wrist encased in plaster. Discovering the constant sweat and heat made it rot he had it reset on several painful occasions. When it was finally removed, everyone was shocked to see his arm had the appearance of a shrivelled, dried up, shrunken old rag. "A fucking dead man's arm," as Morgan had put it. Thankfully, it only took a couple of weeks before it returned to its normal condition. In truth, Aerial complained more about his broken teeth than he ever did about his arm.

Both Shanks and Aerial left Shaibah not long after the end of the war.

Baz and Morgan remained at the airfield well past the long hot summer of 1946, the hottest one ever experienced at Shaibah.

Major John Maschino and the rest of the Americans only stayed for a short while. During that time Morgan had warned them to be careful if they were ever to frequent the lanes at Al Basrah. "Americans are bloody popular or your dollars are anyhow," he told them.

At first, the Americans reminded Baz of how his team used to look when initially arriving at the airfield, but as time went on he spotted small changes in them, just as he had with his own men all those years ago. They began to shave less, their clean cut crisp uniforms started to hang more limply and displayed the usual indelible sweat stains. After a while individual characteristics began to become less noticeable, the only way Baz could recognise them through their stubble was by the way they chewed their gum. "Show me a yank's gum action and I'll give you his name," Baz told Morgan.

"Be careful where you say that Sarge," was the reply.

If only for their own sake, Baz was quite relieved when the Americans were given their orders to move on. "At least you weren't completely contaminated by Shaibah," he told the Major on the morning of their departure. During their time at the airbase, Baz discovered he had a fondness for salted popcorn, air conditioning, Jack Daniels and a strange game called craps, which he judged to be pointless. Not one of them owned a chess set or even seemed to know how to play the game. He decided games of skill appeared to have bypassed American culture. Baz especially liked air conditioning.

In October that year, Baz and Morgan departed Shaibah for the long journey home. "Roll on that fucking boat." Only there was no fucking boat, not to begin with anyhow. The first leg was a long flight over to Egypt. The Catalina they flew in never seemed to go much faster than a car and the trip felt like an eternity. Why anyone would plan a flight across the desert in a flying boat was beyond reason. Relieved to reach Alexandria, they crossed the Mediterranean by ship to Toulon in France. Finally! "Roll on that fucking boat." From there they boarded a train to Calais. When the ferry arrived at Dover the first place they had to visit was the Demob Centre. It was here Baz and Morgan went their separate ways. "Have a fucking good life Sarge. You deserve it," were Morgan's departing words.

Baz was a civilian again.

As for Sergeant Tretyakov, it was just a few days after that fateful day in the desert, Baz had seen the Russian Sergeant a few hours before retiring to his tent. Everything appeared to be normal, maybe he was drinking more vodka than usual, in a way that was normal. Next morning when his bunk was found empty, nobody thought much about that either, until he hadn't turned up for lunch, neither was he seen the day after. In fact, the Russian Sergeant was never seen again, he had vanished from the face of the earth. Rumours spread amongst the aircraftmen from both countries that he just walked out of Shaibah, then carried on walking, until he couldn't walk any further.

The strangeness didn't stop there either.

A couple of days after his disappearance, one of the Russian mechanics handed Baz a screwed up piece of paper with Sergeant Albright written on it, he said he found it under the sergeant's pillow. As Baz unrolled the paper, a small object fell out into the palm of his hand, he recognised it instantly. William's pawn, the brothers of the board pawn. In large hurried writing was 10. P-B4! That's all, nothing else. 10. P-B4! The exclamation mark filling the note from top to bottom.

The move Baz should have made.

IV

ROBERT BLAKENEY

ONE FAMILY, TWO GRAVES, THREE NAMES

IN A DARK CORNER

MRS CHATTLE

I KILLED A MAN ONCE

THE PRIEST'S HOUSE

THE TEMPLE

EDDIE

A DROP OF ACID

JOHN WATERHOUSE'S NEIGHBOUR

YOU SAID YOU KILLED A MAN ONCE

PORK LOIN OR RIB-EYE

PASANG

THE RAID

Maureen Downes named Robert Blakeney after Dr Roberts. The
midwife had never known the doctor's Christian name, or even asked
him. Being at Robert Blakeney's birth also meant she was present at
the tragic death of his mother. Inquiring after the doctor's first name
was not foremost on her mind that afternoon.

It had began when Nurse Downes was put on the spot after she
handed the baby over to the staff at the hospital. She had been told it
was tradition for abandoned babies to be named after their discoverer,
the decision had been made that the same protocol should also apply
in this case. Nurse Downes thought Maureen would not be appropriate
for a boy and felt extremely self-satisfied when the name Maurice
came to mind. She thought it was a nice name, she even thought it
suited Robert.

"Far too French!" the formidable matron said, no one disagreed.

Robert Blakeney had come into this world having never met his
mother or knowing who his father was.

After a brief stay in hospital and before he was even two weeks
old a new home had been found for Robert. The very much misnamed
Village Angels Orphanage. An oppressive eighteenth century rust
brick abbey with large ornate stone windows and an abundance of tall
red chimneys. The cold interior seemed to have more nooks and
crannies than a termite mound. Despite the amount of years Robert
had spent at Village Angels and with his in-depth knowledge of the
abbey, he was sure there were rooms he hadn't yet seen. A child could
vanish for hours on end and many did, most on purpose. In his later
days Robert was permitted to join in with a search. In truth, it had
become a necessity. After all, he was an orphan himself and if anyone
knew the hiding places, then Robert certainly did. Whenever he heard
a priest or sister scurrying past declaring "God Bless..." followed by
the missing child's name, Robert immediately knew a search was on.

The orphanage was located on high ground where it surveyed the
many rolling hills and clusters of woodland for miles around. It was
set in its own vast estate overlooking a small farming hamlet in the
valley below, awarding it an erroneous stately importance. A small,
squat towered church, built solely for the original occupants stood

slightly further up the hill. Robert was told that this was where God could keep an eye on all the orphans in the world. Especially the ones that misbehaved. Hell was a word bandied around a lot by the nuns and priests, usually ensconced in some kind of threat.

For nearly two hundred years Crichton Abbey was home to a devout holy order of Franciscan Monks before becoming a Catholic school. Closed for vital maintenance work in 1929, the pupils were integrated into a secondary school close by. None returned, the maintenance work was deemed too expensive to finish. Crichton Abbey metamorphosed into Village Angels orphanage in 1929. There were no parents to complain about leaking roofs and the lack of heating.

Any children that were aware of the outside world knew only two ways out of Village Angels, three ways if you included death, which you would have to on seven occasions while Robert was there.

Apart from a special ward allocated for babies, the orphanage was divided into two sections, the girls division supervised by nuns and the boys division by priests, both presided over with the utmost strictness. For the first four years the two sections might as well have been in separate worlds, then in their fifth year for five minutes before the short walk to church on Sunday, the nuns and priests allowed them to mingle, mainly for siblings to reunite. This practise was stopped soon after Robert had reached his sixth birthday.

Sometimes the outside world would come to them. Doctors, dentists, workmen, busybody social workers, also God himself, until Robert discovered it was actually Bishop Noad. Then there were the prospective parents, Robert could see them approaching a mile away, and to him, a mile away was the closest he would ever get. He might as well have been invisible.

The nuns and priests had a well proven and practised way of breaking in a child entering the orphanage who had passed a certain age, who had become used to a way of life on the outside, who had decided to rebel against their loss of freedom and the loss of their parents, who had never heard the word anarchy but was the greatest exponent of it. What was left behind of the child afterwards? Certainly not defiance anymore and not much else for that matter.

Strictness and discipline went hand in hand in Village Angels. It was in the walls and the floors, it was in the ceiling, it was even in the air, it filled every second from the time the orphans woke to the time they fell asleep. In truth, sleep was their only means of escape.

The Second World War and the few years following gave the orphanage the largest influx of children they had ever had in their history. Bishop Noad took the decision not to accept any Jews escaping from the tyranny of Nazism. "We are an orphanage, they are not true orphans, it was their choice to leave," he had argued. After the war, the Bishop thought he had filled his quota by allowing a fragile, grey haired, middle aged jewish nurse to work in the orphanage. A kind, gentle woman, who was the closest to a mother figure Robert had ever had at Village Angels. It was years later he found out the reason for her having the thinnest and wispish hair he had ever seen on a woman. Father Nolan had told him it was yanked out by the Germans in a concentration camp. In all the conversations she had with Robert, the poor woman never mentioned the torment she must have suffered. It was then he learnt there were people far worse off than himself. Anyhow, Village Angels was well past its maximum capacity by the time Robert had arrived.

The orphanage had one goal, to mould children into God fearing, educated and well-mannered individuals, ready to be absorbed into family life with the least disruption, although any disruption to the child was not taken into consideration.

There were two ways, not including death, to escape Village Angels Orphanage: one was to get a placement with a family, and if the child was accepted after an initial trial period, a permanent adoption. Baby boys were the most popular, then baby girls, the cuter the better. In other words, if you were not adopted by the time you had passed the baby stage, the chances of getting a placement would dramatically fall. It was decided a few years after the war that siblings would have more chance if separated, hence terminating the practise allowing them to mingle before the Sunday walk to church. Occasionally a couple would turn up at the orphanage and leave with a child on that same day: strangely, not long after, money would be found for some much needed maintenance.

Although prospective parents of the Catholic religion were always preferred, a family outside of the faith would not be discouraged. "They are open to any persuasion," if the question were ever to arise.

Robert had missed being placed at the baby stage (not cute enough, mainly on account of his rounded back and lost gaze), he then missed the toddler stage, then every stage after that. Which leaves us with the second way of escaping Village Angels. The child has to cease being a child. It would be at this stage a foster home or some temporary residential institution would be found, a transitional period before entering the pitfalls of society and falling into some kind of degenerate pit which was what most experienced. By the time Robert had departed the orphanage, he had made it to an age never before attained by an orphan.

In his last years he had become as much a part of the orphanage as the assorted crucifixes and portraits of the popes adorning the walls. To the sisters and priests, Robert had become the child that could never be adopted, some even said he would be at Village Angels forever. To the other orphans he was just Robert, a name, some thought of him as neither a member of the diocese, nor an orphan. Robert was, well, *just there*.

The priests left Robert to his own devices, no one had any need to tell him what to do. He knew when to wash the clothes and when the huge boiler made sounds that were not part of its usual repertoire. He knew the songs of every bird and the names of every tree. He knew how far apart to sow the carrots and when to feed the hens. He knew which of the younger boys needed help at mealtimes and how to quieten them at bedtimes. Robert knew the rules better than most of the Fathers or the Sisters.

Many nuns and priests had come and gone in the time he was at Village Angels. Some priests had become, as Robert put it, 'The Chosen Ones'. This was not, as you might think, some ascendancy to a higher spiritual plane but only a placement to a diocese. 'A parish adoption', as Robert put it. A few had even departed for a missionary posting in a remote corner of some great continent. Always priests and always a hurried departure as though they had committed some ghastly misdemeanour. Sometimes a lack of cuteness, a rounded back and a lost gaze can be an advantage.

"You could enter a seminary, join the priesthood," Father Nolan suggested to Robert. "Return to Village Angels, carry on the good work. You probably know it better than most of the Fathers anyway."

Robert had a special affection for Father Nolan. He thought his first name might have been Patrick but he wasn't sure. He just knew it wasn't Father, he also knew he wasn't his real Father, even though the Father did call him 'my son' most of the time.

Father Nolan's bedtime stories were famous amongst the boys at the orphanage. Robert could remember listening to that creamy Irish brogue as far back as his memory would allow. Any further back and he would enter into a place of darkness where only the sound of a woman's bone chilling screams could be heard. Even now, through a child's nightmare or just the innocent shrieks of a daylight tantrum, Robert would curl up in the nearest safe haven he could find.

"Sorry Father Nolan, but I don't feel the call, well, calling me. Anyway there is something I must do first." Robert sensed the Father knew what he was about to say. "The rule about the orphans not knowing who their real parents are. That they should have a fresh start with their new families. Even letting the adoptive parents change their names if they wish, which I have never agreed with by the way Father." The old priest smiled through the deep creases of his crows feet. "I'm not like them Father Nolan. I have never been adopted and I certainly haven't got a hope in hell now."

"Nor on earth my son."

"Sorry Father."

The old priest paused in thought. "It is us that have failed you." He clasped his hands under his chin. "I know what you're about to say Robert." Father Nolan tightened his mouth. "You know the rules my son."

"What else have I got, I don't know if they're dead or alive or if they would even want to know. Maybe it's because I haven't been adopted," Robert's tone changed, "I need to find them Father."

The old priest put both hands to his lips in the shape of a church steeple, Robert just thought he was in prayer again, Father Nolan always looked as though he was in prayer.

"You nearly said it yourself Robert. 'If he would want to know you.' Have you thought about that?"

"Well if they don't, then maybe I will join the priesthood." Robert drew his head back. "*He!* Father you said *he*, you didn't say *they*, you said *he* father."

"I know what I said Robert, let us take a walk through the garden." Father Nolan crossed his chest. "God forgive me," he said as he rose from his chair.

They strolled between the apple trees and along the grass paths separating the vegetable beds. Father Nolan told Robert about the records that are kept on every child, especially the circumstances behind their arrival at Village Angels.

With the sensitivity only an old experienced priest could muster, the Father told him about the tragic death of his mother during childbirth. "I'm afraid it was your birth my son." Father Nolan stopped walking and waited.

"Oh," was all Robert said after a long silence.

"Who your father was? That had not been written in the notes." Father Nolan stopped under the arched hedgerow leading out of the garden. "I'll make a pact with you Robert."

"Go on Father, I'm listening."

"You stay here at Village Angels, until your twenty-first birthday, I will find out what I can. If you still feel the same then, well, you must do what you think best. I will pray for you on whatever journey you choose."

On 17th July 1963 Robert was summoned by the old priest. They talked for hours that afternoon.

"How will Village Angels manage without you my son?" were the last words Robert would ever hear Father Nolan say.

ONE FAMILY, TWO GRAVES, THREE NAMES

"I'm catching the ferry back tomorrow," Violet said with her arm coupled around Baz's elbow.

Baz had only seen her once since she moved to France and that was at least ten years ago. He was glad to see his sister had lost none of her feminine elegance.

They stared down at the explosion of colour from the flowers Violet had placed at the headstone, a stark contrast to the rest of the overgrown and tired grave. Even the once pristine grey stone was showing the mildewed signs of time.

"Maybe I'll get over to France to see you one day," Baz said.

"I'd like that," Violet replied, then added softly, "It's difficult to remember what they looked like."

"I know what you mean, twenty years is a long time."

"Twenty years," Violet said, stretching the words.

"I wish Dad was still alive Vi. He never asked for much but I bet he would have liked to have kept his life."

"That's because mum wanted everything. If Dad couldn't give it to her, then he wouldn't have it either, Dad was a special person Baz." She paused for a few seconds. "He was like my David."

It was late afternoon, April 22nd 1943 when Violet said goodbye to her husband from the front step of their house, a date she would remember for the rest of her life. It was also the last time she felt his soft lips on her cheek, the last time she heard his voice or saw the face that had shown her so much love and devotion.

During the war David Peveler had been dropped by parachute into occupied France. His superiors thought he was the perfect man for the job, cool, calculated, intelligent, neither brave nor foolhardy. David Peveler was no hero.

It was his unfaltering command of the French language that made him ideal for this mission. His instructions were to liaise with the resistance fighters, complete his task and get out of France quick. What that task was? Only a handful of people had ever known, Violet was not one of them. David's only weakness, he was married, he had so much to live for. Then again, maybe that was a strength.

David Peveler never made radio contact with the return aircraft, nor was he present at the pickup point. He *had* completed his task though. David Peveler *was* a hero. An unsung hero. A *missing* unsung hero.

Why, where and what happened? All remained unanswered for Violet. In the following years so many lines of enquiries only ended in frustration. Her life had become accustomed to disappointment, she expected nothing else. Then in 1951 when all hope had virtually faded, she received a letter from a Claudette Vezier. It recounted how she had met a man fitting David's description, only for a short time though, probably less than an hour. She said her family had helped an injured Englishman trying to escape to Spain. It must have been him, everything seemed to fit. Soon after, Violet resigned from her job as a teacher and moved to Beaune in Burgundy, the town where Claudette Vezier had met him. Violet has never given up her search.

Fifteen minutes earlier, in an older corner of the cemetery, Baz and Violet gazed down on the first grave they had seen that day. This one had been almost obliterated by weather and time itself, forty-five years of it. The same flowers that adorned their parents grave also lay beside the small virtually toppled headstone. The chiselled words nearly honed flat by the elements. Both sister and brother knew exactly what they said.

Norma Jane Albright

1906 -1918

Our flower sleeps

"One family and two graves."

"Three names."

"Two dates."

"We've forgotten Oliver!" she exclaimed. "What about Oliver?" slowing her words.

"How can we *ever* forget Oliver?" said Baz. "Or William, or Garage, or Mikhail."

"Who?"

"So many, I can't name them all. We are surrounded by names of the dead."

"Not David! Not yet."

After a long pause. "Do you miss Ruby?" Baz asked.

"We keep in touch, she sends photos of Christopher and Hannah, she's five now."

Ruby's husband Peter was not a man to rest on his laurels. He knew if nothing was done, his prospects were going to be no more than they were already. Peter was a man that wanted to give so much more to his Angel; his Angel was a woman who wanted her husband to give her so much more.

It was while he was sitting in the Dog and Badger at the end of a morning shift, Peter lit his roll-up, took the first mouthful of ale and with a rustle and a flick he opened the day's newspaper. It was at that moment Peter knew his and his Angel's lives were about to change forever 'COME TO A SUNNIER FUTURE' the large bold type inside a thick black bordered advertisement said. The more he read, the more the words wrapped themselves around him with a warm hug. 'ONLY TEN POUNDS PER ADULT' the subtext yelled out and that was that, nothing felt more right, a lifeline of hope had been thrown out to him. "He who waits," he said quietly to himself, then thought about his Angel.

Peter waited for the ideal time to tell her, 17th February 1948 in fact. It was perfect, wet, cold and windy, only a snow blizzard could have improved it. Over breakfast he put his two options to Ruby. Either they both remain in England and accept their lot, he as a railway worker and she as a shop assistant, or they leave the little they have behind and emigrate to Australia, "Where the weather is always sunny. Where, my Angel, we will make our fortune."

One year later, the soles of their shoes kissed the warm Australian earth, Sidney Harbour to be precise. Hundreds of other eager, like minded folk followed them down the walkway and onto the docks.

Life was not quite as expected at the beginning. For six months they lived in a hostel and performed menial jobs. Peter always remained the optimist, Ruby a lot less so and she also hadn't lost any of that volatile enthusiasm in letting her husband know.

After saving enough hard earned Australian dollars, Peter persuaded his Angel to move to Adelaide, a city paved with gold he was told.

Life at the start was as tough as it was in Sydney but gradually they were becoming acclimatised to their new way of life, they were making friends, and more importantly, Peter was making contacts.

Ruby qualified as a teacher, that was Violet's idea. Ruby loved teaching, she was born for it. "It's all the experience you had with those kids back in Paddington station," Peter told her.

It was after a few beers, one of Peter's friends told him. "Adelaide streets are paved with gold, liquid gold, making money Cobber."

"Oh yeah, how?"

It was only when he arrived at the doorstep and surprised Peter with a couple of old beehives, everything came to light. Through his thick Australian accent Peter realised he had said honey, not money. Anyhow, one year later Peter owned a shop selling honey and beehive equipment. Not quite liquid gold but life was becoming easier and it even made a small profit. He proudly owned up at his friend's barbecue a few years later that growing a moustache was the hardest work he had done that year.

Peter went on to become the foremost bee expert in Adelaide, having over fifty hives dotted around various areas in the outback, only Peter knew the exact locations. Not that anyone would want to steal from a swarm of irate honeybees in one of the most inhospitable areas in South Australia. Along with Ruby's money from teaching they built their own house in a middle class suburb of the city. In May 1954 Christopher was born. After a couple of miscarriages, Hannah followed four years later.

"Would you have liked to have had children Vi?" Baz asked.

Violet dropped her head. "Yes," she replied softly. "Fate has delivered me my cards though."

"What about you?"

Baz smiled, "Poor blighters had a lucky escape."

"The Albright name stops here then," Violet said.

Baz continued to stare down at the grave. "Do you believe in the soul?"

"You'd be better off asking them that," she said, widening her eyes to take in the rest of the graveyard.

"I did."

"And what did they say?"

"They were keeping it to themselves."

Violet laughed, something she rarely did these days and when she did it was mostly for the pleasure of having done so.

"What is a soul Baz? I don't even know what a soul is. Is it our thoughts? You know, our minds, or is it this thing that leaves our body when we die. Whatever that may be?"

"I thought I asked the question Vi."

"OK, would you like to have a soul? Whatever it is?"

"We *are* in the right place, there's probably a few knocking around here somewhere."

She laughed again. "No! I'm saying if you had the choice?"

"That's not answering the question, is it?"

"Turn around Baz," she said, gently rolling his shoulders to face him away.

"How do you know I'm here?"

"I can hear you."

"OK. I'm going to stop talking."

The seconds ticked by. "I get the message," he finally said, turning back.

"Like I said Baz, it's your choice. If you want there to be a soul, then for you there is one. You can even choose the kind of soul you would like. I would have a rich one, if I was you."

Baz thought for a moment. "Have you created a soul for yourself?"

She smiled at Baz. "No, but that doesn't mean I won't when the time comes."

A moments thought. "Why is it there always seems to be a cold wind in a cemetery?" he said.

"You're right, it is getting a bit chilly, let's make our way back." As they strolled between the graves Violet asked Baz, "Who are Garage and Mikhail anyway?"

He told her about his time in Shaibah and the people he knew, including Morgan with his colourful language, then about Mikhail and Garage. He tried to keep the narrative light, purposely omitting the details of that fateful day beside the truck.

"The war has been terribly hard on you Baz," her voice softening.

Baz didn't reply.

In A Dark Corner
1964

The constant drizzle began to ebb away, leaving shimmering white and yellow crucifixes reflecting on the wet pavement from the street lamps. Everything else was dark, even the unbroken line of three storey townhouses had shut down for the night. The only noise was from a random taxi hoping to boost his earnings with a late night fare, and a newspaper van revving loudly as it accelerated away in the distance.

It was the middle of the night, three o'clock on an early May morning and Baz was crossing the junction at Castle Street. He was not alone.

Baz had just reached the middle of the road and glanced upwards to the top of the street. They were still there. Only this time it was different.

The first time he saw them was three junctions back. At the time, Baz thought they were stragglers from a party or an after hours bar.

He crossed the second junction. While he waited for a car to negotiate the corner he looked up the gentle ascent to the top of Needham Road, the same dark figures had appeared again. Stopping in a small huddled cluster on the pavement all four were staring in his direction. Baz looked around for anything unusual, there was nothing, he would even take something usual, something normal, he saw nothing that could possibly warrant their attention. Only himself.

Several seconds later he arrived at the next junction and again he glanced up to the top of the road. Lit by the streetlamp above them the strangers stood in a line strung across the width of the road, like four broken links in a chain. Three were men wearing dark suits, one was tall, a large chested black man, one of far eastern origin and one white man, all in their thirties or forties, the oriental and white man both had shaven heads glowing white from the light above. The fourth person was a woman, short and delicate in stature with shoulder length fair hair and a pale complexion. She wore a knee length raincoat pulled tight around her waist, her dark stockinged legs lifted high by tall stilettoes. She was in her forties, maybe fifties.

Baz stepped onto the pavement opposite and took three long strides forward. Hidden behind the large white cornerstones of the building he stopped and waited; taking one step back he glanced up the road once again. A panic rushed through him. In the centre of the road and walking towards him were the woman and the bespectacled black man towering beside her. There was no sign of the other two.

Baz glanced towards the next junction, expecting to see the other two suddenly appear in front of him. Without stopping, a taxi swung around the corner and spluttered past only a couple of feet away. Why didn't I hail it down, he thought, the driver was even looking at me. Baz turned to look behind him, the black man and the women hadn't appeared yet, they must only be seconds away. He knew if he carried on in the direction he was walking the other two might suddenly emerge in front of him. What do these people want? I have no money. They've probably got knives, maybe a gun! Baz began to foresee his own death, robbed and left to die in some doorway, no witnesses, no clues, it will be the perfect crime. Maybe these people enjoy killing just for the sake of it. I'm probably not the first and I won't be the last.

Any second now he would be caught between the four of them. Like the fork in a chess manoeuvre, even the most stupid of novices wouldn't fall for that one. I could run, fifty years of age, I can still run, he hoped.

Baz bolted across the main thoroughfare of Parkside Avenue and into the street opposite, another road bordered by tall Georgian terraced houses. Fronting them were ornate iron railings uniformly swinging around and up the few steps to one side of their front doors, only to start their journey again from the other side. Baz was halfway along Wyndham Street, his eye caught by one of the railings, not the railing itself but what was in it, or more to the truth, what was not in it. A gap where a gate had been left open, leading down to a basement flat, more importantly, a tiny concreted area. Baz looked down the narrow steps, at one end was a door, on the other a row of three dustbins, facing them was a window with six black panes. It was dark down there, in fact, tucked nicely away in the corner was pure pitch blackness.

Baz took a quick glance down Wyndham Street, a car flashed by, for a fraction of a second its headlamps highlighted his faceless enemies.

Without further thought he leapt down the steps, slowing as he entered the damp smelling murkiness of the corner. Baz crouched down, his back against the cold, dank wall, a forlorn shadow of a figure as he curled his arms around his knees. No one could see him, no one could hear him, he tried to swallow, his mouth was too dry.

A small creature moved only feet away, with stealth like confidence it slyly prowled in-between the bins, disappearing for a second then appearing again to sniff a small piece of discarded food. Like two floating green marbles its eyes stared directly at Baz, as though he was about to give the game away. In one flowing movement, it gracefully sprung onto one of the dustbin lids and without pausing, another giant leap where it landed on the pavement. The cat darted away into the darkness.

He waited.

A curtain twitched behind the window, Baz's whole body froze, his mind went numb. A bright light appeared in the cracks between the curtains, enough to slide a ray of light up Baz's legs and onto his face. A few seconds later the frosted large pane in the top half of the door blazed a glow of bright white light, illuminating the entire basement area. With a quick clunk of a bolt and the turn of a key, the door swung open and standing there, silhouetted in the frame was an old woman in a dressing gown, the air in front of her feeling the full wrath of a walking stick.

"Oi you, fuck off! Bloody vagrants, go on fuck off!" she yelled, brandishing the lethal weapon.

Baz held up a clean pair of palms in surrender. "I'm going, only there are people trying to kill..."

"I'll bloody kill you if you don't fuck off."

As Baz passed her, the warm yellow light behind her looked inviting. He could take the old woman hostage, they would never find him in there, he would let her go in an hours time, no harm would be done.

Baz left the old woman standing in the doorway and climbed the steps.

"Hiya fella," an American accent broke through the dark, damp air as Baz stepped onto the pavement.

MRS CHATTLE

If you were going to be born at home then this would have to be the place thought Robert as he looked over the shallow hedgerow towards the whitewashed thatched cottage. He glanced up at the small lead lined windows on the first floor and wondered behind which one was his first introduction to this world. Behind which one did his mother depart hers. A sadness surged through him, his eyes welled up and a dry swallow got caught in the back of his throat. How much he had missed because of what happened here twenty-two years ago.

Robert Blakeney recalled what Father Nolan had told him back at the orphanage. From the years of constant cigar smoke, the old priest's creamy brogue had begun to sound like he was drowning in his own mucous. Robert had hung onto his every word.

Father Nolan said how he had spoken to Nurse Downes. "She was the midwife present at your birth, long retired now. Unfortunately she wasn't the nurse assigned to your mother. Nurse Dosanjh was your mother's midwife and she happened to be on another call that day. I'm afraid Nurse Dosanjh left the area after the war Robert. The clinic where the midwives were based no longer exists." The priest handed a piece of paper over with an address scrawled on it. Robert looked at the name on the top line, Maureen Downes. "Nurse Downes said she would be happy to put you up in her spare room while you are in the area. You'd probably like to ask her some questions." Robert recalled Father Nolan pausing for quite a long while before he spoke next. "The nurse told me she can remember the birth as though it happened yesterday. She had to call out the doctor, Dr Roberts. Where he is now is anyone's guess but it doesn't really matter, Dr Roberts wasn't your mother's doctor anyway, that was Dr Demant. He died around ten years ago, so many loose ends my son. Anyway, Nurse Downes told me you were born at the place where your mother was living." The old priest handed him another piece of paper, Robert remembered reading it out loud. "Yew Tree Cottage, Spade Elms, North Devon."

"Nurse Downes remembers your mother's neighbour at the time, a Mrs Chattle. She also remembers Mrs Chattle fostering an evacuee, a young lad with an East London accent, she thinks he and your mother had become chums. If anyone knows anything about your father then it will probably be Mrs Chattle or that boy."

Father Nolan picked up what appeared to be a burnt, chewed twig from the ashtray and placed it between his lips. With a whip of a match and for the umpteenth time that afternoon, he lit the cigar, his face breaking through the wreath of smoke as he leant forward. He then spoke in a way Robert had never heard him speak before, as though the words were the most important that had ever departed his mouth. "Now, my son, tell me this, tell me as God is your witness, do you really want to find your father?"

Robert did not hesitate, "I can't think of anything else I would want more Father." There was conviction in his voice. The old priest had everything he needed to know.

"Here is another address in London, it belongs to a Father Duffy, he will put you up if need be. Father Duffy, let's say, owes me a favour Robert."

Father Nolan handed Robert an envelope, "Don't open it now my son, you must wait until you are well away from the orphanage."

Robert longed to knock on the small, wooden door at the end of the path. Then wondered what he would say if someone were to answer. 'Can I see the room where my mother died?..Your mother died here?!..Yes, I used to live here...How long did you live here for?..Oh, for less than an hour.' He knew, if he wanted his questions answered, they would have to come from the neighbouring property.

Robert stared at the tiny squares of coloured glass embedded in the wooden door, a shadow appeared behind the small panes, a click of the latch and the door swung open. Standing in green overalls and a headscarf coiled high up on her forehead was a woman Robert thought was probably in her mid-seventies.

"Can I help you young man?"

"Sorry, yes. My name is Robert," he stuttered.

"Good for you young man. My name is Dawn, if that helps."

"Robert Blakeney."

"Robert Blakeney," she said slowly. Widening her eyes as her gaze gently slid down his body. "My, my, how you have grown."

"You *are* Mrs Chattle?"

"Dawn, please."

"Are you busy," Robert asked, looking at the gardening gloves tucked under her arm. "I can just as easily come back later."

"Do you garden Robert?"

"Garden! I was virtually born in..I mean, well you know where I was born. I mean I was virtually brought up in a garden."

"Then you had better come in."

Mrs Chattle led Robert through the cottage and into the garden, stopping beside a bucket full to the brim with discarded clumps of leaves and roots. "I'm clearing this bed for the summer veg. There's a fork behind you, if you would like to help?" She picked up a small hand spade. "The last time I saw you, you were a tiny baby, look at you now," she said, stabbing the earth.

"What's going in here?" Robert trod the fork into the earth.

"Carrots I think, maybe cabbages."

Dawn Chattle knew his mother would soon enter the conversation, in some ways talking about what had happened might also be good for her own peace of mind. Maybe it would dislodge that image of his mother's death embedded in the back of her mind. Receiving the telegram informing her of her husband passing in the same year made the death of Robert's mother even more poignant.

"Tell me about yourself Robert, what has happened since you were that tiny baby? Tell me what brings you here? As if I need to ask."

Robert told her about the orphanage and the meeting with Father Nolan. He told her how he was staying with Maureen Downes. Mrs Chattle had to ask who she was. "I never knew her name," she said quietly.

Robert paused before asking the question she had been expecting. "You must have known my mother?"

For a moment Mrs Chattle continued to stab at the soil. "Your mother had moved next door about seven months before you were born." She ripped out an old root and dropped it into the bucket. "Each week I could see the bump becoming larger. The bump Robert, you, maybe it was me but I had the feeling she wasn't happy, there was something troubling her, something deep." Another clump of spindly roots found the bucket. "I don't know if I should tell you."

"*Please* Mrs Chattle, you must tell me everything," he pleaded.

"Dawn, please."

"Dawn."

"I once asked her, I thought it may have something to do with her husband being away, you know, fighting in the war. I thought she may have wanted to talk about it. She knew my Arthur was away as well, kindred souls and all that." Mrs Chattle stood up, stretched her shoulders back and pushed her hand into the small of her spine. "Gardening is getting such hard work for an old woman like me."

Robert remained silent, not wanting to contaminate the moment.

"She lost a son in the war. You had a brother Robert. Your mother said his name was William, she said he was a fighter pilot." She stopped talking, wanting him to digest the realisation of another loss in his family, even if it was a brother he had never known.

A faceless image of his brother entered Robert's mind. Was he like William? "A fighter pilot, I would never be that brave in a million years."

Mrs Chattle smiled.

"I don't know her Christian name?" he suddenly realised.

"Margaret," she replied. "Your mother had a lovely nature about her Robert. I can see a lot of her in you, she would have been proud of you."

"Did she mention any other brothers or sisters?"

"No. Only William, I'm sure William was the only one."

"Did she say anything about my father?"

"She mentioned him once."

He waited. "And?"

"He was in the RAF, somewhere abroad. That is all she said, she made it obvious she didn't want to talk about him."

"Oh, then you think he was killed?'

"No, I didn't get that impression, I didn't get the impression she was a widow." Mrs Chattle felt she would recognise a widow.

"Father Nolan said you had a young lad staying with you, an evacuee. Maureen said it was the lad she had sent to fetch the doctor."

"Eddie."

"Eddie?"

"I could murder a cup of tea Robert." She kicked her boots off and walked into the cottage.

Robert continued working the vegetable patch until Dawn Chattle called him in. Sitting in a wicker chair by the window he placed his cup and saucer, a plate with three biscuits and a doorstep of a sandwich on the deep recess. Mrs Chattle sat back on a tartan covered rocker.

Opposite him was a cabinet with more photographs than he had seen in his entire life. He picked up one mounted within a large silver frame, a proud looking man in a wide lapelled suit standing next to a girl hardly out of her teens, both wearing the widest smiles.

"You and your husband?" He had forgotten his name.

"Me and Arthur."

Robert didn't know for how long, he lost track of time. Dawn Chattle told him about her life spent with Arthur. He could tell she was speaking deep from her heart, after all, it was where she kept him. She told Robert how they couldn't have children. "In the end we just accepted it, our lives were full with just the two of us, we were not only in love, we had become soul mates. We never even argued, not once, ever, in our entire time together." She told Robert about receiving the telegram from the war office. "Eddie was my saviour at that time, if there is ever such a thing as God given, then Eddie was it. From a fourteen year old he suddenly became a man. I don't think

I could have got through it without him. Do you believe in fate Robert?"

He thought about the search for his father. "Yes, I have to, yes I believe in fate Dawn."

"Do you believe fate has brought *us* together?"

Robert didn't reply, he didn't know how to reply.

"Eddie?" he said, prompting her to continue.

"Eddie Wallace, I used to take him to the pictures, always cowboy films. Too much violence if you ask me but harmless enough, which is a lot more than you could say about life at that time. He had a mind like a sponge, never stopped asking questions, wanted to know everything he did. I had him for over two years, missed him like I would miss my own son after he left," she said the last words with sadness.

"Where did he go after he left you?"

"Back to the city, back to his family. Mind you, if he had had his way he'd still be here now. We kept in touch for a few months, postcards mainly. Why a boy would want to write to an old lady?...Anyway we lost contact."

"You weren't old then."

She smiled. "To a fifteen year old boy, I was old. Believe me, virtually a dinosaur."

Robert suddenly perked up. "If you wrote to him, you must have his address?"

"I have his Mum and Dad's address in Deptford."

As Robert closed the gate behind him he turned to look at Mrs Chattle. "Cabbages will do better than carrots."

I KILLED A MAN ONCE

"I killed a man once and I'll do it again," Baz cried out.

"Hey there fella, no ones doing any killing around here," a reassuring American accent drifted through the darkness.

Baz couldn't see who was talking, it was too dark, he just knew it wasn't the woman.

"We're not here to hurt you. We're here to help you." That was undoubtedly the woman.

244

"Yeah right!" Baz snapped, taking a step back, still thinking their motives were not as they would like him to believe.

"You're free to go if you wish. We wondered if you needed help?" the woman said with a metallic London twang.

"If you're hungry man, we can give you something to eat," the American spoke again.

Baz lingered on the white man with the bald head, his loose posture and calm manner didn't seem to give the appearance of a sadistic killer.

The American accent spoke again, "It's your choice man, you're a free spirit, like the lady said, you can go if you wish. Believe me man, we're the last people who'd want to stop you."

It was when he saw the milky teeth flashing high in the shadows Baz realised the custodian of the American accent was actually the tall, black man.

"Who are you then?" said Baz, "How do I know I can trust you? You might want to..."

Whoosh and a slam as a sash window loudly opened two floors above them, an old head with unruly wispy grey hair appeared. "Do you chaps realise what time it is? *You* may be nocturnal. I am certainly not! Now be good fellows and move along." Another whoosh and a slam and the window was shut as fast as it opened.

"Fucking arsehole," said the woman.

"Who are we? We are devotees of The Living Enlightenment man. How do you know you can trust us? You don't, your choice man. But you'll get a bed *and* you'll get fed."

"*And* you might get to understand the true meaning of life," added an English accent. Not the woman's.

"I'm not a tramp," said Baz. "*And* I've got a bed, *and* I've got food."

"You won't be needing us then," said the woman.

"I don't need anything, but..." Baz paused for a moment. "I wouldn't mind knowing the *true* meaning of life." The true meaning! It's not as though he knew any meaning of life.

"Not needing anything is a good place to start," said the English accent. "Nothing is what it seems..."

Whoosh and a slam, the sash window slid open again. The same head poked out, only a shade of beetroot this time. "I'm calling the

245

pol..."

"Shut the fuck up you obnoxious little shit!" screamed the woman. Quietly adding "Fucking fascist," as the window was slammed shut.

"Nothing is what it seems," said the black man, glancing towards the woman, "especially with Alice."

"Well, all men are fucking arseholes, now that *is* as it seems!"

"Let's make a move before the men in blue turn up," said the English accent.

The four strangers turned on their heels and made their way back along Wyndham Street.

Baz was left staring at the backs of the retreating strangers. "Sod it," he muttered to himself and started a brisk pace towards the four. Now I'm chasing them, he thought. "I'm not waiting for the police by myself," he said. As if it was the only reason he had caught them up. He slotted himself to their left, something Baz always made a conscious effort to do.

After returning from Shaibah, Baz found employment as an engineer with a newly formed airline, British European Airways. The company was created in April 1946, Baz started in October the same year, practically a founding member.

It was eight years later when he and BEA parted company.

Baz had noticed a hearing loss in his left ear; by the time it got to the seventh year, his hearing on that side was virtually nonexistent.

The cause? The pressurising and depressurising of aircraft cabins, a common daily routine in the hangars.

"One eardrum is damaged beyond repair Mr Albright, the other has also stretched. If you continue with your present employment then I am afraid you will lose your hearing completely." The doctor had not minced his words.

With the small amount of remuneration money, which included Baz signing a declaration that no blame would be held against the airline, he moved into a small bedsit in his town of birth.

It felt as though he had gone full circle.

"What's your name man?" asked the American.

"People call me Baz."

Baz noticed his skin was dark as ebony and his mop of black tight curly hair shimmered like wire wool. His bloodshot eyes constantly fixed forward, as if anything to the sides of him were just not worth looking at. His long lolloping strides unhurried, Baz guessed this man had never rushed for anything or anyone.

"What's *your* name?" asked Baz.

"Lennox."

"No, I mean what's your first name?"

"Lennox."

"Lennox?"

"Lennox."

"People call me Issan in The Temple, I was given the name Issan, it means one mountain."

"I thought it might. If I knew Issan meant one mountain, I would have given you it as well. You said the temple?"

"More mansion than temple, more temple than mansion, we call it The Temple man."

"You said back there that you were devotees of The Living..."

"We call ourselves the devotees man, devotees of The Living Enlightenment. We are Buddhists, Zen. My name is An," said the Englishman.

"An?"

"An, it means peace, *and* I only have the one name!"

The next dozen or so steps were taken in silence.

Baz began frantically waving his hand in front of his right ear. "This bloody bee has been buzzing around me ever since we've been walking."

"There's no bee here man."

Baz continued attacking the air. "I can hear..."

"That's Kai-Liang man."

"You have a name for the bee!"

"No man. Kai-Liang. This is Kai-Liang," said Lennox, slowing his pace and allowing a far eastern man with high cheekbones and almond shaped eyes to become visible. Kai-Liang grinned at Baz, in truth, Kai-Liang grinned at everything, his face was a permanent grin, as though he was born that way.

"Kai-Liang thinks he's a bee?"

Everyone chuckled, apart from Kai-Liang, who just grinned, and Alice who never found anything funny.

"No man, Kai-Liang is saying his mantra, he is always saying his mantra. He has said it for so long now, people say he doesn't know how to stop saying it. Some people say they have even heard him say it in his sleep."

"A mantra?" asked Baz.

"Ah, your first lesson," said An.

"A lesson?"

"What are you thinking about now?"

"What a mantra is."

"What were you thinking about five minutes ago?"

"I don't know, I can't remember, probably wondering if you were going to kill me."

"What are you going to think about in five minutes time?"

"I don't know, probably the same. Who knows?"

"Kai-Liang does."

"So what is a mantra?"

"A sound. A sound to remove all thought Baz. The thought that ties you to the physical world," said An.

"The sound of a bee?"

"The sound of Om."

"Are all future lessons going to be like this one?"

"Om is the sound of creation Baz. The vibration of the universe."

"So the sound of the universe sounds like a bee?"

Lennox glanced down at Baz, the first time since they had started walking, his white teeth flashing from a smile.

Alice, who assumed the helm whenever the pavement narrowed, had swung left into a road with a short line of two storey, terraced houses bordering one side. Across the road were the outlines of large, various shaped industrial buildings.

It was approaching four o'clock and the black nothingness above them was now being infiltrated by a blanket of deep blue, the featureless neutral tone of the buildings was gradually being replaced by colour. The day was awakening.

Then Baz saw it. The mansion, The Temple? There could be no mistaking it. It was the big house, the one standing at the end of Haydons Road, the one he used to see as a child. He hadn't even thought about the direction they were taking. To his disappointment, most of the white stone he remembered had gone, or to tell the truth, been hidden. It now looked as if it had taken a giant step back from civilisation, although it still stood out from every other building. Painted on its wide frontage was a huge Sanskrit symbol, looking like a curly number three with a downward sweeping tail. Baz thought it was green, or maybe blue, or was it red, the darkness still masking its true colour. Covering the remainder of the front wall were other symbols surrounding large hand drawn words. Baz imagined in the light of day all the colours from the rainbow had been used. Love and peace and women rule (an Alice creation), there were ban the bomb signs, also one image that appeared in several places in various sizes. An image with seven pointed serrated edged leaves fanning out from a short stem, like a badly drawn maple leaf, a failed Canadian artist, thought Baz.

"Is this yours?" asked Baz, his eyes scanning the building.

"It belongs to everyone man," answered Lennox.

The five spread out as they walked towards the right of the building. It was then Baz had the feeling that he belonged, that he had never felt so comfortable in any other company. Whoever these devotees were, they knew something he didn't.

Less than one minute later they entered through a small side door.

THE PRIEST'S HOUSE

Father Duffy was only able to become a priest because of the intervention of Father Nolan.

It was many years ago before a Sunday morning service, when Father Duffy's call to holy orders was nearly derailed by a slight misunderstanding over an incident with Mrs Lewis the church florist. Anyhow, that is what Father Nolan called it, a misunderstanding. As far as Father Duffy was concerned there was no misunderstanding at all. He had made the promise of celibacy and he was not going to break that promise, even if Mrs Lewis's marriage *was* going through a bad patch.

Back in Ireland and at a very young age, Father Duffy decided join-ing the church was going to be his true calling, his God fearing mother thought the same about her fifth and youngest son. "The Lord Jesus has spoken to him himself." She used to tell everyone with great eagerness, not forgetting her other sons had fulfilled her expected quota of grandchildren.

The priest's house was like a small Catholic commune in its own right. Father Duffy had always liked the company of other clergy around him, probably a throwback to the episode with Mrs Lewis. Nearly forfeiting his vocation because of the advances from an attractive thirty year old florist had quite a lasting effect on the priest, after all he was only human. If he happened to be in the presence of a woman anytime after, apart from the protected enclosure of the confessional box, Father Duffy always made sure he had company, or witnesses if the truth be known, although he would never use that word.

Also in the house was the recently ordained Father Byrne, a young priest with heavily greased, swept back, black hair and a teddy boy like appearance, who wore pointed cowboy boots. If it wasn't for Father Byrne's dog collar, the clergy would be the last choice any person assigning a vocation would put to him. Then there was the seriously serious Deacon Stone and the old widowed housekeeper, Sheila McKinnon. The only woman Father Duffy would allow himself to be alone with, understandable if you knew Mrs MacKinnon. The last intake to the priest's house was Robert Blakeney.

Remember the envelope Father Nolan had given to Robert on his last day at the orphanage. In fact it was four envelopes, although at the time Robert only knew of it as the one, that is, until the day he opened it. Inside the larger outer envelope were three smaller sealed ones. One had 'Open after arriving at Mrs Downes house' written on it. Inside that envelope was a small amount of cash, and a handwritten note...

Dear Robert

I always thank God for small mercies as I am sure you do. Only now as you are reading this letter I feel it is your mother you must thank for her hindsight and the obvious love for her unborn baby.
A hindsight that also realised God can work in mysterious ways.

Your mother had left a trust for you that
matured on your 21st birthday.
A legacy that I believe has left you with
enough provisions to last for sometime into the
future.
Although substantial, it is not limitless and I
trust the common sense that I have witnessed
from you over the past years will still prevail.
You are now at Mrs Downe's house Robert.
In your hand you are probably holding a small
amount of cash, part of which will help you
get to the solicitors, their address is written on
one of the other envelopes. Give that
envelope to a Mr Pickard, and only Mr Pickard, he
will advise you from then on.
May God be with you.

Your friend always
Father Nolan

And on the other envelope? 'Open after your prayers have been answered'.

The months before Robert arrived at the priest's house, Maureen Downes thought she was the closest to a mother Robert would ever get. After all, she was the first person to see Robert enter into this world, it was as though she had given birth to him herself. It was also Nurse Downes who had named Robert...Robert. For over a year she cooked his dinners, washed his clothes and did everything a mother would do for her own son.

Only in the last few months Robert was starting to feel guilty. He had a secret, one he kept from Maureen Downes, a secret he would have preferred not to have been a secret. Robert had never liked secrets, especially after Father Nolan had once told him that they would rot away your insides if kept for too long.

The secret? Robert was still visiting Dawn Chattle, he could sense the unrest whenever he returned from seeing her. Maureen Downes thought she was losing Robert to another mother. For the last few months when he had seen Dawn Chattle, Robert kept it to himself.

Robert didn't choose the time to leave North Devon, it had been chosen for him. Father Nolan was right, the secret *had* begun to rot away his insides.

There was only one person in the priest's house who knew the true reason behind Robert staying there. For this person, not to tell the others was not made out of thoughtlessness, it was just not his decision to make.

On the third day, Robert decided that keeping his secret from Maureen Downes had rotted enough of his insides to take on another one at this time.

"What brings you to the heathen capital of the world?" asked Father Byrne over his boiled egg and bread soldiers.

"Robert is a friend of Father Nol..." Father Duffy began.

"I'm searching for my father," interrupted Robert.

"Robert is searching for his father," said Father Duffy, clearing his throat.

"In this house we feel we have found our true father," Deacon Stone said, in his usual supercilious manner. There was now a subordinate to practice his theologian wisdom on. As Deacon Stone soon discovered, a boy brought up in a Catholic orphanage was not going to be the most accepting of recipients.

Robert told them the entire story, starting with his mother's death and ending with Eddie Wallace. "I'm hoping Eddie will be able to put the first link in the chain," he finally said.

"When did Eddie leave Mrs Chattle's house?" inquired Father Byrne.

"May 1944." Robert knew the details off by heart.

Deacon Stone began prodding the tip of each finger in turn. "Around thirty-six, if my arithmetic is correct," he said. "Let's hope he has a good memory."

"Do you know anything *at all* about your father?" asked Father Byrne.

"He was in the RAF during the war. He served abroad."

"Do you know where?"

Robert shook his head. "He was in the RAF and he served abroad, that's about the sum of it, at the moment."

"That narrows it down to a few hundred thousand," said Deacon Stone.

"If he survived," Robert said softly. "If he is still alive."

"Then we must all pray for Robert that his father is alive," Father Duffy said.

Robert waited two weeks before he took the journey to Deptford. The last few days had been a constant battle, it felt as if common sense had deserted him. The nearer he got to making the decision to go, the closer he got to realising the many consequences. Every day a new emotion would surface. Would he be able to face up to the disappointment? Could he accept the rejection? Could he handle the frustration? How would he feel if his father is dead? What if his father doesn't know he exists? What if he has a family of his own? Maybe he has children of his own; how would his wife feel about his new-found son?

Robert left for Deptford mid-morning and returned late afternoon, but not to the priest's house. A seat on a cold park bench had been his refuge for the last few hours. A place where he sat and watched young mothers pushing prams, children hanging onto a roundabout for dear life, a father with his son kicking a deflated football around, another teaching his daughter how to ride her cycle, her screams of delight pierced through the air. For Robert, these were memories missing from his past.

Only it wasn't the past he needed to think about. His experience in Deptford had left him hanging from a thread. It was his future Robert needed to consider.

As Robert entered the priest's house he knew Father Duffy would be out with Deacon Stone on church business, it was Thursday evening. Father Byrne was in the living room, the telltale sign of strong smelling cigarette smoke always an indication of the young priest's presence. Sheila MacKinnon could be heard clattering around in the kitchen as she stacked the crockery away, finesse was not one of Mrs MacKinnon's strengths.

Robert quietly shut the front door behind him and tiptoed upstairs, his attempted stealth sadly dashed by a loud creak on the fourth step.

"Sit at the table Robert, I'll bring your dinner over," yelled Mrs MacKinnon.

"I'm really not that hungry Mrs..."

"Of course you are Robert. Many a poor child would give their right arm for this casserole."

"Let's hope they're left-handed then," he said under his breath.

Robert sat alone at the table and prodded at the food.

With his back to Robert and hidden in the depths of an armchair was Father Byrne, a rising cloud of smoke followed a long, hard suck of his cigarette.

"Thank God for Thursday evenings," he said, poking his head round the back of the seat. "A sparrow could eat more than you Robert."

"How did you?...Never mind. I'm not hungry."

Father Byrne sprang out of the chair and parked himself opposite. He snatched the fork out of Robert's hand while stubbing his cigarette out. "The old bag will only moan if you don't gobble most of it up." He began spiking the meat. "Did you put the bet on Robert."

"Oh God! Sorry Father, I completely forgot. My mind..."

"Good! Bloody mare came fifth anyway."

Father Byrne continued eating. From time to time he would freeze and like a wild animal in deep concentration, listen out for the old housekeeper. "You have an overpowering odour of disappointment about you my son." Placing the fork on the plate, then quickly turning the handle to face Robert, he said, "that'll keep the old bat happy."

Robert looked up at the young priest with tired eyes.

"Would you like to confess to a young priest with a wise old head?"

Robert pushed his plate to the side. "Eddie Wallace doesn't live at that address anymore."

"What did you expect? It *was* twenty years ago Robert."

"His father answered the door. I tried to explain why I was there, that I was trying to find out about my father. He didn't seem to be that interested. He didn't even seem to want to listen. I asked him if Mrs Wallace was in, he looked straight through me."

"Ah! Brain dead, know the type my son."

"Who's dead?" said Mrs MacKinnon as she entered the room and picked up the plate. "See, I said you were hungry young man."

"Mr Cooper's dog Brian, Brian's dead, Mrs Mac."

"Who's Mr Cooper Father? Be sure to say I was sorry to hear about his dog."

"Will do Mrs Mac."

They waited until the old housekeeper shut the door behind her.

"Then what happened?"

"I asked him straight out. Would it be possible to have Eddie's address? He told me he didn't have it. What could I do Father? I gave him a piece of paper with this address on it. I wrote at the top that it concerns Mrs Blakeney who lived next door to Mrs Chattle. I asked if he would give it to Eddie the next time he sees him, I expect it's in the bin now."

Father Byrne pursed his lips and nodded. "Not if the old guy thinks there's money in it for him. Believe me Robert, you hear of some strange things in my line of business." The young priest paused in thought. "Your Mother Robert, God rest her soul. Tell me everything you know about her, I mean everything!"

"Mrs Chattle said she came from London before she moved next door."

"London's a big city."

"She, they, she had money, quite a lot." Robert thought about his legacy, he didn't expand any further. "She had a son Father. He died in the war, a fighter pilot. William, William was his name." Robert's eyes glazed over. "William *was* my brother."

"That's it!" Father Byrne spurted out and slapped his hand on the table.

"That's what?"

"The chances are he was killed in the Battle of Britain. We find out all the names of the fighter pilots called William that were killed in the Battle of Britain, all the Williams from London that is. If there's one called Blakeney. Then we've picked a winner."

"We? Father."

"How can they refuse a priest with a good sob story my son. Believe me Robert, this white collar is a ticket that'll get you anywhere, and seeing as you just saved me two and six on the three thirty." Father Byrne waited. "Seeing as you just saved me two and..."

"Sorry Father." Robert delved into his pocket and handed over half a crown.

Contrary to first sighting of the anarchistic daubings on the front of the house, The Temple happened to be the epitome of order and organisation. It had rules, lots of rules, cleaning, cooking, gardening and a multitude of other rotas had to be abided by.

Baz thought back to all those years ago in Shaibah. He liked rules then and he liked them now, rules work, even though he had broken a few.

If there was a problem or a dispute then a simple known procedure had to be followed. Inform Issan (aka Lennox, we are in the house now). If Issan felt it was serious enough, then he would request a private audience with The Master. After an indeterminate length of time that could stretch from a couple of minutes to a whole day, a solution would finally be delivered, more often in the form of a philosophical quote, one that would have to be analysed, word by word, sometimes for a couple of minutes, sometimes for another entire day. Time was not an issue in The Temple.

"What did he say?" asked Tylanni, after Issan returned from the master and summoned the entire house to the meeting room, a large, bare room shedding dark green wallpaper like an old skin. Tylanni had been the one to complain after a young devotee had drunkenly tumbled over in the art room, taking two easels, several pots of paint and a couple of nearly completed, yet still wet, works of art with him, including Tylanni's. Her abstract canvas (in the style of Jackson Pollock) had unfortunately finished face down on the floor, with the young inebriated man thrashing around on top like a swatted fly. His only line of defence was that he thought the painting had been improved somewhat.

Issan rose to his feet and looked down on the circle of cross legged devotees. "The Master said we must see The Temple as an island, an island in the centre of a vast ocean. We can swim in it, we can dive into it, we can even fish in it, but like an ocean has salt we will only face madness if we drink it."

There was great debate whether The Master was actually talking about alcohol itself or western civilisation in general. The overriding opinion was that it was most probably alcohol, considering he had used the word 'drink' and it was the reason Issan had been to see The

Master in the first place. For good measure they decided a small amount of western capitalist civilisation should also be criticised. Meeting concluded.

No one disputed the decision of The Master.

Baz...no, not Baz...Butsugen, Baz had a new name. Like all other devotees it was given to him after a few days at The Temple. A visit to the master and Issan delivered the name Butsugen, meaning Buddha Eye. Simplicity itself! After all the names he *had* been called, 'Buddha Eye' was without doubt, the most complimentary.

"Outside man, in the physical world," as Issan had put it, "You are at liberty to revert back to Baz, but while here, in the temple, you will always be known as Butsugen...man."

On that first night at The Temple, when Baz was still Baz, he was fed, watered and given a bed. Not one for craving the company of strangers, Baz gave it until lunch, if he hadn't been told the true meaning of life by then, he would return to his digs.

The next morning, Issan and Alice gave Butsugen a tour of the temple. He was politely introduced to everyone they met, about thirty in total, of varying ages and backgrounds. The oldest was a man, Abhaya, Butsugen thought he was well over seventy. He had a moustache like a frontier gold prospector and a length of grey hair hanging from the back of his bald head like a horse's tail. Some had shaven heads like An and Kai-Liang, including a lot of the women, others had long hair, including some of the men. All wore loose fitting colourful attire, some cloth appeared to be patched together using various fabrics, kaftans and tie dyed t-shirts were popular, also flowing full length linen skirts, many had braiding and coloured beads weaved into their hair.

It was Kai-Liang who had the most affect on Butsugen, at the beginning anyhow and only in a spiritual sense. He seemed to have what the other devotees called the third eye. Along with his permanent grin and that low vibrating buzz, Kai-Liang always greeted everyone with a hug. At first, for Butsugen, this physical uniting of bodies didn't have the same desired comfort that everyone else seemed to attain from it, he just felt awkward, not even a spiritual awkwardness. Then while in the clutches of Kai-Liang's arms one day, Butsugen felt a warmth he had never experienced before, one that seemed to penetrate his thoughts, that made his brain tingle, it was as if someone had wrapped an electric blanket around him.

"The warmth had always been there Butsugen," An told him later. "Only you were not aware of it."

If Kai-Liang knew the truth to life, then he was going to keep it to himself, Butsugen had never heard him speak. His apparent contentment and happiness was going to have to be passed on by some other means. Maybe that's what the hugs were about, Butsugen decided.

To all the devotees, the building in its entirety, bricks, mortar, people, the oxygen they breathed, furniture, thoughts, in fact everything, was known as The Temple, although Butsugen always spoke about it as the big house. No one seemed to mind, they thought it had an adolescent innocence about it.

In its physical form the big house had been built out of white Portland stone blocks, although it was difficult to tell with the numerous colourful representations covering the front wall. Below the large Sanskrit symbol, which turned out to be a kind of reddy brown, were the grand, double fronted doors set behind four white pillars. These held up an ornate, (Parthenon style) sculptured, stone porch, which after years of neglect and children using it as target practice, had finished up in worse condition than the actual Elgin marbles themselves. For the entire time Butsugen was at The Temple he only ever saw the front doors opened once and that was at the end of his stay *and* not by any devotee.

The big house was built at the end of the 1880's by an ageing eccentric American industrialist called Haydon White as part of his 'Great Plan' project. The 'Great Plan' was to have all his factories built on the canal side of the newly laid road, that way, any manufactured goods could be easily shipped in and out, mostly on Haydon White barges. On the other side of the road were rows of terraced houses, all occupied by the rent paying employees of this freethinking, extremely wealthy and powerful autocratic individual. Three years after his 'Great Plan' was conceived, the first stage was complete and standing in all its grand entirety was the proud and magnificent mansion facing down the length of the road. There had been one stipulation in the plans, not one wall or fence should be erected at the front of the mansion. Haydon White needed to be able to view *all* his expanding empire from wherever he was in the building. The row of terraced houses were finished one year later and the first factory had begun to be built.

Haydon White, who covered every conceivable eventuality and also backed them up with every imaginable contingency, had not allowed for one catastrophic occurrence. In 1886, during a banquet at the mansion celebrating the completion of the first factory, Haydon White unceremoniously slid off his chair with both hands clutching his chest. He was dead before he hit the luxurious double yarned deep red woollen carpet.

His son and heir took the helm of the White empire in America and immediately despatched a certain Christian Paige across the Atlantic to oversee the 'Great Plan.' Mr Paige, a close and trusted friend of the late Haydon, had been successfully managing the White's business interests in America while the 'great plan' was developing. The relocation of Mr Paige was thought to be more erasing a threat to the son's leadership than a shrewd business move. To appease and ensure Mr Paige's move was a permanent one, the son, who had shown no interest in the newly built mansion whatsoever, handed it over to Mr Paige. The 'great plan' was back on track.

Because of the dire financial condition the White Industry had found itself in back in America, only half of the factories were ever built and the last ones had to be self-financed by the 'Great Plan' itself.

Christian Paige died a day before the First World War had been declared, some say it was 'the great plan' itself that killed him. It had never been entirely completed.

Before Mr Paige's corpse was cold, Haydon White's son could not offload the White Industries English interests quickly enough and the few factories that had been built were sold separately, for little or no money. Most went to the British Government for use in the war effort.

Mrs Paige, along with two loyal servants stayed on at the mansion, only leaving it on the rarest of occasions. The childless, lonely and heartbroken old widow died there in 1924.

With a great deal of effort and just as much frustration, because of a bitter and protracted legal battle with Haydon's son over ownership, (he was now needing every dime he could get in his sieve like hands), the distant Paige relatives failed miserably to sell the mansion. Discarded like an old shoe, with the legal battle ending in stalemate, the mansion was boarded up and left to the mercy of the elements.

From then on the rats and an odd vagrant would be its only occupants. Aside from broken window panes and some lost roof tiles, the interior fared very well in the four decades it battled against the elements, mainly because of Haydon White's insistence on using only the best quality materials.

An and Kai-Liang had disappeared for the entire second week and most of the third week. Butsugen discovered they were in The Temple section of the house, alone in small separate rooms, meditating and practicing yoga, without one word being spoken or heard, both sleeping on mattressless wooden beds. Once a day the minimal amount of food and drink was brought up to them, the small bowl of rice and cup of water carefully placed outside their doors in complete silence.

They reappeared on the Thursday afternoon, the same day Butsugen and Issan had collected Butsugen's meagre belongings.

"Great to see you're still with us Butsugen," An said, with a cheerful smile and eyes that were surprisingly bright and clear.

Butsugen had never seen anyone look as fresh as An and Kai Liang did on that day, radiating contentment from every pore in their bodies. After weeks of solitary confinement, Butsugen was expecting to see someone that had sorely missed the basics of life, someone that had battled with their thoughts, tormented by the devils within, someone that would return looking bedraggled and withdrawn. He couldn't recall ever seeing two people look so at peace with themselves as they did on that day.

It was after a few months at The Temple, Butsugen asked Issan, "So where is The Master?" Alice gazed up at the large American as if she was also waiting for the answer. The reply was short and sharp. "He occupies six rooms on the canal side of the house. He never leaves his apartment man."

"So who is The Master?"

Issan sighed. "He is The Master man." Butsugen felt the bloodshot eyes bearing down on him. "The Master is not like us man. He is on another plane man. He would just float away if it wasn't for the devotees man." And that was it, conversation over.

The closest Butsugen ever got to The Master was in the apartment's circular entrance hall on the second floor, with its rows of prayer wheels and sweet smelling incense. Half embedded into the wall were two marble pillars, in-between them was a large wooden door with an arced top that would not look out of place in some medieval castle. (The palatial apartment plans had been put together by Haydon White for his own private use). It wasn't too long before Butsugen realised it was only Issan or Alice that ever entered the apartment.

The devotee's bedrooms and bathrooms were all on the first floor. The many large solid doors set at irregular intervals along the main aisle would lead any unsuspecting person to think they were about to enter a stately bedroom suite. Instead they would find themselves in a narrow corridor with five or more smaller doors leading into small rooms, a thin partition being their only separation, *too* thin thought Butsugen, realising a lot of the noises at night were not the pipes banging.

The ground floor was the business part of the house. The art, sculpture, textiles, print, candle making and meeting rooms were all based there. Also, in a reading room with two tall, multi paned windows that made the light sparkle, there were walls packed full of empty shelves. Apart from the absence of books, it wasn't any different from the day it was built.

A large communal room stretched from the back of the house to the front. From the first time Butsugen had entered it he noticed a permanent smell of earthy, sweet musty smoke. It reminded him of the spices back in Shaibah, a multitude of burning incense sticks attempting to douse the aroma always appeared to be in the minority. By the lavishly carved cornices, ceiling rose and doors, it was obvious that this was once Haydon White's opulently decorated banqueting room. Even one of the two original chandeliers remained hanging, although the sparkle had long been replaced by dust and grime. Sofas and armchairs in varying states of condition, huge, bold coloured cushions, an extremely uncomfortable mattress were all ensconced in some part of this room, although the large flower patterned rug appeared to be in a different place every time Butsugen entered. This was the relaxation room, the socialising room, the listening to music room, the smoking room, the getting away from The Temple room. A bright room fuelled with light by the same tall, arched topped windows as seen in the library, four in the front wall and four at the back, the space in-between them adorned with all kinds of revolutionary

261

hieroglyphics and psychedelic posters, a stark contrast to the old masters that once hung there.

From its original state there was one part of the house that had been transformed beyond any recognition. In all those years of abandonment, this was where the lack of any human interference had done the most damage, where nature had reclaimed her land. A beautiful manicured and landscaped garden had mutated into a jungle of weeds and thorny bushes, a dumping ground for any old waste or discarded rubbish. Then, testimony to the hard work the devotees had put in, it had been transformed into a home for vegetable beds, fruit trees, greenhouses, cobbled-together wooden sheds and various colourful, wind protecting tarpaulins. Although it had the appearance of a chaotic allotment, it was in fact, organised to the highest degree, always getting the best yield from the changing seasons and climate. If it could be grown, then it was grown.

The first time Butsugen entered the garden was with An. At its heart stood a ten foot diameter fountain with four cherubs surrounding the feet of an angel, all exquisitely carved in white stone. Butsugen had his suspicions of where he was, this sighting finally confirmed it to him, returning a distant memory from his childhood, even though, at the time he had only seen it for the briefest moment.

"It's had a scrub up."

"One of the first things we did in the garden. We all think it's beautiful, shame about the missing limbs though. In a strange way it kind of says that life is not complete, not whole."

Butsugen thoughtfully strolled over to the far corner, halted and stood gaping at the canal wall.

"You like old walls Butsugen?" An asked.

"No, a hole."

"A hole?"

"*The* hole. There was one just there once. Look, you can see where it's been filled in." Butsugen decided he must be in the exact same spot he had hidden in all those years ago.

A gentle and thoughtful woman named Sonam managed the garden. She was slightly older than Butsugen, although her long coils of silvery hair and the fact she spent most of her time outdoors made her look more in her late sixties. Butsugen decided that Sonam must have 'dropped out' in a well managed and controlled way, one where she had kept her dignity intact. Striking up a conversation with Sonam was not the easiest of undertakings, whenever he tried talking to her about the past, all he got in return was, "Be here now Butsugen." Other times he asked what she hoped for the future, she would reply. "Now be here Butsugen." And if he wanted to inquire about something happening elsewhere, she would just simply say "Here now be Butsugen." It got to the stage where the only subject he could talk to Sonam about was what she was doing at that exact time in that exact same spot, although one time, she surprised Butsugen by talking about finding a human tooth at the back of the garden.

"Sonam, you are talking about the past."

"Yes Butsugen but I am saying it *now*."

Butsugen liked Sonam.

He noticed the sunniest and largest spot was always reserved for one particular plant *or* vegetable *or* herb, whatever it was? One that Sonam left to the other devotees. When he asked why this was? "It makes them happy," is all she said, he missed the satire. At first Butsugen wasn't sure what it was, he knew that it made a nice rustling noise in the wind and was sticky to touch. Maybe it was a highly thought of Buddhist emblem, after all, they had the lotus flower, why not another?

Then one morning, Butsugen had finished an early shift on the cleaning rota and settled down in the communal room. A large man, more width than height, with long, thick, black hair, bushy beard and Father Christmas cheeks had waddled over and sat next to him. He was in his late twenties or was it forties, it was difficult to tell without being able to see his face. Butsugen had only met him on a couple of occasions and then with just a fleeting exchange, passing the time of day. He couldn't remember him from the initial introductions.

"How's things man?" the beard spoke in a hard Northern Irish accent, before looking over his shoulder.

"Fine thanks."

"Little Daibai."

Little! "I'm Butsugen, how long have you been in the house?"

Little Daibai remained silent and took a packet of roll-up papers from his pocket, he whipped three of the wafer thin sheets out in quick succession. "How about you?" After licking along the thin edge of the papers he stuck them together, patchwork fashion. This guy likes large roll-ups Butsugen thought as the Irishman made an open ended boat shape, then placed it in a fold on his shirt.

"Not long." Butsugen finally responded to the question.

From a packet hidden in his breast pocket, Little Daibai slid out a cigarette. His wet pink tongue shot out through the dark fleece and licked along its seam, peeling the cigarette open, he dropped its insides into the paper boat.

"I love the first one of the day," Little Daibai said. Opening a tiny silver box and taking out a small, the only way to describe it was a dark brown, virtually black half inch cube of dirt, a kind of pellet, like a rabbit's dropping. Lighting a match and turning it until the flame stopped flickering, he softened a small part of the brown pellet, sniffing the fumes at the same time. "Nep, best dope going man." Then began breaking tiny amounts from it onto the tobacco.

All Butsugen could do was sit and watch this strange phenomenon happening before his very eyes. "Nep?" He asked, intrigued.

"Nepalese Man, temple balls, best shit going. Takes you higher than a fucking rocket." He tutted cynically. "Temple balls, appropriate." Then began rolling, the white stick getting tighter with each rotation. His tongue shot out again, then as if he was playing a harmonica, he slid it along the sticky edge, finally closing it on the last rotation.

"Best fucking dope on the market man," he added with a voice of conviction. "The grass here is good man but this is pure black gold."

Dope! Grass! Higher! That's it! Cannabis, Baz suddenly grasping what was happening, feeling an idiot not having realised it before.

Little Daibai then tore a small rectangle of card from the flap of the Rizla packet, rolled it up into a small tube and pushed it carefully into one end, tightening up as it sprung open inside the papers. Holding onto a twist he waved it in front of him, like cooling himself with a Chinese fan, the crinkly large roll-up became even more compact, one more twist. One joint, complete! Butsugen couldn't help but be impressed.

So much could have gone wrong and often does: it was some time in the future when Butsugen had been using an album cover (The Times They Are a-Changin by Bob Dylan) as a platform for some joint rolling, Butsugen didn't have the luxury of a Little Daibai belly. As he was heating the hash a bright red ember dropped onto his shirt. It was the burning material he smelt first followed by an instant sharp pain as the tiny cinder reached his flesh, like someone stabbing him with a needle. Butsugen shot to his feet, everything laying on top of the record cover was ejected into the air, the papers, the tobacco, along with its covering of dope was thrown all over the floor, all Baz could see was Bob Dylan staring up at him in contempt. Another time, after a great deal of prodding and poking he managed to shove the small rolled up tube of card (roach) into the end of a joint and waved it in front of him just as Little Daibai had done. Only Butsugen's roach came shooting out like a bullet, hitting a bashful and delicate woman named Wendywee in the eye, splattering her and everyone else in tobacco and grass.

Anyhow, Little Daibai lit the joint in an explosion of flames, inhaling long and hard as a ring of bright orange crackled down the white stick. Butsugen swore Little Daibai's eyes glazed over in a bloodshot pool right there and then. After a good five seconds of holding his breath an endless jet of smoke escaped through his beard. "Fuck! That's good," he said through a long sigh, then drew in another smoke filled breath.

"Here man, take it now, while I can still give it to you," Little Daibai said, speaking as though he was about to suffocate and holding the joint like a rocket waiting to be launched.

"No thanks, I don't smoke," Butsugen said, having tried a cigarette many years ago. He thought it tasted horrible then and didn't see any reason why it would be any different now.

"This isn't smoke man, this is the road to heaven," said Little Daibai, the trapped smoke stifling his words.

Butsugen took it from the clutches of Little Daibai's fingers, thinking it was a lot more preferential than having the glowing ash fall onto his lap.

"Hey Butes." The very attractive, fresh faced Pasang came bounding over and sat on the armrest. Butsugen remembered being introduced to her, any man would.

"Look, watch, I don't smoke ciggies either," she said, sliding down into the small gap beside him, feeling the softness of her thighs pressed against his. "Hold your hand like this," she said, clutching his hand, making a shape as if he was about to play a bugle. "That's it, now put the joint in there." Pointing upwards between his index and middle finger. "OK, now cup that hand over the end of this hand and suck through there. Look, I'll show you before it goes out. Look Butes." Pasang did everything she had just shown him, at first taking short quick puffs until the ash started glowing red again. "Far out Little Dai, nice gear."

Little Daibai grinned and gazed into a faraway place.

"Give it a go Butes."

Butsugen thought she was going to give the joint to him, instead, she put her coiled-up hand next to his lips. "Place your other hand over the end of mine, that's it, now suck in slowly. Move that hand back to control the air."

He cautiously placed his lips around the hole her finger had made. Her flesh felt soft and silky clean, it even smelt nice, still bearing the dampness from her own mouth, it was the first time his lips had touched another female since Mrs Waterhouse. In a strange way it felt just as intimate, flesh against flesh, lips against finger. He started to suck slowly, controlling the air with the smoke, just as she had taught him. Suddenly Butsugen pulled away, heaving, barking and spluttering wet coughs all over her hand.

Little Daibai roared with laughter.

Pasang smiled, patting the top of Butsugen's back. "Don't worry Butes, the first one always gets you like that." Watching his face return to some resemblance of a normal colour, she took another long suck. "Give it another go Butes, it's like learning to ride a bike. You might fall off a couple of times but once you're up, you're up," she said, her eyes beginning to look puffier, narrower, redder, glassier.

"Too right man, when you're up, you're fucking up," added Little Daibai, melting into the sofa.

Butsugen tried inhaling again, this time with a lot more caution, the smoke managing to stay inside without any more humiliating consequences. Pasang had another puff, Butsugen again, then Little Daibai who appeared to take the largest and longest lungful ever known to mankind. Tiny sparks of burning embers floated everywhere. His head flopped down, staring impassively at the sparks as they made contact with the denim. "Fuck, not more hot rot, there goes another shirt man."

Pasang turned her attention to Little Daibai's shirt and the glittering orange circles fading into tiny dark holes, one was so big you could see the white flesh of the Irishman's belly. She began to titter quietly, then a chuckle, then her shoulders shuddered as it turned into laughter. Butsugen, not being able to stop himself was drawn into the absurdity of it all, the three feeding off each other until tears began to flow. Pasang rested her head on his shoulder and patted his chest. "See Butes, it was worth it." The laughter died down.

Butsugen laid his head back and stared up at the yellow stained ceiling, he felt strange, a nice strange, relaxed, content, everything was looking, well, strangely nice, nicely strange. As though it all had a huge significance, a great purpose in life, a reason for being there. Then the strange feeling of being detached from his thoughts, as if they were being created for him, all with a spontaneity and depth he had never experienced before. He felt as if he was seeing himself for the first time, a kind of new, deeper perspective, discovering aspects about his character he had never realised.

He looked down at Pasang and saw the pure silkiness of her cheek, the feminine delicacy of her nose, he saw her lips move, no words, just a smile. He felt a love for her, not an *in* love, more a merging of souls, a deep compassion, a melting of bodies.

His head rolled onto hers, she nestled further into his neck.

"Far out Butes."

She must have felt the same.

The harmonious tones of the Beach Boys began to fill the air.

"Fucking far out man," said Little Daibai.

"Far out," said Pasang.

Butsugen remained silent. He had become one of the Beach Boys.

1965

With a buzz in his ear and a shake of his shoulder, Butsugen had been woken at four in the morning. It had been a year virtually to the minute since he had stepped into the house.

Still wearing his pyjamas, Butsugen followed Kai Liang's beckoning hand upstairs to the second floor until they stopped outside a wooden door, a door identical to all the other wooden doors in the house. Kai- Liang turned the handle and pushed it open.

For the first time Butsugen could see into the vast and dimly lit room they call the temple, the actual temple, the temple within a temple.

His first impression was red and gold, a lot of red, and just as much gold. Deep red drapes hung down the side walls from ceiling to floor, then wood, dark brown, intricately carved. Surrounding the central floor with its rows of red cushions were the teardrop shapes of white glowing flames, there were hundreds of them, calmly perched on milky candles, some in cups held high on tall golden shafts, others placed in saucers seated on small squat tables. There were gold incense pots hanging from long chains, releasing herbal fumes from intricately carved holes, their shapes casting distorted shadows over the walls and ceiling, smoke lingered in the air, giving the room a hazy atmosphere with a sweet aroma.

Covering the entire back wall and softly lit by a line of candles was a magnificent mural. A mural of a turquoise river snaking its way up into the distance, bordered by snow topped silver mountains on one side and beautiful coloured gardens on the other, there were flamboyant trees and elaborate mystical animals and birds. Fishermen casting nets from long canoe like boats, clusters of houses with townsfolk going about their daily chores. But it was the sky that took Butsugen's breath away, or not the sky to be precise. Instead of the blanket of blue with usual cotton wool clouds, at its centre was a blissful face with sleepy eyes and a Mona Lisa mouth, a face that exuded such serenity it was clearly some God, but not Buddha, Butsugen thought it didn't look like any of the images he had seen of the Buddha. Then again, each picture he had seen of him looked different anyhow. Many more images of the same face radiated into the distance, like a starburst, each one with slight nuances and decreasing in size until they were just tiny specks in the corners of the wall. It was like a window into another world, a paradisaical world.

In front of the mural was a large square wooden plinth seated on a gold edged rug. Another plinth, slightly smaller, sat on the first one, then another, seven in total, a multi coloured drape covered the smallest plinth. Sat on that plinth, surveying the room, was a gold statue of the Buddha sitting cross legged on an open lotus flower lit from within, making the statue look as though it was floating in a golden glow.

An was seated about six feet in front, straight backed, cross legged, his feet tucked onto his legs, his hands cupped over his knees.

Kai- Liang indicated to a spot in front of An. Butsugen stepped over and lowered himself onto a red cushion.

"I see you have done well with your hatha yoga." An said. "An ardha padmasana, that is good for meditation. What we offer is the most precious prize of all." An leant slightly forward and raised his eyebrows. "Enlightenment Butsugen," he said in a heavily breathed whisper.

For the next hour An explained the use of breathing exercises and how they help to open the chakras. How there were seven chakras in total, with the first just below the base of the spine, rising up to the seventh at the crown of the head. "Where you will understand consciousness."

"Where I will understand consciousness?" repeated Butsugen, beginning to feel very childlike, especially in his striped pyjamas.

"It will not happen straight away," said An. Then told him to imagine each chakra having a different coloured lotus flower, how each flower would open and release an energy: one truth, another creativity, another love.

"Why the lotus flower?" Butsugen asked, his mouth opening into a yawn.

"Do you want to peel an onion or a lotus flower?" An said, his mouth widening as Butsugen's yawn was transplanted onto him.

"I don't know, what's the difference?" Butsugen slapped his lips.

"When you peel an onion, you get an onion *and...*" An said, moulding a smile out of his gaping mouth. "A nasty sting in your eyes. When you peel the lotus flower you will arrive at the truth."

"The true mean..."

"And it won't make your eyes sting." An turned around and looked at the mural. "Look Butsugen, the river that flows upward, towards the truth. At midnight we are having a gathering."

"Where we will understand the true meaning of life?" Butsugen asked with heavy eyes.

"Maybe, after we have opened the seventh chakra we will chant a mantra."

"Mantra?" Thinking of Kai-Liang's buzzing.

"Om mani padme hum," said An. "It is a mantra Butsugen. We say it with our heart, listen." An touched the tips of his thumb and finger together. *"Aaummm marrrnee pedmmaay hummmm Aaummm marrrnee pedmmaay hummmm...Aaummm marrrnee pedmmaay hummmm.*" He chanted quietly as if the low vibration was being released from every pore of his body.

For another hour An explained the reason behind the mantra. "Relax your body as you have been taught Butsugen, then try to feel the words, not say or think them but *feel* them, be one with them. When you have removed your ties to the physical world then you will feel the compassion." He explained how each word in the mantra has a purpose, how the mantra will purify the mind from pride and jealousy, prejudice and selfishness, aggression and hatred, how it would release him from all physical thought and material desire. "We are on a lower level of consciousness Butsugen, one that ties us to physical emotions. We have this body, this mind, these emotions, we can also use this body to break those links, guide us to a higher consciousness, like tuning into a radio station Butsugen."

"And the soul?" inquired Butsugen.

"The soul Butsugen?"

"Yes An, the soul?" he asked, expectantly.

"We believe there is no soul Butsugen."

"Oh!"

"Not as such, even the Buddha himself saw the soul as an illusion. We have to see through the illusion, the cycle we call Samsara."

"Samsara?" Butsugen recalled hearing that word somewhere else, for the life of him he couldn't think where.

"Samsara, the cycle of birth and death. It is Samsara that gives us the illusion of a soul. The soul is a separate entity Butsugen. Most religions believe in an external creator. For us Butsugen, we will find it within ourselves."

Dr Chopra! Butsugen thought. That's where. "So there is no soul."

"Yes, no, well, we call it rebirth. It is like lighting a candle from the flame of another candle. Look at all the flames in this room Butsugen. they are all lit from the same flame."

An finally rose to his feet. "Midnight Butsugen. It will be your first step to the truth."

Butsugen spent the rest of the morning on the cleaning rota, waking Pasang when she hadn't appeared on time, which she very rarely did anyway. He had become friendly with the carefree imp over the months, contented just sharing the odd joint with her in the communal room, getting high with a beautiful woman was enough for Butsugen.

"Imagination is so much better than reality Butes." Pasang told him once. "Apart from sex," she quickly added.

Butsugen agreed, thinking of his one time with Mrs Waterhouse.

The clouds were toying with the sun after lunch, finally winning the battle around mid-afternoon. Butsugen rolled up a one skinner and smoked his first joint of the day, within a minute his thoughts began to wander around like a rudderless boat. He remembered Little Daibai's words "I love the first one of the day." Butsugen knew exactly what he had meant, even if the high had reacted with his tiredness like a lead weight.

Late in the afternoon and in a trance, Butsugen sauntered to the basement rooms, or one room in particular 'The Lab' as it was affectionally known. One of the shaven heads was there, a black American in his late forties, although Butsugen thought his shiny dome was not shorn for religious reasons. Out of all the devotees, apart from Alice, Kanshin appeared to be the one closest to Issan and very much like Sonam was to the garden, he appeared to be only assigned to the dope rota. There was something else Butsugen had noticed about Kanshin, he had never seen him take a toke on a joint, ever, even when he was in the company of others happily puffing away on their stick of dreams.

"You after some personal Butsugen?" Kashin said.

"Just a tad, thanks Kashin."

"Jesus, half the stuff we produce here seems to go on personal these days." He sounded irritable.

A loud crack followed by a sizzling noise and a brilliant white light suddenly covered the ceiling in the far corner of the lab. Behind a screen draped in silver foil the sunglasses wearing Kashin had pushed two carbon rods together high above a crowd of potted cannabis plants, igniting the electrodes and bathing them in bright simulated sunlight.

Butsugen went on to have dinner, finishing around eight. He had a plate of the variations of stir fry and rice, tomorrow he would have the other choice, variations of pasta. He missed eating meat, or as Sonam put it, dead animal.

It was just before midnight, Butsugen made his way up to the temple and settled down at the end of the back row. The silver ripples of Sonam's hair and the olive skin of Kai-Liang's scalp were the first of the devotees he noticed. He couldn't see Pasang, maybe she's late, she's late for everything else. No Issan, no Alice either, nor Little Daibai or Kashin.

An was seated in the full lotus position beside the Buddha pyramid. He stretched out his arms as if he was going to wrap everyone in a huge hug. He then took the twenty or so devotees through the seven chakras, enunciating every word slowly and clearly, lingering on each for several minutes. Each devotee listened to his instructions with an attentive reverence. An told them when to inhale and when to exhale, what to think and what not to think, he told them what should be felt and how to feel it. He finished by opening each chakra with their particular coloured lotus flower. When he had opened the seventh chakra, the crown chakra, the thousand petals of the violet lotus chakra, he said, "We have now been fully awakened, our consciousness has been balanced, our understanding is complete, we are now free from the cycle of birth, life and death."

After a moments silence An began the mantra "*Aaummm marrrnee pedmmaay hummmm Aaummm marrrnee pedmmaay hummmm...*" One by one, everyone joined in as though they were jumping on a playground roundabout. "*Aaummm marrrnee pedmmaay hummmm Aaummm marrrnee pedmmaay hummmm...*" With every second the vibrating sound became more pulsating. "*Aaummm marrrnee pedmmaay hummmm Aaummm marrrnee pedmmaay hummmm...*" Butsugen jumped in on a pedmmaay. "*pedmmaay hummmm Aaummm marrrnee pedmmaay hummmm Aaummm marrrnee pedmmaay hummmm Aaumm...*" Forget all other thoughts, he thought. "*Aaummm marrr...*" Don't think that. That is a thought, that one as well, and that. "*maay hummmm Aaummm marrrnee pedmmaay hummmm Aaummm marrrnee pedmmaay hummmm...*" Good, I'm following it. Damn, no I'm not, concentrate. "*mmm marrrnee pedmmaay hummmm Aaummm marrrnee pedmmaay hummmm Aaummm marrrnee pedmmaay hummmm Aaummm marrrne...*" That painting on the wall is so beautiful, that sky. I wonder who painted it, I'll ask Sonam. Oh. "*mm marrrnee pedmmaay hummmmAaummm marrrnee pedmmaay hu mmm Aaummm marrrn...*" She'd probably tell me to be here now. "*rrrnee pedmmaay hummmm Aaummm marrrnee pedmmaay hummmm Aaummm marrrnee pedmmaay hummmm Aaummm marrrnee pedmmaay hummmm..."* I wonder if I'm saying it correctly. "*Aaummm marrrnee pedmmaay hummmm...*" Sounds OK to me. "*Aaummm marrrnee pedmmaay hummmm Aaummm marrrnee pedmmaay hummmm Aaummm...*" This shirt I'm wearing is too tight, I can feel it straining around the middle, or maybe I'm just getting fatter. "*marrrnee pedmmaay hummmm Aaummm marrrnee pedmmaay hummmm Aaummm marrrnee pedmmaay hummmm Aaummm marrrnee pedmmaay hummmm Aaummm marrrnee pedmmaay hummmm Aaummm marrrnee pedmmaay hummmm Aaummm marrrnee pedmmaay hum..."* Wow, far out, that's the longest I've aummmmed without a break, see if I can better it. "*mmm marrrnee pedmm..."* How do I count them though, bugger. *Aaummm marrrnee pedmmaay hummmm Aaummm marr..."* Hang on, bloody hell. I can say the mantra and think at the same time. "*...rnee pedmmaay hummmm Aaummm marrrnee pedmmaay hummmm Aaummm marrrnee pedmmaay hummmm Aaummm marrrnee pedmmaay hummmm Aaummm mar..."* No I can't, it's impossible. Now concentrate, I'm not going to get the true meaning of life like this "*mmaay hummmm Aaum mm marrrnee..."* The truth. What is the truth? "*pedmmaay hummmm Aaummm marrrnee pedmmaay hummmm Aaummm marrrnee pedmmaay hummmm Aaummm marrrnee pedmmaay hummmm Aaummm marrrnee pedmmaay hummmm Aaummm marrrnee pedmmaay hummmm Aaummm marrrnee pedmmaay hummmm Aaummm marrrnee pedmmaay hummmm Aaummm marrrnee pedmmaay hum..."* I wonder what happened to Pasang. No! Stop thinking! Concentrate you idiot! Concentrate! Think about finding the truth. "*...edmmaay hummmm Aaummm marrrnee pedmmaay hummmm Aaummm marrrnee pedmmaay hummmm Aaummm marrrnee pedmmaay hummmm Aaummm marrrnee pedmmaay hummmm Aaummm marrrnee pedmmaay hummmm Aaummm marrrnee pedmmaay hummmm Aaummm marrrnee pedmmaay hummmm Aaummm marrrnee pedmmaay hummmm Aaummm marrrne..."*

"Butsugen! Butsugen!"

"Have I reached enlightenment?" he said, feeling a warmth and a bright light glowing before his eyes, then the hand of Buddha shaking him.

"Wake up Butsugen!" the voice yelled.

"The truth Buddha, what is the tru...Ouch!"

Someone gave him a swift, hard slap on the cheek.

"Fire! Wake up Butsugen!"

"Fire?" Butsugen yelled, snapping back to the lowest level of consciousness and becoming aware of Nima's face staring frantically down on him. His body feeling the discomfort of a toppled, long shafted candle holder laying underneath him.

"Get up! Quick,"she shouted.

Butsugen shot to his feet and to his horror saw the drapes closest to him engulfed in bright yellow flames.

EDDIE

1967

"William Pickard, William Hine, Bill Gold, William Moody, William Spicer, William Scott-Malden, Billy Hobbs, William Bankes, William Spencer, Billy Foster."

"Leave ou' the Bills and the Billys, 'e was a William."

Father Byrne continued. "William Armitage, William Berry, William Watermaine."

"Tha's 'im. No, maybe, I don' know. Go on."

"William Merryweather, William Temlett, William Reed, William Kennard-Davis, William Butcher, William Waterhouse, William Kelly, William Peach, Will..."

"'ang on. Go Back."

"William Peach?"

"Furfer."

"Kelly."

"No. Furfer."

"Waterhouse."

"Tha's 'im! William Wa'er'ouse. I'm sure of it. Wa'er'ouse."

It was an hour before when a knock on the front door sent Sheila MacKinnon scurrying off to answer it. Before she could send him packing, a man with a solemn expression and tired clothing made a polite request to the Scotswoman. The old housekeeper called back to the living room.

Robert's first impression on seeing the stranger was he had a face that revealed experiencing more than his fair share of life's struggles, a man with a muscular frame showing the first signs of decline, a man that rarely shaved but had done so that day. Someone that Robert thought he shouldn't know.

"Are you Robert Blakeney?" said the stranger, attempting to disguise his distinct East London dialect.

"Yes I am."

"My name's Edward Wallace." Feeling as though he should shake hands, but didn't.

"I'm sorry?"

"You left a no'e with me farfer, Frank Wallace. You said it was abou' yer muffer."

"Eddie," the word got caught in the back of Robert's throat.

It had been nearly two years since Father Byrne had returned with a list of the Williams killed in the Battle of Britain and no Blakeney. It was at that time all hope had been extinguished. That is until Edward Wallace had called at the priest's house on a Saturday afternoon in late September.

"Eddie! My God Eddie, come in Eddie." Robert virtually dragged him into the hallway. "Father Byrne, Father Duffy, Bernie, it's Eddie," he said, shaking with excitement, as though the man was a long lost relative just returned from some far flung country. To Robert, in many ways, the feeling was the same. "Sorry Eddie, excuse my excitement, please let me take your jacket. Is it Eddie or Edward?"

"Eddie'll be fine. I'll keep me jacket on all the same."

Father Byrne appeared at the living room door, along with his greased back black hair, cowboy boots, white priest's collar and a lot of curiosity. "Hi," he said.

Eddie nodded, not knowing how a clergyman with the appearance of a rock'n'roll singer should be greeted.

"Anthony Byrne," said Father Byrne.

Eddie then produced a crumpled up note from his jacket pocket, Robert recognised it immediately. "The ol' man gave me this, found it in the tin box 'e did, tried to show me 'ow broke 'e was, was only by luck 'e saw it. I fink he would 'ave probably ignored it if it 'adn't been for the name of the 'ouse. Probably fought 'e could sof'en me up wiff it."

"Priest's house?"

"Probably fought old Lucifer 'imself would have taken 'im to the depths of 'ell if 'e 'adn't passed it on."

"I'm sure the Lord will think not passing on a note the least of all sins," said Father Duffy, on hearing the conversation. "I am Father Patrick Duffy young man, call me Paddy," he added, standing up and offering his hand.

Paddy! That was only brought out on special occasions.

"This is my friend Bernadette," Robert said, indicating to an agreeable and cuddlesome woman around the same age as himself.

"Call me Bernie, nice to meet you Eddie. Would you like us to leave you two to talk Robert?"

"No, please, I feel as though we are all family anyway," said Robert.

Deacon Stone looked relieved to be staying even if he hadn't been introduced.

Father Duffy did the talking to begin with; over many years his profession had given him the most tactful of dispositions and within minutes the old priest had managed to break through the stranger's apprehension.

Eddie talked mainly of his two children, avoiding any mention of their mother told his captive audience a great deal. He also told them about his job as a hod carrier, proudly describing how he could earn good money if he kept several bricklayers in mortar and bricks all at the same time.

It wasn't until Eddie and Father Duffy had spent all their words that Robert felt himself become the centre of attention.

"How is your father?" Robert finally said, thinking he should mention Eddie's father, considering he had actually met him once, even if it was two years ago, and then only very briefly. Bearing in mind he *did* pass the note on.

"The same," said Eddie, shrugging his shoulders. "The ol' man said somefing abou' yer looking for yer farfer."

"My father, yes," said Robert stalling. The seconds ticked by as they waited for Eddie to continue.

Mrs MacKinnon walked into the room with a tray of tea and

biscuits, prompting a hard glare for taking away Eddie's attention.

"You knew Robert's mother?" Father Byrne asked.

"A long time ago bu' yeah. She'd be an 'ard person to forget."

"Did she mention my father?" said Robert.

"In the RAF, overseas somewhere I fink she said." His stare turned inward. "I s'pose she felt as though she 'ad to say somefing when I asked abou' 'im."

"Was there anything else? Anything, the smallest of information might help."

"No, sorry, tha's all she said, I guess she didn't really wanna talk abou' 'im."

"Yes, that's what Mrs Chattle said."

"You *knew* Mrs Cha'le?"

Robert described the time after his birth, about the orphanage and Father Nolan, living with Maureen Downes, a story he had told many times. Quickly explaining to Eddie that Nurse Downes was the midwife.

"Yeah I remember 'er, lent me 'er bike she did, I 'ad t' go and fetch the doctor."

Robert told Eddie about the many visits to Mrs Chattle's cottage, how he grew to love her like a grandmother. "She would think it wonderful if you dropped her a line Eddie. I don't want..."

"Yeah," Eddie paused. "I migh' even drop in on the ol' bird." He fell silent for a moment. "Me an 'er wen' frough a lot togeffer. Losing 'er 'usband and all tha'. Then, well, you know, your muffer," lowering his head. "You said you loved Mrs Cha'le like a grandmuffer, I loved 'er like a muffer."

Eddie told them he remembered the day of Robert's birth as though it were yesterday. His lips tightened as he spoke, "I was looking forward to 'olding the baby I was."

All eyes fell on Robert for a brief moment.

Eddie continued, "When you came to the door a momen' ago, tha's the first time I've ever laid eyes on you."

"Mrs Chattle said my mother told her that I had a brother killed in the Battle of Britain?"

"Yeah, she didn't stop talking abou' 'im, 'e was a Spi'fire pilot. A Spi'fire pilot! To a young gu'ersnipe like me tha' was the dog's boll." Eddie glanced towards Father Duffy. "Sorry."

277

"Even dogs need to reproduce," said the old priest with a twinkle in his eye.

Eddie continued. "I asked her, your muffer, so many questions abou' 'er son, a pilot. A four'een year old boy knew nuffing of wha' was 'appening in the world at tha' time. To me 'e was an 'ero shoo'ing down baddies, only they go' 'im instead, didn' they. The 'ero's never ge's killed. Any'ow, no' in the cowboy films I watch."

"You like cowboy films?" asked Father Bryne.

"Still do," replied Eddie.

"'ave you, I mean, *have* you seen The Wild Bunch?"

"Saw it at the Odeon."

"Yeah Ernest Borg..."

"Yes thank you Father Byrne." Interrupted Father Duffy. "Go on Robert."

Robert thought for a moment. "Did she tell you my brother's name?"

"Tha' aint difficult, she called 'im William, every time, it was William." He paused in thought. "One time she did let 'is surname slip ou'. It was when she was talking abou' 'is flying certifica'e. Flying Officer William, It wern't Blakeney, that's for cer'ain. I don' fink she wan'ed to say it, 'cause I can remember 'er expression changed when she 'ad. It was a long name."

"What was it?!" snapped Robert.

"Robert!" exclaimed Bernadette.

"Sorry Eddie, I mean, do you remember it?"

"I'm not sure."

"If we show you a list of names would you be able to pick it out?" added Father Byrne.

"Oh, I dun' know, maybe, it *was* a long time ago."

"What if we read them to you?" said Deacon Stone, realising Eddie's predicament.

"OK," said Eddie, relieved. "Somefing else." He dropped his head. "William's farfer. I don' fink, I'm pre'y sure, 'e's no' your farfer." Then raised his head and looked directly at Robert. "Sorry ma'e."

"I've thought that all along Eddie. Maybe that's why she was alone. Maybe she, you know, went with someone, you know, maybe her husband, you know, threw..."

"Speaking as a woman," Bernie interrupted, saving Robert from drowning in his own words. "If what you say is correct then if it was me I would revert to my maiden name. I suspect she...what was her Christian name?"

"Margaret," Robert and Eddie said in unison.

"I suspect Margaret Blakeney is the name on her birth certificate," she said.

"It's the name on her death certificate," Robert added glumly. Bernie clutched the back of his hand and intertwined her fingers into his.

"I remember she 'ad become worried before the birth. Lost 'er 'umour she 'ad. Something was boffering 'er, somefing important. She loved painting, pre'y ones at first, you know, flowers. Only before the birth they 'ad become, well, religious like, weird it was." Eddie looked at Father Duffy. "I don' mean..."

"Parts of religion are, as you say, weird Eddie. That's why we have faith my son."

"Maybe she thought you were the second coming," Bernie grinned at Robert. "Sorry," she added after hearing Father Duffy clear his throat. His expression was not as obliging to Bernadette as it was to Eddie.

"Go on Eddie," said Father Byrne.

"She said she 'ad only taken up painting since movin' to Devon. She said it was somethin' she 'ad always wanted to do, but 'er 'usband, this Mr Wha's'isname said a woman's place was workin' in the 'ome.

"Do you know where home was?" asked Bernie.

"She lived in big ci'y before moving down to Devon," said Eddie. "No' East London though, she were no East London lass. She was kinda posh, bu' no' snoo'y like, if yer know wha' I mean. I bet she lived in a big 'ouse though."

"Did she mention what part of London she might have come from?"

Eddie slowly shook his head "No." He perked up slightly. "She told me stories about the 'orses working the canals, she used to take William and one of 'is friends to see them at the stables. I fink the friend must 'ave been close to William." Eddie looked up with his eyebrows turned down. "Basil I fink 'is name was, I remember 'cause it was a posh name, yeah Basil, 'e mus' 'ave been posh."

"Yeah, William Wa'er'ouse. Yeah Wa'er'ouse."

"William Waterhouse it is then," declared Father Byrne.

"So what's next?" Robert said, throwing the words out into the room. "I mean, where do we go from here?"

"I'll go back to the Air Ministry, see what I can find out about our friend William Waterhouse, I mean Robert's brother," Father Byrne said. "Maybe it will lead us to your mother's house before she moved to Devon. Maybe William's father still lives there. Maybe *he* knows who your father is Robert."

"There is always the chance Mr Waterhouse *and* your father are dead Robert. They may not want to..." said Father Duffy.

"I know Father. I've known that all along."

"You must hope for the best but be prepared for the worst young man." He then clasped his hands together. "Let us pray."

Eddie dropped his head and listened to the words.

Mrs MacKinnon, whom up to now had been sitting discreetly on a chair in the corner of the room, abruptly declared. "I'll make another pot of tea Father, thirsty work all this detective lark."

"And cake this time Mrs Mac, and cake for our splendid guest."

Eddie stayed for another hour, deflecting any insistence from Father Duffy that he stay for dinner.

Addresses were exchanged and a promise was made to keep him informed about the outcome of their findings.

Father Byrne suggested they try and see a western or two. "None of this lot appreciate a good shoot out," he said. "Butch Cassidy and the Sundance Kid looks a good'n. It's got Paul Newman and the other one *and* I promise not to wear the dog collar either Eddie."

Robert agreed to go with Eddie if he were to visit Mrs Chattle. "I'll come," said Bernie enthusiastically. "I have heard so much about her."

Eddie stepped onto the pavement and returned an enthusiastic wave.

No westerns were seen after that day. Neither was Mrs Chattle. Neither was Eddie.

A DROP OF ACID

1968

Pasang carefully opened a matchbox and dropped two tiny black discs onto the pale softness of her palm, neither any larger than a pin head.

Butsugen gazed down at the two minute objects almost lost in the fleshy creases of her cupped hand.

"So what are they?"

"Acid tabs. Black microdots," she replied. "Lucy in the sky with diamonds," breaking into song. "LSD, a trip you will never forget Butes."

"A trip, where?"

"That's the fun Butes, wherever your mind decides to go."

"I don't know Pasang, the world is weird enough without making it even weirder."

Pasang licked the tip of her little finger, dabbed it on one of the tabs and placed the small black object on the tip of her tongue. "Ih e ere ou?" she asked.

He nodded and watched as she reclaimed her tongue, followed by a quick ripple from her adam's apple.

There was no disguising what was going to happen next as the other tab was picked up in the same way. "Well, stick your tongue out then." Holding the underside of his jaw, "Keep it still Butes," she chuckled. The other tab was carefully dacked onto his curled tip. Butsugen thought Pasang could make any moment feel so intimate. He watched her gaze slide up his face until they were eye to eye. "OK it's there. Well go on then, swallow."

"I onk oh."

"Don't be such a baby Butes. Anyway it's too late, I need company and you wouldn't leave little ol' me to trip on my own now, would you?" she said in pitiful baby speak.

Butsugen's tongue vanished. His body left to the mercy of the tiny tablet.

Both sat back in the sofa and waited.

"How long does it take Pasang?"

"How the hell do I know Butes. This is my first time too. Little Dai told me when you start thinking nothing is happening, then all hell breaks lose."

Neither moved, they just sat there, open eyed, motionless, silent, waiting.

A half hour passed or was it five minutes.

Pasang was the first to speak, nothing in-depth, just a simple extended. "Oh my God."

As she spoke it also began to happen for Baz. It was his mouth at first but mostly his tongue, they had become, well, kind of effervescent, like a gentle form of static electricity. Soon spreading to a tingling sensation under his skin, as though every cell in his body was jostling for position.

Then a doubt crept into his thoughts, a regret that he had taken the thing in the first place, he felt trapped, anxious, paranoid. He had heard so many stories. A woman that now sees everything in brown. Someone who leapt out of a window thinking they could fly. A boy who thinks he is God. Another who had seen God. Anyone would be worried, even scared.

There was nothing he could do, he sat back on the sofa and waited. A poster on the wall began moving, kaleidoscope like, merging into the peeling wallpaper behind it.

He waited.

"Hey Pasang."

Occupied in her own silence, she gazed forward, mesmerised, as if she was watching a magic show. Objects began to lose definition. Hard edges began to shimmer, inert items became animated, patterns began to breath.

"Hey Butes."

Pasang had turned around on the sofa and was facing back, her arms swallowed by the head rest. "Far out man." Stretching her words and tracing out a non-existent shape in the air, both were captivated by the multitude of images it made, a strobe effect of floating fingers, hundreds of them, each one as clearly defined as the other, as though time itself had difficulty keeping up. In a strange way, it reminded Butsugen of the sky he had seen on the temple mural.

"Hey Pasang."

No answer. He didn't need one.

He turned his gaze downward, his eyes fixed on the shifting shape of the rug, watching the sleeping floral patterns beginning to grow, intertwining with each other, around its border red tassels were twisting and wriggling, escaping from the clutches of the fabric.

"Jesus!" Butsugen whispered, or did he shout it. No wonder the rug appeared to be in a different place every time he entered the room.

"Hey Butes," she turned, dropping like a stone on the seat, bouncing several times as if she was on a trampoline, her hair floating

282

in the air.

"Hey Pasang."

She looked down at her purple linen dress and pinched the wrinkled material, a quick flap sent never-ending ripples along the fabric, breaking like waves over her knees, continuing into the air as if it had entered liquid.

"Wow, far out Butes, wow." She sat back. "Wow."

"Hey Pasang."

"Wow."

"What you seeing?"

"Giant diamond I'm in." Her eyes widened. "It's swallowed me."

"Yeah."

"I can see, and more, so much Butes."

"Yeah, life is so...so, I don't know, open. I'm floating Pasang."

Butsugen closed his eyes. He saw pictures appearing and disappearing at will, images splintering into shards of colour. He saw a Greek temple, a galleon in full sail. He saw Julius Caeser shaking hands with President Kennedy, all manner of strange visions, as though time never existed, as though it was all happening at that same moment.

"I am waiting, in my head, I am in my head Pasang."

"Hey Butes."

"I can hear a flute, it's so beautiful." Butsugen whispered.

"Yeah, far out Butes."

"Pasang," Butsugen pointed.

"Yeah."

His eyes closed.

He saw an attractive woman with bright red lipstick holding the hand of a young boy. The boy is becoming animated with excitement, he is pointing down and laughing, tugging hard on her hand, stretching her arm to the limit. The woman releases him, allowing him to race down the hill, his arms flaying outward. 'Not so fast, slow down,' she calls out, laughing as she gives chase.

"Not so fast." Butsugen muttered.

Butsugen kept his eyes closed. It's turned dark, it is night time, a beautiful star encrusted moonlit night. On either side of a hill are cluttered rows of two and three storey terraced houses, all made from black bricks. Some are radiating yellow light through curtainless, broken windows. Black silhouettes of people are in the rooms. Street lamps beaming tunnels of bright white light onto the ground, lighting up garbage ridden, narrow, twisting lanes. In the far distance a vast bridge spans a road. Three small round glows approach from under it, swaying from side to side in a criss cross pattern. Then the clanking and rattling of bicycles, three girls are shrieking in playful delight. Teenagers, dressed in black coats, their faces hidden by dark floppy hats.

Butsugen smiled. "Love, for always love." He felt his eyes well up. "I'm sorry." He waited. "Pasang."

"Hey Butes."

A baby began shrieking, a newborn. He saw a derelict building. A woman, her shoulders bare, pure, soft white skin. She is gazing down with a look of love and devotion, a smile of contentment on her lips. She is talking, maybe singing, maybe a lullaby, her shoulders swaying back and forth. The baby suddenly looks up, glaring directly at him, a stare full of scorn.

With the sound of a gunshot, the door to the communal room slammed shut. Butsugen's eyes snapped open. One of the devotees was bent over, his head facing the floor, hands on knees, it was Hema, panting heavily. A tall gangly thirty something with straggly receding hair and a long sloping forehead, he was gasping as if every breath was his last. Struggling to force any remnant of air into his lungs, his chest heaving like an expanding and collapsing balloon, Butsugen thought he was about to collapse in a heap, expire right there in front of his eyes. Then one of the side doors opened, Charini walked into the room, a stick insect of a woman, one of the youngest in the temple, more of a girl than a woman. Both Pasang and Butsugen stared as she passed Hema, showing no concern for his state of health.

"Hey," said Pasang.

"How's tricks?" Hema said, rippling the air around him into a rainbow of colour as he lolloped past, leaving behind many snapshots of himself, his long willowy legs taking him to a chair by the window. Pasang and Butsugen followed his every move, both mesmerised by his hangdog eyes, pea sized chin and massive bottom lip that protruded like the bow of a boat, like a cartoon character. Which one? Anyone. Maybe Pluto. "Good weather today folks." His words echoed from his large plasticine mouth. "What's so funny?"

284

"Laughing?" said Butsugen, laughing.

"Yeah."

"Hey Hema?" Pasang said. "Far out man."

Hema glared at them, "Enjoy," tutted, rose from the chair and left the room.

"Let's get out of here Butes," Pasang said.

"I quite like it..."

She rose up and grabbed Butsugen's arm, instantly releasing it when she felt her grip was crushing his bones.

"We're walking too slow...."

"No, too fast."

They stepped outside into the midsummer air.

"My God Butes." Pasang paused for a moment. "Jeeeesus."

Butsugen remained silent, scanning the scene with eyes the size of saucers.

"It's alive, it's all alive."

It was like a storm, the strangest storm ever, only without the weather. A storm they had never seen before, or will ever see again. Every plant, every tree, every flower, every blade of grass, every stone, every brick, every bird, every cloud, every structure, every person, every everything rippled as though it was fluid. A shifting multi-coloured liquid of life.

Butsugen saw a magnificent grey horse galloping towards them, its flowing mane dancing behind a long neck, two bulging, dark eyes aimed in their direction.

"Hi Butsugen. Hi Pasang," Sonam said as she passed by them, her words receding, doppler fashion.

Neither replied.

"She knew," Pasang muttered.

Sangmu, a young woman with the appearance of a ragdoll looked up and waved, a wide pumpkin smile stretched across her face, the air around her rippled, her arm like a slow revolving propeller.

"Yeah," Pasang said.

They carefully negotiated the ten steps down to the garden, eventually arriving on the soft grass below, after a moments wait they began walking across the writhing carpet of green.

Pasang coupled her arm around Butsugen's elbow, their chins held high, their heads fixed forward, a married couple on a park stroll.

285

"Say something?" whispered Pasang.

"Hello" Butsugen said, hoping it sounded something like hello, then quickened his pace, soon slowing when it felt like a run.

They reached the quiet area at the back of the garden, a place where the devotees could go for peace and tranquility, where they knew they would be left alone. A place where a stone Buddha statue sat cross-legged on an old paving block, a laughing statue with a massive pot belly and long earlobes, holding the palm of his hand up as if beckoning you in. A weird statue under normal circumstances, but on acid!

"Hey Buddha."

"Hey man."

They lay on the grass and rested their heads on Buddha's feet.

"The sky Butes?"

Butsugen remained silent.

"What colour is the sky Butes?" She waited. "What colour is the sky Butes?"

"Is it day or night?" he finally answered.

"Day, I think."

"Blue."

"Red, and yellow, and..."

"Yeah. I know, a honeycomb of colour."

"A sky built by bees."

"By Kai-Liang." Baz laughed on his own.

"Hey Kai-Liang." She paused "Kai-Laing?"

Baz couldn't explain that one, not then anyhow. "A sky built by bees on acid," he said. Both instantly burst into laughter, remaining that way for ages, until their stomachs started to ache and the tears began to flow, until their hysterics froze into silence.

Pasang delved into her pocket and took out a photo. "My dog Butes."

He studied it for a long while, closing one eye then the other. "Nice dog."

"Her name is..." She paused for a moment. "My God Butes, I've forgotten her name." She started sobbing. "I miss her Butes."

Butsugen brought his hand under her chin and patted her gently on the cheek. She held onto his fingers and kissed his palm, the warm softness from her lips dissolved into his hand.

He remembered the 'brothers of the board' pawn and slid the wooden figure from his pocket.

"What's that?" she asked.

"William."

"Hey William."

"Hey Pasang."

"I like William."

Both left it at that.

As time passed both realised they had reached their hallucinatory plateau, it was a relief knowing their minds weren't going to float away, Baz hadn't jumped from a window or thought he had seen God, or even thought he was God. They knew then, at that time, they would eventually return to their old selves.

How long they had lain in front of the Buddha was anyone's guess. Hours, yes, how many hours? They never knew. Some of the time they remained silent, lost in their world of fantasies and dreams, other times they would talk about anything, mostly about nothing. Butsugen tried discussing their state of mind, how it had altered, why it had altered.

"Simple, a small black pill," Pasang told him. She had a knack for saying it how it was.

On a couple of occasions they had become what only could be described as 'blissed out'. Words normally seen as ordinary, would appear hilarious. Why Americans called dope, pot, became strangely stomach achingly hysterical. Every description of pot had been thought up, each one as farcical as the other.

The evening drew in, bringing an uncomfortable chill.

As they departed from the laughing Buddha, Pasang skipped playfully along the path while flapping her arms like a bird. It was at that point Butsugen knew the trip was on its descent. Although the strobe effect remained, it had lost its intensity, the world was showing signs of returning to normality.

They bypassed the communal room, neither of them were ready for company yet.

Unlike her usual flawless endeavours, Pasang rolled an extremely dishevelled joint in her bedroom, she found getting the gumstrips to line up nigh on impossible. Smoking it brought some remnants of the trip back to life, be it for only a short while.

It was when Butsugen made signs to leave he heard the words.

"I don't want to be alone tonight Butes."

He held her all night, her naked flesh wrapped around him, her warm breath on his neck, her whole being melting into his, he could hear her pulse echoing through the pillow, the sound of Pasang he thought, the sound of life. Was it the acid or was it him, it didn't matter. He had never felt so close to one person in his entire life, even the time he had spent with Mrs Waterhouse.

As Butsugen closed his eyes he knew he was incapable of sleep. His mind remained on the same roller-coaster, the static tingling and strange colour patterns occasionally reappearing, shards of colour momentarily emerging out of the dark.

Time returned, along with the past.

As the night passed by he thought about the afternoon. He thought about how his consciousness, how his perception on life had changed. He thought he had unravelled the secrets of the inner world. All this had happened? Yes, no, maybe. As Pasang said, it had come locked up in some black pill. He smiled to himself, God comes in a tiny black pill.

Pasang didn't sleep either.

"Mustard," she spurted out at one time.

"Sorry?"

"Mustard, that's the name of my dog."

"Oh, nice name, I like Mustard."

"Hey Butes," she said, giving him a squeeze.

In the morning Pasang had given him a kiss on the cheek and a long hug.

They had experienced something neither would forget.

Baz also knew he would never trip again.

That night he could have experienced something else for only the second time in his life. But didn't.

"Never mind Butes, it was probably difficult to concentrate," she said as he left her room.

JOHN WATERHOUSE'S NEIGHBOUR

1970

288

Father Byrne had heard many confessions in the handful of years he had been a priest, the vast majority were mundane and inconsequential, easily resolved with the usual penance or absolution. He had also counselled many people in ways of life he himself had known nothing about. But, the situation he found himself in was poles apart from anything he had encountered before.

John Waterhouse's stare was anchored solely on Father Byrne as they sat in the old man's living room.

"You said you want to speak to me about William, why? For what reason?" John Waterhouse said, his tone displaying a deep air of suspicion. His well-spoken voice had become splintered with the passing of time. He sat hunched up on a worn Georgian chair, his intelligent, almond shaped face exaggerating his sharp features and concave body, the look of a man shrunk to half the size he once was. "How did you find me?" he asked.

"The Air Ministry records, this was William's home address," said Father Byrne. "I am speaking on behalf of one of my parishioners."

"Why is one of your parishioners asking about William? Who?"

After a short pause. "His name is Robert Blakeney."

An intensity masked John Waterhouse's face, he glared long and hard at the young priest. "Blakeney?"

"I know these must be difficult memories. I believe you were once married to Margaret, her maiden name was Blakeney. You both had a son called William."

"What is this about? Who is this Robert Blakeney?"

Father Byrne suppressed the urge to give Robert a swift glance. "He is her son." Studying the old man's eyes for his reaction.

John Waterhouse directed his stare downward, the words appeared to have sapped the little strength he had remaining. "Her son?" he said quietly, more to himself. "Are you sure?"

"Would you mind clearing up a few...confirm some details please," Father Byrne said, sounding more policeman than priest.

"How old is he?" John Waterhouse asked.

"Twenty-eight in June." Robert spoke for the first time.

The old man lifted his gaze towards Robert. "*He* is not my son, if that is what you want to hear?"

Robert diverted his gaze away.

Father Byrne spoke again. "We know that Mrs Blake..."

"Mrs Waterhouse!" John Waterhouse snapped. "We were never divorced. Of all people Father you must appreciate that. I am a widower! William was *and* has been *my* only son." His finger stabbing his chest.

"Sorry, I didn't mean to..." Father Byrne paused for a moment. "We know that Mrs Waterhouse gave birth to Robert on the twenty-third of June nineteen forty-two. I'm sorry if this is difficult for you Mr Waterhouse."

John Waterhouse remained silent.

Father Byrne continued. "She was living in North Devon when she gave birth to Robert. That means conception would have been some time at the end of Septem...."

"You want to know who the father is, don't you?"

"Do you know?" asked Robert.

"No! No I don't." His words tailing away.

"So when did you and Margaret Blakeney part company?" Robert asked. Refusing to call her other than her maiden name.

"Don't *you* mean, when did I leave *your* mother young man?" John Waterhouse waited for a reaction, None came. He continued. "I can see a lot of William in you," staring long and hard at Robert. "The last time I saw William he was around your age." The old man's demeanour softened as he turned to look at Father Byrne. "I have given everything to the Lord and more, much more than I should have. I have given so much and lost everything."

"When you have the Lord you have no need for anything."

"Then why has he tested me at every corner?" His eyes glassed over. "Why? I have done nothing but serve him."

Father Byrne remained silent.

"When I first saw you, when you said it was about William. I hoped he had given me another chance." His eyes closed like two damp scars. "How he has made me suffer for all these years, so many years. Please forgive me," he said.

Father Byrne leant over and placed his hand on the old man's bony shoulder. "God forgives."

Robert looked over at the young priest, a nod, barely visible was returned, as if to say he is now ours.

"You said you were a widower, so you know she is, I mean, you know my mother is dead?"

The old man cleared his throat, retaining his composure. "My sister wrote to me, she had received a letter from a nurse."

"A nurse! Did she say what the nurse's name was?"

"No, why."

Robert slowly shook his head. "No reason. Do you know how she..."

"Did she tell you the cause of death?" Father Byrne interrupted.

"No. The nurse said it was in tragic circumstances, I thought it had something to do with the war, why?"

Maureen Downes had *some* compassion after all, Robert thought.

"How did she die?" the old man asked.

"In childbirth," Robert said forcefully. "*My* childbirth, *I* killed my mother."

John Waterhouse looked at Robert, then the young priest. "Some sacrifice their lives so others can live. Do they not?"

"They do," Father Byrne replied.

"So when did you and my mother part company?" Robert asked again.

"I didn't, she asked, no, that is not true either. She threw me out. It was the same day the telegram arrived. When we heard about William. Margaret blamed his death on me you know." His eyes stared inward. "She wasn't wrong either. I had never seen her like that before, it was as though the devil himself had her in his grasp." Clutching his hands he leant forward, his face becoming even more gaunt, as though the guilt had set into his bones from all his years being alone, when it was just him and his thoughts. "She had so much hatred for me, so much hatred." He lifted his face, trying to retain some dignity. "Anyway, I went to stay with my sister, she and Margaret had always been close, childhood buddies and all that. My sister Jane and I, well, we never saw eye to eye, let's put it that way. Things weren't a bed of roses at her house, Jane only put up with me because of what happened to William. Margaret had made it clear to Jane that she wanted to leave the house, this house, *my* house. Jane and Margaret talked. My family have always...I had a substantial inheritance. They decided I should pay Margaret an amount of money, enough to set her up somewhere else, I would move back into the house and Jane would be free of me. Neat, simple, don't you think?"

Robert thought about his mother's...*his* money, how it once belonged to the man now sitting in front of him.

"Do you know if my mother had any visitors after you moved out?"

"You mean lovers! Men friends. No! Margaret wasn't like that." He paused for a moment. "My wife was a God-fearing woman, as devout as the next person." The old man suddenly stopped talking. "Mr Leitner."

"Mr Leitner?" Robert exclaimed, wondering.

"My neighbour at the time, German, a Jew, although he didn't seem to practice...never mind. He told me he had escaped from the nazi regime just before the war broke out, spoke English exceptionally well, as though he had been here for years. Gone to his maker now I'm afraid, a few years back."

"What about Mr Leitner?"

"Mr Leitner said a young man had come knocking on the door. It was just after Margaret had moved out. He said he had a lazy eye and a round back." John Waterhouse restrained a grin. "That could only be one person." The grin broke free, accompanied by a shake of the head. "Basil Albright! Mr Leitner also said he had seen him a few weeks before with a kit bag. He heard them talking on the doorstep." The grin widened. "There's not a lot passes by Mr Leitner, he has always been suspicious of everyone."

"Who is Basil Albright?" Robert asked.

"He was William's friend until..." halting mid-sentence. "The last time I saw him he was a small boy."

" Eddie, the horses, the canal," added Father Byrne.

Mr Waterhouse gazed at the priest. "You've lost me."

"Nothing, you wouldn't happen to know where Basil Albright is now?"

"No I do not, a lot can happen in fifty years."

"Did my mother sometimes take him and William to see the horses at the stables?"

"She may have done, probably, why?"

John Waterhouse noticed that Robert's rounded back became more pronounced as he leant forward. "Did Mr Leitner say *when* Basil Albright came to visit my mother."

The old man paused in thought, then hacked out a laugh. "My dear boy, your mother, *my* wife, was a woman of refinement, a woman of class and high values. If you think..."

292

"Did Mr Leitner say whether Basil Albright came into the house?"

"John Waterhouse's face froze."

"Did he say how long William's friend stayed for?"

John Waterhouse's head dropped as though a heavy weight had pulled it down. "Most of the afternoon," just audible under his breath.

YOU SAID YOU KILLED A MAN ONCE
1972

"You said you killed a man once and you would do it again?" Alice said.

"Did I?" replied Butsugen.

"The first time we saw you, remember, you *said,* I killed a man once and I'll do it again."

"I remember, maybe I was trying to scare you."

Seated beside Butsugen on the sofa, Alice turned her head and stared directly into the side of his face. "And did you?"

"Did I what?" His gaze remained forward, wishing the conversation would come to a close.

"Kill someone?"

Butsugen thought for a while. "It *was* the war." He didn't say *in* the war, he just said, it *was* the war, as though it was the war's fault. "It's not something I'm proud of."

"Why did you kill him, or her?"

"It was a him." He thought about telling her the whole story but that could entail a long open-ended explanation. Or he could just give her the simplified version.

"It was me or him."

"What did you kill him with?"

"What?! What difference does that make? A knife *if* you must know."

"Oh," she paused for a moment. "Mine was a hammer."

"Sorry?!" Butsugen turned to look at Alice and saw nothing but the truth. "*You* killed someone with a hammer?"

"It was my mother or him."

"Jesus."

"Fucker deserved it Baz."

"I'm called Butsugen now Alice."

"No! You are Baz, Basil, Basil Albright."

"How do you...?" Baz's name went from Baz to Butsugen in the first week, there was no mention of Albright. He made sure of that, his surname was the part of him he was keeping to himself, that was his and belonged to no one else. Yes, Basil could easily be guessed at, but Albright, no way. How would she know Issan had eradicated all evidence of Baz when he had become Butsugen? Rebirth and all that.

"I have lots of dads," Alice said.

"Sorry?"

"I'm lucky I suppose. Having lots of dads."

"Sorry?"

"Not at the same time though."

"Sor..." He stopped mid-word and gazed at her face. Only she wasn't a fifty-seven year old woman and he wasn't Butsugen. He was now a young Baz sitting on a wooden bench at school and she was an eight year old girl. A pretty, mousy eight year old girl with small features, and a yellow fringe cut in a straight line above her dark saucer eyes.

"Only it's the dad I have now. He keeps touching me and makes me touch him," she said, her words tailing away as she watched Baz's gaze turn to shock.

Baz remembered the time he was sitting at the kitchen table with his father, the picture of a young girl on the front page of his newspaper, a face he had recognised. Above the picture written in large bold letters was the main heading, 'NEVER A GOOD DAY FOR A HANGING'.

Baz said the next words slowly and clearly. "He tells me not to tell my mum, or anyone."

Alice sighed. "Only I did tell my Mum."

"Jesus."

"She tried to throw him out. Then I heard the shouting and the screams, horrible screams. I went downstairs. He was standing over her, his fist held above her, her beautiful face covered in blood." Alice froze from the memory. "Anyway, the fucker deserved it Baz." Her manner became very matter-of-fact. "Do you know there is a part of the skull which is quite soft. Anyway, it'll teach him for leaving his tool box laying around, Mum had told him about that. Someone will trip over it and hurt themselves, she had said." She puffed out a snigger. "I found once you start swinging a hammer the momentum takes it the rest of the way, once it's on the way down Baz there's no stopping it." Alice slowly shook her head. "The fucker died instantly, he could have done the decent thing and suffered for a while."

"You just can't rely on anyone," quipped Baz.

Alice continued "I didn't only kill him that day, I killed two people and one was the person I loved the most in this whole fucking, shitty world."

"The newspaper, Mary Chandler, never a good day for a hanging."

"My Mum, she told the police it was her that caved his head in."

Looking back Baz I realise that's when it all started to get a bit surreal. The police knew it wasn't her, in fact, they knew exactly who it was, me! I even confessed. But dear old Mum wouldn't have any of it. She insisted it was her, her story was watertight. She did have a lot of time to think about it though. The police tried to tell her they knew it wasn't her, that they knew it was me. I'm not having my little girl dragged off to some institution, she told them. Maybe I *should* have been dragged off to a loony bin Baz, anyway, stupid cow pleaded guilty to murder."

"She could have said it was in self-defence or manslaughter or something?"

"Smashing a hammer into the back of someone's head. After I told her what he had done to me, she seemed to become quite proud of killing him, or not killing him, I don't know. It all became very confusing for an eight year old. In the end she started to believe her own story." Alice gave a cynical grin. "I even started to believe it myself."

"Jesus."

"It seemed everyone in the country knew it was me, I can remember the way people looked at me." She paused for a couple of seconds. "Anyway, enough about me, tell me about your knife killing."

"Oh that, just a simple stabbing."

"It was a man though?"

Baz nodded.

"Well, that's OK then."

"I can see why you dislike us, I mean men, but we're not *all* like that Alice."

Her eyes softened. "No Baz, not you." She knew what a man was thinking by the way he looked at her, memories that had stuck long and hard, a look she would never forget, one that had burnt itself into her eyes. "But it *was* a man that touched me, that hurt me. It was with my very own eyes I saw a man batter my Mum. It was a man that came to our house and arrested her, took her from me. It was a man that convicted her and it was a man that hung her. It was a man that sent my mum to the gallows, for killing a man." She paused for a short while. "But it was *me* that told her about him."

"*And* you told me."

"Yes Baz, I told you," she said softly. "I had to tell someone. I remember you sitting alone on that bench. I thought you were there just to listen to my story, telling you somehow helped."

For a short while they sat in silence.

"That night, when you took me to the big house, you knew it was me?" Baz finally said.

"About a week before you arrived here, I was alone with Lennox, we were on a return trip from a drop off. We passed you in front of the late night cafe, the light from the window caught your face. You looked right at me Baz. I don't know how but I recognised you immediately, somehow I knew it was you. Afterwards I told Lennox, I told him that there were three people in the whole world that knew about what happened."

"Now we're all under the same roof." Baz raised his eyebrows. "I was eight Alice. I didn't know what you were talking about at that time."

"It didn't matter. A week later we saw you again. We were with An and Kai-Liang this time, another drop off. Lennox likes Kai-Liang to come along, protection."

"Protection, Kai Liang? What's he going to do, hug them to death!"

"Believe me Baz, if you're with Kai-Liang then you're probably the safest person in the country. Anyway, you looked kind of lonely."

"Thanks."

"It's not safe at that time of night Baz. I just wanted to make sure you were OK." Alice smiled and looked at Baz. "You kept running away though."

"I was scared, I threatened to kill you. I killed a man once, remember."

"Why were you out at that time anyway?"

"There's no one around after the drunks have found their way home, it's the peace and quiet. Nobody knows or cares about you." A sharp glance towards Alice. "Most of the time anyhow."

She smiled.

"I blame it on a place I was stationed at during the war, the closest place to hell you could get Alice. People, disease, death, flies, dust, heat, sun. More people, more flies, more disease, more..."

"OK Baz, thanks, I get the gist."

It was where I had the worst night of my life.

"A simple stabbing?"

He breathed a heavy sigh, "Not so simple Alice."

She listened attentively as Baz told her about Shaibah and the events leading up to that day.

"And here we are now, two killers drawn together."

"You could have gone in another direction, I...we did give you the choice."

"I suppose I was coming to a point where my life wasn't going anywhere, nothing seemed that important anymore. I would have probably followed the devil himself just to see if there would be an improvement."

"So you decided to follow us instead?"

"Why not? We are all following someone or something Alice, a lot of people invent some kind of pipe-dream to follow and get loads more people to follow it with them. I was probably searching for something to follow that night. Then you people came along, I stopped searching and started following. Then I discovered An, Kai-Liang and the others were all searching, so I started searching with them. We're all searching for something or following someone Alice."

"And what am I searching for Baz?"

Baz thought for a while. "You're searching for Alice, Alice. You're searching for what you have lost."

"Then I'll *never* have it."

"Yeah you will! We all lose something from the past. What you have lost is different, you have lost yourself, it is *you*, you are looking for, and one day you *will* find you."

"What about your past?"

Alice watched as Baz leant back and pulled an object out of his pocket. "See this Alice, I carry my past around with me," he said, holding up the small scuffed 'brothers of the board' pawn in his fingertips. "This piece of wood holds the secrets of my past Alice."

"I thought you were a bit weird all those years ago Baz, now I'm sure. You haven't got one of those for the future have you?"

"If I had I would have chucked it away a long time ago."

"Sometimes you can guess the future by what is happening today."

"Things change Alice."

"Yes and we need to change them." Alice took a deep breath. "We have a problem Baz."

"We?"

"The devotees, the temple. How many drop offs have you been on?"

"I don't know, a dozen, twenty, maybe more, I don't keep count. What's this got to...?"

"Aren't you scared you might get busted? Alice interrupted. "If you get caught with a weight or two, could be a couple of years."

"Everyone takes their turn, the house can't run on love and devotion alone."

"No one is going to get busted Baz."

"Not if every..."

"*No Baz*, no one is going to get busted, the police make sure of that. Christ's sake Baz, why do you think we don't get raided? It's fucking advertised enough on the front of the building."

He shrugged, "So we pay off the police."

"Yeah but that's the problem, they want more, a lot more, there is another firm in town. We thought they were only interested in moving the hard stuff, you know, smack, coke, amphetamines. These are not nice people Baz, believe me, they are into the lot, prostitution, protection, guns, you name it, they do it. Apparently they weren't worried about us at the start, we were just small fry, you know, religious nuts, only we got a bit too big. It seems like they want a slice of us, in fact Baz, they want the whole fucking cake."

"And if we don't give the police what they want?"

"No temple, no nothing Baz. They'll probably bust a load of us at the same time."

Baz shrugged his shoulders. "Drop the dope then, keep the temple, that's what most of the devotees are here for anyway. There must be another way."

Alice laughed. "You don't get it, do you? When have you ever seen Lennox in the temple? You can count on one hand the number of times either of us have been in the actual house and that's only when there is some stupid problem to sort out. Listen Baz, no dope, no Lennox, no Issan, no fucking temple."

"What about The Master? What does The Master say? Baz slowly stared down at the floor and shook his head. "Jesus Christ! How can so many people be so stupid? No one ever questioned it, we just accepted he existed. Sometimes I would see you go out, you and Issan were always going out." He paused for a moment then started chuckling to himself. "I believed *you,* I believed he was actually up there, it's like religion isn't it, it's just like believing in fucking God."

"You're the one that wanted to follow. Jesus Baz, you didn't honestly think Lennox was in it for the enlightenment did you? Anyway, what are you here for?"

"I've got no idea, I'm the least spiritual person you will ever meet."

"Is that why you tried to burn the temple down?"

"Yeah. I can't even get that one right. What about you Alice, don't you want to be enlightened? Understand the true meaning of life."

Alice threw her head back with a contemptuous laugh. "Jesus Baz, is God a woman or a man? Ask yourself that, when has any religion deemed it fit to have women spread their word. Religion Baz, created by men for men. The only enlightenment religion wants for us is to serve your fucking egos. How many Dalai Lama's have you ever known to be a woman? None, that's how many. Believe me Baz, Buddhism is as bad as every other male dominated religion. The problem is, you are all fucking scared of us women, because we are dangerous, because we have a vagina, because we can while away your petty so called superior thoughts with our rampant desires to get your cocks rammed up us. Well, who has the fucking harems Baz? Who jumps out at women and rapes them?" Her eyes glared wildly at Baz. "Who attacks defenceless eight year old girls then beats up their mothers." For a moment she sat in silence. "That's why I don't want to be fucking awakened Baz. I'm fucking awake enough already."

"Then what about the devotees? What about the ones who thought *they* were going to be awakened?"

"No one has ever made anyone stay, you could have left anytime

Baz. You were right about everyone wanting to follow someone, searching for something, Lennox had that one well sussed." Alice gazed at Baz and shook her head. "It's all fucking greed anyhow. The Master will give you everything you need, all you need is a bit of devotion, some meditation *and* harvest as much grass and make as much hash as possible. There's a lot of money in dope, quick money, enough for the temple, for Issan, for me, An, Kai-Liang, Kashin, and the police. Or so we thought."

"An and Kai-Liang? I thought they wanted to free themselves from this physical world."

"Freeing yourself doesn't come for free Baz."

Baz thought for a while. "How much have you got?"

"Not enough for all of..." she faltered for a second. "One more year, maybe six months."

"Do you know anything about this other firm."

"No, only that it is run by some guy called Golby."

PORK LOIN OR RIB-EYE

The rag-and-bone man's yard had long gone, Baz had known that, but he went there anyway. He went because he had been given some information about what had replaced it. A dirty, square, brick building with black bars covering the windows and huge open metal doors displaying a smoky cavernous space within. In front of the workshop was an assortment of cars in differing states of condition. Beside them were all kinds of automobile paraphernalia, a line of engine bonnets, a pile of headlamps, rusty bumpers, a stack of all manner of assorted engine parts.

Everything about the place screamed out the name of the proprietor, Baz knew it before he arrived, he knew it when he first stared into the yard and he definitely knew it as he looked up to the sign above the doors, 'GOLBY AUTO REPAIRS'.

A strong smell of oil, sweat and old cigarette smoke wafted past Baz as he stepped into the entrance, then the thudding bass from the radio as it resonated around the vast interior. He waited. Feeling as though he would be encroaching on the inner sanctum of a sacred temple if he were to take one more step forward. In the distance a car engine coughed into life, belching out thick plumes of dark smoke, a man wearing greasy, blue overalls was half hidden under a bonnet, an arm poked out, a thumbs up, the engine stopped. Another car had been jacked high above the ground, underneath it stood a spindly man wearing a welding mask and targeting a fierce blow torch under the chassis, orange sparks cascaded down, bouncing randomly off the concrete floor. Close to Baz another man shuffled backwards from underneath a car, he sat up, took one look at Baz, swaggered over to where Roger Daltrey's dulcet tones were blasting out My Generation and slid a finger over the volume wheel, followed by a loud clatter as he threw a large spanner into a tool box. "Fucking Italian shit," he grunted through the dark smudges on his face.

The bristly, bushy eyebrowed man looked at the ageing hippy with a suspicious eye, then glanced behind him. "Yeah?" His only word as he turned back, wiped his hands on a grimy black towel, Baz thought more grease was put on than taken off.

"I'm looking for Zed Golby?"

"Who?" he said, stopping dead.

"Zed Golby?" Baz tentatively pointed his finger to the sign above the door. "You know, Golby Auto Repairs." He waited. "I'm an old friend."

"He aint here. I dunno where he is."

"Tell him Baz Albright was looking for him. I'll come back this time tomorrow." Baz turned and began walking away.

"What did you say the name was?".

"Basil Albright." Baz waited for a few seconds. "I'll be back tomorrow."

It was twenty-two and a half hours later when the same grime camouflaged mechanic caught sight of the approaching hippy and rushed out from the workshop.

Before Baz could say anything. "Do you know the greengrocers next to the record shop?"

"Opposite Altons the tailors?"

"No the, oh yeah, that's right, the snooker hall's above it, yeah Altons, old man Alton, never mind, you got the right one. Tell the man working there you want to buy some rib-eye."

"Rib-eye? Rib-eye steak?" Baz smiled suspiciously. "Greengrocers?"

"Yeah." The man paused. "Or was it pork loin?"

"Pork loin? Do greengrocers sell pork loin? Or rib-eye?"

"You wanna see Mr Golby?"

"OK! Which is it, pork loin or rib-eye?"

"Rib eye, pork loin was last week," the man said, attempting to disguise a muddled expression.

Baz clearly saw the grocer's shop as soon as he turned into the top of the High Street, not easy to miss, considering its fruit and veg' laden tables were spread halfway across the pavement. He double checked, Altons was opposite, the word SNOOKER high above, each letter allotted its own windowpane.

Outside, a man wearing a trilby was spinning a bulging brown paper bag around, he then handed it over to the customer. Baz slowed his pace until the old lady had trundled away with her shopping trolley.

"Can I buy some rib-eye?" he said quietly.

"Rib-eye steak?"

"Yes please."

"We don't sell meat, we're a greengrocers, you want a butchers." The trilby looked hard at Baz. More surprisingly, he never turned to look behind him, Baz thought he was a sure turner, he was rarely wrong. After all, he had a lifetime recognising them.

"Yes! I know that."

"Then why did you ask?"

Baz stared at the beady eyes and sharp features under the trilby. "The man from the garage said to come here *and* I could get some rib-eye."

"We don't..."

"And that *you* will take me to see, you know," Baz said with a raise of his eyes.

"Don't you mean pork loin?"

"OK, fucking pork loin then!"

"What's the name?"

"Never mind the name! Just take me."

Baz followed the man behind a partition at the back of the shop, a large pile of rotting tomatoes had been pushed up against a side wall,

Baz faltered slightly as the smell hit him. The trilby took out a heavy key from his green stained work coat and unlocked a metal door, one that would not look out of place in the vault of some bank.

"Up the stairs," was all he said with an indifferent wave of his finger.

Baz had taken the first couple of steps when he heard a door shutting above him, he looked up and saw two short chubby legs turning the bend on the narrow wooden stairway. But it was who the chubby legs belonged to.

"Little Dai, what are you doing here?"

The rotund Irishman looked troubled as he squeezed passed Baz. Taking ages before he replied. "Just Nep, what's it with you Butes?" he said, the usually confident gaelic brogue stumbling.

"I've come to see an old school friend."

Little Dai glared at Baz with a look of suspicion. "Don't tell anyone you saw me." he rushed away, scuttling sideways down the rest of the stairs.

At the top there was another door set back from the top step. Baz stared at the glass spyhole, tapped his knuckles on the door and tilted his ear closer. A few seconds later the scrape and clunk of four gigantic bolts rammed sideways, the feint turn of a handle and the door slid outward, causing Baz to quickly skip a couple of steps down to avoid being bowled over.

A short, thick set, bulldog of a man with massive shoulders and no neck stood facing Baz. His thick, mousy hair had been combed back from a large chiselled forehead. Sunk under his neanderthal brows were two narrow slits for eyes and a squashed boxer's nose. This man had been carved from rock, thought Baz.

For a brief moment the bulldog stood studying him. "You'd better come in," he said, his mouth gleaming with gold teeth as he spoke.

Baz stepped onto the same level as the stranger, a cold shudder rippled down his body as he passed only inches from him.

A couple of strides along a short corridor and Baz was led through another door, and there, standing behind a solid oak desk, tall and proud was the imposing dark suited figure of Zed Golby. After nearly thirty years his appearance had lost none of its formidable presence. At nearly sixty Zed didn't look a day over fifty. "Baz," he said, extending the word and his hand. Baz knew what was about to happen next, he just hoped the bones would be able to find their own way back.

Zed slid his gaze down Baz's body and slowly shook his head. "You different old friend?"

Baz had let his hair grow to shoulder length. His family on his father's side had always been blessed with a thick mane, even in old age, unfortunately going grey was also part of that same trait, with the darker grey now being replaced by strands of a lighter, whiter tone. Two long, wavy threads hung free from the main mop just either side of his eyes. Adding to his already unkempt appearance was his old oversize, brown leather bomber jacket, the habit of keeping his hands in the pockets had stretched the front downwards and along with his curved spine, the back was pulled upwards. Under the jacket was a smart, high collared colourful patterned shirt. He only wore t-shirts back at the big house, mainly the tie-dye variety, courtesy of the print room. Changing into a normal shirt whenever he left was his way of turning Butsugen back to Baz, although, after his conversation with Alice, he had insisted on reverting back to Baz anyhow. A woman named Rinzen was a dab hand at stitching jeans together from older pairs, all with varying shades of denim. Quite classy Baz thought, in a hippy sort of way, not the scarecrow appearance one might have expected. He often told Rinzen they fitted better than any pair of trousers made in Savile Row, not that he would know. Softening hash was always a precarious business, so the two pairs Baz owned displayed the usual giveaway tiny dark circles of hot-rot. "You can always tell a dope head by the state of his crutch." Pasang once joked. What Baz wore on his feet was governed by the weather, today was desert boots, the alternative would be sandals.

The bulldog sat motionless on a leather armchair to the side of Baz, his sausage like fingers cupped over the ends of the armrests, his gaze unwavering. Pushed up to the opposite wall was a matching brown leather sofa which Zed had instructed Baz to sit on.

"Long time no see Baz."

Baz pursed his lips and nodded.

"What you been doing?" asked Zed.

Baz thought for a moment. "Not much, this and that," he said, returning the bulldog's gaze, trying to decipher if he actually had his eyes open.

Baz wanted to asked Zed what he had been doing since he saw him last but he knew the answer would have been even shorter than the one he gave, that is if Zed said anything at all. Anyway, Baz had a rough idea what Zed had been doing. That's why he was there. Maybe he just wanted to hear him say it. Then he thought Zed would probably appreciate him not asking anyway. Baz remained quiet.

"You remember Billy?" said Zed.

"Sorry?"

"Billy, school?"

It was so obvious, how could he have missed it. He gazed hard into the bulldog's face. Older, yes, but Billy didn't look any different than he had at school. "It's OK Albright I've eaten already," Billy said.

A Billy joke? That would be a first. Although he did have the appearance of a man that could eat someone. "Sorry."

"No satchel," Billy said.

A satchel. It all came flooding back, school, the playground, the hole, William! Zed! The last time Baz saw Billy he was lying in the mud, blood pouring from where his front teeth had once been, Zed hovering over him like a gladiator ready for the kill.

"Billy Keenan," Baz said slowly.

Zed began to laugh. "I help Billy, he was away for a while."

"Seven years and four months to be exact," Billy added.

Billy work for me now Baz, look at us now." Stretching his long arms out in front of him. "Three friends." His laugh becoming more raucous. "Different from last time Baz."

Billy remained stony-faced. "What is in the past is in the past. It's all history Albright."

The room fell silent for a moment.

"What happened to those two friends of yours?" said Baz.

"Friends, I don't have no...oh, you mean Frank and Marvin. Marvin got killed in the war, Burma, and Frank." Billy jabbed his finger downward.

After a second. "Oh! The shop, the trilby, I thought I recog..."

Zed interrupted with a loud laugh. "Frank work for me too." Suddenly Zed stopped laughing. "Why you here Baz?" The last words spoke without any hesitation, catching Baz unawares.

Baz thought quickly. "Does there have to be a reason? Maybe I've just come to see my old friend, friends."

"Why you here Baz?" Zed repeated.

Zed had a hidden talent of knowing when someone was telling the truth, for him it was like an animal sensing fear, Zed could tell that as well.

Baz had thought about the words, what he was going to say, how he was going to approach the subject, how he hoped his old friend would listen. All that had now been forgotten. "I saw Little Dai earlier. He was coming down the stairs as I arrived." A statement he thought was just passing the time of day.

"Who?"

"Little Dai. Oh, you don't know his temple name, Little Daibai." Baz thought for a second. "Come to think of it I don't know his real name."

"Who the fuck you talking about Albright?" Billy said. Baz didn't know it at the time but Billy rarely swore these days.

"The fat Irishman, the one with all the hair. He's just scored some dope from you, you know, Nep, Nepalese, temple balls. His name is Little Daibai."

Billy leant forward, his eyes piercing into Baz.

"You know him?" Zed said. The whole time Baz had known his old friend he had never seen him give away what he was thinking, with expressions or words. Baz saw a glimmer of something else, something dark and heavy. They know about the big house, that's it! Of course, they know about the devotees but they don't know I'm also part of it.

"Yeah I know him. I live in the big house too." Baz felt like apologising for it but that would be a sign of weakness. 'Even if your position is weak, never let your opponent see it,' he remembered William telling him in his chess teachings. Anyhow, Baz wasn't at all sorry, it was his home after all.

"You live in the same house as that Irishman..." Billy began.

"Where is this house?" Zed interrupted.

"The big house, the big house at the end of Haydons, you know." Baz lifted his eyebrows, hesitating before saying his next words "You know, the hole."

"The big house, Haydons Road, where them hippies live? You live with them hippies Baz." Zed's head went back, instantly releasing another manic belly laugh. Billy remained silent, his gaze fixed on

Baz. Then as fast as Zed had started laughing, he stopped. "The Irishman lives there?" he said.

Baz nodded. "Amongst another thirty or so of us, yeah, why?"

"What did this Little Dabby?..."

"Little Daibai."

"What did he say to you on the stairs?"

Baz had to think quick. What was wrong with someone scoring a bit of dope? Maybe that's it, maybe they don't like people knowing their business. Being alone in a room with two ruthless men that were staring daggers at him wasn't doing anything for his nerves either.

"Little Dai doesn't..."

"What's his name again?" Billy asked.

"Little Daibai." Baz waited, nothing. "Little Dai doesn't like the dope back at the house, he says he can get stronger elsewhere. That's why he is here, isn't it?." He waited again. Again nothing. "That's why I'm here."

"You want to score?" said Billy.

"No. There's enough of that back at the house."

"Then why you here Baz?" asked Zed.

"I've come to tell you we're going to pack up shop soon, from the big house that is. We're going Zed, give us another year, probably less and we'll be out of your hair. In the meantime we'll give you a cut of what we grow."

"Why?" said Zed, sitting back in his chair.

"Why? To keep the police of our backs. Alice told me."

"Alice, Alice who?"

"Just Alice." Baz was annoyed with himself that he'd let her name slip out, making her a prime target, as if she didn't hate men enough already. He was starting to feel small, insignificant. "She said you're paying the police to get rid of us." Baz paused for a second, looking for any reaction. Zed crossed his arms high in front of his huge chest and Billy's eyes became even narrower, if that was possible. "If you let us stay for another year then you won't have to pay the men in blue and they won't have to raid us, they'll still get their cut from us and they'll still get their cut from you, in return you get a load of free grass. We'll be gone within a year Zed, I promise, it's win win all round."

"Simple," said Zed.

"What do you say?" asked Baz.

"You old friend Baz. You get out big house fast, that what I say."

PASANG

"Wouldn't *you* be happy being called Pasang if Imogen Gomme was your real name?" Pasang asked.

When Baz arrived at the big house over six years ago, Pasang was already there, not by long though, maybe a few months. Before then she had been on her own, resting her pretty head on any pillow that would welcome her. It was during those times she met a boy who told her he had just been thrown out of the temple for being drunk, but mostly for wrecking someone's painting (In the style of Jackson Pollock). Imogen Gomme was lucky, the boy had told her about the temple but more importantly, he had left an opening, an empty bedroom. She was also lucky because it was not easy to be accepted as a devotee, unless like Baz you had an inside contact. Just like in the real world, it's who you know. The criteria for the acceptance of a new devotee was under the control of one man, Issan. Pasang was on her own, that was one box ticked. No couples were allowed, too much friction, also no down and outs, no drunks, no smack or coke heads and many more exclusions that were only known to the big man himself.

Pasang said she wanted to be awakened, find enlightenment. She lied. Well, not that sort of awakening anyhow. She just loved dope. Or, as she had put it once. "Creating a good mood amongst the population."

"I've been here so long I've forgotten what Imogen Gomme was like," she told Baz.

Whoever Imogen Gomme was and where she had come from Pasang had kept very much to herself, strongly deflecting any intrusive questions about her past. Baz thought she had something to hide, then again, didn't they all, it reminded him of Shaibah. From her articulate and clearly pronounced dialect he guessed she was well educated. That she had had a comfortable upbringing, probably in the country, probably somewhere in the Home Counties, from a much higher social class than Baz's, a class she had dismissed. By her scatty, uninhibited disposition he also guessed she had never quite made the grade, never quite lived up to expectations, a disappointment to her family. He could sympathise with that, thinking about his own mother. Now Pasang was a woman on the search. For what? He could never fathom that one out, he doubted whether she actually knew herself.

"While in The Temple the past gets forgotten, and there's no need to think about the future, is there Butes? Not until now," she said, close to tears.

"Keep the name Pasang, there's nothing stopping you. Call me Baz though, Butsugen has long gone," Baz said.

"Butsugen's gone!" she cried out, as though he was a different person to Baz, which in a lot of ways he probably was. "Issan's gone, The Master has gone." Baz wanted to tell her about the Master, one step at a time. "Alice has gone, Kashin, Little Dai was the first to go," said Pasang, wiping the dampness from under her eyes. "What is going on Butes?"

In truth, Baz never saw Little Dai again, not since that meeting on the stairs. By the time Baz got back from seeing Zed, he had already left the Temple, leaving most of his belongings behind. Baz blamed himself for Little Dai's departure, he obviously didn't trust Baz not to say anything. Baz's visit to see Zed Golby happened to be Issan's and Alice's idea in the first place.

It was when Baz returned, when he told Issan and Alice what Zed's reaction had been to the offer. "You old friend Baz. You get out big house fast. That what I say." Those three short sentences told them everything.

"What's happening Butes?" Pasang said.

"We've got to leave the temple. I'm Baz now Pasang, call me Baz."

"Why? What's going on?"

"An and Kai-Liang are putting something together in South Wales. They know people there, some kind of guru, you can go with them."

"Will there be dope?"

Baz shrugged but remained silent.

"What about you Butes, will you come?"

"I'm Baz now, maybe."

"When?"

"When? A few days, soon, I'm working on the campervan now. I'll have it up and running in a couple of days."

THE RAID

As soon as Baz heard thudding on the front door and the smashing of broken glass, he knew exactly what was happening. It was five o'clock on a dank Thursday morning, a wretchedness surged throughout his entire body. It was too soon. Why couldn't they have waited another day?

His only hope was Zed Golby's henchmen would just kick them out, that's all, no more, just leave them on the streets. His only regret was that he didn't insist on the other devotees leaving earlier, maybe he should have made them aware of what was happening. "Ignorance is bliss," An told him. What else would you expect from a Buddhist teacher.

The screaming started as soon as he opened his bedroom door. His first sight on entering the aisle was Sonan being lifted by a large man wearing a dark uniform, her bare feet and elbows aimlessly targeting her attacker, one swinging arm knocked the helmet over his eyes. Within seconds both disappeared down the stairway with Sonam shrieking descriptive obscenities.

Other devotees began to emerge into the hallway, confused and frightened, most froze in disbelief as they watched the pack of blue uniforms surge from the stairs and into the aisle. One by one, each man and woman was snatched unceremoniously from where they stood. One devotee fought back, only finding himself flung into a headlock and dragged along the hall, Baz thought it may have been Hema.

Baz turned to see a large, dark blue individual with a wild face and flaming bloodshot eyes racing towards him, the equivalent of standing on a railway line and knowing a train was about to smack directly into you, in truth, the result was not that different. A fist thumped him in the middle of his chest with an explosion of pain, instantly forcing any remnant of air from his lungs. That unconscious drawing of life giving matter had suddenly deserted him, leaving him frantically gasping for breath. With the realisation he was about to die at any moment, probably in minutes, if not seconds, his mind failed to register that his arm had been forced high up his back and he was being clumsily frogmarched down the stairway. The policeman stopped at the bottom of the steps. "You got the bastard?" he said in a rough but determined voice.

"We got 'im," was the exhausted reply.

While being held bent over in pain with his chest still heaving, Baz could see a policeman sitting with his back against the entrance wall, his face splattered with blood, another was coiled up on the floor, whimpering like a scolded puppy, his hands tucked in between the top of his legs. Another was crouching, flicking away a mixture of blood and mucus from his nose. Helmets and truncheons littered the floor. In the centre were at least half a dozen policeman on top of one of the devotees, a knee thrust hard into the side of his face. Through all the shouting Baz could just make out the buzzing of Kai-Liang.

With a hard, two handed shove, Baz was sent flying into the communal room. After a moment splayed out on the floor he rose to his knees, clutching his chest. He could hear the air filled with crying and yelling.

The minutes ticked by, the shouting became less intense, the atmosphere began to calm. Baz stood hunched up, one arm flopped numbly down to his side.

"Who is in charge here?" asked a flat capped policeman with a rod straight back. "You!" he said pointing at Abhaya. "Are you in charge?" Thinking old age and a bushy moustache were the necessary requirements for leadership.

"We are all equal here, not like the dictatorial, hierarchical bunch of mindless bullies you belong to," Abhaya replied.

"Fascists!" shouted Sonam, followed by an inharmonious chorus of agreement.

"It will be in your interest if you cooperate with every..." said the flat cap, halting mid speech as a constable walked into the room and whispered into his ear. The flat cap muttered in return, stood back and waited.

"Where is the search warrant?" came a shout from the devotees.

Indrajalin had stepped closer to a young, pale faced constable and began making pig noises. Tashi, a woman, one of the shaven heads tried to poke a flower into another's tunic but was hurriedly scuppered by a thrashing arm.

"Where's the warrant? Came the shout again.

"Don't worry sonny, we have one," said the flat cap.

Only inches from the constable's face, Indrajalin had now begun to incorporate intermittent sheep impersonations with pig snorts.

"Legalise cannabis," came another shout.

"Yeah, legalise cannabis," several of the devotees repeated.

"Legalise cannabis!" the sergeant declared. 'You must be out of your heads."

A roar of laugher reverberated around the room.

The flat cap raised his eyebrows, sighed, shook his head and looked towards the open door with a quick sharp nod. A constable walked into the room with a stack of heavily budded, bushy leaved cannabis plants and dropped them onto the floor. As fast as the devotees laughter had started, it ceased. The flat cap smirked, so did the young constable standing nose to nose with the baying and snorting Indrajalin.

"This is a set up," shouted Abhaya.

He knew four days ago he wouldn't have been able to say that. Not before Kashin, Issan and Alice had cut down every last plant from the garden and grabbed every last crumb of hash. The house since then had been virtually dope free. The police may have found a bit of personal laying around but nothing like the amount in front of them.

"But cannabis isn't legal. *Is it?*" the flat cap said under a veil of triumph. "How long for supplying sergeant?"

"Two, three, maybe four years sir."

"And you found a lot more in the house, didn't you sergeant?"

"A lorry full sir."

The flat cap turned to the door, nodded and waited again.

After a few seconds, a short, pink skinned, portly man with tufts of hair either side of a balding head stepped into the room. He was wearing a dark pin-stripe suit and the shiniest of shoes. Either side of him were two larger men with chiseled faces, also in dark suits but not pin striped.

"Thank you Chief Inspector," said the pin-stripe with an ageing plummy accent. His gaze lingered on the flat cap, the faintest shake of the head was returned.

Turning to the devotees his voice had an air of authority about it. "It would be in your interest to be honest and truthful in your answers." He waited for a few seconds. "These on the floor, these are not *what* you should be worried about," he said, pointing down to the cannabis plants. Then looked at the devotees one by one. "Cooperate and we will leave you to your bacon and eggs."

Tashi turned to the flat cap. "We're vegetarians, we don't like *pig* meat."

The pin-stripe sighed and continued. "You have been harbouring a criminal." The room fell into silence. "In fact, more than a criminal, *a terrorist.*"

"Yeah and I'm Adolf Hitler," said Abhaya. No one responded. "This is another set-up."

The pin-stripe continued to scan the devotees, he waited while each one digested the words, mentally noting their response.

"A terrorist, a member of the IRA."

Even Indrajalin had now taken a step back from the target of his farmyard impressions.

Apart from the aching in Baz's chest, his breathing had returned to his pre-punched self. Incredibly, being told you have a member of the IRA in the big house was not in the forefront of his mind at the time. It was the whereabouts of Pasang, he still hadn't seen her, not even *she* could have slept through everything that had happened this morning. Anyhow, the police had searched every room, he could still hear them rummaging around.

"His name is Eamon Carrick." Loud enough for everyone to hear. Each devotee remained where they stood. The pin-stripe took one step to the side and glared directly at An. "Eamon Carrick, where is he now?"

An returned the gaze, followed by a warm, compassionate smile.

"How do we know what you are saying is true?..." said Sonam.

"He has another name, Little Daibai," interrupted the flat cap.

The devotees froze. The pin-stripe knew why. "You," he said, his glare remaining on An. "Where is he?"

A moments silence. *"Aaummm marrrnee pedmmaay hummmm."* The flat cap hardly saw his lips move. *"Aaummm marrrnee pedmmaay*

313

hummmmn Aaummm marrrnee pedmmaay hummmm." Sonam joined in. *"rnee pedmmaay hummmm Aaummm marrrnee pedmmaay hummmm."*

Indrajalin, Tashi, Abhaya, all merged into the vibrating chorus. *"Aaummm marrrnee pedmmaay hummmm Aaummm marrrnee pedmmaay hummmm Aaummm marrrnee pedmmaay hummmm Aaummm marrrnee pedmmaay hummmm."* All of the devotees were now in a simultaneous ensemble of deep humming. Not Baz though. Bad memories.

The pin-stripe turned to the flat cap. "They are all yours Chief Inspector, throw the book at them."

The air was still buzzing when Baz finally spoke. "If we did have a member of the IRA amongst us, do you think *we* would know about it. I mean it's not going to come up in conversation is it?" Baz unsuccessfully tried to imitate an Irish accent. "Oh by the way didn't I tell you in my spare time I blow up buildings and murder innocent people," he said, sounding more Indian than Irish. "He is not going to exactly admit to it, is he?" Like a bee tiring in flight the humming gradually began to die down. "Yes we knew Little Daibai, we knew Little Daibai as Little Daibai, not Eamon Carrick. Do you think we would have kept an IRA man in this house, we are people of peace. Little Daibai left four days ago. I take it your informant told you that?"

The pin-stripe walked over to Baz and stood face to face, quickly whipping his head around. Appearing nervous, the two non-pin-stripes also turned, checking the area behind, looking agitated they moved closer to protect their boss. Three turners with one look, Baz was beginning to feel better already.

"Tell me more...Mr?" He waited. "*Mr*?" The pin-stripe asked through tight lips.

"Butsugen," Baz replied, reverting back to his Temple name; just for the time being.

"Mr Butsugen."

"We all knew Little Daibai, far as we knew he was one of us. Like my friend said, we only have your word for it that he was actually what you said he was."

"Believe me Mr Butsugen we have known of Eamon Carrick for some time. Suddenly he vanishes, why? Where is he now?"

Baz thought back to the last time he saw Little Daibai bounding

314

down the stairs. How he had become agitated when he saw Baz. How he had left the big house immediately after. How Zed and Billy's attitude seemed to darken when they spoke about him. He had to see Zed again. Zed knows the truth.

"Maybe he knew you were on to him, maybe he's finished planning his evil deeds..Mr?" Baz raised his eyebrows. "Mr?.."

"Commander," the commander replied.

"Mr Commander."

"We were informed some other people left not long after Eamon Carrick. Two black men and a woman, an older white woman." Baz wondered what Alice's reaction would have been if she heard a man call her that.

"People come and go all the time."

"These were more than just people, Mr Butsugen. These were your leaders, weren't they?"

"We have no leaders, we are all equal Mr Commander, even you and me. If you want to know about the three that left, then why don't you ask him?" Nodding towards the flat cap.

The commander cleared his throat. "We have."

"Believe me, there is not one person in this room that can help you. We all believe in peace and love, not war, ban the bomb commander." Baz's eyes widened. "Ban the fucking bomb. Now if you want to arrest us. Fine! We will go in peace, we will not give you any more trouble, you can have my word on that."

————————

Two weeks had passed since the morning of the attack, and 'the attack' is how it came to be known. "It was an attack on our freedom, an attack on peace, an attack on love and an attack on our liberty, there can be no other words to describe it," is how Sonam had put it before she returned to the here and now, and that is how the words stuck. Sonam had never smoked dope, or taken any drugs, or even drank alcohol for that matter. Out of all the devotees, she was the most justified for feeling aggrieved.

The only person arrested on the day of the attack was Kai-Liang. He was sentenced to three months but only served one.

"Clocking three policemen was probably very highly thought of in prison," Baz told him after his release. Kai-Liang agreed with a grin and a buzz. If only the authorities had known that being confined in a room for hours on end was Kai-Liang's idea of freedom anyway.

Something very strange happened after the police left the house that morning. Whether it was out of stupidity or intentional, no one could decide, even after they had debated it to death. The cannabis plants that were thrown to the floor, the ones the police tried to blackmail them with, well, they had been left behind. Anyone that had had a smoke from them, including Baz, were convinced beyond doubt that it was the temple dope anyway.

Baz immediately went looking for Pasang after the attack. Just like Issan, Alice, Kashin and Little Dai, she had vanished from the face of the earth. It was that same day he realised the only people he had never seen visit the temple were Issan, Alice, Kashin, Little Dai and yes, Pasang. Sometimes you just can't see the wood for the trees.

Fearing the worst after several newspapers reported the raid, many of the devotees had already left the house. Harbouring a member of the IRA, even if it was unknown to them at the time would not sit very well with the general public, although most of the papers did report it solely as a drug bust. It was also in the police's interest that a member of the IRA, even an ex-member, slipping through their net and now at large, was best kept to themselves. The Daily Telegraph got a sniff that a high ranking anti-terrorist officer had been present at the raid but that one line of information managed to get lost in the columns of editorial. One newspaper even described the house as a 'peace camp' pleasing many of the devotees, better than the drug den the other rags had described it as.

An was continuing to organise the move to South Wales, the remaining devotees were to go with him. A nameless rock star had been funding a new Buddhist centre there. The chief Lama heading the centre was known to An from his time spent in Nepal. It was also in Nepal he had met Kai-Liang and Lennox, not at the same time though, both having completely different reasons for being in Katmandu.

Parked in a side building, amongst a horde of other rubbish was an old Volkswagen camper van once belonging to Abhaya. Baz had managed to fire it up a week ago in a plume of black smoke and was continuing to carry out minor adjustments. The van would have to make several trips to relocate everyone, then it could return to the state of hibernation it had been accustomed to for all those years.

"I beg one thing from you," An had asked everyone after 'the raid', "we wait for Kai-Liang."

Not one devotee disagreed.

As Baz approached the greengrocers for the second time, he could see the tables of fruit and veg' had managed to occupy even more of the pavement. Under Frank's straw trilby Baz could see a glimpse of recognition from the schoolboy face he had known all those years ago, even if his sharp features had become more honed over time.

"Hello Frank.

"Rib-eye?"

"No pork loin today?"

"You want a butchers," Frank said with a lipless grin.

Baz remained straight faced. "You never were funny Frank."

Apart from the absence of Little Dai bounding down the stairway everything happened as before. He was led into the flat by Billy, whose stare still managed to send a cold shudder through him, then shown to the same sofa after his hand was crushed yet again by Zed.

"I thought I see you again Baz."

"How's things Zed?"

"Good."

"Why?"

"Why good Baz?"

"No, why did you think you would see me again?" said Baz, thinking this was not going to go the direct route he had hoped.

Zed looked hard at Baz, if Billy's gaze made Baz shiver, then Zed's could freeze him into the depths of darkness.

"You old friend Baz."

"Is that it?"

"You tell me Baz?"

There was a short pause before Baz next spoke.

"Little Daibai," Baz said, then waited. "Remember Little Daibai?"

Zed and Billy remained silent, it gave Baz the answer.

"The Irishman, the one that ate all the pies, remember?"

"I remember Baz."

"The police came looking for him, at the big house, before the sun woke up and they didn't wait for us to answer the door either."

"And did they find the Irishman there?"

"No, he left before I got back, before I got back from seeing you. That's the last I saw of him. Do you know who Little Daibai is?"

Zed and Billy remained silent, again.

"His name is Eamon Carrick, the police say he is, was a member of the IRA."

Zed's hands raised up to below his chin, his two index fingers tapped his mouth. Billy's gaze withdrew from Baz and studied Zed.

"Little Dabby, Eamon Carrick, whoever he is," said Zed. "His..." He paused for a moment. "His friends want from me."

"His friends, you mean the IRA?"

"No Baz, Snow White and the seven fucking dwarfs," exclaimed Billy, annoyed his swearing was returning.

"They wanted your business?"

Zed raised his eyebrows but remained silent.

"The IRA were knocking on your door?"

"The Irishman, he was explos...," halting mid-speech. "He run from IRA, that is why he hide in your house, change name to Little Dabby."

"Little Daibai."

"IRA find him, use him to talk with us, he live."

"And if *we* decided to kill the Paddy, no one would miss him," said Billy.

"Then he saw y*ou* Baz."

"I was the cat amongst the pigeons."

"Fucking feathers everywhere," Billy added.

"The plods find IRA man, he go to prison for bombs, long long time, *or* he help plods."

"No fucking contest," said Billy. The swearing returning to its old involuntary self.

"Whoever find him." Zed pointed a finger at his head and pulled it like a trigger.

"Us, IRA, plods, whoever gets there first, Little Dabby will not be Mr Popular," said Billy.

"Jesus."

"This Irishman, he desperate man, he like Billy the Kid." A cold shiver surged through Baz's body as Zed spoke.

"Don't forget Albright, your enemies watch you a lot closer than your friends," Billy added.

"You're quite the philosopher Billy."

"He could kill you or he could get out," said Zed. "You lucky Baz, he got out, Irishman not happy Baz. The IRA look for him, *now* the plods look for him."

"We're not that fussed Albright, only the Irishman's a moron, and morons act on instinct, like an animal; that makes him dangerous to everyone, including us." Billy said, remembering not to swear that time.

"I told you Baz, I told you, get out big house fast."

"Jesus."

"He see you on stairs, he think you tell me where he live, he think I tell plods, you dead Baz."

Baz felt he had been punched in the stomach. "Well, did you tell the police?" Baz said, looking shocked when Zed roared one of his manic laughs. Even Billy began laughing, flashing his gold teeth and sounding like an approaching steam train.

"You insult Mr Golby," Billy said.

"We tell police nothing Baz. If I tell police, then Billy kill me." His laugh stopped as fast as it had started. "Irishman think same as you. he get out big house, like you should."

"So who told the police?" Baz questioned.

Billy shrugged his huge shoulders. "Little Dabby probably thinks you did," he said. "That would be my guess."

"Anyone leave house?" asked Zed.

"People come and go all the time."

"No Baz, someone never come back."

Baz thought for a moment. "Issan, Kashin, Alice, Pasang." His heart sank. "Pasang."

"Pasang, you lot have the strangest names in that house Albright. Only the Irishman probably thinks it was you," Billy said.

For a minute the three sat in silence.

"So the IRA wanted what you had, is that it?" Baz put his hand on his forehead. "I'm confused."

"Little Dabby got greedy."

"The world is a greedy place Albright," said Billy. "Take, take,

take, no one knows when to stop fucking taking."

"He saw you on stairs Baz, he think you work for me, like I said Baz, you get out big house fast."

———————

As soon as Baz returned to the big house he headed straight for the campervan . A few more tweaks and the VW will be purring like a cat that got the cream.

After, he would try to persuade An to leave for South Wales, maybe the next day. Hopefully arrangements for Kai-Liang to sign on at the police station in Llanelli would be in place by then.

As he had done many times in the last week, he lifted the engine cover at the back of the vehicle.

For Baz, the flash of blinding light and the thunderous noise that accompanied it lasted less than the tiniest fraction of a second. In truth, it was instantaneous.

V

HAS THE PAPER BOY BEEN?

LITTLE DAIBAI, EAMON CARRICK, THE IRISHMAN

SUNNYBRIDGE

BAZ'S BENCH (3)

BAZ'S BENCH (4)

BAZ'S BENCH (5)

THE SPICE OF INDIA

BAZ'S BENCH (6)

THE LETTER

THE TREES ECHO

BAZ'S BENCH (7)

WHERE SALMON GO TO DIE

THE FAIRY FELLER'S MASTER STROKE

A COLD WIND

As he dialled each number Father Byrne waited impatiently for the telephone wheel to return to its home position, every rotation felt like an eternity. Finally the eight digit number was complete. Again he waited as he put the receiver to his ear and listened to the short double drones of the dialling tone.

A click. A feeling of relief. "Hello," came the soft female voice over the sound of a screaming baby.

"Bernadette, it's Father Byrne."

"Sorry Father, Archie is a bit grumpy this morning." Her voice distancing itself as she spoke. "Aren't you, my little poppet."

"I must speak to Robert, Bernadette," Father Byrne said hurriedly.

"Hang on Father, he's upstairs, I'll give him a shout."

Father Byrne heard the sharp tap of the receiver on the cabinet surface, then the call of Robert's name, quickly followed by his own.

He waited, the seconds passed by slowly.

"Hello Father. How are you?"

"Fine" Father Byrne blurted. He calmed his voice. "Thank you Robert, have you read the papers this morning?"

"Bernie." Robert called out. "Has the paper boy been?"

Father Byrne heard a muffled reply.

"Yes. I mean no, I haven't had time, what with Archie..."

"But the paper boy *has* been Robert?"

"Yes Father."

"And you still get the Mirror?"

"Yes Father."

"Go and get it Robert."

"Yes Father, why?"

"You'll see, now go and get it," his impatience returning.

Another wait.

"OK Father. What now?"

"Page four."

Father Byrne heard the tap of the receiver on the cabinet again, followed by the rustling of paper.

Tucking the phone between shoulder and ear. "OK, page four."

"The heading Robert, car explodes at hippy commune."

"Ummm. Car exp, oh yeah, got it."

"Read it Robert." Father Byrne tried to suppress his anticipation.

Robert had become bemused by the priest's restless insistence. The reason, as he was about to find out, was the last thing on his mind.

With Archie upstairs crying himself to sleep and Bernadette standing only a few feet away, Robert started reading aloud from the short column of type.

> "A car exploded yesterday, seriously injuring a fifty-eight year old man in the grounds of a religious hippy sect. The explosion took place at a canalside mansion, well known to the police for being a place of drug taking and devil worship. Chief Inspector Tucker had reported that the drug factory was only raided a week before. One man was arrested for assault during the raid. The injured man, believed to be working on a Volkswagen camper van at the time has been named as Ba..."

Robert stopped reading as soon as he saw the next two words. Bernadette looked over his shoulder, cupped her hand over her mouth and slipped an arm around her husband's waist.

"Carry on Robert, read it." Father Byrne said, impatiently.

> "The injured man, believed to be working on a Volkswagen campervan at the time has been named as..."

Robert paused again.

> "as Basil Albright..."

"My God."

"Read on Robert."

> "The man, also believed to be a member of the same religious cult is said to be in a critical condition and is not expected to live. The police have been informed that Mr Albright's only surviving family is a sister in

Australia and another in France. The police said they
have no reason to suspect foul play was involved."

Robert stopped reading, his gaze facing inward.

"Robert." Father Byrne raised his voice. "Robert! Are you
listening?"

"Yes Father, sorry."

"I will find out which hospital, don't do anything until I contact
you." Father Byrne waited. "Did you hear me Robert?"

"Yes Father."

LITTLE DAIBAI, EAMON CARRICK, THE IRISHMAN

With a flick of his fingers Billy rapped the top of the driver's arm and
pointed to the clean shaven man with short, black hair striding along
the pavement.

It was late evening.

"That's him." Billy looked from side to side, turning his head he
peered through the rear windscreen. "OK Teabags...(named because
of the four teabags he has in each mug of tea, although, he was mainly
known for his sublime driving skills; one time it took twelve squad
cars to finally bring him to a halt after the infamous post office chase).
"When he passes that second car."

"Who's doing the cutting Billy?" asked Joey.

"I'll have that pleasure Joey boy. You get in front of him Teabags,
Frank and Joey, you get behind. He might be carrying, so don't hang
about!"

With the headlamps turned off the Mercedes poodled along the
road like a sinister black shadow, far enough not to be heard, close
enough not to lose their quarry. Like a pride of lions following their
prey, the wide-eyed occupants watched the victims every move.

"Now!" Billy exhaled.

A sharp downward yank of the steering wheel and the Merc roared
into life, shooting forward at great speed to the other side of the road,
bouncing a wheel onto the curb as it screeched to a halt in front of the
unsuspecting victim. Frank and Joey were the first to leap out, swiftly
followed by Teabags. The shorter, stockier and wide shouldered profile

of Billy strolled around the front of the Merc, as if he had all the time in the world.

The man had been half expecting this moment, whoever his assailants were, he knew instantly what was going down. A metal object glinted from the glow off the street lamp as his right hand withdrew from his inside pocket, before he could raise it, his chin met with Joey's knuckle dustered fist. The target's face was flung sideways, whipping threads of blood over the Mercedes roof, the firearm dropped with a succession of clonks.

From under his belt, Billy took out a foot long, inch thick iron bar, it even had a name, 'Thug,' only because of the thug he had snatched it from, Billy didn't know his actual name at the time. In truth, the thug wasn't in a position to tell him, or ask for his weapon back either. Anyway, out of respect for his victim putting up a good fight, Billy kept the weapon and named it Thug.

Billy smashed Thug hard and fast onto the left shin, his favourite spot for inflicting damage, mainly because of his short height. Many a larger man had suffered this same fate. At the same time the spine-chilling sound of a bone snapped, along with a gaelic cry that could be heard on the other side of town. Thug was then smacked hard into the other shin, another crack. Billy caught the scruff of his collar just before he crumpled to the ground, then crashed Thug into the bridge of the nose. Billy was always mindful to avoid the victim's mouth, something to do with an experience he had had in his childhood.

The man released a long gurgling groan.

Billy hauled the heavy body over the boot and held him down with a forearm thrust into the back of his neck. He handed Thug to Teabags and opened the Merc's rear door.

"You're not taking him with us Billy, Mr Golby said not to..." Frank began to say.

With the strength of ten men, Billy lowered the victim's head into the entrance of the car door.

"Fuckin' 'ell," said Joey, screwing up his face. "This is goin' to fuckin' 'urt."

Billy slammed the heavy door. Thud! The head shuddered. He slammed it again, harder. Thud! And again, harder still. Thud! And again. Crunch! And again. A softer crunch! And again. Nothing.

Silence, as though the door had hit a cushion. Billy discarded the limp body onto the pavement as if he was throwing away a piece of litter.

"Get the Merc to the garage Teabags. I think it's going to need a new coat," were the only words Billy spoke on the way back.

Little Daibai never smoked another joint. Eamon Carrick never detonated another bomb. The Irishman never inhaled another breath.

SUNNYBRIDGE

1973

Sunnybridge was a substantial country house with a delightful manicured garden, not that Baz could relate to the size of any object larger than the span of his outstretched arms, neither could he relate to the beauty of anything, unless it was described to him as such and then only if the person sat on his right side and then only how skillfully it had been articulated. He soon realised, relying on others for his eyes on the world would always be a hit or miss affair.

The explosion had ripped through the campervan just above the chassis. Small fragments of metal were propelled indiscriminately into the air, causing untold damage to anything or anyone in its proximity. Fortunately, the engine held steadfast, acting as part barrier for the accompanying fireball.

Unaware of the danger she had put Baz in, the Irishman's source, in all her innocence, had furnished Eamon Carrick with the details he had needed to plan out his strategy. Like all good explosives men, he had been meticulous with his homework.

From then on Eamon Carrick was well aware that this was an operation based on revenge: that had always been his weakness: that was why he was on the run from the Provisionals in the first place. The Irishman had grown to despise himself, if only for his failings.

Eamon Carrick had made a mistake somewhere along the way. Probably due to the positioning of the bomb and an underestimation of the campervan's strength. Forgotten skills and all that. The intended target had survived. Although it did take Baz a long time to abandon death as his preferred option.

To the outside world it was just an unfortunate fuel tank explosion.

These hippies will go smoking their happy baccy around petrol, what do they expect?

During his initial time spent in hospital, Baz had had many visitors, although he was never aware of their presence, or anyone else for that matter. In truth, not being able to see his visitors at that time would pale into insignificance when Baz finally learnt the extent of his injuries.

On first sighting of the completely bandaged head and knowing his chances of survival, Robert thought that this was probably going to be the only image of his presumed father he would ever see. Although he had convinced himself long ago that this faceless person was, in fact, just that, his real father. All those years of searching and there he was, only feet away from him. Basil Albright might as well have been on the other side of the world.

Imogen Gomme had visited on several occasions and would sit with her Butes for hours on end, talking about everything and anything. Pasang had reverted back to her birth name, for Imogen Gomme, Pasang no longer existed.

All the devotees at one point had come and gone.

Soon after Zed Golby had left the hospital he gave Billy instructions to find the Irishman. One high ranking policeman had been extremely instrumental in that undertaking. The rest is history.

Violet had not seen her brother since that day at the cemetery. Immediately returning to France in a state of distress, it took several days before she was able to write to Ruby.

Baz had third degree burns to his upper torso and face, having had several operations to remove pieces of metal and dead tissue. More were to follow, mainly for the grafting of skin. If he could get through these procedures without infection, his chances of survival would increase, although the doctors had expected his heart to give up at any time.

For the first months Baz's body was awash with high doses of powerful antibiotics and the most potent painkillers known to man. If the explosion hadn't blown all thoughts from his mind, then the drugs certainly had.

A few days before the bandages were removed for the last time, Baz was informed of his worst injury. That flash of blinding light, the one that had lasted less than the minutest fraction of a second, the one that was quicker than his ability to blink, it was during this shortest period of time, the most serious damage had occurred.

Baz would never see again, he was blind, his eyes had been destroyed. There was no nice way of putting it and the doctors couldn't find one either.

Two nurses led Baz upstairs to his room. They had introduced themselves as Nurse Maddy and Nurse Francis. Both knew to stand to his right, after all, it was in his report. Baz held lightly onto Nurse Maddy's arm, just the way he was taught. His comprehensive guide to a sightless world.

Accept it or drown in the blackness, that was the mental battle Baz had been fighting over the past months. Walking a tightrope tied together with loose knots was the best way he could describe it, even if only to himself.

Looking down into the darkness and seeing nothing, looking up and seeing, what? More darkness, more nothing, looking back and seeing, forgotten memories. Looking forward and seeing? How does a blind man take his own life? Drive to the nearest cliff? Take an overdose? Cut his wrists? Now that one was worth thinking about.

The colours had gone, so had the faces and shapes. The outside world had gone. There was only one option, he could think of no other way.

'No, I must believe that life is worth living, I cannot do as much as I could before but I can do something, however small it may be, for that reason alone, it is worth living. That belief must come from somewhere. Where? Self pity does not win battles. I can think, I am aware. Life has just thrown me another challenge. My life has been full of challenges. This is just another one. I didn't have much before, I have even less now and I will have nothing in the future. Someone wrote Freedom's just another word for nothing left to lose. Then I am free. Be here now. For Christ's sake. Be here now. The light *is* inside me anyway, I must be here. I must believe. Drifting aimlessly in my black world, if anyone can find me then I must.'

Baz made it through. If only just!

"You can call me Fran, most residents do," Nurse Francis said.

"Call me Maddy, Basil, it's short for Madeleine but you can call me Maddy, I won't answer to Mad though," Nurse Maddy added. She sounded quite a bit older than Nurse Fran.

"A lot more appropriate though," said Nurse Fran. Baz knew by the changing tone in her voice that the words were spoken behind a smile. Guessing the expressions on people's faces was becoming second nature. He hoped.

Nurse Fran was impatient, Baz was certain of that, seeming to be a person always on a mission, striding away in the distance with Baz and Nurse Maddy having to play catch-up.

"Call me Baz, not Basil, only my mother called me Basil," in a tone that said it wasn't through affection. The nurses led him up the stairs. His main concern at that moment was wondering when he would reach the last step, knowing his foot would hang in mid air, searching for that elusive rise, then drop with an ungainly jolt. This he knew would happen, if only by experience. These were the little things that annoyed Baz the most, the little things *not* in his comprehensive guide to a sightless world.

"Last step," Nurse Maddy said. "How is your memory Basil?" she added as they paused at the top.

"I've forgotten," he replied. "And it's Baz."

"Now start counting your steps, *Baz*," said Nurse Fran, quickly.

"Four," said Nurse Maddy as they stopped, then held his hand out so he could touch the wall. Painted plaster, he thought, definitely not wood, nor brick, probably magnolia. That was a guess though.

"Keep your hand on the wall, now turn right and start counting again."

"Your room is down here Baz," said Nurse Fran, her voice fading with the distance.

After seventeen steps and two closed doors later, Baz reached a gap in the wall.

Nurse Maddy and Nurse Fran escorted Baz around his four room domain, gently holding his wrist they placed his hand wherever there was an object to be touched. A wardrobe, a bed, a sink, towels, the light switch, "oh, sorry Baz,' Nurse Fran said, 'I didn't think." A radio, the radio's tuner, the radio's volume knob, the doorhandle to the bathroom, the bathroom, a painting on the wall, which Baz was reliably told was a watercolour of a horse and cart by a lake. "It feels remarkably like glass." An ashtray. "I don't smoke." Shelves, the toilet basin. "Believe me, it is there," said Nurse Maddy keeping his hand at bay. His fingertips were wiped over the cold glass of a mirror. "It feels like a watercolour of a horse and cart by a lake," he remarked.

"We'll take the mirror out."

"No, leave it."

Every object, every nook and cranny in his small enclosed world was eventually caressed by Baz's fingers. A mental note was taken of their position and a picture was formed in his mind, just as he was taught. Again, his comprehensive guide to a sightless world.

"We'll leave you to get used to it Basil," said Nurse Francis, as her voice vanished down the corridor.

"Baz!"

"OK Baz," she shouted back.

Sunnybridge had a wooden bench in the garden. It came to be known as Baz's bench and that is where he could be found most of the time, weather permitting, although the rain and cold wasn't always an obstacle, just another sensation. It was positioned at the side of the far left corner, slightly set back from the circular gravel path surrounding the central lawn and close to the beech and oak trees towering behind. It was at this spot Baz could hear the changing rhythm from the fountain as the water tumbled into the pond below. It was where he could hear the stones crunching underfoot from anyone approaching along the path, Baz thought it sounded like they were walking on small animal bones. It was where he could hear birdsong and the wind brushing through the leaves, like a distant roar on more blustery days. There were even moments when he felt mildly contented with life. But there was another reason why he had chosen this particular one out of the other seven benches. It was far enough away where he knew no one could see him.

Baz knew exactly what people could see, he hadn't been told, but he knew all the same. He knew by the tightness and smoothness of his skin, not that soft, silky, tactile type smoothness but a cold, flat, vitreous texture. He knew by the mass of pot-marked scarring, by his stretched pulpy lips, he knew by his featureless nose, by the bare, hairless patch on top of his head hidden by a blue baseball cap, now a permanent feature. He knew by the flaps of skin that were once his ears. But mostly he knew by the advice he was given to constantly wear sunglasses, the ones that completely hid his eyes from the outside world, the ones, he thought, probably made him look like a blue-bottle. He knew exactly what people could see by the long pauses and the sedate way they spoke to him.

The days when people would just simply look behind were now deep in the past. What Baz would give to have them back.

Over the first weeks Baz took fifteen minutes to walk to his bench, a sighted person would probably do it in less than three.

Nurse Fran and Nurse Maddy had decided to leave Baz much to his own devices. Sometime in the future he would have to experience life on his own anyway. "Flying solo," as Nurse Fran put it once. Probably from the comprehensive guide to a sightless world. "Do I get a certificate?" Baz asked. "A blind licence?" On a few occasions his hands had left the security of a wall or another familiar object, when he found he had lost all bearings, as if he was in a vast empty space without a compass, floating around in no-mans-land. It was then he had to rely on a smell or a sound or just a simple guess, he couldn't remember that being in the comprehensive guide to a sightless world either. Walking in a randomly chosen direction was always an interesting experience for Baz.

BAZ'S BENCH (3)

Baz was sitting on his bench, a cool breeze stroking his cheek. For him there was nothing like the feeling of cold air on his skin, a psychological residue from his days back in the burns unit. Two people crunched their way along the small animal bones in his direction, crunches he didn't recognise. One was heavier with long loping strides, the other had shorter, snappier steps with a sound that was hardly discernible. Their pace slowed significantly as they got within sighting distance, the heavier of the two stalled completely. First timers, Baz thought.

Both eventually came to a standstill, the one slightly to his right was very tall, their deep breaths coming from the clouds. The lighter of the two faced directly onto Baz but remained silent, she was a woman, he could smell her.

"You're blocking my view," Baz said.

A pause. "You haven't lost your sense of humour then?"

"Alice?" the trill of her voice easily recognisable, "Alice?" He paused for a moment. "And Issan, it's you, isn't it Issan?"

After a short silence. "Yeah man, it's me, Lennox, I'm not in the temple now, remember."

"I remember, come into my office," Baz said, patting the wooden slats. His head remained motionless, never deviating from facing forward, he waited for them to speak. Nothing. Only to be expected, he thought. "We keep meeting on benches Alice, have you another confession?" Baz waited, neither said anything. "You never said goodbye Alice, that's twice now."

"Shit life isn't it?" she said.

Baz wasn't too sure whether she was talking about not saying goodbye or because of what had happened to him.

"A lot has happened since I saw you last," Baz said, cynically. Silence. He waited. "Kashin, is he good?" Someone had to say something.

"He's back in the states man."

"Oh, good."

"Did a runner. He got busted."

"Oh." Baz turned his head as if he was looking at them. "So did we."

"Yeah man," spoken with a mixture of acknowledgment and remorse.

"You three got out just in time, I hope it was worth it?" Baz said. Neither answered. "It had nothing to do with Zed Golby though did it?"

A long silence again. Baz waited.

Finally, Lennox spoke. "We were told Golby wanted rid of us, we thought our time was up, we had no choi..."

"At that time we didn't know he had nothing to do with it," interrupted Alice.

"You trying to justify *not* killing another man?"

"You weren't killed," she said, her words tailing away.

Baz faced her long and hard. He could guess her reaction.

Alice continued, "I wish we never had that discussion," she sounded sad.

331

"You mean the last one, or the one fifty years ago."

"I'm sorry," she said after a pause.

Baz took a deep breath. "Someone was playing games with the police *and* you *and* Zed Golby. Too many games. To this day I still don't understand what happened."

"We weren't living by the rules man, that's what happened," Lennox said.

A feeble reply thought Baz. "It was Little Daibai," he said quickly.

"Yeah man, we heard."

"So you heard that Little Dai wasn't Little Dai. Little Dai was Eamon Carrick. Little Dai *was* a member of the..." Baz paused for a second. "The fucking I...R...A." He said the three letters slowly and deliberately.

"Jesus man how were we supposed to know?"

"Then guess who saw me going into Zed Golby's place?"

"It was when we sent you, wasn't it?" Alice asked.

"He thought I worked for Zed, or the police. Anyhow, he thought I was on to his little game, I signed my own death warrant. *He,* was an explosives man back in his heyday. To Eamon Carrick I was just another lamb to the slaughter."

"Shit life isn't it,"Alice said.

Baz turned his head towards Alice again, he wanted her to have a good look at his injuries. "Yeah Alice, shit fucking life, isn't it."

"Jesus man, we didn't know he was playing everyone off each other," Lennox said.

"Little Dai, Eamon Carrick, was working for the IRA, or so they thought. And then Zed. Believe me, that is not a good idea, I mean fucking with the IRA *and* Zed Golby."

"So why did they bust us?"

"They didn't bust you, they busted us remember," Baz said. He missed looking people straight in the eye, even if it was with just the one. "Little Dai did a runner. In fact, they didn't bust us, they were looking for Eamon Carrick, or anyone who knew where he was. Only one certain high ranking rosser wasn't looking for Little Dai, not for the right reasons anyhow, he was on Zed Golby's books and guess what? They found him."

"What happened man?"

"Zed Golby got there first or his henchman did."

Lennox paused, "Oh."

"It doesn't matter, the outcome would have been the same whoever found him."

Alice and Lennox pondered the demise of Little Dai. Neither knowing how to continue.

Baz finally spoke. "Tell me something Lennox, did you own the big house? I mean, *own* it, you know, the bricks and mortar, I don't mean the people. You wouldn't think you could own them, *would you*?"

"No man. I own nothing."

"So who does the house belong to?"

"The Master man."

"The Master," Baz said. "I might be blind and half deaf but I'm not a fucking idiot!"

"No man, The Master *did* exist..."

"As a person, as a normal, average, fucked up man," interrupted Alice.

"He owned the joint man, Martyn White was his name, he was the great grandson of the original owner. Mart's great grandfather built the fucking joint man. When the old man died, Mart's grandfather gave it to some other guy, nothing was signed though man. Mart's father told him the story but did nothing himself, something about an ongoing legal case, then he died. So Mart ignored the lawyers and just claimed it back. We and a few other dudes came over to see what it was all about.

"Other dudes? You mean Kashin?"

"And An, and Kai Liang, we all met in Katmandu."

"And Alice?"

"No man. That's another story."

"Lennox got me off the hard stuff," said Alice, then paused for a second. "*And* the streets. Fucking men, that's all they're good for anyway."

Baz wasn't too sure whether she meant fucking men or *fucking* men.

"You *were* past your prime old girl," Lennox said, trying to mimic a well-to-do English accent. "Mart lived in the apartment, we called him The Master, only as a joke at first but the name stuck. After all it was his place man. Some other dudes started drifting in, it became a kind of commune man. We started growing some gear, An and Kai Liang started the temple. Life was kinda good man, we were free."

"And out of your fucking heads," said Alice.

"We started selling some gear, then began making money man," sounding as though it was a surprise.

"Capitalists," Alice puffed out.

"So what happened to Martyn White?"

"Dead," replied Alice.

"Oh."

"White family couldn't get any man past the age of fifty."

"Became a smack head man, he *was* a wild one."

"Wild! He was an eighteen carat fucking arsehole," said Alice.

"A dead eighteen carat fucking arsehole" Baz added.

"Anything could happen when Mart was around."

"And usually did," said Alice.

"Looking back I suppose it was inevitable," Lennox shook his head, not that Baz knew. "One evening we went upstairs to the apartment, and there he was man, dead, overdose, bad smack or good smack or something." He then lowered his voice. "You know where we used to grow the grass plants?"

Baz thought for a second, not about where the plants were grown but what was under them. "No," he finally said, drawing out the word in a long breath. "You didn't bury..."

"It was what he would have wanted man," Lennox said.

"Pushing up daisies," chuckled Alice. "Pushing up cannabis, same fucking thing."

"I've been smoking Martyn White?"

"You got stoned, didn't you?"

"What about his family?"

"None."

"What could we do Baz," Alice said. "Tell the old fucking bill, think about that one Baz. A hippy commune with a dead fucking heroin addict man, and a load of dope. Then a bunch of fucking rossers come swarming round the place."

The three sat in silence again.

"So *that* was The Master," Baz finally said.

"Shit life, isn't it," Alice replied.

"Yeah, shit life."

They spoke for a while longer, mostly small talk, mainly about people and events when they were back in the house. Baz was aware from the tone in Lennox's voice that he had been truly humbled. Alice had been through too much in her life to have anything affect her. Seeing Baz got pretty close to it though. In the end it was Baz who had to ask them to leave. "It's getting chilly," he said.

That was the last time he would hear of either Alice or Lennox.

BAZ'S BENCH (4)

Rolo was a Sunnybridge attendant, a jovial man who wore chalky white trousers and a thin, half length, white lab coat. He was also large, Baz knew this because his deep rolling voice came from high above. Also, the heaviness of his crunches on the small animal bones was the loudest in Sunnybridge, not the quickest though, Nurse Fran carried that mantle. He was also black. "You have a slight Caribbean accent," Baz told him on their first meeting.

"Probably watching too much cricket," Rolo replied and confirmed that he was indeed, in his own words, chocolate coloured. "The ladies love to lick chocolate," he added.

The answer reminded Baz of Mikhail.

Anyhow, when this man told Rolo he had come to visit Basil Albright and he was a relation, but declined to offer what relation. Rolo, forever protective of Baz, viewed him with a lot of suspicion.

"You have a visitor Baz," said Rolo. "He says he..."

"My name is Robert Blakeney," Robert quickly interrupted.

Rolo waited for a reaction from Baz. None came. "I'll be watching," he whispered to the man as he began to crunch his way back.

"Hello," Baz said.

For Robert, this was it, the culmination of all those years of searching. Now he was facing his father, his presumed father. All he could see was a baseball cap pulled down low, throwing a shadow over his disfigured face, the eyes hidden behind large black glasses. Now Robert was finding it hard to think. "Hello," he finally said, stuttering through the word.

"I'm Basil Albright." Baz thought it was another psychologist, the second one that week. He did enjoy talking to the mind men though, often turning the conversation around to people's beliefs and faiths, their self-proclaimed intelligence not denying him any opinions they had on the subject. None had the answer though.

"I'm Robert Blakeney," he said, nervously.

Not Doctor Blakeney, thought Baz, or Mr Blakeney, if he was a consultant. "Do you like the sound of water Mr Blakeney?"

"Yes I do." His voice settling slightly. "Please call me Robert."

"Peaceful, isn't it Robert, the sound of water I mean. And calming. Peace and calming are, well, relaxing, everyone should have a fountain."

"Yes they should," Robert replied with conviction. "May I call you Basil? Mr Albright."

"No."

"Oh."

"But you can call me Baz though."

Baz waited through a long pause, he knew Robert was looking at him by the warm breath on his cheek.

Robert tilted his head. "I can hear a chaffinch, listen, there it is again. It's coming from that elm tree, there's another one, the male has a reddish breast and a blue head Baz."

"You know your birds Robert."

"I lived in an orphanage for a long while, I spent a lot of time outdoors."

"Orphanage to doctor, you have done well?"

"No, no I'm not a doctor."

"Oh, OK."

The conversation lapsed for a short while.

Robert eventually broke the silence. "I'm sorry to hear about what happened. I read about it in the papers, that is where I saw your name, in the Daily Mirror. It must have been the fuel tank."

"So you want to find out why the van exploded. Have you got a VW camper?"

"No I haven't."

Baz felt relieved, he didn't fancy explaining that one. "Then are you from the papers? You're a reporter?" Thinking he had solved the mystery.

"No! No I'm not and why I am here has nothing to do with...with what happened." Robert's words tailed away.

"Is this some kind of game Robert? Great! I like stupid word games," Baz said, sarcastically. "You don't have to see words, do you?"

"No, no it's not a game." Now or never, thought Robert. "You were once a friend of my brother *and* you also knew my mother."

"Your brother?" Baz paused. "*And* your mother?"

"Margaret was my mother's name," Robert said, then waited.

"No." Baz shook his head. " Margaret Blakeney means nothing..."

"She was Margaret Waterhouse when you knew her."

"Mrs Waterhouse," he turned to face Robert. "Your mother?"

Robert felt as though Baz was actually looking at him, he couldn't see he wasn't.

"And William?" Baz said quietly.

"He was my brother...half brother."

"William was your half brother? I suppose he must have been if Mrs Waterhouse is your mother, I would like to say I can see the resemblance. William was my friend. Did you know I was the last person to see him alive?" sounding proud of it.

"No I didn't."

Baz slid his hand into his trouser pocket and pulled out the pawn. "This belonged to your brother, the first time I saw it was over fifty years ago, we were just kids." Baz paused as he recalled that exact moment. "I call it William, it reminds me of your brother." He wrapped his hand around the small figure. "And your mother."

Robert watched as Baz returned the chess piece to the confinement of his pocket. "You are wondering why I am here?" he said quietly.

"Because you want to ask me about William? Your mother must have..."

"Yes. I need some questions answered."

"How did you know I existed at all? I suppose your mother must have..."

"Mrs Chattle was the first to mention..."

"Who?"

"Mrs Chattle, then Eddie, but that's another story. It was John Waterhouse that told me your name."

Baz paused. "John Waterhouse?"

"Yes. No one knew if you were still alive and if you were, well, we

337

couldn't find you, there appeared to be no record of you ever existing."

Baz recalled when he had entered the house, also Wing Commander Batty changing his war papers, it must have been like vanishing from the face of the earth. Two rebirths thought Baz.

"Then the newspaper article," Robert said.

"The newspaper article?" Baz sighed deeply. "I don't read the papers."

"No, sorry, they said your name. There can't be that many Basil Albrights."

"Mrs Waterhouse, she married a Mr Blakeney. I hope she was happy. Your mother is a nice lady Robert. Where is she..?"

"She died in childbirth. I never knew her. Blakeney was her maiden name, there was no Mr Blakeney. I never knew who my father was."

Baz felt a surge of sadness. "All those years and I never knew. I thought about her often."

"It was my childbirth, I killed her."

"Oh." A long pause. "Maybe, maybe John Water..."

"No! No he's not, my mother is buried in North Devon. She moved down there in nineteen forty-two."

"Then she met someone while she was down there?"

"I..." the word got caught in Robert's throat, "I was conceived before she moved. After John Waterhouse, after her husband had moved out of the house and before she moved to North Devon. I am thirty-one." Robert said assertively. "I was born on the fifteenth of July, nineteen forty-three." I was conceived in September, nineteen forty-two."

Baz took a deep breath. "She died during the war. Childbirth, all the killing at that time and she died from childbirth." There was a long silence, one that left him with one thought. "Do you believe in God Robert?"

"Yes! I am a Christian," Robert said proudly.

Baz thought he sounded smug.

"Do you believe in the virgin birth?"

"Yes of course, I *am* a Christian."

"Well, you could be from a virgin birth then?"

"That's ridiculous!"

"You believed in one virgin birth, why not another?"

"Then do *you* believe in the virgin birth?" asked Robert.

"There *was* no virgin birth Robert. If *he* did exist, then Jesus's father was probably a drunken Roman soldier, maybe Jesus's mother was raped, maybe *your* God is a rapist."

Robert crossed himself. "How can you say that!?"

"Because more women get raped than there are virgin births."

An uncomfortable silence.

"*Did* you have sexual intercourse with my mother?" Robert finally blurted out. "You know, when you returned William's kit bag."

Baz's mind wandered back to that afternoon spent with Mrs Waterhouse, he thought about the smoothness of her body, her gentle touch. He thought how he would give anything to experience it one more time. He also thought it was above any denial.

"Yes."

Another, longer silence.

"When?"

Baz angled his head towards Robert but not directly at him. "Nine months before you were born."

It was those last words Robert had been waiting for, ten long years had finally come to a close. "So do *you* think you *are* my father?"

Baz paused for a moment. "Probably." Another pause. "Yes," then lifted his hands up to Robert's face. "Don't be afraid." For the next minute he carefully felt around Robert's features, as he was taught in his comprehensive guide to a sightless world. "Close your eyes." He knew it was his son he was touching, his son, his own flesh and blood. "Yes," he said again. "It looks like we both killed her."

Robert no longer saw the horribly scarred featureless face with the oversized black glasses. Robert saw only his father.

Baz saw nothing but felt everything.

Robert stayed for another hour, telling Baz his entire life story, about Bernadette and Archie, about the search and Father Byrne, not one stone was left unturned. When Robert asked about Baz's life, Baz replied with the only word that came to mind. "Unfortunate," then added, "up to half an hour ago."

Baz felt for the radio's on-off knob and released Bob Harris's whispered tones into his bedroom, a mellow introduction to Pink Floyd's 'The Dark Side of the Moon.' He then heard a delicate but subdued tap on his door, followed by an unfamiliar fragrance entering the room.

Over the weeks, Baz had got to know every odour of every nurse and attendant. A nurse's perfume would always be a favourite topic for conversation and Baz had become quite an expert on identifying the different brands. Only this one was different, more natural, like teddy bear fur.

Without any warning, Baz felt the warmth of moist lips firmly being planted on his right cheek, not a quick smack of a kiss but a cushioned softness that remained for several seconds. Since the explosion, no one had dared touch his face, he could even sense when a person couldn't bear to look at him. But a kiss, with lips!

"Hi Butes."

"Pasang!"

A wailing noise erupted in front of him as she slumped on the edge of the bed, flinging both arms around his neck and dropping her head onto his shoulder.

"Sorry Butes. I promised myself to stay strong," sounding as though she had just emerged from a long dive under water.

"You have nothing to be..." Baz said, halting as he felt two fingers press on his lips. He tried to reassure her by stroking her arm, feeling the loose sleeve from her flimsy kaftan rise above her elbow, it reminded him of how warm and silky her skin felt. Her weeping settled into rhythmic sobs as she nestled deeper into his neck. Baz wanted to tell her that nothing had changed between them, that nothing need be said, inside they were still the same people. He didn't, he knew it wouldn't be true. He then recalled the last time he had touched her in the same way, laying in her bed, coming down from the acid trip. When sex was out of the question.

"I'm so sorry Butes," she whimpered.

Baz remained silent, just holding her was enough. He pulled her closer, feeling her shoulder submit under his grip. He remembered holding her the same way on that night, when she had wrapped her legs and arms around him, enclosing him in like a parcel.

"I have so much I want to tell you." Her voice sounded shaky. "I'm so sorry Butes."

"Sorry, there's nothing to be sorry about Pasang."

He felt the dampness of her cheek sliding on his neck.

Then what happened next took him completely by surprise. His first thought was, why now? Why not that night? That was it, he thought. That was the problem. He wanted it. Now he didn't. It did! And the more he didn't, the more he couldn't stop it. What did his father say? "The best way to get something is not to want it."

And what was it? His penis had moved. A slight stiffening.

"I was in the house when the bomb exploded Butes," Pasang said, her sniffs filling the spaces between the words.

Baz placed the other hand on her cheek. A horrible thought entered his head. Was his bedroom door still open? What if someone had passed? Human traffic was always at its busiest after lunch. An image entered his mind, a picture in a book he had seen many years ago, a Minotaur in his labyrinth, picking at the bones of a beautiful woman. Only this was a faceless monster wearing huge black glasses, a bulge developing in his trousers, the flat of his hand holding the face of a beautiful sobbing blond into the crook of his neck. People have probably been arrested for less, he thought.

Pasang slid her hand around his waist.

It was only when Baz held her wrist he realised her elbow was resting firmly on his erection. The response was spontaneous, an involuntary throb that pushed upward. Did she feel it?

"I'm so sorry about what happened Butes."

"It's fine," he gasped.

Pasang responded with a loving squeeze, causing a downward movement from the point of her arm, resulting in Baz's defiant muscle pushing up one more time. To his surprise she nudged down, followed by a reflex reply from Baz. Slowly lifting her elbow she pushed down again, only this time the pressure had become stronger. Baz responded, another longer shove upwards, it was as if his penis and her elbow were in communication with each other. Down once again, this time she added a slide to the repertoire, a sensation rushed up his body. Then up again, then down again, then up again, then down again, then up again, his entire being becoming completely under the

341

control of her elbow. With every push, every slip, every nudge, every rub, every throb, he felt himself hardening that bit more. Then suddenly it felt different, something stirred, his penis had stiffened to the peak of its hardness and there it remained, like cast-iron, in a state of hardened suspension. The pressure from Pasang's elbow held fast, along with Baz's breath, his stomach and every muscle stiffened, his hips thrust upwards.

Baz felt a warm liquid trickle between his legs.

A minute passed and Pasang peeled herself away. "You'll need to change Butes, I'll wait outside."

A feeling of relief as Baz heard the bedroom door slide on the carpet.

'And who knows which is which and who is who' the radio sang out before the click from the volume knob extinguished the music.

Ten minutes later they walked onto the terrace decking at the back of the house. "I love that fresh smell after the rain," Baz said with a deep breath, as though he had been given some kind of deliverance. "As if life itself has been cleansed." For the first time in a very long time he was feeling content, human again.

Pasang's arm linked around Baz's elbow as he led her along the small animal bones, both enjoying the warmth as the sun dispersed the last of the clouds; it reminded him of their stroll in the temple garden when they were tripping, nothing ever seems normal with Pasang he thought.

Baz heard a conversation to his right end abruptly. "Baz!" Nurse Fran called out as she paced along the path with swift methodic crunches. "You've forgotten your hat. I'm sure your niece will not want you to get sunburnt."

"This is Pasang. She is not my..."

"Imogen," Pasang interrupted.

"This is Imogen. She's not my..." halting as he heard Nurse Fran disappear into the distance.

Baz thought for a moment. "Imogen or Pasang?" he asked.

"For you Butes, Pasang, only for you though." She dropped her head on his shoulder and placed her hand into his. "And Butes, not Baz, always Butes." Then added. "It will be our little secret."

"You said you were in the house on the day of the explosion?"

She intertwined her fingers into his. "I came to see you Butes. I watched you from the window, you were walking down the street, then you disappeared around the side." Her words tightened. "Then I heard it Butes. Everyone ran outside, we thought you had been killed."

He remembered Mary saying those exact same words in the war.

"You were just lying there. Then an ambulance came and took you away. A few days later we were told you were going to die." A determination entered her voice. "But I knew Butes, I knew you would pull through."

"I remember the morning of the attack, the raid, you weren't there, you were there when I went to bed but you weren't there in the morning, I remember searching for you after the police had gone. I thought you had..." Baz halted mid-speech. "You weren't there."

Baz waited through the silence.

She took a deep breath. "It was a few days before the raid, the police stopped me. I was on a delivery, I had this feeling they knew I was carrying. You know, they didn't look surprised when they found the gear. They sat me in the back seat of a squad car. There was another man already seated in front."

"What did he look like?"

"A suit, I didn't see him, he kept facing forward." She waited for Baz to respond. Nothing. "This man, he didn't seem interested in the dope, he was asking me about Little Dai. So many questions, I didn't know anything about Little Dai then, well not about what he was asking."

"What sort of questions?"

"Had I seen Little Dai? Did I know if he was going to leave the house? Where was he? I told him he had disappeared for days on end before but had always returned. He asked if he had met anyone that I hadn't seen before and about some guy called Golby. Who is this Golby?"

Baz thought before he answered. "He's an old friend of mine."

"An *old* friend?"

"It's a long story."

"Do you know what Butes?"

"They didn't arrest you for the dope, they let you go."

"Wow! How did you know? A whole weight of weed, can you believe it, they *actually* gave it back to me. Then they told me that it would be good for my health if I wasn't in the house that Wednesday night, but not to tell anyone. If I did then they would charge me with supplying and I would go to prison. In fact, they told me not to go back to the house, ever. I was scared Butes, you must believe me, I wanted to tell you but I didn't want to go to prison."

"You weren't going to come back?"

"I was scared Butes."

"So where did you go?"

"My sister's, I hated it. Her husband's a suit, straight as you can get. I even had to sneak out just for a puff."

"That's bad Pasang," he said, mockingly.

"I dropped a tab while I was there, just to break the boredom. Jesus Butes, weird or what, never trip with straight people, especially when they don't know you're on acid. Bummer or what."

"Yeah bummer."

"I left their flat one day and guess who I met walking along the street?"

"Little Dai?"

"Wow! You're so clever Butes."

"Go on." As though he knew what was coming. "What did he say?"

Pasang spoke softly. "He asked me what was happening back at the house. I told him we were going to South Wales, I told him you were doing up the old camper. He was very friendly, after all it *was* Little Dai Butes. He asked me if anyone else was working on the camper." Pasang barely whispered her next words. "Not to my knowledge, I said. He asked me a lot of questions about you Butes, he wanted to know every little detail. He even asked me about this guy called Golby. *Who* is this Golby?" She started sobbing again. "You must hate me."

"Why would I hate you Pasang? You said you came back to the big house."

"It was at my sister's, halfway through the night I had this horrible feeling. I thought it was the acid coming back." Pasang hugged herself. "It was horrible Butes. Then it came to me Little Dai asking all those questions about you, I don't know why Butes but I had to see you. Warn you, about what, I had no idea. I left for the temple straight after breakfast, only you weren't there. An told me they were going to South Wales soon and I could go with them. He told me about the raid and how they were going to wait for Kai Liang to come out of

344

prison. I couldn't believe it Butes, what Kai Liang did to those policemen." She puffed out a laugh. "So much for peace and love. Then he told me about Little Dai working for the IRA and he wasn't Little Dai at all, he was this Carrick guy and that he used to be a terrorist. Jesus Butes, what was happening? Nothing made sense anymore. I was beginning to think the acid trip at my sister's had messed up my head."

"Believe me Pasang, it wasn't *your* head."

Sonam said you would be back soon. She thought you had gone to get some parts for the van. Then I saw you walking up the street, I was so happy to see you. You looked in a hurry. I had a giggle to myself because I thought you must have sensed that I had rolled a mother of a joint, just for you Butes. Then you went around the side. I rushed round to see you." Pasang went silent for a couple of seconds. Baz felt her breath on the side of his face. The next words sounded automatic, as though they had lost all emotion. "Then the noise, I will never forget it. Half a minute later and I would have been by your side Butes."

"It was good it happened thirty seconds earlier then." Baz thought for a moment. "You're still here though, I mean you're not in South Wales?"

"No." The word fell to the ground.

"Why?"

"All that chanting and bendy exercises." She told Baz how she had only been to the actual temple a couple of times, stopping after no one seemed to care whether she was there or not. "Besides where would I get my gear from? You know me Butes, can't live without my blow."

"*Why?*"

A long pause. "OK, you Butes." She smiled. "You need to get your relief from somewhere."

They talked for a while longer, mainly about the strengths of the new dope on the market, Pasang's favourite subject. "There's some real good Red Leb on the streets, I'll bring some along next time," she said.

"I don't smoke any more." Concerned whether he could handle the paranoia, the anxiety, especially after what had happened. He knew how dope could have adverse effects.

"You didn't smoke the first time."

345

Pasang left after giving Baz a long hug and a kiss on the lips, telling him she would visit him often. She kept to her word.

THE SPICE OF INDIA

Zed Golby walked everywhere, he never drove, in fact he had never learnt to drive. Strange for a man who owns a garage. He once said that a horse and cart was the only way to get around and since nobody had ever driven a horse and cart, apart from Zed that is, no one could disagree, or would want to anyhow.

Whenever it was necessary, Teabags was his driver, Teabags was happy to be his driver. Teabags got to keep the Mercedes Benz 450SEL and looking very shiny with its re-spray of deep royal blue it was too. Most people thought that every year, for the past three years, Teabags had been given a new car. Most people didn't know it was the same one with a change of colour and new plates. A necessity in this particular Merc's line of business.

On a warm clear day and wearing his usual tailored, dark suit with an open neck shirt, Zed had left his office above the greengrocers and began the short walk to the Spice of India. Not to eat though!

The evening before.

Mr Gupta, the owner of the Spice of India had phoned the snooker hall, the one above Altons, remember. Mr Gupta asked for Joey, the snooker hall manager. Joey, at the time, was busy smashing the butt end of his snooker cue into a glass fronted one arm bandit. Unfortunately for the machine, Joey had just lost twenty-five quid after missing a simple pot *and* the game. In truth, he had lost more than the twenty-five quid, Zed Golby not only owned the snooker hall, he also owned the one arm bandit. Joey's wages were going to be light that week.

After Joey had managed to calm down, Mr Gupta told him that five yobs in the restaurant were causing trouble. What would a restaurant owner be doing phoning a snooker hall manager about some unruly yobs? Simple answer, for the past ten years Mr Gupta had been paying Zed Golby a monthly insurance premium to remedy such problems. In fact, most of the restaurants in the area paid the same premium. This insurance premium would be more commonly known, for those officiates of gangster movies, as protection money. Hence, trouble in these particular restaurants was very rare. Strangely, the few restaurants that had refused to pay the premium, seemed to have more than their fair share of misfortune. Anyway, Mr Gupta thought, it's only right that the vast amount of money he had handed to Zed Golby over the years, should now be justified.

Joey, not in the best of moods after his monetary loss, relished the chance of busting the heads of five drunken yobs. Five, Mr Gupta had said, five Joey had thought, probably two too many for him to handle by himself.

"Fancy a Ruby tonight boss?" Billy asked Zed, as he returned the telephone receiver to its base.

Curry was by far Zed's favourite meal. Zed liked it hot. A madras was his favourite but many had seen him attack a vindaloo barely breaking a sweat. It also wasn't unusual to see a waiter place a small plate of green, finger chillies in the centre of the table and to anyone that happened to see this phenomenon, watch him happily munch away as though they were sherbet lemons.

Zed hadn't had a curry for over a week, neither had he eaten that evening. "Two birds, one stone," Zed replied. Billy translated that as actually meaning, five yobs, three curries.

Most of the diners knew as soon as Zed, Billy and Joey casually entered the restaurant. The only people that appeared not to know were the five drunken yobs.

Zed and Billy despised drunks and they despised drunkenness even more. Neither drank alcohol, one of the reasons they had grown a mutual respect for each other. Billy had a very good reason for his hatred of alcohol. It was alcohol that drove his mother away, it was alcohol that stole his childhood and it was alcohol that drowned his father's liver. Zed was different, his dislike of alcohol was simple. For a big man, he was a lightweight when it came to drink, even half a pint would turn his mind into a woolly version of its former self.

Mr Gupta shook Zed's hand first, then Billy's, Mr Gupta knew the order of priority very well. Being completely ignored by the restaurant owner did nothing to ease Joey's already stretched disposition.

"As always Mr Golby sir, we have saved the best table for you." Mr Gupta clucked, presenting Zed with a continuous bow as the three followed his outstretched arm towards the back corner.

Five tables lined the opposite wall from where Zed, Billy and Joey sat. The yobs had spread themselves around the central one and much to the annoyance of Mr Gupta, had also appropriated the two tables either side. Broken glass, flicked food, and the contents of a dropped ashtray surrounded the floor below them. Joey saw the table with the remnants of what Mr Gupta had tried, unsuccessfully, to explain to him on the phone. One of the yobs attempting the whipping away the tablecloth trick, without success. "They whipped my tablecloth away," the restaurant owner had cried down the mouthpiece much to Joey's confusion.

A young indian waiter with a large silver wristwatch and a red waistcoat furnished Zed's table with a tower of sauce trays, a large jug of water, a pint of ice cold lager for Joey and as always, a complimentary plate of green finger chillies. Zed had taken one as soon as the plate touched the table, quickly biting it in half. Then, wearing his usual roguish grin, he did what he always did at this time and offered up the plate under the noses of Billy and Joey. Never, at any time, in the entire history of the Spice of India had anyone taken one.

The noise of breaking glass, followed by raucous laughter broke through the air from the opposite side.

Joey, although dying to vent his suppressed anger on the noisy uncouth yobs, knew only too well the rules of combat. Talk normally or remain silent and under no circumstances look across to the intended victims. 'Staying downwind,' Billy had fittingly named this rule.

From his inside pocket, Zed took out a small notepad and pen, strange for a man that could hardly read or write. He quickly scribbled something on the top sheet, tore it off, folded it in half and slid it under the table mat, a fraction remained poking out. With the slightest movement of his huge index finger, the young waiter scampered over to the table. Mutterings were imparted.

The waiter followed his orders to the letter, he wiped the tablemat and the small piece of paper vanished. The next time it appeared was in the hands of the yob sitting with his back to the three men, another yob leaned over to see what was written on it. Soon after a third yob abruptly snatched it away from him, each gaze followed by a confused expression. Lastly it was handed over to the yob slouched with his back to the wall. He turned it over and gazed at the blank side, turned it back again and studied the mark one more time, screwed it up and lobbed it at the waiter.

What was written on the paper? Just a simple cross, not an x type cross, more like a plus sign. Everyone knew the formula. Beneficiary (Yob) + Benefactor (The Spice of India) = well, that would be up to the yob. A simple killing wasn't out of the equation, remember the Irishman.

Zed, who had been watching all this without actually turning his gaze towards them, now knew who the head yob was. Another rule, always find out who the leader is. Appendix to that rule: always bust the leader's head first!

"Oi! Paki. Come 'ere," the head yob slurred. The young waiter held his ground. "Oi, you fucking Paki, was that some sort of fucking joke?"

Mr Gupta had lost all concern at the condition his restaurant might end up in. Worse than calling a *Pakistani* a *Paki*, never, ever, at any time, call an *Indian* a *Paki*. Mr Gupta wanted blood. The waiters wanted blood. The diners wanted blood. Joey, especially, wanted blood, the lost snooker game and the demise of the one arm bandit, not yet forgotten.

Like a giant shadowy ogre, Zed apathetically rose from his chair and carried the plate of green finger chillies over to where the yobs sat. Billy and Joey followed.

For several seconds Zed stared at each yob one by one. To him, these were kids, snotty youths barely out of their teens, he sighed and shook his head. Zed Golby really had no time for upstarts like these.

The yobs looked up at him the same way someone would stare up to the top floor of a skyscraper. Then looked at Billy, who was probably wider than they were tall. Then Joey, who had all the weather-beaten hallmarks of having spent the majority of his adult life in some kind of institution, which, of course, he had.

Zed picked up a chilli, bit it off from the stalk and happily crunched away, his eyes firmly fixed on the yobs' leader, finally swallowing it several seconds later, his expression remained deadpan throughout. "Eat whole chilli, if no tears like real man, you leave restaurant." He paused to study each yob in turn. "If not eat nice chilli, if cry like girl..." he stopped talking and looked at Joey.

"Fucking crushed skulls," Joey said, thumping a fist into the palm of his hand.

"Sounds good to me boss," said Billy.

"If not eat nice chilli, if cry like little girly, two choices. Clean up this mess..."

"Boss!" exclaimed Joey.

"*And* pay Mr Gupta for damage...or..." Zed turned to look at Joey again. "You take chance." Zed sighed again, "our skulls, your skulls, you take chance."

Everyone in the restaurant waited.

"Skulls it is..." Joey began to say as he took a step closer, only to see a hesitant hand stretch across and pick up a chilli.

The head yob bit into the green vegetable leaving only the stalk between his thumb and forefinger. The first few seconds seemed to pass without effect. Suddenly the yob's face froze, large droplets of sweat began oozing from every pore, his eyes widened into two protruding bloodshot balls. His mouth opened wide, as though his chin was being pulled down by a heavy weight. He spat out the half chewed chilli on to his lap, followed by short splutters as he tried to eject each seed. His face jerked round in different directions, a look of panic as he saw every glass empty. Zed strolled over to a table where two diners sat and took a single red rose from a tall slender vase. "Do you mind," he said.

"Be my guest Mr Golby."

Zed returned and the yob snatched it away, guzzling every last drop of water, spitting out soggy cigarette butts as he did so. "Water, more water."

Zed nodded to the waiter. The yob was now his.

"Chilli?" Zed said, displaying the plate to the other yobs.

One yob quickly shot up from his chair and made a dash for the door. Strangely, no one made any attempt to stop him or even acknowledged any concern. A great sense of freedom must have rushed through the yob's body as he reached the handle unhindered.

Another rule, this one well known by Mr Gupta, *always* lock the door.

The yob turned to see Joey nonchalantly strolling towards him. Joey was going to get to bust a skull after all.

Mr Gupta directed operations as the yobs cleaned the area around them, finally leaving it as they had found it. And the one at the door? Joey was just left shaking his head with frustration, the yob went down after the first punch.

The day after.

Zed was alone when he crossed the High Street. In front of him was the Spice of India with its gold script lettering on a green glossy background and bright red paintwork on the door and window frames. Mr Gupta's wayward colour scheme was the last clear image Zed Golby would ever see.

As he stepped from in-between two cars and onto the pavement he felt something hit him in the side of his stomach. Only this was like no other punch, this one was so powerful it had rendered him motionless, as if the blow itself had entered his body and wrenched out all of his considerable strength. Zed dropped onto his knees clutching his side, his head bowed, the warm blood seeping between his fingertips and trickling down the back of his hand, the redness spreading as it soaked into his crisp white shirt. Then the burning pain, like nothing he had felt before, as though acid was eating him away from inside. A woman screamed, shoppers stopped in their tracks and stared at the fallen giant. Mr Gupta and two waiters came running out from the restaurant and coaxed his limp body onto the ground. "Very hot chilli, Mr Gupta," were Zed's parting words.

"I'm still a rag and bone man, just different rags and different bones." Zed Golby told someone once.

His enemies were mainly people the same as himself, empire builders, duckers and divers, gangsters, sometimes working below the line of the law, sometimes above, sometimes with the law, sometimes they were the law themselves. He had come in contact with the Krays and the Richardsons, even crossing paths with the IRA at one time, as we know all to well.

So you would think if Zed Golby was going to meet his end before the allotted time, it would be in the midst of rival gang warfare.

Zed Golby was killed by a boy, a nobody, an insignificant drunken yob that held a grudge. All because of a tiny vegetable called a green finger chilli.

And the killer?

Yobs do not plan ahead, they work from their pent-up delinquent emotions. 'There he is, I've walked up this stupid street long enough, I've waited all morning for this scum, now he's going to know not to fuck with Ryan Rigby'.

Only Ryan Rigby's thoughts could only think so far ahead. This particular yob cannot expect to do what he has just done *and* escape that easily. The 'Swede' from the secondhand store saw the stabbing as it happened. Sitting outside on his wicker chair and puffing away on a joint he watched his boss cross the road. It took him several seconds to realise what he had just seen, but long enough to realise the person wearing the hooded anorak had to be stopped. The Swede quickly rose from his chair and began pointing at the yob. Chopper George from the butchers (different bones) was the first to grab the youth, soon followed by Frank Harman, then Jack 'the bear' Brown. The three managed to grab the yob and drag him into the combat clothes shop (different rags). From there he was quickly transferred to the old workshop.

Billy met up with them two hours later, directly after leaving the morgue.

Billy Keenan is not evil, well, not as such, he was just good at being evil. The man on the street may think he could impose evil on to another, only when it came down to the nitty gritty, he would soon find thinking or imagining it was far easier than carrying out the evil deed. Far too many emotions, guilt, fear, paranoia, even just thinking that your actions are doing actual harm to someone. Billy had served his apprenticeship, starting as a school kid, then managing to keep his evil hand in, building up his evil repertoire and with that, an evil reputation. Even the incident with the Irishman and the car door had come as no surprise to anyone. Billy Keenan's evilness was infamous.

What happened next would curl the blood of the toughest of men. All I can tell you is that two heavy duty cast iron vices, a blunt two inch chisel, a five pound hammer, a four inch thick wooden bench, a dirty cloth and a pair of welding gloves were involved.

The yob was dumped from the back of a van outside the hospital entrance. A note tied around his neck.

ZED GOLBY'S
KILLER

The yob would never have the use of his hands again and even if he did want to masturbate, it would be out of the question anyway. His penis was now feeding whatever creatures reside at the bottom of the canal.

Billy Keenan's evilness was now legendary.

BAZ'S BENCH (6)

"Did you find your soul?" asked Violet.

"Did you find your husband?" replied Baz.

"Not yet."

"Nor me, but while I'm trapped in here, I'm having a good rummage around."

Violet wanted to smile but she wasn't ready for that yet. "When I find my husband, then I'll start looking for my soul," she said.

"He's dead Violet," Baz told her bluntly. He would liked to have said those same words many years ago. Maybe not having to see the reaction gave him the courage to tell her.

"I know Baz," she said quietly. "I've known for nearly thirty years, in truth I hardly think about him now. Sometimes hope is all we have, sad isn't it?"

"Be here now," said Baz, thinking what Sonam used to say to him whenever he hoped for something. Three words he used a lot recently, sometimes repeating them over and over again, like a mantra, as An had taught him. If nothing else, Baz said it just to break up the boredom. That was not in his comprehensive guide to a sightless world. Although in doing so he never found it getting him any closer to enlightenment.

"Sometimes when you hope for the best, you end up getting the worst," he told her. "You hope for heaven, you get hell. Life's full of fu...," he stopped mid-sentence, "surprises." Baz had never used strong language in front of Violet. Even now he still felt like the little brother. "What do they say, love is blind Vi, we can't have two blind people in the same family."

353

Again, she tried to smile, still not ready. "Maybe it's just the hope I got off on, maybe we would have argued all day, maybe he would have hated me, maybe I'm just a lonely old spinster living on hope, maybe... "

"Be here now," said Baz.

They sat in silence.

Violet perked up the best she could. "I remember when you used to sit on your bench at school. No one else sat there because it only had two slats. I'm glad to see this one has got *all* its seat." Violet's voice sunk back to where it was. "You struck a lonely figure back then Baz."

"And I don't know, nothing's changed in sixty years, has it? Deafer, blinder, uglier." Baz paused in thought. "Maybe I was being prepared for this moment, maybe then is now, maybe..."

"Be here now," interrupted Violet, managing to break into a grin.

"I used to like it back then, seeing people when they couldn't see me. Now it's the other way round, now everyone looks at me, only they don't see *me,* do they? *And* I don't see them."

"Then knowing what you are looking at, isn't that what is important?" asked Violet. "To see," she corrected herself, "to *feel* the sun and know it's the sun."

Baz thought for a second. "To know it gives us light and where there is light, there is dark. I'm just on the wrong side Vi."

A minutes silence. "You're fifty-nine now Baz, I'm sixty-one, so much time has passed by, we have been through so much."

"Then look forward Vi."

"I have, so what do you see Baz?"

"How much closer to death I am."

Violet wrapped her arm around Baz's arm and squeezed it tight.

Another minute of silence passed by.

Violet watched as a light penetrated through the trees and dappled the lawn in front of them. She turned to gaze at her brother, the tight scarred skin, his misshapen lips and nose, those black glasses. A wretched sadness came over her.

"You're looking at me." Baz said.

"*And* I can see *you*, I will always see you Baz, I will always see *my* brother." She waited for a moment. "So what do you see Baz?" she asked again.

"Nothing, I have *always* seen nothing." He paused in thought. "What do you see Vi?"

Violet looked around. "I see green hills and trees. I see a big house and a fountain. I see people."

"Oh that seeing." Baz lifted his chin in pretence concentration. "Still nothing, only black this time, a black nothingness *but* if I close my eyes I can see green hills and trees, a big house and a fountain, I can see people. *Now* I can see everything."

Violet plucked up courage through another long silence. "Tell me what happened to you Baz?"

She had wanted to know as soon as she sat down on the bench but was worried her probing might be down to her own selfishness. Maybe it would be better not knowing at all, save her brother the torment. Only she had to know, she had the right, she was his sister after all.

As soon as Violet sat down, Baz knew she would want to know what had happened. Out of anyone, surely out of anyone, a sister should have the right to know. He decided to tell her everything. It might even be good for his own peace of mind, put the details into some kind of perspective. In the past year he had only thought about it in fragments, as separate pieces from a jigsaw.

Baz spent the next half an hour joining the pieces together. "I was rescued." He told her how Alice, Lennox, An and Kai Liang had found him one night. He then told her about the dope.

"Drugs!" she exclaimed.

Then about the temple and the devotees, she didn't seem to mind that so much.

"You didn't tell me where you were. I was angry with you," she said, "For Christ's sake Baz I'm your sister you should have at least told me you were safe." The anger in her voice mellowed, she felt as though she was being selfish again. Baz heard her take in a deep breath. "I saw you laid out on that hospital bed, I cried and cried, I couldn't stop, sorry. God Baz, I'm beginning to sound like Ruby, I, I, I."

Baz then told her about Alice and her mother's execution. "She went to St Josephs," he said. Violet tried to recall the faces. "She was invisible, like me," Baz said. Then he told her about the visit to Zed Golby and Billy Keenan, about Little Dai, alias Eamon Carrick and the IRA.

"You certainly kept odd company."

But there was something far more important Baz wanted to tell Violet. Since the beginning of her visit he had thought of nothing else.

"Have you heard from Ruby?"

"A Christmas card with a short note. A grandmother, twice over."

"A grandmother, twice! You should get over there and see them Vi, report back, be my eyes."

"At least we now know the Albright bloodline will continue," she said.

Baz waited. He missed the chance. "What about you Vi? Wasn't there ever a debonair Frenchman that swept you off your feet."

"Once," she replied. "Well, a few times, only they were too much like David. That was the problem Baz, I only seem to like one type of man, the ones like David. But they reminded me too much of him. You hope for the best and get nothing."

"You deserve nothing less than the best."

"What about you Baz? Was there a girl in your life?"

She's asking me about other women. Mrs Waterhouse, Pasang, no not Pasang. Mrs Waterhouse is Robert's mother, I'm Robert's father. Jesus, why is this so difficult?

He remembered one of his father's quotes. "The consequences of an act are sometimes more important than the act itself." It seemed to fit.

"My God, you sound like Dad Baz, that is just like something he would say. I never understood him then and I certainly don't understand you now."

"It *was* one of his."

"Oh."

"There was one."

"One what."

"Someone in my life."

"Oh yes. What happened? Was she nice? I bet she was..."

"It was just a quick fling, we had a son, it was during the war, she was quite a bit older than..."

"What did you say!?"

"It was during the war, she was quite..."

"No! Before that?"

Baz angled his head towards his sister. He wanted to feel as much of the reaction as he could. "We had a son."

"*You* had a son?" Violet pronounced each word precisely.

"*We* have a son," Baz said copying her exactness, speaking as if Mrs Waterhouse should not be forgotten.

"You have a son, why haven't you told me Baz?"

"I only found out myself a few weeks ago and there is something else."

"More!"

"My son, Robert. Robert has a son, Archie, I have a grandson."

"What? Robert, who is the mother?"

"Margaret Blakeney."

"Oh, tell me about her?"

"She's Mrs Waterhouse?"

"*Mrs*, Mrs Water...*Mrs Waterhouse!* You mean...."

"Yes Violet, William's mother, Mrs Waterhouse."

"She is married!"

"No, was, well, separated at the time." Baz started the second story that day, not that there was much to tell, not from his perspective anyhow. He just said they were both lonely, both upset after William's death, that they had comforted each other. "And Robert was conceived," he simply added. Then he told her about Mrs Waterhouse's death in childbirth and Robert's long search for him, how he had taken Mrs Waterhouse's maiden name, Blakeney.

"Robert, Bernadette and Archie Blakeney are our family Violet," Baz said as he ended the story.

Violet sat in silence, digesting everything she had just heard. The revelation of her brother's newfound family seemed to outweigh everything else.

As Violet took everything in, Baz thought about Robert and Mrs Waterhouse. Then he thought about William, he felt the brothers of the board pawn through his trouser's pocket.

"Have you still got father?" he asked.

"Sorry!" Violet exclaimed in confusion. "Father? Oh Dad. The chess piece, the king, he's on my bedside table."

Violet's tone perked up. "Ruby still has mother you know, she told me she keeps it in pride of place in a glass cabinet." She blew out a cynical breath. "The queen."

Robert carefully placed the creased envelope on the dining room table as though it was the most fragile object he had ever touched.

Bernadette, Father Byrne, Father Duffy and Deacon Stone were also present. Sheila MacKinnon sat in the window chair holding Archie's attention with an assortment of distorted facial expressions.

"Open after your prayers have been answered," Father Duffy said, examining Father Nolan's scrawled handwriting on the front.

"It looks well travelled," said Bernadette clutching a cushion to her chest as though she found it necessary to hide her ample frontage.

"Father Nolan was a wily old fox," said Father Duffy. "It's probably got this years Grand National winner in it."

"We *all* know the winner," said Father Byrne rolling his eyes. "The Grand National was run several months ago."

"But not known seven years ago," added Deacon Stone, taking the older priest's side, or the opposite to Father Byrne's if the truth be known.

"Then it would..."

"It hasn't got the Grand National winner in it." Robert said abruptly.

"You should open it in your own privacy," Bernadette said. Her eyes fixed firmly on Archie's reactions to the housekeeper's pouting.

"I just feel I need to share this moment," Robert said. "I have a feeling this is going to be something special."

He poked his little finger in a hole where the flap hadn't stuck properly and ran it along the top fold, only the tear sliced downward, cutting through the wording and twisting the thin paper wallet into a distorted cone.

"Maybe I should have opened it on my own." He gazed into the gash.

Bernadette put her hand on her husband's shoulder. "Slow Robert," mouthing the words.

Robert took a deep breath and enticed the contents out as if he was performing an intricate, surgical operation. Held in his fingers was a letter straddling another, smaller envelope.

Robert glanced at the writing on the small envelope. Neat, scripty and confident, a woman's hand. His mother's? He carefully placed it face down on the table, enticing his audience as if playing some kind of card trick. Seeing the writing made him feel as close to her as he would ever get, too intimate to share at that moment.

Robert unfolded the letter and began reading aloud from the crisp, nearly transparent paper.

Dear Robert
As you read these words, you now know that
the time has come to realise the truth. I hope
your prayers have been answered.
With God's love I have now moved on to serve
Our Lord within the walls of His glorious city.

Father Nolan had known he was dying when he penned this letter, he also knew he was dying on the day Robert left the orphanage. Father Nolan had been diagnosed with emphysema many years earlier and died from a lung infection soon after Robert had arrived at the Priest's house. "Those bloody cigars," a distressed Robert said at the time, it was as if he had lost a father.

Enclosed with this letter is another envelope.
This was given to me by your mother's solicitor;
Mr Pickard from Pickard, Pickard & Glass in
Barnstable. I was instructed by Mr Pickard that
this letter should be given to you on the day you
leave the orphanage and should only be opened by
yourself when you have discovered the truth.
It was found on your mother's writing desk at
the cottage when you were born.
When you have realised the truth Robert.
When you have found your father.

In God we trust
Father Nolan

The room fell into a sombre silence. Robert carefully folded the sheet and returned it to its place on the table, then tentatively tapped it twice as if to thank Father Nolan for having completed his mission.

"And *have* your prayers been answered Robert?" Father Duffy asked.

Robert stared at the priest, then Bernadette, then Archie. Then thought about Baz. "Yes Father, they have."

Father Duffy returned a priestly nod.

"To my unborn..." Robert read from the small envelope.

"Wait!" Father Byrne interrupted as he rose from his seat and collected a silver letter knife from the cabinet's top drawer. "Let's not make a pig's ear of this one Robert."

With a shaky hand and after several near misses, Robert just managed to poke the trembling point of the letter opener into the hole at the top of the flap. Bernadette wrapped her fingers around her husband's wrists and slowly lowered his hands down onto the table top.

"Sorry, all fingers and thumbs today," he said.

With a confident sawing action she sliced through the envelope "Do you want me to take out the letter?" she asked.

"Please."

"Would you like me to read it?"

"Please," he repeated. "Woman's voice and all that."

"*To my darling unborn child. Only open when you have realised the truth,*" she said softly, reading from the face of the envelope.

"The truth?" said Father Duffy.

Robert shrugged. "My father I suppose?"

Bernadette released the velvety sheet from its thirty year internment.

To my darling unborn child.
As the ink from my pen bleeds onto the paper, it feels as though another has stolen my thoughts from me. Another who is aware of the destiny that awaits us both. A destiny with an outcome that is as unsure to me now as the world is as uncertain to all who now live in it.

My darling unborn child, I do not know your name. I do not even know whether you are a boy or a girl, fair or dark, tall or short, of a good nature or a wayward disposition. I know as much about you now as if I am a stranger arriving in a strange land.

Yet here you are, safe in the confinements of my own body, a part of me, a part of my own flesh and blood as if you are my heartbeat itself. I am as close to you as any one person will ever get to another. Your life depending on my breath, reliant on my sustenance. In a day or two your journey will start with the first breath of your own, the first suckle of my milk. A journey of love and healing and teaching.

Now we are alone, living in a world intent on self-destruction, where so many are making sacrifices, where news of death and losses are commonplace. No one knows this more than myself. My darling unborn child, we are in a world that needs deliverance. More than any other time, this is the time the world yearns for a saviour.

Yet, what if our destinies are written in stone, our fate has been mapped out for us already. What if the forces that are guiding my hand have designed our lives to be lived in righteousness. For in a few days I feel my work will have been done.

My darling unborn child, you can return this letter to the vellum skin it came in and bury it deep in a place where neither you or anyone else will ever find it again.

Or you can read on and realise the truth.

For you will have to believe the unbelievable. You will have to accept in your own heart that a miracle is happening in our time. There can be no other alternative.

Bernadette suddenly stopped reading. "What!" She cried out in disbelief. Her lips remained tight. Her eyes widened as they moved silently and swiftly from side to side and down the sheet. "I'm not reading this."

"What is it?" Asked Robert.

"It is *not* realising the truth Robert. That is what it is *not*."

"What does it say? Give it to me Bernie."

"No!"

"It is *my* letter."

"You're better off not..."

"He *is* better off knowing my dear," said Mrs MacKinnon.

Bernadette still reeling from the words in the letter failed to notice the housekeeper approach and lower Archie onto her lap, snatching the sheet of paper from her fingers.

For the next few seconds Sheila MacKinnon scrutinised the writing. "Oh dear?" she finally said.

"Would someone please?..." Robert began to say, only to be struck dumb by the hard Glaswegian voice.

There can be no other alternative

My darling unborn child, for how you entered into my body was a matter that cannot be explained under any normal circumstances. I have been pure and free of sin for the past many years and I have come to accept the inevitable, as you must now do yourself.

My darling unborn child, I have been blessed with the immaculate conception. Through me you have been given to the world by the God Almighty himself.

In a few days time we will be saved.

Bless the Lord for he has found the way.

Your loving and devoted mother.

The room fell into a stunned silence.

"She was obviously not thinking straight when she wrote the letter," said Bernadette. "I mean it *was* the war, she *had* already lost a son. She was alone and going to give birth in a few days." Everyone remained speechless. "My God that would send anyone over the edge." She waited. "Somebody say something!"

"You believed in one virgin birth, why not another?" said Robert. "What!"

"That's what my father said. "You believed in one virgin birth, why not believe in another."

"Don't be stupid Robert. You can't even open an envelope!"

"She knew that she was going to die?"

"She didn't actually say that Robert. She *said*, 'in a few days I feel my work will have been done.' *In fact*, she said the first suckle of my milk. She *thought* she was giving birth to the Messiah. *In fact*. it was just you Robert."

"Thank you for that vote of confidence Bernie."

"How many miracles have you performed in the last ten years?"

Robert looked around the room as though the actual truth had become lost somewhere.

362

"You don't *really* think *you* are the Messiah, do you?" she said.

"This is not the shoot out at the OK Coral. *No* one is the Messiah," declared Father Byrne. "Your mother was obviously in denial." He added with a calming voice.

"Sorry Father?"

"That afternoon she spent with your father. She cannot accept what happened. She has blanked it from her mind. To her it was as though it never happened."

"What if something bad happened to her on that day," said Mrs MacKinnon.

"Sorry Mrs MacKinnon?"

"*It* would explain the reason why she blanked it from her mind."

"Then you had better say it Mrs Mac," said Father Byrne.

"Maybe this Basil Albright..."

"*This* Basil Albright is my father," said Robert.

"Maybe he forced himself on your mother."

"What!? Forced! What are you saying?"

"Let us not jump to conclusions. Without any evidence that is a very serious accusation Mrs Mac," said Father Byrne.

"Because more women get raped than there are virgin births," Robert muttered under his breath.

"Sorry Rob?"

"Oh, it's just something my father said. He said, 'maybe Jesus's mother was raped. Maybe *your* God is a rapist' and when I asked him how he could say such a thing, he said, 'because more women get raped than there are virgin births.'"

"*See*, he said it himself Robert. Your father *might* be a rapist," said Mrs MacKinnon.

"Or God!" Robert snapped back with cynicism.

"Or God! Mary, Mother of Jesus," Sheila MacKinnon said, crossing herself. Then quickly added. "You saw the newspaper. He was a druggy, a devil worshipper. Who knows what..."

"He and my mother, they, it was in the war, years earlier ,and just because he said it, does not mean..."

"This is ridiculous, Bernadette is right," Father Duffy finally spoke. "Alone in the world. The birth of her child due any day. The chemicals in her body being pulled in all directions. Losing her son and hearing of thousands more dying everyday." Father Duffy glared at everyone in the room. "I would also have given anything to see our Saviour at that time."

"There is something else wrong." Deacon Stone drew everyone's attention towards him. "The Immaculate Conception does not refer to the conception of our Lord Jesus but to the Blessed Virgin Mary by *her* mother." He repeated. "*Not* our Lord Jesus. The Virgin Mary was born without sin and lived without sin, therefore she received the divine sanctifying grace to *become* the vessel for our Lord. I believe your mother, although a God fearing woman had a son already. In God's eyes she was not without sin, *she* could *not* have carried the Son of God."

"So when she wrote, 'only open when you have realised the truth,' she wasn't talking about my father."

"No Robert, I'm afraid as much as you, or she," Father Duffy's eyes sparkled, "or we would have liked you to have been the Saviour, I'm afraid you are not. As for the words on the envelope, we've all got it wrong Robert."

THE TREES ECHO

1974

Baz couldn't remember who, but someone had once said. "Imagining can be better than the reality itself." It sounded like one of his father's, definitely not Zed or William, maybe Pasang, whoever said it, wasn't wrong.

He had spent the last half hour thinking about writing a book, finally deciding that for a blind man there were too many obstacles to overcome, too many people he would have to rely on. Nevertheless it made him feel good. Even managing to think of the first sentence, 'Basil Albright, born to die' or even just 'Born to die', maybe that could be the title. Maybe both.

It was early evening in late September and the weather had remained unseasonably humid; it was warm and that was good enough for Baz. A good time to be out in the open air, to be at one with the sounds and smells of nature, to be at one with his own thoughts.

Also, Baz was high.

Pasang had been on a visit at the weekend and had left him a dozen

joints. "Thai sticks," she said. "It'll turn your mind inside out Butes."
She was right. In a strange way, he also thought being blind and stoned
went hand in hand, looking inward, and all that, or was that just the
dope speaking again.

Baz took the last puff of his one skinner, scooped away the lit end with
a slip of his fingers, squashed the remnants into a tiny ball and kept it
in his hand, ready to be dropped randomly onto the small animal bones
as he returned to the house.

The only problem Pasang had foreseen was when to smoke the
joint, especially voicing her concern about the tall red headed nurse
"The one in a pinball machine," as she had put it.

Rolo knew though. He was standing on the other side of the garden
when the strong smell of sweet musty weed was carried over on a
breeze. The big attendant knew the aroma well and it wasn't too long
before Baz knew that Rolo knew.

"We have a mutual respect for trees," Baz told Nurse Fran after she
found it odd they had both taken to going for strolls in the woods. "I
like the sound. It echoes."

"Baz can now sense a tree without touching it," Rolo had added. It
was true, he could. Something to do with the noise as he trudged
through the undergrowth.

Aside from Zed's funeral, Baz also had quite a few other excursions
out into the big wide world, all under the auspices of his improvement
sessions. This *was* in his comprehensive guide to a sightless world.
The trips were usually accompanied by an attendant, mostly Rolo.
Mind you, being blind and stoned while tackling a crowded pavement
always appeared to end up with some intriguing encounter. Who could
blame a blind man?

Anyhow, Baz couldn't stay at Sunnybridge House forever and the
doctors had made their decision. Baz had completed his recovery, or
as much of it as he would ever achieve. A home would be found on
the outside within the month. In fact it was one week.

BAZ'S BENCH (7)

Even after everything he had heard while sitting at his bench, one more

365

surprise was going to come Baz's way. A surprise that would eclipse all others, including finding out he had a son. Because this surprise was a miracle, a 'resurrection', for the want of a better word.

Baz heard two people approach. One was the unmistakeable heavy footsteps of Rolo, only his strides were narrower, irregular, slower than usual, finding it difficult to adjust to the person he was accompanying. The other person's footsteps were new to Baz. Listening to a person walking on the small animal bones was like hearing someone's voice or recognising their face, everyone's crunch was unique.

Rolo had stopped a good ten feet before he reached Baz. After a long silence he heard him return to the house. The shorter crunches continued, soon stopping in front of Baz.

Baz's immediate reaction was memories of the Golby's old yard, the odour of old clothes. It was a man, he could tell that much. It also sounded as though a lifetime of smoking was now taking its toll, as if each wheezing breath would be his last. Baz thought an old mangy dog with a bad cold would be more pleasant on his senses. The man remained standing, he coughed, not bothering to cover it, Baz held his breath, the wheezing continued.

The man finally spoke. "Black man in white say what happen."

Not English thought Baz, although the accent was familiar, even if it was choked behind a chalky and laboured voice.

"You change, my friend."

Not a doctor, Baz was certain of that, no doctor could sound that bad. Definitely foreign but not middle or far eastern, nor Indian or Caribbean. You change, what's that supposed to mean? Also, the words my friend, it sounded as though he wanted to sell him something.

"Time is long Sergeant." the man said, sucking in the word. Sergeant, Baz thought. No one had called him that since the war. The man coughed again, Baz held his breath again. He was half expecting to hear a loud crunch as the man dropped onto the graveyard of small animal bones.

"You should see a doctor, there are probably some knocking around here somewhere," Baz said.

"Ah doctor, not like doctor in Shaibah..." The stranger paused. "How do you say? English sarcasm Bazil."

Bazil, only one person had ever pronounced his name like that. Only that one person was dead. He tried to think. It sounded like Mikhail, but Mikhail was dead. Although, no one else had ever called him Bazil like the South American country. He wished he had the proof of sight.

"I sit Bazil, legs not good."

"Mikhail?" Baz said, a quietly spoken question, as if he felt stupid just saying it. He thought back to that night they spent in the truck. How could he forget it? The vodka flask with the bullet hole. Mikhail was the luckiest man alive, but he was alive, Baz remembered that much. He tried to think what happened after, he vanished, that's it, he just vanished one night. Everyone assumed he was dead. Mikhail had walked into the desert in the night. No one could survive out there. It was even written in the rules. He killed himself and his body got eaten by whatever eats things in the desert. Maybe his luck had continued, maybe he did survive. No one could cheat death twice.

"Yes, my friend, it me."

"You're not dead?"

"Maybe in minute Bazil. Sarcasm yes, I get good."

"But we thought you had had enough and just walked into the desert, no one could survive out there."

"Shaibah not kill Mikhail Tretyakov, Bazil know bullet not kill Mikhail Tretyakov."

Baz heard a match spark up, soon followed by a loud hacking cough.

"Many vodka, many cigarettes, they kill Mikhail Tretyakov." He stalled like a spluttering car. "Mikhail Tretyakov not many years." He coughed again.

"I have some whisky in my room," Baz said, then wondered why he had, although it was true, he did, a present from Pasang.

"Now you kill me Bazil."

"No, I didn't mean, I thought..."

"Vodka?"

"No, sorry, only whisky."

"Not vodka," Mikhail sighed. "You not believe it me. Redhead nurse and black man in white not believe it me, I say I comrade from war. It me Bazil." Mikhail took a long drag on his cigarette. "Remember scorpion." He knew that was something only the two of them knew about.

"I remember."

Silence. Baz sensed Mikhail looking at him, he always knew what followed a glaring silence.

"Black man in white say you hurt in explosion."

Baz nodded.

"You not see Bazil. Hear one ear."

"The hearing had nothing to do with the explo...Never mind." Baz turned to face the Russian and tried to conjure up a picture of what he looked like now. Imagining him to be a ghost of his former self. "I can still smell though."

"You smell Shaibah?" said Mikhail, missing the sarcasm.

"I can." That was something else he would never forget about Shaibah. He wondered if Mikhail smelt this bad back then. It was hard to tell, everyone must have reeked in the sweltering heat of that airfield, even himself. At Shaibah the smell seemed to be everywhere, rising up from the earth, blowing in with the wind, even appearing to float on the water.

Baz felt a sadness in the knowledge he would never be able to see Mikhail. How far had his jowls dropped? Had that blanket of dark fleece finally covered his entire body? "How did you find me?" Baz asked. "And *what* are you doing in this country? You are Russian. Are you allowed out?"

"Many questions my friend, how find you Bazil? I know many things, I know many Englishman. How English say? You scratch back, I scratch back."

"Then who scratched your back Mikhail?"

"No speak Bazil, no can speak, if Bazil my friend, no more ask."

"Sounds like Plan B again."

Mikhail remained silent. Baz even heard him hold his breath, appearing ages before he exhaled again.

"Then what are you doing in this country?"

Mikhail spat out a chuckle, Baz thought it sounded fake, it had the sound of a condemned man attempting to keep his dignity. "I English Bazil, now I same as you. Russia not good, England good, now I on good side of Iron Curtain."

"Then *how* did you get on good side of Iron Curtain?" asked Baz, then thought it sounded condescending.

Mikhail choked out a nervous laugh. "Small hole, Mikhail Tretyakov squeeze through." The laugh swiftly died down. "Comrades want me back. Send to Siberia, nothing change Bazil. They not find Mikhail Tretyakov," he said proudly. "We end talk now Bazil. Good you know nothing. Not tell black man in white my name. Not tell fast lady with red head. Not tell them I Russian, not tell anyone anything! Tell I comrade from war"

"Plan C?"

A short silence.

"You Bazil, what happen?"

"A car I was working on exploded."

Mikhail paused. "Why car explode Bazil?"

"Just unfortunate Mikhail."

More silence.

"Not good, upset IRA man, not good Bazil."

"You know! How?"

"Mikhail Tretyakov know everything."

Another silence.

"What happened Mikhail? I mean after that night in the truck. I can remember you before then," Baz shook his head slowly, "but after that you just vanished."

"This I want to tell you Bazil, tell you story, not good story Bazil, not good." Baz could hear Mikhail's words sinking under a deep breath.

"Russian officers come Shaibah, take me in night, two days after Plan B. Take me to ship in Al Basrah. Russian officer say he see me with Stepan and Daniil and Igor. Ask many questions about them. Not let me sleep, keep asking questions, keep asking if Daniil is Alexander Novikov's son."

"Who?" asked Baz.

"Alexander Novikov, Soviet Chief Air Marshall."

"He ask if Daniil is Alexander Novikov's son? I thought Daniil was Stepan's son. Why would he ask if he was this Chief Air Marshall's son?"

Mikhail, in the best way he could, told Baz what had happened at the port.

"I told officer not know who is Daniil. Stepan said Daniil is Novikov son, first time I hear."

369

"That wasn't in Plan B."

"More not in Plan B Bazil."

"Oh."

"Russian officers take me desert." The Russian stopped talking. Baz heard him take a deep swallow. "Tent in desert Bazil. British soldiers with guns stand around tent." His breathing quickened. "Russian officers take me in tent, see three bodies covered in sand, see blood, throats cut, hole in head, not forget Bazil. See now, how do you say? As yesterday. I know bodies." Another long pause, another deep swallow. "Stepan I see first, then Igor, then Daniil."

A longer pause, Baz waited.

"I hope kill Stepan before Daniil. He not see son killed." Baz heard a throaty groan. "Russian officer roll Stepan over, legs and hands tied, all legs and hands tied. White sand cover face, how do you say? Like ghosts."

"I'm sorry Mikhail." Baz said quietly.

Mikhail wiped his hands down his face. "British officer come in tent, ask other officer question, but I understand, he not know I speak English good. He say local boy tell him these three killed because three Arabs killed." Mikhail hacked out another cough as he lit another cigarette. "They ask me about Arab's death, I know nothing I tell them, I say not know bodies, only know them at port."

"My God Mikhail, we had to save ourselves. We weren't to know, it was the war, people died."

"Not war kill them Bazil."

The two men sat motionless.

"What happened then?" Baz finally said.

"They send back to Russia, many questions. They think Daniil is Novikov's son, much confusion, Novikov think son is dead. Send me to front line, I watch many die. Then, how do you say? Cold War Bazil. I not tell I hate Russia. Bad leaders. I want your country, I help English, now I English, I die English, I die happy."

Baz suddenly remembered the pawn in his pocket, the one he had given to Stepan, the one returned to him wrapped up in a note. Baz pulled it out of his trouser pocket and held it up between his fingers. Baz knew the Russian was looking at it. "Pawn to bishop four Mikhail! This is the pawn I gave to Stepan, remember, instead of the bullet on the chess board."

Mikhail spoke quietly. "Yes, it has name, I forget name. Stepan gave me to give you. Said you should have...Um?"

"William."

"Yes, William."

Before leaving, Baz told Mikhail he would be leaving Sunnybridge soon and would let him know his new address.

"No contact me, I find you my friend, I always find you. How do English say? I like bad smell."

WHERE SALMON GO TO DIE

Baz didn't have much time to think about it, he was told a place had been found on Wednesday and he would be moved in over the weekend. He thought the decision not allowing him to dwell on it was probably deliberate.

Baz's new abode was a ground floor one bedroom flat in a converted house owned by the local council, not far from where he had been born and close to the cemetery where his parents and sister were buried. They decided knowing the roads would be an advantage. "You are returning to your roots," Rolo told him, overplaying his Caribbean accent.

"Returning home to die, more like it," said Baz.

Rolo's large lips moulded into a grin. "Like a salmon, after a good shag."

Nurse Maddy glared at the big attendant wearing the deepest of frowns.

"What?!" exclaimed Baz.

"Salmon return to where they were born to spawn, then they die, it's a known fact," Rolo added.

"Is that right?"

"It's the everlasting circle of life Baz."

"You don't know a Doctor Chopra do you?"

"Is he the foot Doc..?"

"Never mind Rolo, I'll avoid shagging a salmon just to please you."

Rolo sounded like a chiming clock as he laughed.

"Basil!" said Nurse Maddy, her voice pitching several notes higher.

The conversation finished there and then.

It was the first Saturday in October and Baz could smell the air turning to autumn. He had said his farewells to Sunnybridge for the last time.

Baz and Nurse Maddy sat in the front two passenger seats of the ten seater transit with Rolo driving at his usual snail's pace. The rust ridden and ramshackle vehicle would shriek out a thunderous rattle every time it hit anything resembling a pothole, so much so that Baz thought it was going to fall apart around his ears at any moment. Only the melodic drumbeat of reggae blasting from the cassette player kept away thoughts of their imminent death. Rolo liked Bob Marley, so did Baz, even more so today. Engelbert Humperdinck was more to Nurse Maddy's liking.

Feeling like the journey had eaten up most of the day, they finally arrived in the residential back road late in the afternoon. "How many lights work on this rust heap is anyone's guess," Rolo declared, hinting the need to leave before sunset. As much as possible in front of Baz, he avoided words that related to not being able to see.

The flat was bright, newly decorated, Baz could smell the paint covering the woodchip wallpaper. Magnolia he was told. "What else," he replied.

It had a large window overlooking the front road, not that Baz would ever have firsthand experience of life on the outside of his flat, apart from one of the sash windows shuddering as a car passed.

At the back was a small galley kitchen leading into a walled yard permanently draped in cold, dark shadow. Set against the whitewashed wall to the side of the yard was a tiny bench. In his naivety Rolo thought Baz might have been pleased. "Am I sharing with eskimo dwarfs," Baz had said to him after he sat on it. The only time he ever did.

Their first task was to meticulously relocate all the furniture to suit Baz's sightless needs. Every piece had been moved, like footballers jostling for position, sometimes more than once, sometimes four or five times, testing the big attendant's patience to the limit. "No more bruised shins." Baz told him when they had finished.

Baz had insisted that Rolo should lead him around the flat after all the furniture shifting, several times in fact. Each time counting the strides from one piece of furniture to the window, from another piece to the other window, from one wall to the armchair, from the armchair to the fridge, from the fridge to the table, every possible variable had been tested. "It's like the moves in a chess game, there is always an alternative," Baz told him.

Nurse Maddy waited patiently before putting away his clothes and any other personal essentials, all under the scrupulous guidance of Baz. His comprehensive guide to a sightless world.

After a cup of tea, which Baz managed to make with the slightest of spills, the three said their goodbyes. With a bang and a clatter like an old lawnmower, the vehicle burst into life, taking several corners before the rattling finally faded into the distance.

Baz was now alone in his dark world. And I mean really alone, alone alone, the first time since the explosion.

Pasang visited Baz on the second day. "We must paint the walls," she said on first sighting, leaving Baz picturing the same colourful images that adorned the front of the big house. Pasang also imagined the same. She brought a number of goodies of the edible kind, plus a small replenishment for his tobacco tin. Her visits were numerous, at least once a week, sometimes more, usually with the same merchandise. Not always grass though, she said it was getting harder to come by. "Bendy black," as she called it, had flooded the streets. "A large shipment must have got through," she added, then would sit for hours rolling the single skinned joints, one after another, occasionally lighting one up for herself and Baz. With her concern over him burning the flat down, a very large glass ashtray was skillfully appropriated from the Dog and Badger. Bendy black was famous for its hot rot.

Getting stoned and escaping into his own world was now a necessity in Baz's life. Who was it that said, "imagining is better than reality?" The place where there are no obstacles to get hung up on, where you can choose your own destiny, where everything can be created perfectly to suit your own desires, then the ideal conclusion, even conclusions, each one better than the last.

On some of her early visits she had brought some relief to Baz, mostly by hand, on two occasions she had used her mouth. Pasang knew she had lost that feminine dominance over Baz and was forever striving to win it back. After a couple of months he had decided the act was getting too automated, the relationship was, as he said, "Like a hooker and client, I'm beginning to feel like a dirty old man, anyway I can do it just as well by myself. Dope, blindness and a good wank were made for each other," he joked.

"What you need is a girlfriend," she said.

"A blind date?" Then added softly, "she would have to be."

"It's Robert," the voice crackled through the intercom.

"Wait there Robert. I'll come and let you in." Baz left his door on the latch as he counted the four and a bit steps to the outer main entrance. "You've brought a friend Robert." Baz pretended a sniff. "I smell God."

"Actually it's Father Byrne."

"The detective, the man who can get into places no ordinary man dare tread and I'm not talking about up there."

Baz waited for the seconds to pass as Father Byrne became acclimatised to his face.

The Father cleared his throat. "Just the Air Ministry, Mr Albright. It seems a white collar and a blessing are all you need to get into most establishments, not that it did much good. Pleased to meet you. And how did you know? You know, the God bit."

"Lucky guess. Well, it was obvious you were a man. Youngish, clean shaven. Old Spice I believe." Baz inhaled again. "Brylcream, quite a lot of it. You like cowboy films and country music."

"It's you that sounds more like the detective Mr Albright or should I say Mr Holmes."

"Also, Robert *has* mentioned you quite a lot." Baz heard Father Byrne beat out a rhythmic laugh. "And call me anything but Mr Albright, most people call me Baz." He showed them into the living room. "And what do I call you?" asked Baz. "Only one person in my life has ever had the right to be called father."

"Anthony."

"As in St Anthony, the patron saint of lost property, good choice Robert. No wonder you found me."

"No Baz, as in Father Anthony Byrne and you seem to know your saints?"

"Lucky guess."

"Another?"

"And does your white collar get you into places *not* of this world Anthony."

"Only if I repent my sins Baz, same as any other person."

Baz stretched his lips. "Oh dear."

"Do you get out much?" said Robert, not knowing why he said it.

Even with his hearing getting worse, Baz could still detect that melancholy tone in his son's voice, as he had when he phoned him with his address. He knew Robert wasn't really interested in the answer either. "Not much, I have people that get me everything I need," Baz replied bluntly. Then felt guilty over the cold way it came out.

"Nice flat," Robert said.

"Is it, that's good," Baz replied. "How are Bernadette and Archie, I still have to meet them." Baz knew too well why Robert hadn't brought Archie round to see him. How do you say to your father, I don't want a faceless monster scaring my only son to death?

"Maybe you could just come with Bernadette?" Baz waited for the reply, none came, only a thick silence.

"So what is your take on the soul St Anthony?"

"Saint." Father Byrne laughed again "I think you're mistaking me for someone else. I have a long way to go before I reach those Godly heights."

"Is that what you are looking for, Godliness? Like the Buddhists are looking for enlightenment."

"We believe in the miracle of heaven, yes." Father Byrne said, putting on his feathery priest's voice. "Some people find it comforting."

Baz caught the suggestive tone.

"I believe in what is here, not what isn't here."

"God is everywhere."

"I've been places where even *your* God wouldn't tread. *And* the soul Anthony?"

"The soul Baz?"

"Yes Anthony, *what* is the Catholic Church's take on the soul?"

"The bible says God created us in the image of himself, I believe it is our soul that is that image, our immortal soul and it is our soul that will be judged after death, when *we* will be judged Baz, judged by God himself for what we have done in this world." Father Byrne's tone became more forceful. "It is then God will decide, heaven or the fiery pits of hell."

"The fiery pits of hell, maybe he's started early on me," Baz said flippantly. Unaware Robert was glaring wide-eyed at Father Byrne, even *he* hadn't heard the priest speak like that before. "So that is it, no second chance. Then I had better be good in the one life I do have."

"Would you like to confess your sins Baz? You don't need a confession box you know."

"Yes! Confess your sins," added Robert. "It might help."

"Help me?" Baz thought about what his father once told him about Catholics wiping the slate clean. "Confess my sins and go to heaven, that's far to easy. Sin, confess and God will forgive."

"Yes, you're right, God will forgive," said Robert.

"Is this the same all loving all forgiving God that sends you to the fiery pits of hell."

"You can still confess, repent your sins," Robert repeated.

"You can't change what you have done just through a confession." Baz quoted another one of his father's sayings. "You don't know where you are going to until you know where you have come from," he said rhythmically.

"Some people get punished *in* this world," said Robert.

"Then I'm paying my dues, is that what you are saying? You must think I have done something pretty awful Robert."

"Have you?"

"Hasn't everyone?"

"Not our Lord Jesus, not our Blessed Mary. They are without sin," said Father Byrne, continuing with his righteous tone.

"But Mary is not your God, Jesus is not your God."

"No Baz. Our God is God."

"For *all* have sinned and fall short of the glory of God, isn't that what your bible says. *All* have sinned, doesn't that include Jesus *and* his mother."

"Scripture, Romans three twenty-three. You know the Bible as well as the saints Baz," said Father Byrne authoritatively. "Or was that another lucky guess?"

"Then Jesus and his mother are sinners, the same as the rest of us." Baz waited for a reaction, none came. "They were human, just like the rest of us, then Jesus was conceived, just like the rest of us."

"Then tell us under what circumst..."

"Then tell me more about *my* mother," Robert interrupted Father Byrne, drawing a stony glare.

"Your mother, from discussing Mary to wanting to know about your mother. Is that a large leap or a small step for you Robert? Maybe you're thinking there is some kind of comparison." Robert and Father Byrne waited in silence. As though they didn't want to contaminate the moment. "The truth is Robert, I never really knew your mother. When you are a young lad you don't take much notice of your friend's mother. Do you? She always dressed immaculately, I remember that much. I remember her being very kind to me *and* she loved William, very much." Baz paused for a moment, he thought about his own mother and how different she was. "She was so happy when me and William were playing, sometimes I think she was even happier than us and thrilled that William had a friend. We were brothers of the board," Baz said proudly.

"Brothers of the board?" inquired Father Byrne.

"Don't get excited Anthony, it's not some holy order." Baz pulled the pawn out of his pocket and told them about the pact they made. "You could say this is my soul Anthony. It is this that will judge me, not your God, *your* God needs to judge himself first." Baz could sense Father Byrne's reaction.

"What about the day you returned William's kit bag? Tell me what my mother was like then," Robert said, his words becoming tighter.

Baz understood the question was a son wanting to learn about his mother. "There's not much to tell, I returned William's kit bag."

"A child isn't conceived by returning a kit bag?"

"You don't want to hear about that though, do you?"

Baz heard the crackling of paper followed by an extended silence.

"My mother left me this letter, they found it on the day I was born. The same day she died," Robert said, in a matter-of-fact tone. Then he began reading "To my unborn child..."

"There is no need, this is your lett..."

Robert ignored Baz. "As ink fom my pen bleeds into the paper..." For the next four minutes Robert spoke slowly and precisely. Baz listened, without interrupting.

Robert finished. "In a few days time we will be saved. There can be no alternative..." He paused for a moment. "Your loving and devoted mother." The last words barely audible.

Baz waited, he had never felt a silence so intense. "May I hold it?" he finally asked.

Baz sandwiched the velvety sheet between his palms, as though he was in prayer, as though he was reading the words through his hands. "A fine letter," he said softly, returning it to Robert, feeling the note slide from his fingers. "If not a bit odd," he added. "This is your letter Robert, she wrote it to you, you should make of it what you wish."

"I will, she denies, well, ever having a relationship with you."

"She denies ever having a relationship with anyone and yet here you are."

"I can't understand why my mother, this beautiful, sophisticated woman would, well, would have, you know, a relationship with an ordinary mechanic. And not long after her son, my brother had been killed."

Baz puffed out a laugh "An ordinary mechanic, in fact I was a leading aircraftman." he said sarcastically. "She was lonely, I was lonely." Baz turned his face to where Father Byrne was sitting. "Two souls coming together. It always comes back to souls, does it not Anthony?" He turned his face back towards Robert. "Maybe that was it Robert. For that short space of time, we both felt the same." As Baz's next words came out he knew he shouldn't have said them, it happened too quickly, they were in the air before he realised. "Plus she had a few drinks."

"Are you saying she was a drunk?"

"No! I said she was drunk, in fact, we both had a few drinks."

"So you took advantage of a vulnerable woman?"

"Well at least you're accepting what happened *and* who I am."

"I've accepted what happened already."

Baz felt the words cut through the air. His heartbeat stepped up a gear, his throat became dry. "What is this really about Robert? *Who* is this really about? I don't understand." He made an attempt to rise from his chair. "I need to get a glass of water..."

"I heard you mumble under your breath, you didn't think I heard it, but I did, you said it was you that killed her. You also said," Robert took a deep breath. "Maybe Jesus's mother was raped. Maybe *your* God is a rapist."

"I was talking about Jesus's mother, *not* your mother. We were discussing religion, remember."

"Because more women get raped than there are virgin births. *You* said that."

Baz was half expecting Father Byrne to intervene, the young priest remained a silent observer. This was Robert's and Robert's father's argument. He knew from counselling married couples, it was always best to let quarrels come to their own conclusion. Although accusing someone of rape was new territory for him.

"What are you saying? This is ridiculous."

"If you did rape her, you wouldn't admit to it, would you?"

"If I didn't rape her, I wouldn't admit to it either, would I? And I didn't. In fact Robert if you want to know the truth." Baz then thought about his next words. It *was* the truth. Then say it. "In fact Robert, she seduced me."

"What! My mother was better than that," Robert snapped.

"You didn't know her, I did! You just can't bear the thought of a blind faceless monster laying on top of your mother. Well I haven't always looked like this."

It was Robert's turn to say something he wished he hadn't. "Then maybe what happened to you *is* God's revenge."

"This is what it is all about isn't it. You were expecting your father to be someone different. Someone that could play with your son, my grandson, at Christmas. You can't bear who I am. It is you your mother would be ashamed of, not me!"

"But I'm not a rapist..."

"Stop it Robert," yelled Father Byrne.

"I thought God was in the business of forgiveness Anthony, not revenge."

"So you think you need forgive..." Robert began to say.

"He is Baz. I think we should go," interrupted Father Byrne.

"You wouldn't need to ask for forgiveness if you hadn't..."

"Come on Robert." Father Byrne waited. "Come on Robert!"

"Goodbye Baz," said Father Byrne as they stepped through the front door and onto the street.

"Goodbye Anthony."

"Goodbye Robert," Baz said, then waited, nothing. "Goodbye son," he murmured as the sound of the lock clicked behind him. "I'll pray for you."

THE FAIRY FELLER'S MASTER STROKE

Rolo paid two more visits to Baz, one in each of the first two months. Baz had decided the reason was probably down to Rolo's inability to score. More would have followed, apart from, well, a slight transgression, let's put it that way.

It was on the first visit when the big attendant had taken him to the cemetery to search out his parent's grave, not that this was the reason behind Rolo's visits ending, not directly anyhow.

'Touch is the most beautiful of all the senses,' Baz once told Pasang, boasting that he could feel better than most people could see.

It was the second visit that was to be Rolo's last. The reason? Shame, along with guilt, but mostly shame.

As Rolo put together a joint, he joked about life back at Sunnybridge, especially Nurse Fran, always a good candidate for a Rolo joke. It was when he gave back the shrunken knob of dope that Baz came straight out and said it. "If you had asked me Rolo, I would have given you some, probably not as much as you have just taken though."

Baz thought it was sad having to listen to this proud man apologise like a scolded schoolboy. "Now it Is out in the open, keep it," Baz told him. However, the small piece of hash, no bigger than a kidney bean was returned.

As Rolo left the flat, both knew that it would be the end of their friendship. Stealing from a blind man haunted the big attendant for a long time after.

As promised, Mikhail had found him again. Baz introduced Mikhail to dope, along with the vodka and the misplaced sarcasm, conversations had become even more surreal. "You have to be stoned to appreciate him though," Pasang had once said. In truth, Pasang would have to be stoned to appreciate anything. It could be said that Pasang was incapable of doing anything unless she was high. "I'll just roll another before I go to the shops...We'll have a toke with our cup of tea...One more for the road."

Mikhail stopped calling round to the flat after the second year.

Weeks passed with no sign of him, then months, then years. "Strange how that stinky Russian suddenly stopped coming around Butes." Pasang had said.

"Mikhail has a habit of vanishing," Baz replied. "Anyway, the smell was reassuring in a strange sort of way."

Baz guessed that Mikhail's body had finally given up on him. In truth, he was surprised he had even lasted this long. Baz also guessed that only one anonymous person knew Mikhail had actually existed at all, the only person who would know if he had died, but probably not as Mikhail Tretyakov, more likely under some pseudonym. He also knew this one person would not know of the existence of a blind man living in a small flat. Baz's only hope was that he had had a decent burial.

Violet travelled over from France on several occasions. Each time they would visit the cemetery. It had been a number of years since either had been to the older part of the graveyard. After a good half hour of fruitless searching in the undergrowth, which left Baz feeling frustrated that he couldn't help, Violet eventually gave up looking for their sister's headstone, both walked away realising Norma's last attachment to this world had finally disintegrated.

Billy had taken over the Golby empire, a natural progression, and just as if it was Zed himself, no one disputed it at the time, or had wanted to. Only Billy Keenan didn't possess that Zed Golby subtlety, that ability to fly under the radar. Unfortunately for him, at the same time the police were becoming less corrupt and Billy's greed for power even more fanatical. Having never lost his flair for making enemies at every corner, Billy's legendary evilness deemed too dangerous to leave unleashed. The Mercedes Benz 450SEL was shot up in a hail of gunfire. Out of the five bullets, it wasn't known which one ended Billy's life. Teabag's demise was clearer, just the one hole to his head. Everyone said if Teabags had chosen how to depart this world, it would have been in his beloved Merc. Frank and Joey went into hiding at the safest safe house they knew.

"In fact, it is the only safe house we have left," Frank said.

In a strange way Baz was thankful for the company. It must be a desperate world when you need gangsters for companionship, he thought to himself.

On the second night Frank explained to Baz how Billy had gone back to his old ways. "The schoolboy thug had returned."

"Stealing food from satchels," Baz added.

Frank and Baz explained to a bemused Joey what had happened behind the hole. "So that's how he got his gold teeth, I never wanted to ask." Joey said afterwards.

Frank and Joey would have stayed longer if it was not for Pasang throwing them out. "He won't see the bullets coming," she had yelled. Baz never heard from either of them again.

Baz's occupancy of the flat was in its eighth year when Pasang met someone, a Dutchman. "There are coffee houses where you just go downstairs and smoke dope to your hearts content," she told Baz when explaining the reason for going to live in Amsterdam. On her penultimate visit she even brought her Dutchman round to meet him. Baz thought he seemed nice enough, not as expected though, his face felt like the fisherman type, puffy cheeks, an under-chin beard, no moustache. The poor fellow was obviously dumbstruck by Baz's appearance, probably wondering what his girlfriend was doing knowing someone like him. Anyhow, Baz was happy for her, even if he was undecided whether it was the coffee houses or the Dutchman behind her move. He gave her the benefit of the doubt. "For a long time you've needed someone to love more than someone to love because you needed to," he told her, with himself in mind. "One of my fathers," quickly adding, "I think."

The last time Baz had seen Pasang was the afternoon before the raid. When I say seen, I mean actually seen, with his eyes. Then she was a fresh faced beauty with long willowy golden hair and a free spirit. Baz's blindness meant the last memory of her had always remained the same, to him she would always be that fresh faced beauty.

She gave him a lock of her hair, explaining that a part of her would always be with him. "I will never forget you Butes." Were her parting words through a stream of tears.

"Yeah you will." But he knew she wouldn't. Neither would he forget her.

1992

Baz's worst nightmare had begun, his right ear was losing its ability to hear. His doctor had told him he would be totally deaf within a couple of months, he was not wrong.

Live, sink, or die? That was the question Baz had to battle with. He had been there many times before.

It wasn't a case of there was nothing out there, don't think that, there was plenty. He always had smell, touch, speech, as far as he was concerned he was still three fifths up, even if it was one way traffic. In truth, his remaining senses had become infinitely more enhanced. Often sitting hidden behind the curtains from his open window, feeling the vibrations from the outside world, taking in the multitude of odours, experiencing whatever rode in with the wind, discovering what the neighbours were having for dinner, breathing in the smoke from a passing pedestrian, feeling the air ripple from a speeding car.

The world hadn't gone anywhere. Neither had he.

How did Baz feel? Well, to be honest, he was expecting it, in a lot of ways he had prepared himself already. To him it was always going to be the natural progression, all be it the worst kind. Some courageous people under the same circumstances may have even preferred death. Baz had never been that brave.

Boredom was probably his worst enemy, no new incoming information to ponder over. Although, he had always been a person that lived in his own head, never one to get too close to another, loneliness was not going to be an issue for Baz. He thought he had experienced more in life than most anyhow.

He thought about An and Kai Liang, how they used to disappear for weeks on end, meditating, emptying their minds of all emotion, attempting to escape from the physical connections tying them to this world. Baz thought he had arrived at the same place, only through the back door. For him, there was not one shred of emotion remaining. How could there be? How could he possibly afford to have them? Revenge, hatred, sympathy, guilt, self-pity, desire, pride, sorrow, they had all gone. Not love, he had kept love. Love for his sisters, for the memories of those departed, love for friends now gone, love for life, what was left of it.

He missed Pasang. A lot! Especially her little gifts. He thought it was now, more than at any other time, he could do with getting high. Play around with his thoughts, allow his thoughts to play with him. His secret thoughts, wise thoughts, clever thoughts, creative, inventive thoughts, toxic thoughts.

As for the soul, if anyone was in a situation to find it, Baz certainly was. After all, his physical world was gradually disappearing, but he was no closer than at any other time in his life. Baz decided he had to wait to die for that one.

For two years he remained in the flat, refusing to step out under any circumstances. An enigma to the occupants from the other three flats in the house, rumours about a blind and deaf monster must have been rife.

"I've seen everything on the outside I've ever needed to experience. I wasn't impressed with it then, so not being able to see or hear it won't change that now," he had told the Social Services in no uncertain terms.

Two people were assigned as Baz's carers, one woman and one man. This way he would get to know their individual ways of communicating. They both used the same technique, only with slight nuances. A letter would be drawn onto the palm of his hand, spelling out words that would eventually make a sentence. For Baz, he just spoke, like he had been doing for his entire life, only now there was no sound, just an inner vibration, a kind of hum. Baz could feel himself talk.

The woman, whose name was Florentina, used her talon like fingernails to scratch the letters on the palm of his hand. After spelling out her name F L O R E N T I N A, she then tried telling Baz its sound was like the football team, only that was Fiorentina and they were Italian and she was Spanish. It was a kind of touch small talk, something on their first day to break the ice. It had in fact, taken most of the afternoon. Baz took a long while to decipher what she was actually saying in the first place, considering he had never heard of a football team called Fiorentina. She also misspelt many of the words. Occasionally a sentence made no sense at all, a shake of his head would indicate Baz's lack of understanding. After each word had been completed she would tap the top of his fingers and Baz would have to say the word. He could sense her impatience when the tap evolved into a slap. "It is not my fault if you can't use the Queen's English," Baz said forcefully. Well, he hoped he had said it forcefully, the strength of the hum told him he had. From her first touch Baz had decided Florentina was an older person, it was the way her long fingers would wrap around the back of his hand, cold and furrowed, a grip from where there was no escape. It was the same day she told him her age was thirty-four.

The man, or boy, or girl as Baz first thought was named "T H O M A S" but Thomas had traced. "YOU.CAN.CALL.ME. T O M."

"My name is Basil but call me Baz, with a z," Baz hummed.

From his first feathery touch, Baz had determined Tom's hand had not held a manual tool in its entire life. On occasions Baz wondered if Tom was actually touching him at all. The contact was as soft as whipped cream and so light it took some convincing that Tom wasn't actually a woman after all. You can have George, Ashley and Lee as girl's names, why not Tom, although, neither could come up with a girl's name starting with those three letters. Baz said he even smelt like a woman. Now that was an interesting conversation between speech and touch. Apart from getting Baz to hold his private parts, which he thought was probably not appropriate, if not illegal, Tom told him he would just have to take his word for it. Unlike Florentina's quick cuff of his fingertips, when Tom had finished a sentence he would lightly rub the tip of his finger in the same spot on Baz's palm, as though he was drawing the full stop itself. Baz enjoyed their touch-talk conversations, which could cover everything from art to flying Spitfires. "I kept Spitfires in the air during the war." Baz had told him once. Tom understood that this meant he was once a fighter pilot in the Battle of Britain. "W O W." Tom had replied. The pressure of the full stop on Baz's palm showed how impressed he was. A simple aircraftman must have been an honourable trade after all, thought Baz.

It was when their combined ability to communicate got to an all time high that Tom tackled his most difficult task yet, his greatest professional test, you could say. The description to a deaf, blind man, as Tom put it with a creamy stroke of his finger. "THE. GREATEST.PAINTING.EVER."

"Wow." Baz used that word a lot now, he thought it must be the *in* word, how would he know any different? He also liked the vibration it made in his head.

"THE.FAIRY.FELLERS.MASTER.STROKE."

Baz repeated it. "The Fairy Fellers Master Stroke...Wow."

"RICHARD.DADD.WAS.THE.ARTIST." After a short pause.

"1855.TO.1864."

"He was nine years old?..Wow!"

Tom squeezed Baz's hand as though he was laughing, several squeezes, if it was really funny.

"NO.IT.TOOK.HIM.NINE.YEARS.TO.PAINT.IT."

Baz stretched his lips. "Richard Dad with two 'd's."

Tom squeezed Baz's hand again. "YOU.SAY.IT.LIKE.DARD.BAZ."

"I would love to see it," Baz said. Tom squeezed Baz's hand again.

"I.WILL.DO.MY.BEST."

Tom cut out a picture of the painting from one of his art books and flattened it on the coffee table. He told Baz how the viewer sees the painting as though he is hiding in the grass. "A SECRET. CEREMONY." He held the tip of Baz's forefinger on the picture and swiftly stroked it along the paper, following the lines of the grass blades, as if Baz was painting it himself. He went on to explain how it was a fantasy picture about the afterlife, the dreams of people between life and spirit. "THE.SOULS.OF.PEOPLE.IN.WAITING." Tom stroked. He then went on to tell Baz about Queen Mab waiting for her carriage. "TO.TAKE.HER.TO.THE.SPIRIT.WORLD."

"A place where souls go," Baz hummed.

He told Baz the Fairy Feller had searched for the perfect nut. "HAZELNUTS.LITTER.THE.GROUND."

"Messy," Baz said. Tom squeezed his hand then rubbed the tip of Baz's finger on each of the nuts. He described how the feller, holding an axe above his head, had just been given the order by the wise old wizard with outstretched arms and a crooked hat to crack open the chosen nut.

"EVERYONE.IN.THE.PICTURE.IS.WAITING.FOR.THAT. MAGICAL.MOMENT.IT.WILL.BECOME.THE. QUEENS.CARRIAGE.BAZ."

"To the world of souls?"

"YES."

"If such a world exists?"

"NO." Tom paused. "OR.YES"

Tom went on to describe the forest folk dressed in their earth coloured clothes.

"WATCHING.FROM.LEDGES.ON.A.ROCKY.HILL.SOME.EVEN. LOOK.LIKE.THEY.ARE.PART.OF.THE.

ROCK.ITSELF."

Each time he described a detail from the painting, Tom would trace Baz's finger over it, then pause, Baz guessed he was studying the picture, searching out the next part to describe.

"IN.THE.TOP.LEFT.A.GRASSHOPPER." Tom floated Baz's finger above the picture for a couple of seconds. "OR.IS.IT.A. DRAGONFLY.ANYWAY.IT.IS.PLAYING.A.LONG.GOLDEN. TRUMPET.A.DARK.BLUE.MOONLIT.SKY.IS BEHIND IT." He told Baz there were huge daisies growing out of the stone.

"I had an acid trip like that once," said Baz. "Only it was a rug."

Another squeeze of the hand, several squeezes in fact.

"NOTHING.ABOUT.YOU.SURPRISES.ME.ANY.MORE.BAZ."

"You never know."

The description continued.

"IT.IS.A.SECRET.CEREMONY.BAZ.ONLY.THE.LUCKY.FEW. ARE..." He suddenly stopped tracing.

Baz waited. "Go on Tom."

"ALLOWED.TO SEE.IT."

"I'm glad you are one of the lucky few Tom."

"I.WISH.YOU.COULD.SEE.IT.BAZ."

"I can see it with my heart."

"WOW.THAT.IS.BEAUTIFUL."

Tom went on to describe how Richard Dadd was committed to a mental asylum for killing his father. "HE.ONLY.PAINTED.THE. PICTURE.TO.PROVE.HIS.SANITY."

"Mmmm?" Baz hummed.

Tom's communication became a lot more confident after that day. He drew simple pictures on Baz's hand to depict certain words, a woman when short strokes protruded from the top of a circle, a man if the hair came from the bottom, like a beard, after all Tom was an artist. It wasn't too long before their conversations got to be nearly as fast as two people speaking.

Tom told Baz he was twenty with a receding hairline, adding he would be bald by the time he reached thirty. He also said he lived with his friend Paul.

1994

387

"YOU.WILL.HAVE.BETTER.CARE," said a strange woman through the end of Tom's finger. Immediately after and with great clandestine speed, Tom had traced. "C H E A P E R." then squeezed Baz's hand. That would be the last time Baz would feel either the gentle touches of Tom's fingertips or the sharpness of Florentina's talons. The local council in all its wisdom had decided an eighty year old deaf and blind man would be better cared for in a nursing home.

Baz's new home consisted of a small bedroom with a door leading into an even smaller bathroom. The usual fake wood furniture, not much more to say about it really. A bit like his room at Sunnybridge.

Each day was the same, a monotonous, repetitive routine of identical procedures.

Then one became different to all the others.

A new odour had entered his room, nothing unusual about that, new odours enter all the time. But this was not a new carer, or a nurse, not that they all smelt of disinfectant or cheap perfume. Baz just knew this person was different, a women, much older, even older than himself. How did he know? Many reasons we five sensed mortals could only guess at. The breathing, the shuffling of the walk, maybe the smell, Baz knew though. Anyhow, under normal circumstances, it was not the kind of visitor he was used to. Baz sensed it was someone that knew him well, no overstated welcoming. Whoever it was had sat down on the chair in front of him.

"Who are you? I know you are there. It's you, isn't it Violet?" Baz said. He then felt the willowy soft leather of cool fingers turn his own hand over, expecting a letter to be traced onto it any moment. Instead, a small object was placed on his palm.

For ages he just held it in his clutches, remembering the shape, feeling its contours through his palm. The cross protruding from a strong bulbous head, its wide circular base, that thin tapered body. A chess king, but not any chess king, this one he knew well, he had touched it many times in his past, decades ago, in his childhood.

"Violet," he said quietly.

Baz felt her hand gently open his fist and remove the king, she then replaced it with another wooden object. Baz rubbed his thumb over the coronet shape of the crown, the queen.

Baz slid his hand into his pocket and pulled out the pawn. He let it be taken from him, something he had never allowed since the day it was returned at Shaibah. The cushioned tip of a finger gently touched his palm, a touch he had never felt before, the touch of an angel. The first letter was slowly drawn out, an "R". For a few seconds the finger remained, then he felt it brush over him again, another letter, "U", the same procedure followed, this time a "B". As she began stroking the last letter.

"Ruby!"

She finished the last one "Y."

"Ruby," he repeated, softly. She picked his other hand up and placed it against her cheek, he felt the warm dampness of her tears coat his palm.

"And Violet?" Baz said so quietly he hardly felt the hum in his head. Ruby pressed his palm harder into her face. A long silence. "How long?" Ruby began to speak "Two week..." She suddenly realised. "2WEEKS." She traced.

"Two Weeks." After a short pause. "How?"

She moved her finger slowly and carefully. "H E A R T."

"A broken heart," he hummed softly. Ruby stared at him. Through the featureless scarred face, the dark glasses, the hairless patchy scalp, through everything else. It was only then she could see the brother she once knew.

"Peter?" he asked. He felt her head drop slightly.

After a moments silence. "Sorry."

Ruby stayed for another three hours. With the best strokes her finger could muster, she told Baz about her children and grandchildren, that she now lived in Perth. She also told him that she had to travel back to Australia the following day. When she had finished she held Baz's hand, it felt as if an angel was holding him, a grip that said everything. But most of all it said they would never meet again. She left with a kiss on his forehead. Baz insisted she take the King and Queen with her. "Think of Violet, think of Father and Mother. Think of Norma and Oliver." He paused. "Think of me. Look at them and think of us." Were his last words to her.

1996

Baz's shouts for help would often be ignored. Sometimes he felt he had been calling for hours, even days. The smell of food being brought

389

in, that same rotting smell, that same tasteless fodder, this would wake him from his incarceration. Then he would feel the cold sharp tap of a spoon on his lip, he would let the stodge be shovelled in, one spoon after another, one choking swallow after another.

Then there were the visions. For Baz, a blessing, an escape from the nightmare that was his awareness, until they became as real to him as reality itself. At first he was afraid, other times he felt anguish, desolation, a helplessness. Then he would feel bliss, euphoria, a contentment in finding the refuge he was finally at peace with.

Only the pawn he kept faithfully for all those years, the object that contained the memories of his past, the living vehicle that informed him whether he was in the real world or his transcendental world. This was his pawn of souls. The souls he had once known, souls long departed. If he could touch the wooden figure then he was in the real world, his world, his world of torment, the world that held him to his powerless existence, the world he no longer desired. If all feeling from the small object had gone, if its smallest molecules had dissolved with his own body, then he would be in his world of dreams, the place where they had become one. Where the embodiment of all that he had experienced was united into a single understanding of life. It was there he found a world where he felt at peace, where there was no pain or misery, where he felt free. Then it was easy, nothing to care for, nothing to fight for, a world where he could see and hear again.

A COLD WIND

"There are three things you wouldn't want to know about my life."
   "Three?"
   "My world is black."
   "Isn't everyones?"
   "My world is silent."
   "Love is silent."
   "My world is not a happy one."
   "Wanting to be happy will not make you happy."
   "You sound like my father. Who are you anyway?"
   "You know who I am. Look, so what do you see now?"
   "Nothing, I just told you, and I *don't* know who you are."

"Yes you do. Look again, look, now what do you see?"

"I see a burning red sky, I see flames devouring a vast forest, I hear animals wailing, I see a small cove, a rowing boat floating out in the water. People are fighting to get in it, they are trying to drown each other, trying to kill one another. There are bodies being washed up on waves of blood. Great birds of prey are soaring overhead, they are casting huge dark shadows over everything. The shadows feel so cold."

"Now look again, look inside yourself, *now* what do you see?"

"I can see islands in the ocean, islands bathed in a radiant white light. I can feel their rays, a feeling of compassion and love; and the wind, it is so warm, it feels so much more than just warmth. I can hear the beautiful soft sound of flutes whispering through the trees, the music feels as if it is entering my body. I can see that same boat again, a cold wind is blowing it towards me.

"Now look again, look this way, look towards me. What do you see now?"

"I see me."

THE END

one golf course, one gang, one war,

one winner!

driver
boy

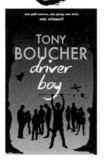

TONY
BOUCHER
driver
boy

Barney is a fifteen year old boy living in a rural town
called Pinnton. The year is 1969, the second week of
the summer holidays.

Barney is bemused with the world, coming to terms with his
transformation into adulthood, questioning life with a
naivety and innocence only someone of his age could.
For Barney and his friends there is one thing they have been
preoccupied with for the past three years - to win the war!
Barney is a member of a gang and they are at war with the
town's golf course. The fairways and greens are their battleground, the whacks (golfers) and dibbles (greenkeepers)
their enemy.

'Driver Boy' spans a single week. Through humour and
tragedy, along with its many eccentric characters, it tells of
the events leading up to the downfall of the golf course.

The prequel to The Drowning Mary

THE TUKUL
with the
BLUE DOOR

Recently employed by The Way for Life
charity, Norris Kinley has been sent to
Breidjing Refugee Camp in war-torn Chad
to organise the transportation of food aid.
But is this the true reason why he is there?
Five days after his expected return to the
UK and no one has heard from him.

For Teresa Flores the operations director
at the charity and Crystal Bullion the
camp manager at Breidjing, one word
instantly comes to mind — kidnapping.

Spanning four weeks and three countries,
the truth of what happened to Norris
slowly unravels.

The sequel to The Tukul with the Blue Door

THE DROWNING MARY

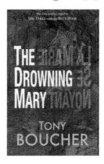

**TWO MURDERS, ONE SCANDAL AND
THE PLIGHT OF TWO REFUGEES...
ALL CONNECTED BY ONE PAINTING.**

THE PEOPLE

Lucile and Norris attempt to unravel the mystery of
the Markovic Affair. At the same time Crystal and
Teresa help Jamia and Ali escape from Chad...
Their paths will soon cross.

THE SCANDALS

In 1968, secret photographs involving the
future French president's wife had rocked the
foundations of the French political establishment...
A prostitute killed fifteen years later.

THE FAMILIES

Two families obsessed with revenge...
There can only be one outcome.

THE DECEIT

When a person's name is not their own...

THE CLUE IS THE DROWNING MARY!

'Anna is pregnant with a cartoon rabbit and
Sir James is plain old Roland Budd.

Both are on a mission to reach the site of the legendary
1970 Isle of Wight Rock Festival.'

Every Sunday lunchtime Anna is instructed
to pick up Sir James at his cottage and take him back
to the Dog and Duck. This is only so he can tell the
unsuspecting clientele his knightly tales of
crumbling bridges and unfaithful artists.

Today is different though. Today Sir James needs to scatter
his wife's ashes at the place they met fifty years ago.

This is an extraordinary road story between
eighteen year old Anna and the octogenarian Sir James
as they travel from the village of
Crendham Hook to the Isle of Wight.

The prequel to 'CLOSE'

'ALONE' MAY BE FICTION
BUT CAN IT SEE THE TRUTH?

For his entire sixteen years Owen Roberts has
been living a teenage boy's idyllic lifestyle,
until one phone call that is, a phone call that
will change it and him forever.

President Carter Ward has sanctioned the
assassination of one of his agents, not
realising the catastrophic results it will have
on the world, nor knowing this will leave one
teenage boy in another country
alone in this world.

Owen discovers he is not the only one who has
survived, his only goal is to reach the others.

The sequel to 'ALONE'

Also published together to
create one remarkable story.

Owen and his granddaughter
are the only people remaining in the
country, if not the entire world.

After returning to Buncies Cottage to see out
his last hours, Owen thinks back to his life.
The time spent in the city with the
remaining survivors, the move to a
small fishing village on the south coast,
his journey to see his family and to find other
survivors. Owen thinks back to the horrifying
sights he has seen and to the people he has lost.

Together, Alone and Close are a warning to us all.